Praise for Minerva
THE ACADEMY OF LOVE series:

"[A] pitch perfect Regency .... Readers will be hooked." (THE MUSIC OF LOVE)
★*Publishers Weekly STARRED REVIEW*

"An offbeat story that offers unexpected twists on a familiar setup."
(A FIGURE OF LOVE)
Kirkus

"[A] consistently entertaining read."
(A FIGURE OF LOVE)
Kirkus

Praise for **THE MASQUERADERS** series:
"Lovers of historical romance will be hooked on this twisty story of revenge, redemption, and reversal of fortunes."
Publishers Weekly, STARRED review of THE FOOTMAN.

"Fans will be delighted."
Publishers Weekly on THE POSTILION

Praise for Minerva Spencer's *REBELS OF THE TON* series:

NOTORIOUS
★A *PopSugar* Best New Romance of November
★A *She Reads* Fall Historical Romance Pick
★A *Bookclubz* Recommended Read

"**Brilliantly crafted...an irresistible cocktail of smart characterization, sophisticated sensuality, and sharp wit.**" ★*Booklist STARRED REVIEW*

"*Sparkling...impossible not to love.*"—*Popsugar*

"Both characters are strong, complex, and believable, and the cliffhanger offers a nice setup for the sequel. Readers who like thrills mixed in with their romance should check this out."
—*Publishers Weekly*

"Packed full of fiery exchanges and passionate embraces, this is for those who prefer their Regencies on the scandalous side."—*Library Journal*

INFAMOUS

"Realistically transforming the Regency equivalent of a mean girl into a relatable, all-too-human heroine is no easy feat, but Spencer (Outrageous, 2021) succeeds on every level. Lightly dusted with wintery holiday charm, graced with an absolutely endearing, beetle-obsessed hero and a fully rendered cast of supporting characters and spiked with smoldering sensuality and wry wit, the latest in Spencer's Rebels of the Ton series is sublimely satisfying."
—Booklist STARRED review

"Perfect for fans of Bridgerton, Infamous is also a charming story for Christmas. In fact, I enjoyed Infamous so much that when I was halfway through it, I ordered the author's first novel, Dangerous. I look forward to reading much more of Minerva Spencer's work."
—THE HISTORICAL NOVEL SOCIETY

Praise for S.M. LaViolette's erotic historical romance series *VICTORIAN DECADENCE*:

"LaViolette keeps the tension high, delivering dark eroticism and emotional depth in equal measure. Readers will be hooked."
-PUBLISHERS WEEKLY on HIS HARLOT

"LaViolette's clever, inventive plot makes room for some kinky erotic scenes as her well-shaded characters explore their sexualities. Fans of erotic romance will find much to love."
-PUBLISHERS WEEKLY on HIS VALET

Praise for Minerva Spencer's *Outcasts* series:

"Minerva Spencer's writing is sophisticated and wickedly witty. Dangerous is a delight from start to finish with swashbuckling action, scorching love scenes, and a coolly arrogant hero to die for. Spencer is my new auto-buy!"
-NYT Bestselling Author **Elizabeth Hoyt**

"[**SCANDALOUS** is] A standout...Spencer's brilliant and original tale of the high seas bursts with wonderfully real protagonists, plenty of action, and passionate romance."
★*Publishers Weekly STARRED REVIEW*

More books by S.M. LaViolette & Minerva Spencer

THE ACADEMY OF LOVE SERIES
The Music of Love
A Figure of Love
A Portrait of Love
The Language of Love
Dancing with Love*
The Story of Love*

THE OUTCASTS SERIES
Dangerous
Barbarous
Scandalous

THE REBELS OF THE *TON*
Notorious
Outrageous
Infamous

Phoebe

The Bellamy Sisters
Book 1

Minerva Spencer

writing as
S.M. LAVIOLETTE

Crooked
Sixpence
CS
P
Press

CROOKED SIXPENCE BOOKS are published by
CROOKED SIXPENCE PRESS

2 State Road 230
El Prado, NM 87529

First printing May 2022

10 9 8 7 6 5 4 3 2 1

Photo stock by Period Images
Printed in the United States of America

This is dedicated to my Proofer Gang: Brantly, George, Linda, Marla, & Shelly.

I couldn't do it without you guys!

Chapter One

Lady Phoebe Bellamy stopped yet again to wait for her younger brother Dauntry—or Doddy, as his family called him—who had been dragging his heels in a way that only fourteen-year-old younger brothers could do. Phoebe huffed out an exasperated sigh and turned to scold him.

But Doddy wasn't behind her.

No, the only thing she saw was a rather spectacular butterfly.

"Why, look at you," Phoebe murmured, pausing to admire the large black and crimson specimen. "What are you doing all by yourself, Your Grace?"

The butterfly hovered closer and then landed on her shoulder.

It was an entrancing insect—large, brilliantly colored, and sufficiently ducal—and only the second Duke of Burgundy that Phoebe had ever seen.

If there was a butterfly within a quarter of a mile, it would land on Phoebe. And if she stood there long enough, more of the gentle, shy creatures would find her.

"Have you seen my brother?" she asked the butterfly, which was opening and closing its wings in a languid, showy fashion. "Yes, that is very nice," she said absently, raising her hand to shield her eyes against the sun and scan the area for Doddy.

She shifted the parcel of old clothing she was holding and clamped the awkward bundle between elbow and hip so she could cup her hands around her mouth.

"Dodddddyyyyyyyy!"

Her voice sounded unnaturally loud and Phoebe felt ill-mannered to be caterwauling amid such pristine quiet. It certainly convinced the Duke of Burgundy to flutter away and seek a quieter resting place.

She listened for a reply, but all she could hear was the low buzz of insects and the occasional *tweet* of a bird.

"You little wretch," she muttered, laying her Sisyphean burden in the grass before stomping back down the path that led to Queen's Bower, the quaint Tudor house she shared with her family.

Phoebe never should have invited the little monster to come along, but he'd been so downhearted lately that she had given in against her better judgement.

Not that Doddy was the only one who was downhearted.

It was difficult to remain cheerful when one's circumstances worsened daily and one's mother took every opportunity to point out said worsening to one's father—loudly and often.

Phoebe cursed her brother beneath her breath as she trudged back in the direction she had just come.

She had hoped to deliver the clothing and be back in time to speak with Mrs. Parks, their housekeeper/cook, about the weekly menu.

It was Phoebe's task to stretch the meagre weekly food allowance so that it would feed not only the eight members of her family, but their three remaining servants as well. Mrs. Parks would be delighted to hear that Phoebe had—thanks to several small economies—scraped together enough money to afford a leg of lamb for Sunday dinner.

After Phoebe finished her marketing, she wanted to nip over to Nanny Fletcher's cottage to help with her weekly baking. At ninety years of age, and nearly blind, the old family retainer shouldn't be allowed near a hearth, but she dearly loved her cream buns.

It was a shame that Nanny couldn't live with them, but there simply wasn't room for her at Queen's House. There was barely room for family, as her mother, the Countess of Addiscombe, was so fond of reminding her husband and children.

Phoebe had been so busy gathering wool that she was half-way home before she noticed.

"Blast!" She stopped and shouted again. "Doddy!"

"Over here, Pheeb!"

She shrieked at the sound of Doddy's muffled voice. "Where?"

"By the stream."

"You little rotter," she muttered. "Just wait until I get my hands on you." Phoebe stepped over a fallen log and picked her way through the trees, glimpsing her brother's bright flaxen curls—yet another reason to be irritated with him. Why would God give a glorious head of hair like that to a mere boy?

Phoebe shoved the thought aside, along with the long, snaky bramble that reached out to snag her skirt.

Her brother was standing beneath a monstrous horse chestnut tree, staring up.

"You promised you'd behave and not make trouble, Doddy."

Dauntry Bellamy's blue eyes were enormous, limpid, and deceptively innocent as he turned to her.

Her brother reminded Phoebe of the brightly colored jungle creatures that her sister Aurelia was frequently paid to illustrate. The animals were lovely, but only so they could lure their prey close enough to sting, bite, or poison them into submission.

Doddy looked like an angel, but he was a hellion from the soles of his scuffed boots to his curly blond head.

He pointed up at the immense tree. "It's Silas, he won't come down."

"You brought your *rodent* to deliver clothing to the poor."

His mouth tightened dangerously. "He's a squirrel, Pheeb, as you are perfectly aware."

"Don't call me Pheeb."

Phoebe lived in the rapidly dwindling hope that her family would stop using her appalling pet name if she was adamant enough.

"To answer your question, *Pheeb*, I didn't *bring* him, he brought himself. Silas is his own master and goes where he pleases."

"Fine, then let him find his own way down from the tree."

"It's too dangerous."

Phoebe had to bite her tongue; she would only look like a fool if she argued with her irrational little brother about his verminous pet.

She planted her fisted hands on her hips. "Call him, then!"

Doddy squinted up into the tree's frilly canopy, his brow furrowing. "I did. He is refusing to come down."

"I'm sure he can find his way back home." Phoebe gestured to the parcel she had tasked him with carrying. The brown paper bundle was dirty and battered as though he had kicked it all the way from Queen's Bower. "Pick up the clothes and come along. We've not got all day."

"I can't leave him here."

"He's a squirrel, Doddy, he'd be happier living outside. He probably hates living in a hatbox in your messy room."

"He's only ever lived inside—he wouldn't know what to do out here, all alone." His lip quivered.

"Ha! Nicely done, Doddy."

Her brother's pitiful, beseeching expression dissipated faster than a cream cake at tea.

Phoebe clucked her tongue. "You little faker."

Doddy looked proud at the accusation and crossed his arms over his chest. "Either you help me get him down, or you can take the clothing yourself."

"I can't believe you'd forego your duty to deliver much-needed clothing to your very own people to fish a rodent out of a tree."

"Do you really believe Mrs. Thompkins wants my worn-out knee breeches and your threadbare old petticoats?" He fixed her with a sneering look that made him appear far older than his years. Phoebe thought of it as his *lord of the manor* look, which would serve him well when he became earl—if there was anything left to become earl *of*. "Give me a moment to get him down and I will go with you."

Phoebe scowled. "Fine. What do you want me to do?"

Doddy's triumphant grin showed off two rows of white, straight teeth that were more perfect than they had any right to be.

Phoebe self-consciously tongued the chip in her own top front tooth, a result of sliding down the banister at Wych House when she'd been ten.

"I'll do the hard part," he told her. "You just stand as close to the base of the tree as you can."

"Why do I need to do that?" she demanded.

"Because if you're near the trunk, he won't see you."

"Why does that matter?"

"He won't jump down if he sees you." Doddy gave her a head-to-toe dismissive look. "He doesn't care for you."

Phoebe snorted. "I'm crushed. If you don't have your rat by the time I've counted to one hundred, I'm leaving without you. And then *you* can explain to Mama why you didn't do what she asked."

Fear of their mother's wrath put him in motion. He went to the lowest branch—which was still a good six feet off the ground—and sprang straight up like a monkey, chinning himself up to the next branch before throwing a leg over it.

"Do be careful, Doddy."

He grunted but otherwise ignored her, scampering up the tree as nimbly as the creature he was trying to capture. She watched until he disappeared into the canopy and all was silent but for the rustle of leaves.

Phoebe examined her gloves while she waited. They were a disgrace; her little finger poked out of a hole in the left glove and she could see her right index finger beneath a few strained threads. The leather had originally been a buttery tan but was now dishwater gray.

"Found him," Doddy called down in triumph.

Phoebe looked up to see a section of the tree shaking. "You're terribly far up. *Please* be careful."

"I'm coming down."

Leaves cascaded around her, and Phoebe's heart pounded like a runaway horse. She had to bite her lower lip to keep from screeching instructions and startling him. But when his foot slipped, a shriek broke out of her all the same.

"Bloody hell!" Doddy's curse was punctuated by the distinctive sound of wood cracking.

Phoebe was staring straight up, mouth open wide, when a rectangle of reddish fur fell from the sky.

"Doddy!" Her screaming joined with high-pitched rodent squealing and Phoebe staggered blindly away from the tree, as if she could outrun the creature scrabbling on top of her third-best hat.

Something boy-shaped slammed into her and rough hands grabbed her shoulders.

"Hold still, you barmy female. Here, stop squirming and let me get him. You're terrifying him."

"Get him off me!" Phoebe shrieked, backing into a tree.

Doddy's fingers dug into the flesh of her upper arms. "Bend down, Pheeb."

She hastily dipped her head, her eyes squeezed shut in case the little rat got through the hat, which Phoebe could hear it chewing. "Will you *please* hurry up?"

Doddy yanked her down and Phoebe slid to her knees, reaching out to break her fall and encountering an exposed tree root which ripped the thin palm of her glove.

"Ow!"

"Oh, hush," he muttered, tugging on her hat hard enough to yank off her right ear.

"Wait, Doddy—let me untie it."

Phoebe jerked the frayed old ribbon over her chin, taking some skin with it, and then shoved the hat—with the squirrel still attached—at her brother.

"Careful, Pheeb," Doddy chided.

Phoebe shoved her hair out of the way and gaped at the straw wreckage in his grubby hands.

"Oh, Doddy, just look at my hat—it's ruined."

In less than a minute,   Silas had chewed a hole the size of a grouse egg into the crown.

My hair!

Phoebe's hand flew to the top of her head and she heaved a sigh when she didn't encounter a bald spot.

"You're a very naughty squirrel, Silas." Doddy's loving tone was completely at odds with his scolding words.

The small rodent wrapped its tiny hand-like claws around her brother's finger and then scampered up his arm, crouching low on his shoulder beneath his ear, its black, shiny eyes fastened on Phoebe.

She made a sound of disgust. "That little brute knows exactly what he did to my hat!" She snatched her ruined headgear from her brother's unresisting hands.

Doddy rubbed his cheek against his pet. "He didn't mean any harm. It must have terrified him when I slipped."

Phoebe didn't bother telling her pest of a brother what his near fall had done to *her* heart, which might never be the same.

Just like her hat. She frowned at the battered crown and shook her head.

"Do you want to go back to the house to change your kit?" Doddy asked.

"Mama would have you beaten if she heard you use such cant as kit."

Doddy shrugged. "So, don't tell her. Are we going back or not?"

Phoebe wanted to change her clothes, but if she returned home, she'd have to endure a lecture from Mama about going out dressed like a ragamuffin.

Besides, if she went back then she'd never have time to go to Nanny's and keep her from scalding herself or burning down her cottage.

Phoebe sighed. "No, Mrs. Thompkins will hardly care about the wretched state of my hat."

"Maybe you should stuff it in with the other castoffs?" Doddy suggested with a laugh.

She scowled up at him as she struggled to her feet, clutching her battered hat in one hand while she beat the dirt off her skirt with the other.

Her dress had a tear near the knee and dirt smudges where Doddy had pulled her to the ground. Her brother might be right: perhaps Phoebe would do better to ask Mrs. Thompkins for *her* castoffs.

They took a few moments to fix clothing, hair, hat, and—in her brother's case—situate Silas inside his coat, where he caused a slight bump under the lapel.

Soon they were on their way.

Having the squirrel in his coat made carrying the bundle difficult, and he kept dropping it as they made their way back down the trail.

"Oh, give it to me, Doddy. I'll carry it until I collect mine, but then you'll have to take it because I can't carry both. Look," she held it up for her brother to see the tear in the brown paper the housekeeper had wrapped around it. "Everything will spill all over the road if you don't show more care."

Doddy ignored her.

Instead, he pulled his mouth harp from his pocket and launched into one of the merry jigs he'd no doubt learned from some stable boy, back when they'd still had horses and servants to care for them.

Phoebe ruffled his hair, unable to stay angry at him for long, and couldn't help noticing that her little brother was now taller than her—which meant little as Phoebe was only a smidge over five feet.

In addition to his spun gold hair and limpid blue eyes, Doddy had also inherited their father's lithe, slender build.

Phoebe, on the other hand, was as neither lithe nor slender. She'd once overheard her mother describe her as a *stout little dab* and had cried herself to sleep for a week afterward.

But that had been years ago, and she had long since accepted the fact she was the plainest among her siblings, all of whom were exceptional in their way.

She would never be willowy and elegant like her elder sister Aurelia; golden and angelic like Selina; slender and green-eyed like Hyacinth, or an auburn-haired beauty like her youngest sister, Katie.

No, she was just brown eyed, brown-haired, *stout little dab*, Phoebe.

"Pheeb?"

"Hmm?"

"Do you think Papa will lose Queen's Bower to dunners and we shall be without a home?"

Phoebe stopped and turned to her brother. "Wherever did you hear such a thing?"

He shrugged, the skin over his high cheekbones flushing.

Phoebe had a pretty good idea of where he'd heard the rumor. They only had three servants left and Doddy loved to loiter in the kitchen. She would need to speak to Mr. and Mrs. Parks and Maisy about curbing their gossip in front of her brother.

Of course, it was their father's fault that the servants possessed such gossip to begin with.

The earl had sold the last of their horses—two rather aged hacks—and got rid of their remaining groom and stable lad just two months earlier.

Doddy had been inconsolable since then. It had been the first real hardship he'd had to endure. The rest of them had been living through their steady downward spiral into poverty for years.

First, they'd been forced to lease Wych House and move into the far smaller Queen's Bower.

Then a much-truncated Season for Aurelia—who'd been relieved, rather than hurt.

Right on the heels of that, the London house had to be leased to bring in much needed money.

No house in London had meant no Season at all for Selina, which was criminal since she had to be the most beautiful girl in England.

Finally, two years ago, her father had sold the London house.

Now there was an ugly rumor that her father might be forced to sell Queen's Bower if he couldn't find a tenant to lease Wych House.

"Pheeb?" her brother prodded.

"We won't lose Queen's Bower," she assured him with far more confidence than she felt.

"Mrs. Parks said Papa gambled it away."

She gritted her teeth. Yes, she'd have to speak with Mrs. Parks.

"Papa doesn't play cards anymore, Doddy."

"Yes, he does—he plays all day long in the library."

"I meant that he no longer plays for money."

"Then why did we have to sell Castor and Pollux and let Jem Philpot go?" His narrow, boyish features were pinched with anguish.

Phoebe's heart bled for him. He would one day be the Earl of Addiscombe and she doubted there would be anything left.

Not that the future looked any rosier for Phoebe and her sisters.

Unless one or more of them could marry—and who would marry dowerless girls?—they would soon need to find positions as governesses or companions just to keep a roof over their heads.

Phoebe looked into her brother's worried blue eyes and forced a smile. "Come, let's walk and I'll try to explain why we had to sell the horses and let poor Jemmy and Ned go."

Phoebe started walking. It was getting hot, and she already felt as though she'd been marching back and forth on this road for hours.

"Wych House is empty now, and until Papa can find another tenant, we must pay the servants and all the other expenses. Everything will be fine once there is a new tenant."

"Why does nobody wish to lease it? Wych House is beautiful."

Their family home was magnificent, but it was in dreadful repair. Oh, Phoebe wanted to weep just thinking about it.

The home farm hadn't produced enough food to supply even the main house in years.

Worst of all, her father had sold off all the unentailed property, so there was very little land that went with the estate. The few tenant farms that remained were in such poor condition that half of them were uninhabited or had very short, unprofitable tenancies.

But she couldn't burden her little brother with all that.

Instead, she said, "Wych House requires a very special tenant, Doddy— somebody who won't mind spending a great deal of money on a house they can never hope to purchase."

In other words, only an idiot would want the ramshackle property at the price her father was asking.

They arrived where she'd left the parcel on the side of the dusty lane.

Phoebe handed Doddy the bundle she'd been carrying. "Here, hold out your arms."

He did so, and she had to bite back a smile at the picture he made. He'd outgrown his coat, and the sleeves exposed boney wrists and arms as thin as toothpicks. His breeches had belonged to their father and had been remade for him, but with a growth spurt in mind so they hung off his narrow hips like drapes.

Doddy was at that awkward point between boyhood and becoming a man.

Something about that made Phoebe's throat burn, and she swallowed down a sudden urge to cry.

They resumed their walk.

Phoebe had hoped her brother was finished with the subject of Wych House, but it was not to be.

"If Papa cannot find a tenant for Wych House, then perhaps *we* might move back in and he could rent Queen's Bower instead."

It was far more likely that her father would have to sell Queen's Bower, and they'd be forced to rent somewhere small and horrid where they would languish, waiting for somebody to lease Wych House.

Once again, she did not say that.

Phoebe shifted the parcel higher onto her hip and held it in one arm, draping her other arm around Doddy's angular shoulders.

"Things might seem grim right now, but we'll come about. There have been Bellamys at Wych House for six hundred years. We've weathered civil wars, plagues, and worse. We'll weather this."

He smiled up at her, but she could see he wasn't convinced.

Well, neither was Phoebe.

***

By the time they'd dropped off the clothing—much appreciated, it turned out—and joined the Thompkins for tea, it was the heat of the day.

Doddy's steps slowed and his cheeks became flushed as they walked, his blond curls sticking to his forehead. The road offered no shade until they reached the shortcut they always used to avoid walking past Wych House, a view which all of them except Doddy found unspeakably depressing.

"Do you want to rest?" she asked.

He shook his head even though he had bright spots of red on his pale cheeks. He'd been terrifyingly ill two years earlier and had not been robust since.

Phoebe was just about to insist they stop when the sound of galloping hooves came from just beyond the rise ahead.

They'd just stepped off the packed dirt into the weeds when a horse and rider crested the slight hill.

Doddy made a noise of male appreciation and Phoebe couldn't help staring either.

The horse was big—huge, in fact—perhaps seventeen hands. Even so, its massive rider dwarfed the giant beast.

The man belatedly noticed them and slowed his pace to a trot.

His clothing was that of a gentleman, but he was built like a farm laborer—or, more accurately, like an ox—and what seemed to be acres of black superfine stretched over massive shoulders. He wore no overcoat in deference to the heat, but even his black clawhammer coat must have been uncomfortably warm on such a day.

His cravat was blindingly white and simply tied, his breeches a dark buckskin that was almost black and his boots—even with a haze of dust on them—were the finest, glossiest pair Phoebe had seen in years.

A high-crowned beaver was rakishly tilted on short but stylishly cropped dark brown hair, and his face, Phoebe saw as he drew closer, was not at all handsome.

Indeed, he was downright ugly. His jaw was chiseled but heavy, his lips thin and unsmiling, and his nose an aggressive jutting blade.

His eyes were cast in shadow by the brim of his hat—which he didn't bother to tip or remove—and his expression was flat, dismissive, and arrogant.

"I am looking for Wych House, boy."

His voice was as harsh as his person, and the flat vowels were those of a cit and completely at odds with his gentlemanly attire.

Doddy was so enrapt by the horse that he didn't appear to hear the question. He approached the monstrous black beast with his hand outstretched.

"Boy!"

The word was like the crack of a whip, and both Phoebe and Doddy startled.

"Are you daft?" the man demanded, holding his head at such an angle that she could finally see his glaring eyes.

They were a shockingly pale gray, the pupils mere pinpricks against the blazing sun.

"Step back," he barked rudely. "Coal would love nothing more than to take a chunk out of your hand."

Coal. What a perfect name for his magnificent horse, which was a deep, velvety black.

The horse looked no friendlier than its master as it stood with its neck arched, eyes disdainful.

Indeed, the beast—which was better groomed than Phoebe—seemed to study her chewed up hat, ripped and stained skirt, and sweat-sheened face with derision.

"The directions to Wych House, and be quick about it, boy," the man repeated.

Doddy's eyes narrowed dangerously at both the stranger's tone and being called *boy*

Suddenly, his normally straight shoulders sagged, and he doffed his hat.

"Oh, aye? Wych House?" He scratched his ear. "Hmmm." He glanced about gormlessly, scuffing the dirt into little puffs with the toe of his battered boot.

Phoebe had to bite her lip to keep from laughing and giving away her brother's masterful performance.

The stranger heaved a sigh, reached inside his coat, and drew out a small leather purse.

Doddy's eyes widened comically. "Ah, *Wych House*," he said in sudden comprehension, his greedy gaze on the purse. "Go back the way ye came but take a left at yon fork. It be less than a mile on."

When it looked like Doddy might hold out his hand, Phoebe grabbed his arm and yanked him away, forcing him to turn his back on the rude stranger.

The sound of hooves followed them, but Phoebe refused to turn.

A deep voice called out, "Look sharp, lad."

The tone seemed impossible to disobey, and both Phoebe and Doddy spun around just in time to see two coins sailing toward them, glittering under the bright sun.

Phoebe glared up at the giant stranger with open loathing, but he never even glanced at her. Instead, he lightly spurred his horse, turned the beast in a half-circle, and galloped back the way he'd come.

Doddy dropped to his haunches in the scrubby weeds beside the road.

Phoebe gave a disgusted huff. "Look at you, Viscount Bellamy, scrabbling about for a penny."

"I'm not too proud, Pheeb. Besides, I think one of those coins was a half guinea."

Phoebe couldn't help smiling, even though it physically pained her to see the next Earl of Addiscombe behaving like a street urchin.

"Ha!"   Doddy grinned up at her and held out his grimy palm on which not one, but two, half guineas glinted. "Cor, Pheeb! He must be as rich as Croesus to throw away so much money."

"Indeed, he must," Phoebe mused, her eyes narrowing as she looked at where the arrogant, obnoxious man had disappeared over the rise.

So, he was looking for Wych House, was he?

With his accent, he was probably a secretary for a wealthy merchant; the sort who called themselves *men of business*.

No doubt his employer was looking for a fancy aristocratic estate to use as a showpiece where he could bring all his vulgar merchant friends.

Phoebe snorted softly. Well, luckily for her family, Wych House would not be what he wanted, and they'd not have to bear the thought of such an encroaching cit living in their ancestral home.

"Do you think he wants to lease Wych House?" Doddy asked. His furrowed brow told Phoebe that her brother wasn't sure how he felt about that.

"I daresay he is a servant employed by a wealthy man to find suitable property."

"His employer must be terribly rich if can mount his servant on such a horse."

"Indeed."

Phoebe smirked as she pictured the arrogant man's expression when he saw their lovely, but terribly neglected, family home.

"I doubt Wych House will be up to his standards." She turned to her brother. "If I were the wagering sort, I'd bet your new coins that today was the first and last time we'll ever set eyes on that crude, overbearing cit."

Phoebe would have good reason to remember those words later.

Chapter Two

As Paul rode away from the ragged and rather witless looking boy and his companion—whose battered straw hat looked as if it had been ravaged by weasels—he shook his head in disgust.

He wasn't just disgusted by the poorly garbed yokels he'd just encountered—which were walking, talking proof that the Earl of Addiscombe failed to take care of his people—or the neglected state of the farmland on both sides of the road.

No, what really disgusted him was that he had ridden all this way to see the state of the place when he should have guessed how matters lay.

Paul was mad at himself for being such an idiot.

He also reserved a little anger for his man of business, Harold Twickham.

It had been Twickham who'd piqued Paul's curiosity and sent him to the Earl of Addiscombe's godforsaken little corner of the world.

"The Earl of Addiscombe is desperate for funds, Paul. I daresay he'd offer you a lease for a song," Twickham had said a mere two weeks earlier at their monthly financial meeting.

"I don't want to lease Twickham. I want to build my own house, not pour money into some nob's castoffs."

The older man had winced at the word *nob.*

Twickham was something of a nob, himself, as he was the grandson of a baron. But his family had fallen on hard times when he'd been a young man and he'd been forced to seek employment. That was how he'd met Paul's father—John "Iron Mad" Needham—almost fifty years earlier.

"I have seen the architect's plans for the house you wish to build and it will take at least two years to finish it," Twickham said. "It was my understanding that you were looking for somewhere that Mrs. Kettering and her daughter could live in the interim."

Paul had sighed. "I can see you won't be happy until you tell me more about this earl—Addiscombe? I've not heard of him."

That wasn't exactly unusual. Even though Paul was the second Viscount Needham, he eschewed moving in *tonish* circles.

"The Bellamys are one of the oldest families in Britain and—"

"Now that has to be one of the stupidest things these toffs say about their families," Paul scoffed. "*Everyone* comes from somewhere, Twickham—even the lowest chimney sweep could trace his bloody lineage back six hundred years if he had the leisure and money to do so."

Twickham ignored the interruption. "Their country seat is Wych House—"

"*Witch* House? What the devil kind of name is that?"

Twickham sighed, his features wearing the patient expression he probably used with his fractious two-year-old grandson.

"It is w-y-c-h, as in wych elms. Several fine specimens of such majestic trees can be found on the grounds of the estate. This is not the original house—which burnt to the ground during the Civil War—but its replacement, which was built in the late 1660s and is an excellent example of the Carolean style." He hesitated. "Carolean means—"

Paul threw back his head and laughed. "Lord, man, you're worse than my old housemaster. I know what it means—Latin for Charles—that would be Charlie the second, not to be confused with his headless papa."

Twickham pursed his lips and shook his head at Paul's disrespectful levity. "Wych House is a spectacular structure in need of a great deal of maintenance, and the earl is looking for someone who will lease the property."

What a surprise.

"I suppose this *spectacular* property includes a great many dogeared tenant farms and falling down outbuildings?"

"The current earl sold off thirty-two thousand acres several years ago, which was everything that wasn't entailed. What remains is four-thousand acres and the home farm."

"I don't suppose you know who bought the land?"

"Albert Freemantle."

"Freemantle?" Paul frowned. "He just lost his shirt—and probably his breeches—when that hurricane sank three-quarters of his fleet."

"That is true. He is eager to divest himself of property, which is one reason I am recommending you look at the house. I know you had your eyes on another piece of land in Devon, but this might be had for a song and you could lease Wych House and be close during the construction phase of the new house."

"How long has the house been sitting vacant?"

"A naval man leased the property for four years but broke his lease three years in, forfeiting his last year's payment just to get away."

Paul laughed. "So I will have to pour my money into the earl's estate if I want to live comfortably. Then, in four years' time—or less—I can hand it back to him in pristine condition."

A sly expression flickered across the older man's face. "Actually…"

"Yes?" Paul prodded. "I know that expression, and it usually means something that makes us both a great deal of money."

"Leasing is only one part of the plan."

"Go on, you've got me interested now."

"The earl is amenable to an action for common recovery."

Paul shook his head. "I'm confused. If his heir would offer no resistance to breaking the entail, then why is he fussing about with leasing?"

"His son is not yet fifteen."

"Then he'll have to wait years—six of them—until the boy is no longer a minor to begin an action in common recovery."

"Well, that is true… in a way."

"What do you mean, *in a way*? Either the lad is a minor or he isn't." Paul frowned. "Why do you look so damned guilty, Twickham?"

The older man cleared his throat. "While a minor may void a contract, the contracts entered into by minors are not in themselves void."

"Why is that relevant?"

"Have you heard anything about the sale of Lord Hightower's property in Cumberland?"

"I know the matter was dragged through the courts for several years. Why?"

"While the case yielded no firm precedent, it created some interesting possibilities."

Paul sighed. "Speak plainly, please."

"Well, what happened in Hightower's case was the usual recovery action—"

"Which is already a twisted legal fiction," Paul couldn't help pointing out.

Twickham didn't deny it. "In Hightower's case, the buyer turned around and sold the property almost immediately to a third party, who in turn sold it to another and—"

"Good God, Twickham—is there a point to any of this?"

"I'm getting to it," Twickham insisted. "These transactions happened four years before Hightower's heir reached his majority. The last sale took place between buyers that were far removed from the action in common recovery and the court—in this case, at least—was unwilling to overturn the sale."

"Bloody hell, that's confusing. And it also seems… unethical." Even to Paul, whose morality on matters of business was more than a little elastic.

"I agree it appears a bit murky, but not when you consider Addiscombe is on the verge of losing the little cottage where he and his family have lived since being forced to abandon Wych House. When that happens, he either must move back into the house—which he cannot afford to operate—or take his family to a less than desirable location. The man really has no other choice."

Paul stared for a long moment before asking, "How do you know Addiscombe would be amenable to such an idea?"

"Because he's been casting out lures." He hesitated, and then added, "Nathan Malvern is his first nibble."

Paul gave a hoot of derisive at the mention of his longtime nemesis, a conscienceless shipping magnate who had never forgiven Paul's father for receiving the title that Malvern himself had aspired to for decades.

"You are only dropping Malvern's name to pique my interest," he accused.

Twickham didn't deny it.

"I know there is something you aren't telling me, Uncle."

Twickham wasn't really his uncle—or any relation at all—but he was closer to Paul than his own father had been.

The papery skin over Twickham's cheekbones darkened once again at Paul's words.

"Out with it, you old scoundrel."

"Addiscombe has five daughters, all unmarried."

Paul laughed. "It is past time you remarried!"

Twickham clucked his tongue at Paul's teasing, hesitated, and then said, "I know you promised your father on his deathbed that you would—"

"If I were you, Twickham, I wouldn't be so eager to bring up my father's ambitions for me. I'm sure you recall what happened the last time I tried to please him," Paul said, no longer amused.

Especially since the last *episode* was the reason Paul was still unmarried at the ripe old age of thirty-five.

Twickham looked so chastened that Paul felt guilty about snapping at him.

"Fine. Tell me about these daughters; I take it all of them are bran-faced," Paul said.

"No, I recall seeing his eldest daughter several years ago, and she was lovely. The second oldest girl, who must be in her early twenties now, is said to be a diamond of the first water."

"Why is it I've never heard of this nonpareil?"

"Addiscombe hasn't been to London since selling his town house. It is my understanding that they don't even socialize much in the country. I daresay that isn't from choice but from the need to retrench."

"Lord, he really must be skint if he can't even take his daughters to country assemblies." Paul sighed. "Other than your desire to match make, what do his daughters have to do with all this?" He snorted. "Is Addiscombe actually requiring potential buyers to marry one of them as part of the bargain?"

"No. In fact, it is Malvern who is insisting on marrying the second oldest—the beautiful one."

Paul's stomach churned with disgust. "Good God! The man is a revolting, diseased deviant. Is Addiscombe really considering it?"

"He isn't happy about it—nobody in their right mind wants to have anything to do with Malvern. But the man is too wealthy to ignore. Especially for somebody as desperate as Addiscombe."

Twickham, wily old bird that he was, let Paul stew on that thought for a moment before adding, "Even if you decide not to marry one of the earl's daughters, this is an incredible opportunity, Paul. Wych House might need a great deal of money, but you could never build a house even half so grand. And with your interest in agriculture—"

"I only have a scientific interest in farming, Uncle, not a desire to become an actual farmer. Besides, I doubt there's enough land available—"

"There would be if Freemantle could be brought to sell," Twickham insisted.

"—to even support this massive pile of bricks," Paul finished, ignoring his uncle's interruption.

Twickham was undaunted by Paul's arguments. "Even if you aren't able to buy the land from Freemantle, you don't need it to be self-sustaining."

No, Paul's pockets were deep enough to support a dozen Wych Houses.

"But I know you, Paul. You love a challenge. Unlike many of these aristocrats—who are unwilling or unable to adjust to the changes—you have the skills and ambition to make such an enterprise sustainable. It is men like you who will own this new age, Paul."

Paul wasn't interested in engaging in philosophical discussions about impoverished aristocrats or money-grubbing merchant-cits like himself.

"You might be right about the property and land, Uncle. But what in the world makes you think I want a wife?"

"You've spoken about wanting to establish your daughter, Paul. A bachelor cannot launch a young girl; if you should ever decide to do so."

"And how do you think my prospective wife will feel about *launching* my bastard daughter? How will an earl's precious daughter feel about my reputation, my life, my background?"

"Women of the aristocracy are bred to overlook and endure such things, Paul."

He laughed, but there was no humor in it. "Bloody delightful. So she can pinch her nose and close her eyes whenever she needs to look at, speak to, or fuck her barbaric husband?"

Twickham sighed. "For all that you like to *behave* like a barbarian, Paul, you are a highly educated man and we both know it. No matter what pains you take to hide it. And it astounds me how you refuse to accept that you are also a peer in your own right."

"My title is so new as to be offensive to this sort of people. Not only that, but I am—unapologetically—a merchant. I will continue to engage in business no matter how much money my father put into turning me out like a lord. We both know that would horrify an aristocratic woman."

"It is true that your title is new and that you are not accepted by the highest sticklers. But with the proper wife, you could enter the upper orders of society."

"Yes, but why would I want to?" Paul retorted.

"Lucy is thirteen, Paul. If you have any hope of establishing your daughter as anything other than—"

"I don't need any advice about my daughter." Paul didn't raise his voice. In fact, he'd lowered it—but it had the desired effect on the other man.

And yet Twickham's words had stayed with Paul and caused a noxious stew of guilt and anxiety to grow in his stomach.

Neither Lucy nor her mother, Ellen, liked London and Paul knew the city was bad for Ellen's health. She needed clean country air but refused to go to any of the usual seaside towns or watering holes—at least not without Lucy. And Paul, selfish man that he was, didn't want to be away from his daughter.

Paul had been searching for somewhere to lease—a place the three of them could move quickly—because the house he was going to build would take so long that Ellen wouldn't live to see it.

Paul sighed, met Twickham's eager gaze, and said, "Where did you say this Wych House was?"

Twickham struggled to smother a grin and failed. "Near the market town of Little Sissingdon, a picturesque village unspoiled by coaching inns or commerce or—"

"Or collieries or iron works?" Paul asked wryly.

"Er—"

Paul snorted. "Don't worry—I might own such places, but I don't wish to live near them, either." He'd narrowed his eyes at the older man. "But before I go anywhere to look at anything or talk to anyone, I shall want you to get me more information."

It had taken Twickham a few weeks to gather the Earl of Addiscombe's disastrous financial details, and Paul had also hired a private enquiry agent to pay a visit to Little Sissingdon and collect some information about the Bellamy clan and their much-reduced circumstances.

First, there was Queen's Bower. The quaint Tudor manor where the family now lived was all Lord Addiscombe had left to sell if he didn't find a wealthy, clueless tenant. Soon.

Second, there were Addiscombe's six children, all of whom were unmarried and living at home.

At twenty-five Aurelia Bellamy, the eldest, was an attractive and accomplished artist who'd been supplementing the Bellamy family income for years by illustrating naturalist publications under the alias Jacob Forrester. Aurelia was the only Bellamy who'd had a Season.

Next was Hyacinth, who, at twenty-two, was something of a dark horse. The sparse information the agent had dug up painted a picture of an awkward woman of no great beauty who lacked both the social aptitude and desire to socialize. Like her elder sister, Lady Hyacinth did her part for the family economy by dressing as a boy—the agent had noted the disguise was entirely convincing—to play cards in the rural gambling dens around the area. Unlike her father, Lady Hyacinth had come away with money in her pocket all three times the agent had followed her.

Selina Bellamy, at twenty-one, was widely considered the most beautiful women in the county. She possessed no peculiarities or odd hobbies like her older sisters, a fact which made her number one on Paul's tentative list of marital prospects—not that he had decided to offer for one of the earl's daughters *or* connive with him to break entail.

A fourth daughter, Phoebe, was twenty and agreed to be the least accomplished or attractive of the Bellamy brood. She spent most of her time taking care of household matters at Queen's Bower and shouldering tasks that should have belonged to her mother or father.

Interestingly, Phoebe was the only Bellamy sibling to have been betrothed. Her engagement to Sebastian Lowery—the son of a local squire—three years earlier, had only lasted a few months before she ended it.

The consensus is that she broke off the betrothal after discovering her father had dissipated his daughters' doweries. Whether she received pressure from Lowery to end the engagement is unknown.

Katherine Bellamy, at barely seventeen, was reckoned to be both a beauty in the making and something of a hoyden.

The heir and only son, Dauntry, Viscount Bellamy—also called "Doddy"—was almost fifteen. He'd never been to school and was tutored by the local vicar and his elder sisters.

And then there were pater and mater Bellamy.

The earl and countess, by all accounts, hated one another's guts and had done since their fecund and infelicitous union began twenty-six years earlier.

Lady Addiscombe was born plain Helen Framling, the daughter of a wealthy dry goods merchant from Bristol. Helen brought a much-needed infusion of brass to the tottering earldom, which her new husband set about spending at an alarming rate.

Gerald Bellamy, Seventh Earl of Addiscombe, had been a close associate of the Prince Regent for decades.

The earl was generally liked by his peers, although acknowledged to be something of a loose fish. He'd not sat in Lords since leaving London and had done precious little in his capacity as earl before then. By all accounts, he was a man infected with a fatal case of gambling-fever.

All that information had combined to pique Paul's interest enough that he was currently sitting astride Coal and staring at a crossroads.

The road on the right led to London and the road on the left—according to the young ragamuffin who'd directed him—led toward Wych House.

Paul was, literally, at a fork in the road.

The symbolism did not escape him.

Twickham had known exactly how to describe Wych House, the Bellamy family, and the earl's desire to break entail in such a way that Paul—a man whose instincts for profit were as deeply ingrained as a shark's instincts for blood—had packed a bag and ridden all the way to Little Sissingdon.

Although he had not yet seen the famous—or infamous—Wych House yet, the air of neglect that pervaded the village, the surrounding area, and its impoverished denizens was palpable and was causing him to regret setting off on what increasingly felt like a harebrained journey.

Harebrained? Not at all! This is a perfect opportunity for you, my boy, said a wheedling inner voice that sounded exactly like his dead father.

Paul wanted to ignore the voice, but it was as loud and insistent as his father had been in real life.

With your wealth, you can elevate everyone in the area, Paul—not just save a noble old house. That little village you passed through sits on land the earl sold to Freemantle and it is dying of neglect. If you bought the house and surrounding property, it would be your land and the inhabitants would be your people.

Paul snorted at the absurd claim. *You make it sound as if I'd become a feudal lord, Father. Besides, I already own a great deal of land around all my houses, so why would this be anything different?*

Here you wouldn't be the ugly son of a grasping upstart. Here you could build yourself in a new image and become a proper lord of the demesne.

Paul laughed aloud.

Although his social-climbing father was long dead, this entire arrangement was exactly what John Needham had dreamed of all his life: somewhere he wouldn't be known as "Iron Mad" Needham, but Lord Needham.

This was your dream, Father, not mine.

You promised me, Paul. Remember...

Paul snorted. *I'm unlikely to forget the foolish deathbed promises you squeezed from me.*

He sighed and patted the stallion on his glossy black neck. "Well, Coal, what do you think? Should we turn tail and scuttle back home? Or would it be cowardly to leave without even seeing this so-called masterpiece of architecture?"

His horse shifted restlessly but offered no opinion.

So, the decision was up to Paul, then.

"Very well, old boy. You asked for it," he muttered, and then urged his mount toward the lefthand fork and the road that led to Wych House.

Chapter Three

Describe him again, Phoebe," Aurelia ordered.

"Good Lord, Lia, I've already described him three times," Phoebe complained, squinting at the three-inch rent in her skirt that she was trying to mend without leaving any trace. It wasn't likely to happen, as she was a dreadful hand at needlework.

All six Bellamy siblings were sitting in the large attic room that had been packed with rotting furniture and chests full of moldering old clothing when they'd moved into Queen's Bower.

Lady Addiscombe had showed no interest in the dusty, stuffy, cobweb-festooned space so the six of them had salvaged what they could of the moth-eaten furniture, gradually creating what they affectionately referred to as The Lair.

It might be hot and miserable in the summer and freezing in the winter, but it was the one place in the house their mother was unlikely to come looking for them.

Selina held out a hand for Phoebe's mending. "Here, give that to me, Pheeb. You're making a dreadful hash of it. I'll see to it while you tell us about the man again. This time, leave nothing out," she chided gently.

Selina did everything gently.

Even though her sister was firmly on the shelf at twenty-one, she seemed to grow more lovely with each passing year. She had a complexion like fresh cream, golden-blonde hair with a natural curl, and thickly lashed sky-blue eyes. Not only did she look like an angel, but she also possessed the temperament of one.

"Describe him again," Katie urged when Phoebe hesitated.

"Oh, very well. Why not?" she muttered.

After all, what else did they have to talk about? They never socialized or went anywhere interesting, so encountering a stranger who might want Wych House was the most exciting thing to have happened in months.

"He was an immense man, quite the largest—"

"He was even bigger than Papa's old tenant, Zeb Cantor." Doddy cut in from his position on the floor, where he was lying on his back with his squirrel lying on his chest, the two of them gazing lovingly into each other's eyes.

Phoebe glared down at him. "Excuse me, my lord, but would *you* like to finish this story?"

"I'm sorry," he said, not very convincingly.

"Yes, he was even bigger than Zeb," Phoebe said. "Although his expression was far less—"

"Witless?" Doddy suggested as he scratched Silas behind one ear and reduced him to a drooling lump of fur.

"The word I was going to say was *pleasant*. Anyhow, he was dressed in clothes just as nice as Papa's—"

Katie snorted. "Then perhaps he wasn't looking to lease the house at all, but was an impoverished peer seeking a game of cards?"

"Katie!" Selina admonished softly.

"Sorry," Katie grumbled. At barely seventeen, their youngest sister was sharp-witted and sharp-tongued. She also bid fair to rival Selina as the family beauty—but without the gentle temperament.

Phoebe continued. "It was clear he'd purchased his clothing from the finest clothier on Bond Street—"

"Just like Papa," Katie murmured, unsuppressed.

This time Selina didn't bother scolding her sister. After all, what Katie said was true; while the rest of them re-made their gowns and wore castoffs, their father still visited London twice a year to purchase new garments.

It was hardly fair that the person who had done the most to plunge them into penury was the least affected by his actions. But then life wasn't fair, was it?

"Pheeb," Doddy whined. "Are you going to tell it or should—"

"As for the rude stranger's horse," Phoebe said loudly, talking over him, "He was—"

"Smashing! Bang up to the knocker," Doddy cut in.

"Mama will confine you to bread and water for a week if she hears such talk coming out of your mouth," Katie said.

"It was the finest piece of horseflesh I've ever seen," Doddy went on, his tone reverential.

"Oh, and you are *such* an expert on such matters," Katie taunted.

Doddy bristled. "It's better than being a stupid girl who is afraid of a little spider and cries if she gets a splinter in her finger and—"

"Children," Aurelia warned.

Doddy opened his mouth to argue with his eldest sibling—one of his favorite hobbies, even though it was as dangerous as bearbaiting with a sister who was more likely to box your ears than report you to their mother—when Hyacinth spoke.

Their second eldest sibling was so quiet that it was often easy to forget she was in the room. And she spoke so rarely that everyone paused to hear what she had to say.

"You say he was dressed like a gentleman yet spoke like a cit. If his horse was of the caliber you claim, then he does not sound like a rich man's servant, but a rich man himself, coming to inspect a country house. That sort of man likes to be in control. They don't delegate important details to mere servants. That is something Papa would do."

Trust Hy to reduce matters so quickly and easily.

Their quiet, introspective sister was the cleverest person Phoebe had ever met, which was not something Phoebe envied Hy. After all, being an intelligent woman was considered a defect among their class.

Added to Hy's unfortunate intelligence was her unwillingness to speak more than ten words a week. Her narrow face was pale and freckled and her hair was as orange as… well, an orange. She was so tall, thin, and gangly that she resembled a boy even though she was a twenty-two-year-old woman.

When you added all that together, you had a woman who was unlikely to catch a husband even if she'd been an heiress.

Phoebe's chest hurt just contemplating Hy's future. Of all the Bellamy children, she was the one least likely to escape the dreary future of living and dying at Queen's Bower with their parents.

"Whoever he is," Katie said, cutting into her grim thoughts, "he doubtless took one look at the dreadful state of poor old Wych House and ran as fast as he could back to his manufactory or coal mine." Katie's words were flippant, but her tone—just like all their moods—was pensive.

While none of them wanted some merchant upstart in their ancestral home, what would happen to them if their father could not find a tenant for Wych House?

"I received a message from our Aunt Fitzroy," Hy said, speaking for a second time in one day. "She wishes me to come to London for the Season."

The Lair erupted in gasps.

"But Hy, you would hate it. Wouldn't you?" Phoebe asked.

Before she could answer, Katie piped up, "Why didn't she ask Aurelia? She is the eldest and should be—"

"I already had a Season. I don't want another," Aurelia declared coolly.

"I trust Mama knows of this?" Selina asked. "If she does, then you shan't be able to escape the invitation, dearest."

"She knows. I am to leave in four days," Hy said, as expressionless as ever.

A stunned silence filled the room.

Surprisingly, it was Doddy who broke it. "You cannot go to the city and prance about in gowns at balls, Hy." He pushed himself upright, dislodging a sleeping Silas. "You hate that sort of mummery—it would kill you in a week." He snorted. "Or, more likely, you would kill somebody else." His slight smile slid away. "None of you will sacrifice yourselves like this; I shan't allow it." He met each of their eyes in turn, six centuries' worth of aristocratic breeding turning his angelic features hard, determined, and far too old for his years.

"I will be Addiscombe one day, and it is *my* duty to save you." His blond brows snapped into a straight, golden line. "*I* am the one who is going to marry a rich, vulgar heiress and we shall all live together at Wych House. I'll settle monstrous sums of money on each of you and you shan't ever have to marry unless you wish to." He grimaced, once again resembling the boy he was. "And who the devil would wish to marry if they didn't have to?" He shivered, demonstrating just how selfless the offer he'd just made was.

His chivalrous words diffused the somber atmosphere Hy's announcement had created and all five sisters jumped on their beloved little brother, kissing him, ruffling his hair, and generally horrifying him.

Phoebe knew that as much as they might laugh and play now, behind all their smiles were crushing worries just waiting to erupt.

If the cit they'd seen today—or another one like him—leased their ancestral home, it would be just one more humiliation. But if he didn't want Wych House? Well, that would be a hundred times worse.

Once they had tickled Doddy breathless and driven him from the room, Selina turned to the rest of them, her expression firm and resolved. "Let us not allow our imaginations to run away with us. Nobody needs rescuing from anything. Yet."

***

A scant three days later, Selina had to eat those words.

"Four months—that is all the time Papa has to pay the money on the loan. If he cannot pay, they will eject us from Queen's Bower," Katie said, eyes wide.

Normally, Aurelia would scold their youngest sister for her nasty habit of listening at doors, but this time, she remained quiet.

It was just Phoebe and her sisters in the Lair. Doddy was at the vicarage, where he took his lessons three days a week, which was just as well, since the last thing their little brother needed to hear was something like this.

As Aurelia put aside her mending, Phoebe couldn't help noticing that her oldest sister did not appear as surprised as the rest of them.

"You knew about this, didn't you, Lia?" Phoebe asked.

Aurelia nodded. "Mama told me."

"Why didn't you tell us?" Selina asked, clearly hurt by her sister's omission.

"Because I needed some time to think."

"Think about what?" Katie asked.

"About what we should do." Aurelia looked around at the rest of them, her expression one of grim resolve. "We cannot depend on Papa to save us. If we're going to find a way out of this horrific disaster, we'll need to find it ourselves."

The words were unsettling when said out loud, but Phoebe knew it wasn't anything they'd not all thought privately.

"Lia is right. *We* need to get the money," Hy said quietly.

"But how?" Phoebe demanded.

Hyacinth and Aurelia exchanged a look that Phoebe couldn't decipher.

"Marriage?" Selina suggested, her face paler than ever. "But… we never go anywhere or meet anyone."

"That needs to change," Hy said. "I'm off to London tomorrow, and I've been thinking about our aunt's invitation." She looked at Selina. "It should be you who is going to have a run at a Season. You would actually enjoy it and you *want* to get married."

"I can hardly thrust myself into your place," Selina said.

"No," Hy agreed. "But Aunt Fitzroy mentioned one thing in her letter that was very interesting. Her mother-in-law needs a companion, and our aunt is on the hunt to fill the position for the *fourth* time."

"She must be a difficult old lady," Katie said with a grimace.

"Dealing with a crotchety old lady is more in my line of things than going to balls," Hy pointed out.

Nobody argued with her. Hy had more patience than the rest of the family combined.

"What are you thinking?" Phoebe asked.

"I shall suggest to Aunt that I am the solution to her mother-in-law dilemma. At the same time, I'll let her know Selina is champing at the bit for a whack at the Season."

Phoebe smiled; knowing Hy, she would use exactly that same street cant to speak to their aunt.

"What if she has already engaged somebody as a companion by the time you get there?" Katie asked.

"If she's already run through three ladies in only two months, then I'm guessing the position will be vacant soon enough."

"But…" Phoebe bit her lip.

"Yes?" Hy prodded.

"I don't see how a companion position will help get the money we need?"

The rest of them nodded.

Hy's pale cheeks flushed faintly, an unusual sign of emotion in their normally phlegmatic sibling. "I have saved up almost three hundred pounds."

Everyone gasped.

Aurelia clucked her tongue. "Oh, Hy. Cards?"

Hy flashed one of her rare smiles, a humorous glint in her pale green eyes. "Yes."

"But, dearest, we've all seen how risking one's luck at the card table turns out," Selina said.

"What we have seen is how a terrible card player fares." Her lips curved into a faint, almost predatory smile. "I do not rely on luck and I'm a far better card player than Papa. I've won this much money, and that was only by playing for chicken stakes. In London, I would have access to far better games."

"But they'd never let a woman play," Katie said.

"They don't let a woman play *here*," Hy pointed out dryly.

Only Aurelia didn't gawk at their sister.

"You knew she was dressing up and sneaking out, Lia!" Phoebe accused for the second time that day.

"I did," Aurelia admitted. "And while I can't approve of cards, I have to admit that Hy knows what she is about." She shrugged. "Hy is a woman grown. It is her own decision."

"You really dress like a man?" Selina asked.

"Yes. And nobody has ever questioned me," she said, looking unperturbed at the admission. "I can at least make enough money to hold us over until one of you, er, well, does the deed."

Phoebe glanced around at the others, expecting to see disbelief or disapproval.

But her sisters looked thoughtful.

Truth be told, they were simply too desperate to rule out any possibility, even dreaded cards, which had led their family to ruin.

"It doesn't seem fair to put all the burden on Hy—or Selina, if Aunt Fitzroy invites her," Phoebe said, her mind racing how she could help.

But she had no way of earning money and the only gentleman who'd ever shown any interest in her had turned out to be a repulsive, manipulative cad.

Aurelia cleared her throat, and they all turned to her. "I respect Hy's plan to save Queen's Bower, but it has become increasingly clear that we cannot stop our father from"—Aurelia paused, obviously searching for some way of calling their father a feckless, thoughtless gambler without using those words.

"Losing our home," Katie supplied grimly.

Aurelia nodded. "Yes, losing our home. So, that is why I've come up with a plan of my own." She reached into her needlework bag and took out a folded sheet of newspaper, which she handed to Phoebe.

It was an advertisement for an illustrator.

The suitable applicant would be required to work with field journals and samples at the employer's residence for the duration of the project. Ability to collate data—whatever that meant—would be an added benefit. The job was expected to last six months, with a salary to be agreed upon.

"Surely the employer will expect a *man*?" Phoebe asked, handing the clipping to Selina.

"I applied for the job under my nom de plume," Aurelia admitted. "And I included several drawings. When the gentleman—Lord Crewe—offered me the position, I wrote to him and confessed my identity. He wrote back and said my gender was irrelevant, but that I must begin work by the end of the month if I wanted the position."

They all spoke at once.

"A lord?" Phoebe repeated.

"Is he wealthy?" Katie demanded.

"Is he married?" Selina asked.

"I read about Crewe in the *London Examiner*," Hy said.

Aurelia answered her sisters' comments in order, "Yes, I don't know, no, and so did I." She smiled and added, "He is a widowed gentleman who is a naturalist of some renown and was badly injured on his last expedition to America."

"His wife was killed by a wild cat and he was badly mauled," Hy said.

"A *cat*?" Katie scoffed.

"It was a panther," Aurelia said quietly. "And yes, he was *severely* mauled. His wife was also a naturalist, and the two had always worked together. It was quite a tragedy."

"Is he an invalid?" Phoebe asked.

"I don't know," Aurelia said.

"Is it wise to live in a widowed gentleman's house?" Selina asked. "Won't it harm your reputation beyond repair?"

Aurelia shrugged. "I will use my alias on his work. In the past, that has kept our family name free of any scandal that would come from being associated with a *woman* earning money. Besides, although I know it is selfish of me, I really do not care if I ruin my reputation. This is the best opportunity I will ever get. Lord Crewe is a fellow of the National Geographic Society. If my work pleases him, the potential for new commissions is immense."

"Well done," Hy said softly, her pale green eyes glinting with respect.

The others nodded.

Aurelia flushed at their quiet praise. "I know it will not be enough to save Queen's Bower or do anything about Wych House and poor Doddy's situation, but if the sum Lord Crewe and I agreed on is indicative of how much this sort of work pays, then I could eventually afford a little cottage." She gave one of her rare smiles. "It might be a bit cramped for all of us, but at least we wouldn't have to live in fear of it being taken away."

The room was quiet as they considered their sister's words.

Phoebe finally broke the silence. "The rest of you have already put so much thought into how to help. I've done *nothing*."

Selina squeezed Phoebe's hand. "Oh, dearest, you are invaluable here! You are the one who makes sure we have meat to eat and a bit of sugar for our tea."

"You knew who to summon when the ceiling collapsed in our bedchamber," Katie chimed in.

"Without you to manage the accounts, there would be even fewer little luxuries," Hy added.

"And somebody will need to watch over Doddy and you are by far his favorite," Aurelia pointed out—unjustly in Phoebe's opinion; their little brother loved all of them equally and would miss his sisters desperately.

"If Hy wins a fortune or Selena marries a wealthy, handsome gentleman who adores her, then you can come home, Aurelia," Katie said, her brow creased with hope.

Aurelia sighed. "I know this will sound ungrateful, but I don't wish to be a pensioner in any of your homes if you marry. And while Hy might earn enough to avert disaster for the family *this* time, who is to say what will save us the next?" She gave a bitter, very un-Aurelia-like snort. "The last ten years—especially since leaving Wych House—have been filled with constant worry and dread. Henceforth, I wish to make my own way."

Hy nodded. "That is wise. While our goal should be to keep Queen's Bower and preserve something for Doddy when he inherits, we should pursue our plans regardless of whether the others succeed or fail." Hy glanced around. "Pax?"

The four of them nodded. "Pax," Aurelia, Selina, and Phoebe murmured.

"Wait! What about me? I want to help," Katie said. "What can I do?"

Selina smiled. "You are too young to either seek work or marry."

"Mama married at seventeen."

"And look how that turned out," Phoebe said tartly.

"Phoebe!" Selena gasped.

"Phoebe only said what all of us have thought on more than one occasion," Aurelia said. "I want to say one more thing. I know we are all hoping to rescue the family fortunes but let us agree that *none* of us will form a union as ill-advised as that which our mother and father did. You must all promise me you will not sacrifice your own happiness for the rest of us. I would not want to save our family at the cost of your happiness."

Again, the others nodded.

Phoebe wondered if any of them would really let their own personal happiness impinge if there was a chance to save the others.

She knew what she would do if faced with such a decision.

Chapter Four

Eleven Days Later …

Phoebe nervously smoothed her already smooth skirt. Again.
Katie fidgeted on one side of her, and Aurelia remained as motionless as a statue on the other.

Phoebe couldn't help envying Hy and Selina—whom their Aunt Fitzroy had invited, just as Hy had predicted—who were *not* sitting in a row like items perched on a shelf in a shop window.

For Sale: Three Females of Various Ages and Appearances. Maidenheads guaranteed intact. Inquire Within.

A nervous giggle bubbled up in her throat, but Phoebe prudently forced it back down.

She twisted slightly to look at Aurelia, but her sister appeared to be entirely consumed by her embroidery.

If this horrid meeting had occurred even one day later, then Aurelia would have escaped it entirely. Because tomorrow she would board the mail coach that would take her to Scotland, to her new job.

Phoebe was proud of her sister, who'd stood her ground even when their mother had harangued her to stay every day for the past three weeks. But Aurelia was serene and immovable. And tomorrow she would be gone.

"Katie!" Lady Addiscombe's voice was like the crack of a whip in the quiet, cramped drawing room.

"What is it, Mama?" Katie demanded, looking up from the lovely embroidery piece she was working on.

For all that her younger sister was often as scuffed, stained, and dirty as Doddy, she possessed the most exquisite needlework skills in their family.

But she squirmed, seemingly unaware of her body's gyrations.

"Will you *cease* your incessant thrashing, or must I bind you to your chair?"

"I'm sorry, Mama," their usually irrepressible hoyden of a little sister murmured.

Not even Katie, the bravest of all the Bellamy children when it came to open defiance of their mother, was foolish enough to antagonize the countess today.

Indeed, nobody had wanted to be in the same room with the countess after she had learned that Viscount Needham, one of the wealthiest industrialists in Britain, was to lease Wych House.

"Needham is not *tonish*," her ladyship had conceded, "but situated as we are… " The countess had shrugged, not needing to complete the thought: that—thanks to their father—the Bellamy family could not afford to be choosy.

Unfortunately, it wasn't the leasing of Wych House that had them all sitting and waiting in the parlor.

No, they were there because Lady Addiscombe was *determined* that Viscount Needham would marry one of her daughters.

"I am actually relieved Selina is in London," the countess had said earlier. "Your sister would be positively *wasted* on such a man."

It had been difficult to keep a straight face.

"Do sit up straight, Phoebe."

Phoebe stiffened immediately at the sound of her mother's command.

Once again, the room settled into silence, only the warring ticking of the ormolu mantle clock and longcase clock disturbing the tomblike atmosphere.

They'd been assembled and waiting in the drawing room for over an hour—since well before the viscount's arrival.

He'd arrived in a sinfully luxurious traveling coach that was pulled by *six* matched black horses.

"Oh, poor Doddy," Aurelia had murmured. "It is a shame he is missing those horses."

Phoebe had certainly never seen the like before. The animals were identical, their coats glossy black, their tails and manes stylishly plaited.

Of the viscount himself, all they'd seen was a pair of long legs in buff pantaloons, monstrously broad shoulders, and a top hat.

Phoebe had seen enough to say, "Yes, that was the man Doddy and I saw."

So, not a servant, after all…

"There is nothing vulgar about either his equipage or his servants' livery, Pheeb," Katie had—rightfully—pointed out.

"I didn't say that he or his possessions *looked* vulgar," Phoebe had protested.

"Everything is of the first elegance," Aurelia had commented.

Phoebe had to agree.

His swaggering postilions and grooms wore tasteful black coats and breeches that matched the glossy black carriage and horses. It was all unimpeachably stylish.

She was still struggling to reconcile such opulence and luxury with the harsh, ill-spoken creature who'd barked at them and flung coins.

The door to the sitting room opened and snapped Phoebe from her reverie.

"Ah, yes, here they are," the earl said, as if he hadn't known exactly how long they had been waiting.

Phoebe had believed that her memory had exaggerated the man's size, but the opposite was true: he was bigger than she remembered. He *towered* over the earl by at least six inches and seemed to be twice as broad as their slender father.

Gerald Bellamy, at sixty, looked a good decade younger than his wife, who was his junior by almost fifteen years. Phoebe had never been able to decide if her mother's premature aging resulted from living with her father or from giving birth to nine children, three of whom did not survive infancy.

Whatever the reason, her father had remained handsome and youthful, no matter how little he might deserve it.

The earl smiled vaguely at his wife. "My dear, may I present Viscount Needham." He nodded at the tall peer. "Needham, my wife, the Countess of Addiscombe."

The giant took her mother's hand and bowed over it, his movements neither clumsy nor especially graceful, but merely perfunctory.

Phoebe hadn't seen him so closely the last time. Also, the sun had been glaring in her eyes and his face had been shaded by his hat. But her first impression had been correct: his features were harsh. He had a heavy, square jaw and a chin that was determined and jutting. While it would have been unfair to call him *ugly,* he was very close to it.

And yet he was not difficult to look at. Indeed, it seemed hard to look away. He appeared to possess that undefinable quality that drew one's attention. Perhaps it was his great size or the aura of power that hung about him.

He was, Phoebe realized, the most masculine man she had ever encountered.

Not that she was entirely sure what that entailed or what about him had led her to that conclusion. Indeed, never in her life had she considered what constituted masculinity, but something about the viscount encouraged such thoughts.

Just like his impeccable clothing, his dark brown curls were fashionably cut and tousled. Everything about him except his size, face, and abrupt manner was that of a gentleman.

Phoebe's face heated at her thoughts.

Was that really what made a gentleman? Fine features, an impressive lineage, and courtly manners?

Suddenly that struck her as being terribly shallow.

She pushed away the sobering thought and studied their guest from beneath lowered lashes.

His pale gray eyes—his only attractive feature—were fringed with black spiky lashes and heavy-lidded. In fact, they were so hooded that he appeared to be brooding.

Maybe he *was* brooding.

He certainly wasn't smiling.

Judging by the harsh brackets around his mouth and the downward pull at the corners of his thin lips, he was a man who was a stranger to merriment of any sort.

"Thank you for receiving me today, *Lady* Addiscombe." His lips curved faintly— almost mockingly.

The countess flushed at the slight emphasis on her title and what his sly look implied—that Lord Needham and the countess were cut from the same merchant-class cloth.

Lord Addiscombe's eyes bounced between Needham and the countess and he looked positively gleeful at the viscount's needling and its effect on his wife. He turned away from the show with obvious reluctance.

"This is my eldest, Lady Aurelia."

Needham bowed, his expression once again brooding rather than mocking. "Lady Phoebe."

If looking at him was distracting, being looked *at* by those pale gray eyes was well…

Her face heated and breathing seemed like something she had to force herself to remember.

The viscount's lips flexed, but no smile reached his eyes. He inclined his dark head and turned to Katie.

And then he deliberately turned back, and his eyes widened in recognition. Amusement transformed his face into something that—if not handsome—was certainly appealing.

His cruel-looking lips curved, and kept curving, until Phoebe saw a flash of white teeth. The skin around his eyes crinkled and his eyelids lifted enough to expose more of those remarkable irises.

"Lady Phoebe," he repeated, humor glinting in his gaze. "We've met."

His flat vowels confirmed her memory that he spoke like a clerk, although not with the heavy Northern brogue one would expect.

Because his disgraceful behavior that day deserved no answer, Phoebe merely inclined her head.

His smile grew broader, his bold gaze moving over her face, throat, and bosom in a way no decent man would look at a woman.

Phoebe swallowed hard and blushed harder. *Wretched man.*

Her parents looked confused, and Phoebe realized that neither of them had put this man together with the stranger from several weeks earlier.

"Last, but not least, is my youngest daughter, Lady Katherine." The earl's smile spoke louder than words. Katie—although only just turned seventeen—had been brought out for Needham's inspection just in case the wealthy peer preferred her dewy freshness over Aurelia's superior, but more mature, beauty.

As for Phoebe?

Well… Phoebe harbored no illusions that Needham—who was as rich as Croesus and would have his choice of beautiful debutants—would ever be interested in her.

"We have two other daughters who are visiting their aunt, Lady Fitzroy," the earl said. "I hope you will call upon them when you return to London." He beamed. "You can introduce yourself as our newest neighbor."

Phoebe cringed, ashamed of her father's willingness to barter his children. Especially when it was all to pay for *his* mistakes.

"Perhaps I shall," Needham agreed quietly. He wore a faint, derisive smile, obviously amused that the earl was hawking his daughters as if they were bloodstock.

"Please, have a seat." The earl gestured to the only chair that was likely to hold the viscount.

Needham flicked aside his cutaway tails to sit, briefly exposing a glimpse of hips and thighs that were so thick and muscular they filled the entire chair, his shoulders broader than the wingback.

For all that he was so large, he seemed to be utterly at home in his skin, his posture one of ease, as if he were lounging in his own home rather than visiting strangers.

Phoebe bristled at such arrogant confidence and resolved not to fawn over him, no matter what the countess had ordered when she'd learned that he was coming to *inspect* them.

"Lord Needham will commence occupation of Wych House immediately," the earl said.

Phoebe could see by the lights in her father's green eyes that he was already mentally spending the money.

"How nice it will be to have somebody at Wych House," Aurelia said in her cool, well-modulated voice.

Needham looked amused by her haughty tone and inclined his head. "Thank you, Lady Aurelia. I look forward to deepening my acquaintance with my neighbors."

Phoebe couldn't help noticing that even her unflappable sister's pale skin tinted beneath Paul Needham's raptor-like gaze.

The silence stretched and the countess gave Phoebe a pointed look.

"Will you have any family living with you?" Phoebe asked.

"As a matter of fact, my daughter Lucy will join me."

The countess stiffened at this information. "I must apologize, my lord. I wasn't aware that you were a widower."

"I'm not. Lucy is my natural daughter."

Nobody moved or spoke. The shock that pervaded the room was so thick it was palpable.

"My daughter is just turned thirteen and has always lived with me," the viscount went on, as if nothing were amiss. And then his eyelids drooped even more, and he added, "As has her mother, Ellen Kettering."

An odd, almost animalistic noise came from Lady Addiscombe right before her hand flew to cover her mouth, as if she might be physically ill.

Phoebe was almost more stunned by her mother's unprecedented public display of emotion than she was by their guest's outrageous declaration.

She could only assume their parents were terribly mistaken—that Viscount Needham was not in search of a wife—and they had all made fools of themselves today.

Phoebe turned to her father, wondering what he would do—what he would say? Would he call Needham out for saying such crude things in front of them?

Rather than glaring angrily at the viscount, the earl was smirking at his wife.

Phoebe recognized the gleam in her father's eyes and knew, without a doubt, that he had engineered this meeting to punish and shame his wife.

The countess's hand was still over her mouth, but otherwise she'd not moved. Her face was chalky white with two bright spots of color, and her chest was rising and falling in shallow, rapid breaths.

"Share your good news with my wife and daughters, Needham," the earl said, as if nothing were wrong.

Needham swept them all with a slightly contemptuous gaze, which Phoebe was beginning to suspect was his natural expression.

His eyes settled on her and did not move.

Phoebe swallowed; the weight of his stare was like being slowly squashed.

"I will give a ball at Wych House as soon as I have settled in," he finally said. "I hope you are all able to attend."

Their mother shot to her feet, followed instantly by the earl and Needham.

The countess swallowed convulsively, her eyes darting wildly between her husband and the monster in gentleman's clothing who'd invaded her sitting room.

"I—I beg you will excuse me. I have just remembered…" Her hand fluttered like a frantic moth. "Something."

She bolted for the door in a swirl of dove-gray muslin, but Lord Needham needed only two long strides to get there before her and open the door.

He bowed. "My lady."

The countess fled.

The earl clapped the enormous man on his shoulder. "Jolly good, my lord!" he said, grinning up at his wife's newest tormentor. "I'm sure all the young ladies in the neighborhood will be in high spirits looking forward to a grand ball at Wych House."

Needham ignored her father and turned to Phoebe and her sisters. "Your father tells me you have always used the estate woods, walked its trails, and enjoyed the stream. You must continue to treat Wych House and its environs as you've always done. It has been a pleasure meeting you." He bowed and turned to the earl. "I shall see myself out, my lord."

Their father opened his mouth, but Needham left before he could get a word out.

When the door shut soundlessly behind him, the earl turned back to his daughters, his smile dimming at whatever—likely shock and anger—he saw on their faces.

"Well," he said, rather lamely. And then turned and left without another word.

Katie was the first to recover from the shock. "When he said *her mother*, did he mean—"

"Katie, darling," Aurelia broke in. "Will you look in on Mama and make sure she isn't in need of something?"

Phoebe and Katie could only stare.

If there was any child Lady Addiscombe cared for less than the others, it would be her wild, auburn-headed youngest daughter. Sending Katie to wait on their mother was like throwing pitch onto a fire.

Aurelia tilted her chin down and gave Phoebe a significant look.

"Ah," Phoebe said, seizing her sister's meaning. "Yes, Katie. Find Mama. Tell her we will be up to wait on her shortly."

"But—"

"Katie." When Aurelia used that tone—remarkably like the countess's—it usually got her siblings moving.

Katie flounced toward the door. "Oh, very well! I know you are just sending me away so I won't ask questions."

Neither of them denied it.

Katie slammed the door behind her.

"Do you—" Aurelia began.

"How could—" Phoebe started.

They both stopped.

"You first, Lia," Phoebe urged.

"I don't believe I've ever heard such a thing before."

"I certainly haven't. But perhaps we might look on the bright side?"

"Which is?"

"At least this puts an end to our worries that Mama would force one of us to marry him."

Aurelia gave an unamused bark of laugher. "Are you so certain about that?"

"Are you mad, Lia? Neither Mama nor Papa would consider such a union. Papa only did what he did today to torment our mother—you know how the two of them are. But neither of them would allow one of their daughters to marry a man who keeps his love child and *mistress* in his house and makes no bones about it. No. Impossible." She shook her head vigorously. "He is so far beyond the pale there should be a new phrase for it."

"He is beyond the pale," Aurelia conceded. "Unfortunately, his great wealth will cause all the influential people in the area to flock to him." She frowned, deep in thought. "I dislike admitting this, but if it looks like the neighborhood is on the catch for Lord Needham, then Mama will relent. You know she would encourage us to marry Beelzebub himself if she thought one of her neighbors might marry him and inhabit Wych House as its mistress."

Phoebe stared at her sister as the horrible truth of what she was saying sank in.

"Mama is upset right now," Aurelia continued. "But by the time Needham's wretched ball comes around, one of us will be engaged to marry him—mark my words. She will exert all the pressure she can to encourage one of us to capitulate. As for Papa, I suspect he has formed some arrangement with the odious man."

"An arrangement? You mean you think Papa has agreed for one of us to marry that—that *monster*? Would *you* consent to such an arrangement?"

"We might none of us have a choice, Phoebe."

How could her sister sound so calm?

"But Aurelia, now that Papa is leasing Wych House surely the money problems have been settled?" Phoebe asked. "Surely they won't expect any of us to—to do such a thing?"

"Have they been settled?" Aurelia's eyes were flinty and grim. "Will father *ever* settle such problems? And what about us, Phoebe? Do you believe Father wants the burden of five unwed daughters for the rest of his days?"

Phoebe's brain raced to come up with a convincing counterargument. What her sister was saying could *not* be true.

Could it?

"I don't believe it will be me Viscount Needham wants," Aurelia continued relentlessly. "Nor do I think it will be you or Katie. Thanks to Papa's invitation to *view* his other daughters in London, the viscount will take one look at Selina and want her. Who wouldn't?"

"No!" Phoebe jumped to her feet. "Absolutely not—it is unthinkable."

But even as she spoke, she knew Aurelia was right.

And Selina, their selfless sister, was so kind and sweet that she would sacrifice herself for them.

Unless one of them came up with a way to stop him.

Chapter Five

Aurelia left the day after the dreadful meeting in the sitting room.
"Do nothing rash or foolish," had been her last words to Phoebe.
The countess did not leave her room for three days—not even to bid Aurelia goodbye—and when she finally did emerge, she didn't say a word about the vile cit occupying their ancestral home.

Indeed, after a week had passed with nothing being said at home or in the village, Phoebe was feeling as if the entire episode had never occurred.

But then the invitation to Needham's ball arrived.

Even though the glorious event was still weeks away, the entire area erupted with eager anticipation at the treat in store for them.

Phoebe had seen their family's invitation, but neither her mother nor father made any mention of it.

She wasn't sure what that meant.

Had her mother torn it up without opening it, or was she watching and waiting to see how their neighbors reacted?

Could Aurelia possibly be right? Would their mother encourage a match between one of her daughters and Needham if it appeared their neighbors welcomed him?

Four days after the invitations had been sent out, Phoebe and Katie were at Burton's Mercantile when Agnes and Susannah Lowrey, Squire Lowrey's identical twin daughters, entered the store, chattering nineteen to the dozen.

They didn't immediately see Phoebe and Katie behind the bolts of fabric, so they made no effort to curb their conversation.

"—and can you believe Susan's mama chose that wretched primrose muslin for her ball gown?" one twin asked in a carrying voice.

"It makes her look positively pasty!" Sister Two answered.

"And here I thought it was impossible for her to look any worse than she did at the Hitchen's ball," Sister One said.

The two tittered like peahens.

Sister One lowered her voice, or at least tried to. "Mama says he is worth as much eighty thousand pounds a year."

"Eighty thousand pounds," Two repeated in awe. "It could almost make one forget how ugly and huge he is."

Her twin gasped. "You are cruel and wicked!"

Again, they laughed.

"As hideous as he is, at least he dresses well," Two pointed out.

"Mama said it was clear that he bought his clothes on Bond Street."

"Oooooh, Bond Street," the two cooed together, and then dissolved into giggles.

"We should wear blue the same shade as a bluebell," One said, suddenly serious.

"You chose our gowns the last time, Agnes!" her twin retorted. "It is my turn now."

They began to bicker, their voices becoming louder.

Katie and Phoebe exchanged an amused look.

As they could hardly lurk in the tiny fabric section all day, Phoebe nodded to Katie and the two of them left their covert.

"Oh!" both twins exclaimed when they saw them. "Hello, Lady Phoebe. Lady Katherine," they chimed in unison.

The sisters really *were* identical, and they made it even more difficult to tell them apart by dressing the same.

"Aren't you simply delighted about the ball?"

Phoebe only knew it was Agnes because her sister had already identified her.

"You must be pleased that you'll be able to attend a ball at Wych House," Susannah added.

"Yes," Katie said, with a faint smile. "We're *overjoyed* to attend a function at our own house."

The other women blinked, clearly trying to assess whether this was sarcasm.

The Lowery twins would have been Phoebe's sisters if she had married their brother Sebastian Lowery—the man Phoebe had briefly been betrothed to several years ago. While she did not especially like the girls, she could tolerate their brainless, self-absorbed nattering.

Katie was not so forbearing.

"Will you be taking a journey to Brighton for your ballgowns?" Phoebe asked, not because she was interested, but so the girls would leave Katie alone.

Sir Thomas Lowery wasn't a wealthy man, but neither had he gambled away all his money and daughter's doweries, as Phoebe's father had. He was a generous and indulgent parent and his children were always the best dressed in the small community and his son the best mounted. But, for all that, they were still country gentry and not at all tonish.

Their brows puckered, and the same expression of discontent shifted their pretty features.

"No, not Brighton," Agnes admitted. "But there is a new seamstress in Upper Coombs who has only recently moved there from London."

Upper Coombs was a nearby village that was about twice the size of Little Sissingdon.

"Oh. Upper Coombs," Katies said with a dismissive smile. "Not exactly the hub of fashion, but I suppose it will do."

Both twins scowled—albeit genteelly. Two identical pairs of sky-blue eyes flickered over Phoebe and Katie, both of whom were wearing gowns that had seen better days.

"And what about *you* two?" Agnes asked, a sly smile on her pretty face.

Phoebe opened her mouth.

"*We* are getting our gowns in Brighton," Katie said.

Phoebe turned to stare at her sister, but Katie refused to meet her gaze.

What could Katie be *thinking*?

Yes, Wych House was leased. But there were piles of bills that needed to be paid and dozens of repairs that needed to be made.

Phoebe had already begged Papa to have the roof fixed before anything else, but he had pooh-poohed it because *his* chambers did not require three buckets to keep dry when it rained.

Katie knew perfectly well there would be *no* new gowns—even if they *were* going to the ball.

The Lowery twins appeared displeased by Katie's lie, a reaction which clearly delighted her sister.

Phoebe was about to drag Katie from the store before she told any more lies when the bell over the shop door rang and in walked the very subject of their conversation.

Lord Needham's strange, pale eyes moved over the four of them, his expression one of polite disinterest.

"Good afternoon, my lord." The twins dropped graceful—and identical—curtseys.

"Ladies." He inclined his head.

"Ah, good afternoon, my lord." Mr. Burton hurried out from behind his counter, where he'd been slowly unpacking a large crate filled with new fabric.

The new fabric was the sole reason that Phoebe and Katie had lingered so long; they'd wanted to get a peek at the newest bolts before they were all snapped up.

Needham turned to the shop owner. "Good afternoon, Mr. Burton."

Although the viscount spoke quietly, his voice was so low that Phoebe could feel the vibration in her chest even ten feet away.

"Are you here to see about that special order you made, my lord?"

"Did it arrive?"

"Yes sir, just this morning, in fact. If you want to inspect it, you can come round back and—"

"No, no, that won't be necessary. I'm on my way to London and only stopped to show you a list of items I need. If there is anything on the list that you might have difficulty procuring, then I shall order it in the City."

Burton rubbed his hands together, his eyes sparkling at the thought of a large order. "It'd be my pleasure to take a look, sir."

Lord Needham pulled a piece of folded parchment from the pocket of his exquisitely cut coat and handed it to Burton.

While the older man studied it, the viscount turned back to the twins, who'd edged so close they were at his elbow.

He smiled coolly. "Miss Lowry, Miss Susannah."

The twins' jaws dropped in tandem.

"You can tell us apart," the one he'd called Miss Lowry said. "*Nobody* can ever tell us apart!"

The viscount looked amused. "You won't be able to say that again, will you?"

Predictably, the twins giggled.

He turned to Phoebe and Katie, who'd been inching toward the door, trying to escape before he saw them.

"Good afternoon, Lady Phoebe, Lady Katherine," he said, inclining his head.

They stopped and dropped curtsies, the gesture instinctive.

"My lord," they both murmured.

"We have a question for you, Lord Needham," Susannah said, clearly unhappy that his attention had turned away from them.

"Yes?"

"My Papa says you will bring an orchestra *all* the way from London to play. Is that true?"

"Yes, it is."

"And he also said—"

Phoebe had no interest in hearing their conversation. She clutched Katie's arm and gave it a tug. "Come, we are leaving," she said in an under voice.

"But what about—"

"We'll come back later," she hissed.

Katie dragged her feet, forcing Phoebe to all but drag her out of the store.

"Wait, Pheeb," Katie complained once they were outside the shop. "My sandal is broken."

Phoebe glared at Lord Needham's black coach and six identical horses, which took up most of the street. Four outriders stood around the coach, awaiting their master's return.

Phoebe sneered. "Just look at that vulgar excess. He travels as grandly as a royal duke."

She turned her back on the grand carriage and frog-marched Katie around the corner of the store, to where there was a wooden bench.

She pushed her sister onto the seat and dropped to her haunches before taking Katie's foot in her hands.

Phoebe looked from the tattered shoe to her sister. "Why on earth did you wear these, Katie? They are almost worn through."

"I wore them because they looked best with my gown."

Her *gown* was a faded sprigged muslin that had belonged to all four of her elder sisters before it had been refurbished for her

Katie leaned forward and pointed to the place where two of the six straps flopped loose. "Just tie the two front straps to the back."

"These two?" Phoebe asked.

"Yes. Why did you drag us out of there, Pheeb?"

"Because the last thing I wish to do is stand listening to that vulgar upstart puff off his wealth and consequence to those two vapid ninnies."

"But we might have heard more news and now *they* shall have all the latest *ondits*."

"I find it difficult to believe that vile, hideous, encroaching cit has anything of value to impart about *anything*." She snorted. "Other than the latest developments in ironmongery."

When Katie didn't laugh, Phoebe glanced up at her and saw her sister staring over her head, gawping like a stunned carp.

A throat cleared behind her.

Phoebe tried to turn without standing first and fell onto her bottom in the dirt, sending up a small puff of dust.

Lord Needham stood mere feet away. His face was as harsh and expressionless as any other time she'd seen him.

For one long moment, she thought perhaps she'd been lucky.

But then she noticed the faint streaks of color on his cheekbones.

No, he'd heard her.

Phoebe briefly squeezed her eyes shut, wishing she could simply burrow into the dirt like a gopher.

But there was no escape from this situation.

She might have continued sitting there, eyes shut tight, if he'd not said, "Let me help you up, Lady Phoebe."

Phoebe forced her eyes open to find him looking down at her in a way that made her stomach clench, his huge, gloved hand in front of her.

Phoebe stared at it.

The last thing she wanted to do was touch it, but her only other option was to ignore him and hope he went away. Clearly her insult hadn't driven him off, so pretending he wasn't there wouldn't work, either.

She took his hand, painfully aware of how grubby her cotton gloves looked compared to the sleek, soft black kid.

He raised her up as if she were a feather.

The instant she was on her feet, she yanked her hand away.

Only then did she realize how close she was to him, her eyes barely inches from the top button of his elegant clawhammer coat.

She stumbled back and would have fallen *again* if he'd not reached out a hand to study her.

"Thank you, my lord," she said, and then jerked away her elbow with the pretext of swatting dirt from her gown.

"My pleasure."

Phoebe continued to beat her clothing, even when no more dirt came off.

Why didn't the wretched man *leave*? Why was he standing there? What did he—

"I plan to call upon your Aunt Fitzroy on this visit to London."

Phoebe's head whipped up at that, and she saw he was smiling down at her.

It was the sort of smile that villains in gothic novels wore right before they shoved the unwanted heroine off a cliff.

It was the sort of smile that made hairs she'd never noticed before stand on end.

It was the sort of smile one received from one's mortal enemy.

"They were not at home the last time I called," he said, the words sending yet another bolt of fear to her belly.

Oh no! He had already called on them?

"Are there any messages I might pass along for you?" he asked, his gray crystalline gaze so cold and sharp it was like being stabbed with two icicles.

Phoebe had to force herself to hold his gaze.

She also had to force herself to keep from shouting, *stay away from my sisters!*

Instead, she said, "You are most kind, my lord. But I have no messages."

It was a lie; she actually had *plenty* of messages, but not the sort she'd ever tell *this* man.

The countess had, suddenly, forbidden Phoebe or Katie to write to their two sisters.

When Phoebe had asked why, her mother had snapped, "The last thing this family needs is to spread the news of our disastrous new tenant to London. Your sister may have an opportunity to make something of the Season. Just leave her be."

Phoebe and Katie had known *which* sister the countess had meant.

She wondered what her mother would think when she learned Needham was calling on Selina...

Lord Needham's nostrils flared slightly as he stared down at her, like a predator scenting something new and intriguing.

Phoebe took another step back.

One side of his thin-lipped mouth pulled up into a tiny smile and he touched his hat. "If you have no messages for me then I bid you both good day."

Only when he turned the corner did Phoebe release her pent-up breath.

Katie came to stand beside her and they both crept closer to the building so they could peek around the corner in time to see him climb into his coach.

As well-sprung as the expensive vehicle was, it still bowed under his considerable bulk.

Neither of them said a word until the grooms resumed their places and the magnificent carriage rolled down Little Sissingdon's tiny main street and out of sight.

"Phoebe!" Katie said, turning on her with eyes as round as an owl. "That was *dreadful!*"

Yes, it had been. Even though he was a man of low birth—who exhibited even lower behavior—she had behaved reprehensibly.

"You could have told me he was standing right behind me," Phoebe snapped, striding toward the path that would lead them back to Queen's Bower.

Katie had to trot to keep up with her, even though she was two inches taller than Phoebe.

"I didn't see him until it was too late, Pheeb. I'm *so* sorry." She sounded on the verge of tears.

"It was entirely my fault," Phoebe said.

"But—do you think he will change his mind about inviting us to his ball now?"

Phoebe laughed at her sister's question, which had been the farthest thing from her mind.

"It's entirely likely that our mother won't permit us to go, Katie. Besides," she snarled, becoming more furious—at herself? At Needham?—with every step, "after what he said in our sitting room, I wouldn't go to his wretched ball if he begged me on his hands and knees."

Chapter Six

Y ou are going to Needham's ball, and that is my last word on the subject!"
Sparks flew from Lady Addiscombe's cornflower blue eyes as she glared at
Phoebe. "I am not in a mood to be trifled with," her mother warned when
Phoebe opened her mouth to argue.

As if that were something new. As far as Phoebe could tell, her mother had been
in ill humor since birth.

Normally, Phoebe would have bowed her head like a dutiful daughter, but not
this time.

No, not this time.

"How can you ask such a thing of me? Don't you care what he said to you in
your very own house, Mama?"

Her mother seemed to double in size. "Do *not* think to chide me in my own
home," she said in an awful voice. "If you believe there is even one aristocratic male
in the nation—no matter their lineage—who does not keep mistresses or visit houses
of ill repute, then you are too ignorant for your age."

Phoebe reeled under her mother's assault. "But—but to bring such a woman into
his *home*—"

"Trust me, my girl, whomever he marries will be grateful for the diversion of
having a trollop so close at hand."

Phoebe gasped. "Mama!"

Her mother gave her a dismissive sneer. "It will not only relieve his unfortunate
wife of certain onerous duties, but she also won't have to watch as her husband drains
the family coffers to set up his light skirt in an elegant and *expensive* establishment."

Phoebe had never heard her mother speak with so little sensibility before.
Normally, she was the epitome of propriety. Now, suddenly, she was crude and
agitated.

It was… upsetting.

"Every eligible young miss in the entire *county* is on the catch for him, Phoebe.
Do you really believe I can bear to watch one of those Lowery chits sit at the foot of a
table that should be mine?" Spittle flew from her fastidious mother's lips and she
didn't even appear to notice. "You *will* go to this ball if I have to drag you by your
hair. And you *will* do your best to secure this vulgar mushroom's interest." Her
mother's eyes narrowed, fury in her gaze. "Because if you believe the money from the
lease is enough to save us all, then you are a fool."

The countess turned on her heel and left Phoebe standing in the middle of the
room, mouth agape.

***

Phoebe stared in horror at the letter in her hand, Hy's chicken scratch penmanship dancing on the page.

"Lord Needham took Selina driving in his phaeton—twice. Aunt Fitzroy believes he is smitten. She says Selina may snare him without lifting a finger.

Selina is trying to put a good face on regarding the potential match, but I know she is horrified, Phoebe. Given what you said about that dreadful meeting at Queen's Bower, it is shocking that mother would have written the last letter she did. A letter which all but commanded *poor Selina to secure the wretched man's interest.*

Phoebe dropped her hand, the letter crushed between her fingers. The memory of Needham as he'd looked outside Burton's Mercantile—harsh and satanic—lodged in her mind's eye.

"Oh, poor, poor Selina," she whispered.

What can I do?

Phoebe's mind raced round and round as she stood staring at nothing.

No matter how long she pondered the matter, she arrived at the same conclusion.

There was only one way to save her sister, and there was only one person who could do so quickly.

Phoebe shoved the letter under the pillow on her bed, snatched up her bonnet and cloak, and went to pay a visit on her new neighbor.

***

"There is a young lady in the sitting room, my lord. She claims to be one of the Earl of Addiscombe's daughters." Paul's staid butler, Davis, hesitated and then added, "She is unattended, sir."

Paul had met all five of the earl's daughters, and there was only one of them who'd looked forthright enough to call—unattended—on a bachelor who'd announced that he would install his mistress and love child at Wych House.

Paul smiled at his servant. "Show her in."

"Did I mention she is without a companion, sir?"

Paul almost laughed. "Thank you for reminding me, Davis. Send up a tea tray."

The butler's pause was just long enough to convey his thoughts on such behavior. "Very good, sir."

Paul pushed aside the stack of ancient architectural plans that lay open on the desk and removed the spectacles he used to read.

He'd been at Wych House not quite three weeks and had become obsessed by the old structure. It was a magnificent, one-of-a-kind house.

Every instance of neglect Paul found only served to make him more determined to help Addiscombe break entail and take the property for himself.

Addiscombe had practically broken into song when Paul had accepted his offer. Paul knew the other man had already rushed off to London, ostensibly to speak to his own men of business, but likely to spend the first lease payment.

Breaking the entail and acquiring the property was time-consuming and, by necessity, convoluted, so the sooner Paul began it, the sooner he could get what he wanted.

Although the agreement with Addiscombe left him with a nasty taste in his mouth, he was not the one who was doing his own son out of his inheritance.

No, but you are the vile, hideous, encroaching cit who is making breaking entail possible, a voice in his head whispered.

Paul chuckled just thinking the words. He had been called many, many things in his life, but never had he been so brutally and efficiently summed up.

And now the young lady who'd conceived of that delightful epithet had come to pay a call.

Paul felt like it was Christmas morning and his birthday, all wrapped up in one.

The door opened, and Davis ushered her into the room.

Paul stood. "Ah, Lady Phoebe. What a pleasant surprise." He glanced behind her, as if looking for something—or someone, even though he already knew she was alone. "Where is your maid, my lady?"

She flushed at the implication of impropriety—especially coming from a vile, hideous, encroaching cit—but set her jaw. "I came alone."

Paul raised his eyebrows and turned to Davis, who hovered in the open doorway. "Send in one of the maids and leave open the door."

"Yes, my lord."

"Really, my lord," Lady Phoebe said after the butler had gone. "That is hardly necessary."

"Oh, but I think it is." Lady Phoebe looked like a skittish filly, so Paul was careful to keep any amusement from his face or voice.

He gestured to a cluster of chairs in front of the dormant fireplace. "Please, have a seat."

Paul had just sat when a maid skidded to a halt in the open doorway, breathless, her eyes wide. She dropped a curtsey. "Mr. Davis sent me, my lord."

"Yes—Becky, is it?"

"Aye, sir." The girl looked pleased that he'd recalled her name, apparently unaware that Paul always remembered servants' names.

"Come in, Becky. You may sit in the window seat and rest your feet." He gestured to the window that was farthest from them.

Becky nodded uncertainly but obeyed.

Paul turned back to Lady Phoebe, who was openly glaring at him. "I am not a young, ignorant miss whose reputation requires protection, my lord. In the past month alone, I've had unchaperoned meetings with a roofer, butcher, and a chandler."

Paul was amused at being grouped in with tradesmen and merchants.

He ignored her objection and rested his booted foot on his opposite knee, the action drawing her eyes to his riding boots.

"I apologize for receiving you in all my dirt, Lady Phoebe, but I wasn't dressed for visitors." He paused and then added, "Because I wasn't *expecting* any visitors. Especially not unaccompanied young ladies."

She bristled at his criticism of her behavior.

"What I have to say shan't require very much of your time," she said stiffly.

He rested his elbows on the arms of the chair and steepled his fingers. "Oh?"

"But it is rather… private."

"Becky is too far away to hear us."

She chewed her lower lip as she glanced toward the maid.

Paul raised his eyebrows and waited.

She swallowed, and he could almost *hear* the struggle occurring inside her.

The door opened, and another maid entered, sparing her from having to answer.

"Ah, here is tea." Paul gestured to the low table in front of his guest. "Will you do the honors, Lady Phoebe?"

Her eyes slid to the tea tray—which was laden with fancy biscuits and tarts and whatnot that Paul's pastry cook baked fresh daily for his atrocious sweet tooth—and such hungry desire flickered across her face that it left him breathless.

She wrenched her greedy gaze away from the food.   "Tea isn't necessary, my lord. I will not be—"

The maid hovered uncertainly.

"You may go," Paul said to the maid who'd delivered the tray and was hovering uncertainly. He turned to his agitated, clearly hungry guest. "Share my tea with me, please. It seems Cook has sent up enough food to satisfy an army."

That was a lie. Paul would have eaten everything himself if he were alone and Cook knew it.

He watched the struggle take place inside her as if it were a stage play.

He was charmed by her innocence, which was completely at odds with her air of competence in more mundane matters. She was as transparent as a pane of glass, with none of the guile a woman her age and class would have if she'd had a few Seasons.

Paul rarely associated with such young women. He did not attend *ton* functions in London—although he received hundreds of invitations every year—nor did he socialize with anyone but men of business when he visited the nation's capital.

While he'd enjoyed many lovers in his life, almost all of them had been women of experience.

Not that Paul was contemplating taking her as a lover, of course.

Although the thought gave him pause.

While she wasn't pretty, she was attractive, with her flashing hazel eyes and lush figure. Her true beauty, however, was her feisty intelligence.

She looked up and caught him watching her.

Whatever she saw on his face made her blush wildly. It was a response he'd never had from one of his mistresses and it made heat pool in his groin.

"Will you pour, my lady?" he asked again.

She gave a jerky nod and pulled off the most pitiful gloves Paul had seen in ages—perhaps ever; he caught glimpses of pink finger pads where the kid had worn through.

Her gown wasn't gray as he'd initially thought, but a faded blue, scrupulously clean but so threadbare he could see the warp.

And she wore the smallest pair of ankle boots Paul had ever seen. Like the rest of her ensemble, the boots were religiously polished and carefully patched, the leather so old and thin it had molded to the contours of her feet.

She wore these signs of her family's poverty with a quiet pride and resilience that humbled him and plucked at his conscience, a part of his brain he'd only been on nodding terms with for years.

What a strange effect she was having on him!

Send her packing right now, his newly awakened conscience ordered.

She's an earl's daughter! his father's voice—gleeful and determined—chimed in.

Paul knew that whatever she had come to negotiate, he would end up the victor—just as he always did.

Did he really want to be victorious over such an impoverished, unworthy foe?

Since when did you equate a lack of money with unworthiness?

The thought was like a slap and it shamed him to his expensive, handmade, polished-to-a-gloss boots.

Paul pushed his shame away—there was no reason in the world for him to feel ashamed. After all, if the action in common recovery worked and the earl could break the entail on Wych House, then Lady Phoebe and the rest of her family would have enough money to afford decent gloves *and* anything else they wanted.

That's if her father doesn't gamble it all away again…

Paul blinked at the thought.

Well, that would be unfortunate, but it was no problem of his, was it?

"How do you take your tea, my lord?"

Paul jerked his gaze away from her old boots. Her hazel eyes were cool, but her jaw was rigid with tension.

"Black and strong."

He watched as she gracefully poured a cup—weaker—for herself and then gestured to the tray of biscuits. "Do you have a preference?"

"I am not hungry," he lied. He was hungry, but, oddly, he was even hungrier to observe her without the distraction of eating.

Her pupils flared like those of a lover as she surveyed the bounty on the tray.

Paul smiled at her covetous expression; she was like a little girl peering in a shop window.

And Paul was the shopkeeper who could give her a sack of sweets.

But only as a distraction—so you can take something else from her.

He scowled at his interfering conscience. Why had it chosen to rear its nosy head now? He had made hundreds of business deals in his life, many of which had been far more inequitable—not to mention downright illegal—why in the hell was he feeling so guilty about *this* one?

If Paul didn't purchase this pile of bricks from the earl, somebody else— Malvern, likely—would swallow the deal like a hungry trout on a fly. And Malvern wouldn't just take the boy's inheritance, he'd take the earl's pretty daughter along with it. So why—

"Lord Needham?"

He looked up to find her holding a cup and saucer toward him.

"Thank you," Paul said. He took a sip of the inky liquid; it was perfect.

Lady Phoebe had still not chosen a pastry.   Her hand hovered over the sweets, as if she were frozen by too much choice. Finally, she selected a plum tart, one of his favorites.

Paul watched greedily as she took a tiny bite and chewed. Her eyelids dipped slightly, and he swore he could almost taste the sticky sweet delicacy sliding over his tongue and down his throat.

The pink tip of her tongue darted out and swept her plump lower lip for any crumbs.

Paul's mouth flooded with saliva, and he swallowed convulsively at her expression of sensual bliss.

Bloody. Hell. It was the most erotic thing he'd ever seen.

Paul shook his head in wonder; his cock was throbbing, and his balls were tight all because this scruffy chit was eating a tart.

He had paid thousands of pounds for mistresses who were renowned for their skills in the bedroom over the years. Perhaps he should have just given them pastries to eat in front of him?

Paul snorted at the ridiculousness of the situation.

She scowled at his ill-concealed laugh, her face flaming as she realized he had been watching her.

Once again, Paul witnessed a struggle take place inside her.

This time, the fight was between embarrassment and confusion. She could *sense* the charged feeling between them but was too naïve to identify it as sexual tension. Well, at least it was on his part.

Rather than titter or look away, she stared back at him boldly as she struggled to comprehend what she was missing.

The way her hazel eyes brimmed with intelligence and curiosity made Paul wonder why he'd always avoided virginal young women.

You're behaving like a vile pig, Paul, his newly awakened conscience chided.

Well, that was a bit unfair.

Paul wasn't *acting* on his impulses, but he was certainly *thinking* like a vile pig.

It was a damned good thing he'd possessed the foresight to bring Becky into the room to make sure he toed the line.

But the longer she sat there tempting him with her very presence, the harder it would be to continue to deny himself.

"Why have you come, Lady Phoebe," he asked harshly, suddenly quite annoyed that *he* was the one who had to protect her virtue because *she'd* been so foolish as to wander into his lair without a chaperone.

"I'm here about—" she stopped and bit her lower lip, which made *him* want to bite her lip.

And it was a lovely lip, shapely and far fuller than her prim, prissy upper lip.

"Yes?" he urged, impatient to get this over with.

"I wanted to apologize for what I said the other day."

Ah, so that was it.

Paul was more than a little disappointed by her answer. He'd hoped she was there for something less prosaic, although he knew not what.

"Oh?" he asked, yielding to his evil imp and feigning ignorance. "What did you say?"

Her lips parted in shock, the sight doing nothing for his already aroused body. *Quit being an arse.*

Paul sighed. "I am jesting, Lady Phoebe. I know the words you meant — *vile, hideous, encroaching cit*—or something to that effect?"

Those were the exact words, and they were burnt into his mind.

She nodded, cheeks on fire. "Yes, that," she said in a small voice.

"No apology necessary," he told her. "That is a fairly accurate summation of me, after all."

Her jaw sagged even lower.

"Was that all you came to say, Lady Phoebe?"

She closed her eyes, gave a loud, gulping swallow, and then, with her eyes still closed—as if she couldn't bear to look at him—asked, "Are you going to marry one of us?"

Very little surprised Paul anymore, but she just had.

He set down his cup and saucer. "Is that what your father told you?"

She opened her eyes and her pupils fluctuated wildly as they adjusted to the sudden light. "No, my father only said you've taken the lease."

Paul wondered if the earl had suffered a crisis of conscience after all but offering up his daughters naked on a platter.

"It was my mother who suggested you might be, er, seeking a spouse."

"Did she?" he asked, struck by her answer. Lady Addiscombe hadn't liked Paul *before* she'd met him, and after his announcement in her sitting room, she had looked at him with flesh-curdling loathing.

"Actually…" Lady Phoebe hesitated and stared down at the plate of sweets, although Paul didn't think she was seeing them. After a moment she blinked, as if to clear her vision, and straightened her shoulders before looking up. "I think she *initially* believed you were considering marriage but was less convinced of your motives after the announcement you made in the drawing room."

Her carefully crafted response delighted him and, once again, Paul couldn't resist the urge to tease her. "My announcement?" he repeated, willfully misunderstanding. "You mean about my intention to give a ball?"

Her lips parted, but nothing came out.

"I assure you, my lady, I have not changed my mind about giving a ball. In fact, my secretary already sent out the invitations." He cocked his head and gave her a look of concern. "Did yours not arrive?"

He could almost hear her teeth grinding as she considered her possible responses.

Paul knew he was an odious, evil pig of a man to force her to articulate what had transpired at her house that day, but he couldn't stop himself. Something about the proud set of her chin was making him misbehave.

Not to mention the fact that she called you a vile, hideous, encroaching cit.

Yes, it was possible those words might still rankle.

It wasn't her actual insult so much as all the insults it had made him remember, the thousands of slights and cuts he'd endured over the years from people like her.

It had started at Harrow and become worse at Cambridge. But it hadn't stopped there.

Even in the ballrooms of London and at places like Whites, Paul had faced aristocratic derision.

While he might have a title, Paul knew that he never would have gained entry to *any* of those places in a thousand years if not for his mountains of money.

Money.

Oh, the things people would do for money.

Is that why Lady Phoebe had come today? For money?

If Paul had been a decent man, he would have sent her home immediately. Or, even better, he would have sent Davis to tell her he wasn't at home.

But he was not a decent man.

He was the kind of man who would entice her with lovely pastries and lure her deeper into a dark, dangerous place from which there would be no escape.

"No, my lord," she had to force the words through clenched teeth. "I do *not* mean your intention to throw a ball."

"Oh? What do you mean, then?"

"I mean about your m-mistress."

Paul felt a flare of respect for her; he wouldn't have believed an earl's daughter capable of speaking such a word out loud. He waited, but she'd become stuck, like a wagon in a deep, sucking muck. She couldn't go back, but she couldn't go forward, either.

A kind, decent man would help her free her wagon.

Paul just sat back and waited.

When she spoke again, her voice was hoarse. "I understand you took my sister driving in Hyde Park."

"Lady Hyacinth?"

Her mouth tightened. "My other sister."

"Ah, yes, Lady Selina." He nodded his head slowly. "I called on them both. However, it was only Lady Selina whom I took driving. Twice." He smiled and knew it wasn't pleasant. "Your father spoke of her beauty, and I found myself intrigued. I must admit, he did not exaggerate; she is an extremely lovely young woman."

Lady Phoebe looked as if she might weep—and not because she envied her sister her beauty, either.

You are going to burn in Hell, Paul.

True, but he'd burn for a host of other things first.

Paul studied her from beneath lowered lids, unable to pull his gaze from her.

He could have told her that as beautiful as Selina was, she had done nothing for him.

His cock hadn't swollen from sitting next to her in the carriage, taking tea with her, or at any other point during either of his visits.

Paul hadn't wanted to tease and taunt and get under her skin, and he'd had no desire to take her apart and see how she worked.

Indeed, other than her impressive physical beauty, he'd found Selina Bellamy to be positively… boring.

"Selina is not just beautiful, my lord, she is also very kind and good." Lady Phoebe's voice shook, but her gaze was steady. Her throat flexed and produced a labored, gulping sound.

"M-Marrying you would destroy her."

To his utter amazement, Paul felt a small pang of… *something* deep in his chest— shame? chagrin? anger?—at the knowledge that this young woman didn't just think Paul was a *vile, hideous, encroaching cit*. She actually thought he was *evil*.

"I have made you angry," she blurted. "I'm sorry. I didn't mean to insult you. Again." Her face was a mask of fear—almost terror—her brow creased with apprehension.

Paul suddenly found her opinion of him not only deeply offensive, but painful— like a knife between the ribs.

If she thought him such an evil beast, perhaps he should behave like one?

He smiled, and she drew back slightly at whatever she saw. "What would Lady Selina say if I asked her to be my wife?"

Her jaw tightened, and Paul *knew* she wanted to lie. But she was a good girl who'd been raised to tell the truth. He could only assume some decent, upstanding nanny or governess was responsible for that impulse because it certainly hadn't been her parents.

"If you asked her to marry you, she would accept," Lady Phoebe finally admitted.

"She is a woman grown. Is it not her choice to make?"

"She would sacrifice herself for the rest of us."

Sacrifice. What a powerful word.

Even a man without a heart would find her belief that marrying him would be a sacrifice insulting. Paul tried to focus on the amusement he felt at being bluntly told such a thing. But then he noticed her hands, which were clenched together so tightly her tanned skin and work-scuffed knuckles were white. She was terrified at the thought of her sister marrying him.

Not disgusted or contemptuous, but terrified.

And yet she had come here to beard him in his den, to save her sister.

Paul could not recall the last time—if ever—that he had met somebody so… magnificent.

He almost felt sorry for her at that moment. Sorry that she had, inadvertently, made the disastrous mistake of piquing his interest.

***

It was like being trapped in a cage with a dangerous animal—one that liked to toy with its prey before killing it.

Phoebe had no idea what Lord Needham was thinking. She could see expressions, but they were not identifiable. He didn't appear to possess the emotions a normal person did. She'd been terrified that he would be angry at her or insulted by what he'd overheard, but, if anything, he had looked amused. And yet now, he was a silent, brooding enigma.

His pale stare was abrasive—like a razor flaying her skin—but she could not look away.

He stared and stared.

And then his thin, mobile lips curved up at the edges. "You needn't worry, Lady Phoebe. I shan't ask any of your sisters to marry me."

Phoebe felt like she did when she stood too fast and her head spun, her vision blackening around the edges.

Thank God.

She had fully intended to offer herself—a poor substitute for Selina, that was true, but an earl's daughter, all the same. And now, none of them would be sacrificed.

She realized he was waiting for a response and smiled—the first genuine expression she'd allowed her face to show since walking up the front steps to the house.

"Thank you, my lord. Thank you." Her face heated at the raw gratitude in her voice when she recalled exactly *what* she was thanking him for.

"You are welcome."

She picked up her tea; her trembling hands causing the fine porcelain to rattle, and raised the cooling beverage to her mouth, her gaze settling on the almost untouched plate of delicacies as she sipped.

Her hunger—which had fled earlier—returned with a vengeance and her stomach rumbled, thankfully too softly to be heard. She bit her lower lip. Perhaps she could have just one more—

"But I have one condition, Lady Phoebe."

She wrenched her eyes away from a particularly tasty looking cream cake and glanced up to find the behemoth standing.

Phoebe put down her cup and saucer with a noisy clatter and pressed her body against the back of her chair, as if she could get away from him.

"Wh-what? I beg your pardon?"

"I said I had one condition."

"Condition?"

He nodded solemnly as he towered over her chair.

"What is it?"

He dropped to one knee with a swift grace that made her jaw sag. Two huge, warm hands enfolded one of hers.

"I won't ask any of your sisters to marry me as long as you agree to become my wife."

Chapter Seven

London
Ten Days Later

Y ou did *what?*" Twickham demanded.

Paul smiled at the usually imperturbable man's stunned reaction.

They were sitting in Paul's study in his London House. He had completed his business in Yorkshire sooner than expected, so he had come to the city for a few days to spend some time with Lucy, the first person he'd told about his upcoming nuptials.

She had been delighted to learn that she'd have a new step mama and thrilled at the thought of living in the country.

Her mother, on the other hand, had looked distinctly unhappy when she'd heard Paul was marrying an aristocrat and relocating them all to rural Hampshire.

Well, Ellen had some time to get accustomed to the idea, as Paul wasn't moving them to Wych House until after the ball, which is when their rooms would finally be ready.

Paul had needed to engage every tradesman in the county to ensure the formal dining room and ballroom were all fit to be used by the time of the ball.

Although work was progressing nicely on the master and mistress suites, Ellen and Lucy's part of the house was taking longer than he'd expected.

In his London home—where Paul, Ellen, and Lucy had lived together since Lucy's birth—the three of them had occupied the same part of the house.

But Paul did not want to further agitate Lady Phoebe by housing his mistress and her child right near their own chambers, so Ellen and Lucy would be in the east wing of the house, which was as far away from Paul and Phoebe's rooms as a person could be.

Phoebe. Just thinking his wife-to-be's name was enough to make him smile.

"Paul?"

Paul shook away the mental image of his bride—which seemed to appear often in his head—and looked at his oldest friend. "Hmm?"

"I asked you if you were sure of your decision?"

"I thought you *wished* for me to marry one of Addiscombe's daughters?"

The old man gave a choked laugh. "And since when have you ever done anything that anyone wished you to do, Paul? You are the least tractable, most unpredictable man I've ever known. In fact, you can be counted on to do the most unpredictable thing in every situation."

Paul grinned. "I hate to argue," he lied. "But wouldn't *always* being unpredictable actually make me... *predictable*?"

Twickham's nonplussed expression made Paul laugh.

"Come, old friend, let's not engage in word games. Why don't you share a drink with me—congratulate me on my good fortune?" Paul poured them both a stiff brandy without waiting for his answer.

"So," Twickham said, after fortifying himself with a healthy gulp of fifty pound per bottle brandy. "She must be as lovely as they say to make you work so quickly."

Paul raised his eyebrows.

"Lady Selina."

"Oh, I'm afraid you are mistaken—it isn't Lady Selina I'm going to marry."

Twickham lowered his glass. "Isn't she the one you said you'd come specifically to London to call upon—thanks to her own father's endorsement?" He snorted—a rude and uncharacteristic action for a man of his taste and refinement.

"Lady Selina is lovely, but she will not be my wife."

"Ah, you picked Lady Aurelia." Twickham nodded. "Good choice. I've seen her myself and she is quite a beauty. And it is wise of you to take a slightly more mature wife who will understand when—"

"It is not Lady Aurelia, but Lady Phoebe, who has done me the honor."

Twickham's forehead wrinkled as he dredged his mind for the information the Runner had provided in his report on the Bellamy family. "Oh. But isn't that the plain one?"

"She will be my wife, Harold," Paul said, before his friend could stick his foot any deeper into his mouth.

"Ah," was all Twickham said.

Lady Phoebe flashed into his mind, much as she'd been doing several times a day for almost two weeks.

While she was not a beauty, neither was she plain. Indeed, he found her far more attractive than cold Aurelia or colorless Selina.

It wasn't only one thing that made her appealing to him. Paul liked her lively eyes, her kittenish lips, her small, shapely body, and especially her fierce determination.

Even in the face of someone she despised and feared—Paul—she had been valiant in her effort to protect her family. If her father had shown even an iota of his daughter's courage, the family would not be in such a predicament.

She had given no thought to herself when she'd blundered into a dangerous situation, and all to protect her siblings. Such loyalty was rare, and he found it stirring.

And then there was her natural sensuality...

Perhaps there was something to be said for inexperienced ladies, after all?

"Have you told Lucy and Mrs. Kettering you are getting married?"

Paul sipped and nodded. "Yes."

"Will they stay in London, or will you engage a country house for them?" Twickham asked.

"They will stay with me. I have already prepared rooms for them."

Twickham paused, his glass half-way to his mouth. "I beg your pardon?"

"They will live at Wych House." Paul took a drink and smiled at the other man's obvious confusion.

"You will bring them to Wych House," Twickham repeated, uncertain.

"Yes."

"But... you will get married soon."

"Yes, although the exact date has yet to be determined. Lady Phoebe and I agreed we would wait until after the ball to tell her parents about our betrothal."

"That is backward, isn't it?" Twickham looked appalled yet again. "Shouldn't you *ask* her father first?"

"As the earl offered me my choice of his five daughters, I'd say that would be a hollow gesture. Besides, Lady Phoebe's wishes matter more to me than her parents'. She has asked for a small wedding in the family chapel at Wych House immediately after the ball. That is what she will have."

Twickham set down his unfinished drink, shaking his head. "But why would you bring Mrs. Kettering and the child down to Hampshire only to have to move them again? Wouldn't it make more sense to find a place for them where—"

"You misunderstand me, John. They will not be paying me a visit. They will make their home at Wych House. Permanently."

Twickham's brow furrowed. "Where will you and Lady Phoebe live?"

"My wife and I will also live at Wych House."

Twickham gasped. "You can't mean to house your wife, mistress, and bas—"

"It is best that you do not use that word." Paul gave the older man a wintry smile. "Lucy might be offended—hurt, even—if she were to learn that her Uncle Twickham called her such a thing."

"I would *never* say such a thing in front of Lucy."

"Then do not say it behind her back, either. And *never*," Paul added softly, "use that word to refer to my daughter in front of *me*."

Twickham didn't seem to hear the threat. "My God, Paul! Please tell me you will not put your mistress and love child in the same house with your wife?"

"That is exactly what I am going to do."

"What do you think your wife will say when she—"

"She already knows, John. As do her parents."

"But... *how*? Who told them?"

"I did."

Twickham's already pale skin drained of all color. "You cannot be serious. You would not have said such a thing."

"I am and I did."

Several seconds of shocked silence inserted themselves into the conversation.

"Possessing great wealth does not give you the right to be cruel, Paul. Have you given any thought to what a gently bred young woman will suffer? Not just her reputation—which will be irreparably damaged—but her self-worth." Twickham shook his head. "You cannot have thought this through."

Paul set down his drink with exaggerated care before looking up to meet the other man's eyes. "And would it not be cruel to banish my daughter just because I am getting married? To tuck her away somewhere like a dirty secret?"

Twickham sputtered. "No, of course you needn't do that. You could bring her to live with you without bringing her mother. At least—"

"I should tear a thirteen-year-old girl from her dying parent? Put her in a strange place without the person who has cared for her and loved her all her life, so that the adult woman who is marrying me—knowing the situation well in advance of accepting my offer of marriage—won't be offended by my past?"

Twickham gawped.

Paul's face shifted into an ugly smile. "Speaking of great wealth and the attendant responsibilities, perhaps you believe that because I am as rich as the King—or richer, in fact—that I should behave as the royal dukes do? I could build a house—a type of stable—where I could install my mistress and put a child in her once a year and we could call them Fitz-Needhams. And that would be acceptable? Filling a house with a dozen of my *bastards* while I live with my wife and legitimate children in ignorant domestic bliss?"

"You are twisting my words, Paul—taking them in the worst light and—"

Paul slammed his hand down on the desk. "I might be a *vile, hideous, encroaching cit,*" he said with a bitter smile. "But I am not a hypocrite. I am what I appear to be: a man who will house and care for his ailing mistress and child. Lady Phoebe is coming to me with her eyes wide open." He sat back in his chair. "She is not being forced to marry me." He felt a twinge at his words, knowing they were not necessarily true. He shrugged them away, along with the censorious look Twickham fixed on him.

"Your father—"

Paul lunged to his feet, raising his voice for the first time in ages. "Do tell, Harold; what would my father—the man who married two women for their money and then impregnated his housemaid not once, but three times, while he was still married to his second wife, and then kept them all living under the *same roof*—say about my behavior?"

Twickham's mouth closed with a snap.

Paul nodded. "I thought so. Now," he said, dropping back into his chair and opening the ledger they'd been examining before business had veered into personal. "Tell me how we are getting on with our plans for Wych House and the land purchase from Freemantle."

Chapter Eight

Every morning, Phoebe woke up vowing to confess to her mother that she was secretly betrothed to Lord Needham.

And every night she went to bed disgusted with her own cowardice.

The viscount had said he'd return in two weeks and talk to her father. Tomorrow would mark two weeks.

Lord Addiscombe himself hadn't returned from London until yesterday, garbed in new clothes and looking well-tended.

Phoebe shuddered to think how much money it had taken to achieve such a look.

Yet while she hated to think of her father spending and gambling in London, she had also been grateful that he had stayed away. Without him at Queen's Bower to countermand her orders, Phoebe had hired window glazers, a carpenter, and a man to assess the roof for repairs.

In addition to all that, there had also been the preparations for the ball.

Lady Addiscombe had been behaving like a woman possessed. Phoebe knew her mother had decided that Needham—however loathsome he might be—*must* marry one of her daughters.

The countess was so obsessed with the notion that Phoebe was actually afraid to tell her mother about her betrothal; she did *not* think the older woman would take the news well, no matter how much she believed she wanted such an outcome. The countess's crazed eyes made Phoebe think of a martyr just as they were about to set themselves on fire.

Marrying Needham might solve some of their problems but aligning their family with such a man would create new ones.

Phoebe's own mental state was not much better than her mother's.

Although it had been almost two weeks since they'd agreed on their betrothal, she still struggled to wrap her mind around the fact that she would be Needham's wife before the month was out.

Whenever she thought of *him,* Phoebe felt oddly breathless, as if confronted by something massive and awe-inspiring.

The man was too big, too overwhelming, and simply too *much* to think about directly. He was like the sun, best approached indirectly with sideways glances and quick looks.

Even sleep provided no real release from him. She dreamt of him every night, her brain concocting scenarios she never would have imagined herself capable of even imagining. Scenarios that her body already seemed to know... intimately.

At night, in the privacy of her bed, she relived the way he'd touched her, the hardness of his body, the calm confidence of his kisses, and the wordless promise of more in his black, bottomless stare.

During the day, reality impinged on those fantasies.

Phoebe would change her family forever by marrying such a man. While some of those changes would be beneficial, there would undoubtedly be scandal. He had made certain of that by housing a mistress and lovechild in the same house as his wife.

She clung to the knowledge that she could provide at least some financial security for her sisters and brother, although his only words on the subject had been as obscure as everything else about him.

"You can stop worrying, now," Needham had said that day, after releasing her.

Phoebe's body had hummed from his masterful kiss—a kiss that had turned her inside out like a stocking.

His mouth had briefly flexed into an odd smile and he'd reached out and feathered his thumb between her brows, his harsh features as unreadable as Latin or Greek, his palm big enough to—

"Oh, Phoebe! Look what you've done."

Phoebe yelped, jolted, and her head whipped up at her mother's shriek.

For one terrible instant, Phoebe worried the countess knew about the exquisite tightness at the juncture of her thighs.

But then her mother snatched the dress bodice away from Phoebe's unresisting hands.

"Look at this! You've attached the sleeve to the other sleeve. Whatever are you thinking?" The countess did not wait for an answer. "If you ruin this, there is no chance of more material."

Katie took the silk bodice from her mother. "I will do it, Mama. After all, it is for me and I am easily the most familiar with the pattern." She cut Phoebe a small, reassuring smile.

Lady Addiscombe looked like she wanted to argue, but she scowled, cut Phoebe one last glare, and stalked from the sitting room.

Once she had gone, Katie let her head drop against the back of the settee. "How happy I will be when this wretched ball is over! I can't believe I was ever excited to go to it."

Phoebe felt a pang for her younger sister, who was only seventeen and should not, by rights, be going to a ball just yet. But the invitation had included her name, so their mother had been adamant.

Katie had been thrilled to go before the last ten days of slaving over their ball gowns, which they were refashioning from several of her mother's old gowns.

Although the dresses were dreadfully out of style, they reminded Phoebe that their mother had once been a young girl—an heiress—who had gone to balls and probably dreamed of marrying a handsome lord.

And then she had married one.

How sadly a person's life could change.

"I do wish Mama would just let me make these dresses," Katie grumbled. "I could do it faster and better without your help." She grimaced. "I'm sorry. I didn't mean to be rude, Pheeb."

Phoebe smiled. "You are only being honest."

"Here." Katie handed back the piece. "Pick out this stitching for me," Katie ordered. "I need to run down and look through mama's sewing basket for more thread. I shall be right back."

The moment her sister left the room, Phoebe put aside the sewing, laid her head against the back of the settee, and closed her eyes.

She allowed her mind to wander back to that afternoon almost two weeks ago…

"But you said you wouldn't marry any of us," Phoebe had protested as Lord Needham—quite shockingly—sank down on one knee, putting their heads almost level, bringing his face so close that she saw his eyes were the most mesmerizing crystal-clear gray.

His huge hands had been warm and surprisingly soft as they held hers. "No, that is not what I said. I said I wouldn't ask any of your sisters to marry me."

She had tugged on her hand, and he'd released her. But he'd remained on his knee, his gaze holding hers like a snake with a hare.

"Yes, but I thought you meant me, too." Phoebe had flushed at the whine in her voice.

"You must allow me at least a basic command of English, my lady, no matter that my vulgar accent may be difficult for you to understand." He smirked at whatever he saw on her face—likely mortification—as if he could see right into her head. "If I had meant to exclude you, I would have said so."

She'd shaken her head, unable to put together any coherent sentences.

"Does that mean *no*, Lady Phoebe?"

"I beg your pardon?"

"You are shaking your head; do you decline my offer?"

"What if—" Phoebe had needed to lick her lips, which had become so dry they kept sticking to her teeth. "What if I say no? Will you ask one of them?"

"I can't tell you what I will do, but I can tell you what I will *not* do. I will not *not* consider your sisters as prospective spouses."

Phoebe's mind had spun as she'd tried to keep up with his verbal twists and turns. "Then… then you would ask one of them to be your wife."

He'd smiled at her effort to pin him down. "I won't say that I would not."

She had hated him in that instant. *Hated* him.

There he sat—or knelt, rather—in *her* family's ancestral home, which they could no longer afford. He had servants to take care of his every need, his body was clothed in the finest garments money could buy, eating delicacies she'd not seen in years, and speaking with an accent hardly one step from the servants' hall himself and—

He had chuckled then.

"I'm glad you find all this amusing," she'd snapped, and then stood, her action drawing him to his feet as if he were her shadow. She had allowed all her dislike to show, glaring up a good foot to make sure he saw it.

He sneered. "Are you really? Because I thought you looked surprised rather than pleased by my ability to see through your unveiled snobbery."

Phoebe's face had heated. "I didn't—I never—"

"Your disdain for me is obvious. You think me a barbaric oaf who apes my betters—poorly—and aspires to insinuate myself into a class of people who are so superior to me I wouldn't even dare to *look* at them in a rightly ordered world. You consider me an odious upstart who would not only soil your family name, but who would *destroy* your sisters by the mere act of marrying one of them."

He'd spoken softly and coolly, but Phoebe had recoiled as if he were shouting, horrified to hear her own harsh thoughts coming from his mouth.

Was she really so judgmental, prejudiced, and conceited about her lineage?

He had taken a step toward her and Phoebe, whose legs were pressed against the chair, had nowhere left to go.

He'd come close enough that she could feel the warmth from his enormous body and smell the subtle scent of his cologne, something masculine and expensive and utterly foreign to her olfactory organ.

Something she had wanted to inhale more deeply.

Something—

"Becky?"

For a moment, Phoebe had believed that Lord Needham had forgotten her name. "No, I'm—"

"Yes, sir?" The maid's anxious voice had come from the far corner of the room, reminding Phoebe they weren't alone.

"Please fetch another pot of tea—I'm afraid this one has become cold." He stood close enough to Phoebe that the low timbre of his voice sent vibrations through her body.

She didn't want any tea, but she'd been unable to form the words.

"There," he'd said, when the door shut behind the servant. "Now we are alone, the way you initially wished." His hand came beneath her chin and she jolted.

"Shhh." He tilted her face until her neck was craned back so sharply it ached. His lips curved into a smile that never reached his eyes. "Lady Phoebe," he whispered, one corner of his mouth pulled up higher than the other. "I've never known a *Phoebe* before." He caressed her chin with his thumb. His smile faded and his eyelids lowered. "You are the only Phoebe, for me."

He had lowered his mouth slowly enough for her to pull away if she'd wanted.

What Phoebe had done next had shocked her to her core.

Rather than shove him away, she had pushed up on her tiptoes to reach him.

You wicked, immoral wanton! a voice in her head had shouted.

Phoebe had ruthlessly ignored the scolding, intent on her own destruction.

As for Lord Needham, he'd given a low rumble of approval at her indecent eagerness and brushed his lips over hers so very lightly that she wasn't sure it had really happened.

The second time he lowered his mouth, his tongue flicked over the damp inside skin of her lower lip, reminding her that her mouth was still hanging open. He'd stroked her again and again, probing her deeper with each caress.

Her knees had buckled and Phoebe would have slid to the floor if his arms hadn't closed around her.

"Steady, sweetheart," he'd murmured, drawing her closer, until she was plastered against him, his heart beating an amazingly strong *thud thud thud* against her chest.

He'd tilted his head, tasting her more deeply, stroking into her more boldly, the broad palm of his hand cradling her head in a way that made her feel tiny and fragile. His other arm had tightened around her waist, pulling her against a hard ridge which pressed against her midriff—

"Sir?"

Phoebe had squeaked and jolted, but Lord Needham had moved slowly to release her, his actions languid and unconcerned.

He'd looked down at her with eyes as black as pools of ink, his lips suddenly fuller, red, and slick. His hand slid slowly down her neck, over her shoulders, skimming her back in a light caress before it disappeared.

"Thank you, Becky," he'd said to the maid without ever breaking eye contact. "You may place it on the table and leave."

They had stood like statues until the door closed.

"Sit, my lady. Let us discuss my proposal."

Phoebe had fallen into the chair behind her with all the grace of an exhausted toddler, vaguely aware that Lord Needham appeared to be doing something with the tea tray.

"Lady Phoebe."

She'd looked up at the sound of his voice to find him holding out her cup and saucer in one hand and a plate with a delicious looking fairy cake in the other.

"Oh, thank you." She'd taken both from him with shaking hands and set them down on the side table with a clatter.

"Do you need time to consider my offer?" he'd asked, his eyes no longer black, but a dark gray that glittered as he stared at her.

Did she need time? Could she ask for ten years to consider it?

She'd had to grit her jaws until they ached to keep down the hysterical bubble of laughter that threatened to explode out of her.

The choices were simple: either Phoebe accepted his offer or he *might* marry one of her sisters.

"No," she said.

"*No,* you don't accept or *no,* you don't need time?"

"I don't need time." She'd wrenched her gaze off her clenched hands and looked up. "But I have—there are some… things I wish to make clear." Lord! Why did she have to sound like such a bumbling fool?

"Yes?"

Just spit it out, Phoebe—if he can say the word mistress *in your mother's sitting room, surely you can say it back to him?*

She looked up at him and saw that his lips were twisted in a smile so faint it was almost worse than a grin.

"About your… mistress," she'd blurted, suddenly angry that he found her nervousness amusing.

"What about her?"

"Do you intend to keep—" Phoebe had been horrified by the word choices open to her.

He'd cocked his head, as if he were confused about what she was asking.

It had been the final straw. "You know very well what I'm trying to ask!"

His eyes had glinted with humor at her anger. "To answer what I *think* is your question: No, Ellen and I are not lovers, nor will we be in the future."

Heat had bloomed in her belly at the word *lovers*.

"As a matter of fact," he went on, no longer looking amused. "Mrs. Kettering is deathly ill with consumption and I shall be installing a nurse here at Wych House."

Phoebe hadn't known what to say; he was taking care of a dying woman?

There was no denying that Needham's impulses were honorable, even if the way he was going about it would cause Phoebe and her family a great deal of discomfort with their neighbors.

Phoebe knew men—rich and poor—often took their pleasure and left the woman to deal with the results. In fact, she was intimately acquainted with the details of one such incident because it had involved Sebastian Lowery—Phoebe's fiancé at the time—and a parlor maid who'd worked at Sebastian's house.

The maid had claimed that Sebastian was the father of her child. He had called her a liar, and worse, and the girl had lost her job and her family had disowned her.

Phoebe had gone to speak to the girl—for that is what she'd been, only sixteen—who'd told her that Sebastian had forced himself on her not once, but many times.

Phoebe had believed her story and had confronted Sebastian.

He'd denied it at first—repeatedly. Finally, he had snapped. "Is this the sort of shrew you're going to be if we marry, Phoebe?" His beautiful face had contorted with sullen anger—that of a spoiled boy finally called to account for his behavior. "I chose *you* because I thought you'd be sensible about such matters—as you are about so many things."

That's when Phoebe had understood why he'd picked her above all the pretty girls in the area.

Not because she was an earl's daughter but because she was too plain to have expectations of him. He had actually believed that she would be so grateful that he'd married her that she would not care if he raped their servants.

Phoebe had broken their betrothal that day.

"Did you have other questions or conditions of your own?" Needham had asked, pulling her back from that horrible day three years ago.

"Yes, I do have some conditions for marriage. First, I would want my sisters and brother to be welcome to live with us, should the need ever arise."

He was too intelligent not to take her meaning, which was that she wanted a home for her family if her father lost Queen's Bower. Something that was probably inevitable.

"Naturally, your family would always be welcome to live with us. Is that all?"

Think, think, think, she ordered herself. What else was there?

You know about one mistress, but what about the others? Because Needham isn't the sort of man to go without a woman. Although how Phoebe knew such a thing, she could not have said.

"Are you planning to install any more of your mistresses at Wych House?" she'd blurted.

His lips twitched into an almost imperceptible smile. "You would object to that, I take it?"

"I object to the fact that I am forced to have a conversation on this subject—as any decent woman would. So, yes, my lord, I would strongly object to you moving more of your *women* into any house where I would be living."

"Then I shan't move any other mistresses under our roof."

Phoebe had not been impressed by his easy capitulation. Yes, he wouldn't move them into their house, but that didn't mean he wouldn't keep them elsewhere.

Well, it would have to be good enough.

"Fine. I accept your offer."

He'd looked neither pleased nor displeased. "I will take you home and speak to your father."

"He has gone to London and I am not sure when he will be back."

"I shall be away on a business trip for two weeks, beginning tomorrow. I will speak to him when I return. After we have told your parents, I propose we make an announcement at the ball."

When Phoebe hadn't immediately responded, he'd added, "Unless you were hoping to keep it a secret. Forever." He'd sounded wry, but there had been a hard glint in his pale eyes.

"That isn't why I hesitated. I was thinking about the wedding."

"What about it?"

"I would like to have a small wedding—in the chapel here at Wych House, if that is acceptable?"

"That is acceptable. When?"

Phoebe's first impulse had been to pick a date far in the future, but then that would hardly help her brother and sisters.

How did one say *I want to marry right away* without sounding forward?

"Would three days after the ball be acceptable?" he'd asked, putting her out of her misery.

Three days!

"Will that give you enough time to invite your family?"

"I have nobody except Lucy. What of your siblings? Do you want to wait until they can return to have the ceremony?"

The last thing Phoebe wanted was to have to answer her sisters' questions. Especially as they'd all agreed that nobody would *sacrifice* themselves for the good of the others.

"No, I don't wish to bring them back. Three days after the ball will be—"

"Phoebe? *Phoebe?*"

Phoebe's eyes flow open and she jolted, disoriented to find she wasn't at Wych House with Lord Needham at all, but at home in the sitting room, with Katie staring down at her.

"Wh-what did you say?" Phoebe asked, still somewhat dazed.

"Viscount Needham is here, Phoebe! He has come to call on Papa." Katie's green eyes sparkled with curiosity. "What in the world do you think *he* could want?"

Chapter Nine

Lady Addiscombe's blue eyes were creased with apprehension as they rested on her second youngest daughter.

After Viscount Needham's call, the countess had not left her bedchamber for two entire days to recover from the news.

She had emerged only a few hours ago, looking pale and gaunt and sorrowful—as if somebody had died—and summoned Phoebe to the sitting room.

While Phoebe was far from feeling settled about her impending nuptials herself, she was furious at her mother for behaving as if she had committed some atrocity and agreed to marry an itinerant tinker rather than one of the wealthiest men in Britain.

Lady Addiscombe's air of tragedy was especially ironic as she had been grimly determined that one of her daughters would capture the viscount—regardless of what she knew about him—if only to keep any other local girl from marrying him.

Perhaps her mother sensed some of her anger because she greeted Phoebe's entrance with a kinder than normal smile.

"I was surprised by Lord Needham's visit on Tuesday," she said, as if Phoebe hadn't already guessed that. "In addition to his generous settlements, his lordship has also paid the lease on Wych house for the first two years, which will allow us to make some much needed changes."

Phoebe would certainly be making some changes, but she didn't think that's what her mother meant.

"Dauntry will finally be able to start at Eton next term, just as Bellamy men have done for generations."

Phoebe ignored the stab of anxiety she felt about sending her little brother to such a place. Instead, she tried to think of the benefit he would receive from being among his peers for the first time in his life.

The countess cleared her throat. "I am not insensible to the sacrifice you have made for your sisters," she hesitated and then added grudgingly, "for all of us." Her patrician cheekbones, so at odds with her humble background, flushed. "I am going to speak more bluntly than I would normally. You are no longer a girl but a woman and about to become a wife. The viscount made a point to thrust his base, animal nature into prominence with his vulgar announcement a few weeks ago. While his behavior was unfortunate, I'm ashamed to admit that it is far from uncommon for men to have their, er"—her hand fluttered and words deserted her.

"Mistresses," Phoebe supplied.

Lady Addiscombe grimaced and winced, as if Phoebe had poked her in the forehead with a fork.

"Yes, yes—*that*. Based on Lord Needham's remarks, you will be exposed to a level of crassness that… Well, suffice it to say that being forced to endure such ignominy is not unknown to many women of our class." She cleared her throat yet again, and then added, "To me."

So, the earl was not only a gambler, but a womanizer. Phoebe wondered if that was why he'd rushed off to London, to set up a mistress with the money her husband-to-be had just given him.

It was too depressing a thought to contemplate.

"In a way, Lord Needham's behavior is a blessing."

Phoebe raised her eyebrows. "I beg your pardon?"

Her mother blushed. "I only meant that Needham will satisfy his, er, baser needs elsewhere and come to you only for an heir. Or at least it is to be hoped."

It was Phoebe's turn to blush.

Her mother delicately brushed her fingertips against each other, as if she were shaking away the crumbs of an unpleasant conversation.

"As for your wedding," she continued, her expression much lighter. "His lordship has informed me that his secretary will see to all the details of the ceremony and wedding breakfast." She smiled fondly. "I recall Mr. Dixon from when he was just a boy. I daresay he has grown into a fine young man."

Phoebe was amused; her mother finally liked something about her betrothed, but it was his secretary.

"Although there is so little time before the proposed ceremony, I have sent word to Mrs. Debenham letting her know we have *urgent* need of her services. I daresay she will—with proper compensation—be able to quickly make not only a wedding gown but a few other garments for the new mistress of Wych House."

Phoebe felt sorry for the overworked seamstress, who had already needed to engage four additional helpers to finish all the orders for ballgowns.

"Although I would have wished for a London ceremony for you, I think it prudent to remain closer to home," the countess continued.

Phoebe almost laughed. Yes, it was prudent; especially as the countess didn't want anyone to know whom her daughter was marrying.

Lady Addiscombe hurried on. "Your father has given Lord Needham leave to call on you at Queen's Bower and he has indicated his desire to ride with you."

"But I have no hack, Mama."

"You needn't be concerned about that as his lordship will mount you." Her cold blue eyes flickered over her. "I suppose your old riding habit will have to make do. I wonder… Perhaps his lordship might consider postponing the ceremony for a few weeks while we go to London to shop for your trousseau. Actually, Brighton would be even better," she hastily amended, clearly remembering she didn't want the news of Phoebe's unfortunate nuptials to make its way to London and damage her other daughters' chances.

Phoebe shuddered at the thought of an expensive shopping trip. "My old habit has barely seen any use, Mama."

The countess sighed. "Yes, I suppose that is true. His lordship will doubtless buy you everything you need… after." She lifted a hand to her temple, as if thinking about the man gave her a headache. "Lord Needham wants to engage a lady's maid for you and has offered to have Mr. Dixon inquire with an employment agency and engage the most appropriate candidate. If you do not care for her, you may always engage another maid after you are married."

"A maid? But where will we put her, Mama?"

"You must talk to Mrs. Parks about such matters." She gave a dismissive wave. "In fact, you may do so now as I am finished with you." She sighed, as if she'd been awake for a hundred hours straight rather than barely two. "I am going back to my bedchamber."

***

That evening at dinner, the earl and countess had some surprising news to share with Phoebe and her siblings.

"We shall vacate Queen's Bower for a few months directly after your wedding," the countess announced before the dessert was brought to the table.

"But… why?" Phoebe, the first to recover, asked.

"We won't wish to be here while having extensive roof repairs done," the earl said.

That was a surprising admission from a man who'd always insisted there *wasn't a problem with the roof.*

But their mother's next words were even more shocking. "Your father is right." *Your father is right?*

Phoebe, Katie, and Doddy exchanged astounded glances; who would have believed the countess was even capable of speaking that sentence?

"As to where we shall go… Well, several places," the countess admitted. "I have been feeling terribly pulled these past few weeks, so I shall go to Bath to take the waters."

Katie gave an excited shriek and bounced up and down in her chair. "Oh, Bath!" She looked at Doddy. "We shall have so much to do!"

"No, no," the countess said hastily. "Your brother must go to a crammer if he is to start Eton in the autumn. He will spend the summer with one of the housemasters, a kindly gentleman who takes a few fortunate boys into his own home to tutor."

Doddy looked—rightly—horrified at the prospect of being shipped off to school months early. "But Mama! Surely I don't need to do something so… drastic?"

It was a night for surprises because their father said, "Do not argue with your mother, Lord Bellamy. This is not up for negotiation."

Doddy's jaw sagged at his father's unprecedented defense of their mother, stern tone, and use of his title.

The earl took advantage of the silence to add, "It is time you did your duty. You will go and that is the beginning and end of it."

Doddy looked positively tragic.

"You will have fun," Katie said, her cheerful tone not at all convincing. "You will make lots of friends and when you come home at Christmas, I shall tell you about Bath, and you can tell me about—"

The countess cleared her throat. "You will not be going to Bath, Katherine."

Katie's eyes grew enormous. "Where will I be going?"

"You will go to stay with my sister, your Aunt Agatha."

"But Mama, you've always said that Aunt Agatha's head was stuffed with outlandish notions and foolishness."

The earl snickered.

Their mother flushed and scowled at her youngest daughter. "You *must* learn to curb your tongue, Katherine!"

"I'm sorry Mama. But—well, doesn't Aunt Agatha live in some horribly out of the way place?"

"She lives near Norwich, Katherine, and that is where you will be going."

"Why can't I stay with Phoebe at Wych House?"

Phoebe was grateful when her mother and father both gave a resounding *no*.

While she would gladly take Katie at Wych House, she really needed a few months to settle in first.

Dinner was a grim affair after their parents' announcements and the meal broke up early, everyone going off to their rooms to deal with the sudden changes in their own way.

Katie and Doddy weren't the only ones facing unknown futures.

Phoebe's life would soon change forever.

Tomorrow Lord Needham would come to take her riding and she had to admit the prospect of spending time with him excited and frightened her in equal measures.

She knew so little of him, and most of that was superficial.

He might look uncouth and uncivilized, but aside from his background, size, and slight brogue, he dressed and comported himself like a gentleman.

Except for moving his mistress and daughter into your house.

Phoebe grimaced at the unneeded reminder.

Perhaps it was some defect in her character, but even *that* was no longer as offensive now that she knew the reason for it. While she did *not* wish to live with her husband's former mistress, she could not fault him for his motivation.

Indeed, everything he'd done—from caring for a dying mistress to paying handsomely for a property that didn't deserve it to giving two years' lease money in advance—was what she would consider *gentlemanly* behavior.

It was befuddling, really. The earl had dissipated his wife's fortune, frittered away his daughters' dowries, and—according to what her mother had strongly hinted—housed mistresses, and yet he was a friend of the Prince Regent and received in the best houses in Britain.

Yet Needham—her family's knight in shining armor—they were treating as if he were a necessary evil to be endured or a dirty secret to be hidden from the rest of the world.

It shamed her to admit that they had held that attitude even *before* he'd ever mentioned his mistress. Could their snobbery have been part of what motivated him to behave so crudely?

After all, Phoebe and Katie hadn't liked it one bit when the Lowery twins had looked down on them for their worn-out, unfashionable clothing. Indeed, Katie had openly lied to the twins that day in Burton's store.

Phoebe wondered why—after the way she had insulted him—a man like Lord Needham had settled for her.

She had seen by the look of confident amusement in his eyes that day at Wych House that he'd known any of her sisters would have accepted his offer.

Yet he had asked Phoebe.

Why had such a man chosen her?

Phoebe would never forget why Sebastian, her last fiancé, had chosen her—because he'd thought she was so homely that she would be a meek, grateful wife.

What if Lord Needham had picked her for the same reason?

Chapter Ten

The following morning, Phoebe went riding for the first time in almost three years.

It had been a joy to take her forest green habit out of its storage chest after so long.

Phoebe especially adored the coat, which was of a military cut, trimmed with black piping, complete with dull gold epaulettes. The dashing black shako hat, with a patent brim and peacock plume, was the most modish article of clothing she'd ever owned.

She was dressed and ready a full half-hour early, pacing her bedroom, both dreading and anticipating spending time with her betrothed.

A light tap on the door froze her pacing.

Katie poked her head through the gap, her striking emerald eyes dancing. "Lord Needham is here, and he has brought you the most marvelous gift." She grinned. "I'd marry him myself for such a mount, Pheeb."

"You hush." Phoebe shook her head and gave her sister a gentle push.

Needham waited for her outside, standing between two horses. One was the smoky black charger he'd been riding the first day she saw him and the second was a slightly smaller bay with a black mane and black tail.

"My lord." Phoebe dropped a shaky curtsy under his burning gaze. It had only been two weeks, but she'd forgotten how a look from him could discountenance her.

"You look lovely, Lady Phoebe," he said, his gaze sweeping her habit like his hands had swept her body that day two weeks earlier. "That color suits you."

Phoebe ignored her furiously heating face and took a step toward the bay gelding. "He's beautiful." She pulled off a glove and raised a hand to the horse's velvet soft muzzle.

"He comes from one of the finest breeders in the North."

Phoebe stiffened at the word breeder and forced herself to look up at him. "Thank you."

He ignored her thanks. "The man who raised and trained him named him Brandy, for his distinctive color, but you must name him as you see fit."

"No," Phoebe said, stroking the horse's glossy neck. "Brandy is perfect." She turned to his horse, which looked every bit as magnificent as she recalled. "And his name?"

"His name is Coal."

"His coloring is so unusual—almost blue black."

"He came from a stud known for unusual color combinations." He handed his reins to the groom who must have ridden Brandy over. "I'll assist Lady Phoebe," he said, and then turned to Phoebe. "Ready?"

She nodded.

Instead of cupping his hands for her foot, he took her by the waist and lifted her onto her horse.

Although Phoebe was short, she was not especially slender, but his enormous hands made her feel dainty, and he lifted her with ease.

He cut her a brief, brooding look from beneath his thick lashes and then held the stirrup for her while she hooked her knee around the horn.

His fingers curled around her leather-covered ankle. "Is this the right length?"

She knew it was all in her head—that it was impossible that she could feel warm flesh through her boot—but that didn't stop the muscles in her thighs from tightening.

"Thank you," she said in an annoyingly breathy voice.

Once he was astride the huge horse, he had to look down a goodly way to meet her gaze. "I am going to leave the choice of destination to you. After all, it is your home territory."

Phoebe guided Brandy toward the prettiest trail, the one that passed through the woods.

Once they were out of earshot of the stable, Phoebe said, "I wanted to thank you. My mother says you've been most generous with wedding settlements."

She cut him a covert glance and found that he was watching her.

When he said nothing, she continued. "She said your early lease payment is what will allow my brother to go away to school."

He still said nothing.

She turned her body to face him this time. "Have you gone mute, Lord Needham?"

"No. You seemed to be warming up to your task, so I was just waiting until you'd finished."

She bristled at his dry tone. "I was merely being courteous."

"Oh? What does that word mean?"

Her lips parted in surprise, but then she saw the humorous gleam in his eye and scowled at him.

"That's better," he said.

"You are a rude man."

He grinned. "Better still."

She snorted and shook her head. "Tell me, my lord, as I'm not supposed to thank you, then what *should* I talk about?"

He shrugged, his gaze on an old, sick Wych Elm beside the path. "Anything other than thanking me. I don't plan on thanking you for all the lovely things you will do for me." His thin, expressive lips curved into a smile that made her entire body heat.

How did he *do* that?

"You don't believe in showing gratitude?" she asked, her voice a bit warbly.

"Not for the results of a mutually agreed upon business deal."

"And that's what our marriage is to you—a business deal?"

A sly smile curved his mouth, which she was finding more fascinating than she should. "Why, my lady, is there something you wish to tell me?"

"Whatever do you mean?"

"Is this a love match rather than a business deal?"

Her face flushed. "Why must you do that?"

"Do what?"

"Inject such an element of... Oh, I don't know what it is called. But you always seem to take joy in dragging things through the mud."

"Always? You speak as if we've been married for two decades. What else have I done to so offend your sensibilities in the four times we've seen each other?"

"You mean, aside from announcing that you would install your mistress beneath your roof the very first time you paid a call on my family?"

He turned fully toward her, allowing his horse to find its own way, his expression arrested, all his former amusement gone. "I wondered how long it would take for this to come up again."

Phoebe chewed the inside of her mouth, furious with herself for blurting out those words; she vowed then and there that would be the last time she snapped at the bait he dangled.

"Just forget I said anything about it," she said.

"Very well," he said mildly.

Her head whipped back toward him.

He smiled at her, and the lazy, arrogant expression goaded her into breaking the vow she had made to herself only seconds earlier to keep her mouth shut.

"After all," she retorted with more than a little heat in her voice. "I am accustomed to being the butt of local gossip. What difference will one more topic make?"

"I take it that was a rhetorical question?"

"Rhetorical," she repeated, an unpleasant thought blooming in her brain. "Where did you go to school, my lord?"

"School? What do you mean?"

"Yes, school. Surely a man who knows the meaning of the word *rhetorical* doesn't need me to define such a simple word as *school* for him?"

Something flashed across his face. Humor? Respect?

"I went to Harrow."

Her lips twisted bitterly; yet again she had been snobby and judgmental, not to mention foolish, to assume this wealthy, well-spoken man was uneducated.

He had known what she thought and encouraged it. Paul Needham, she was realizing, enjoyed it when people underestimated him. And that is what Phoebe had been doing right from the start.

"You are no stranger to a London Season either, are you, my lord?" she asked.

"Are you interrogating me, Lady Phoebe?"

"Yes."

That made him laugh, which relaxed the stern set of his chiseled features.

Why, he almost looks… attractive.

The thought was like a punch to the midriff and left her breathless.

Luckily, they entered the woods and had to ride single file at that point, allowing Phoebe a moment to collect herself.

When would she stop falling into the same pitfalls with this man? When would she learn he was more than what he seemed?

They rode in silence until they came to the spot where Doddy had stopped to fetch Silas that fateful day all those weeks ago. On impulse, Phoebe cut off the main path and guided Brandy toward the stream.

This part of the woods felt older, almost ancient, and the lacy canopy filtered the sunlight far, far overhead.

Phoebe stopped, and Needham reined in beside her.

"There is a pretty stream, the same one that meanders through the grounds of Wych House. Would you like to see it? We can only reach it on foot."

He dismounted without answering, loosening his horse's girth a little before coming to help her down. He lowered her to the ground in such a way that she slid down the front of his body. When her feet hit the ground, he did not release her. She swayed toward him, as if he exercised some magnetic force.

He cupped her cheek with one warm, leather-clad hand, staring into her eyes, but not attempting to kiss her.

Finally, after a thousand years, he smiled and dropped his hand. "Lead on, my lady."

Phoebe swallowed, thrown off balance by his teasing, flirtatious ways. She walked with the self-conscious gait of a woman who knew somebody was watching her; the gait of a woman whose thighs were tingly.

"Are you ready for the ball?" he asked after a moment.

Phoebe glanced at him, wondering if this question was yet another of his traps.

But he was looking ahead, reaching out a long arm to raise a branch higher for her to pass under.

Phoebe wasn't sure why she wasn't elated about the ball.

Her neighbors would look at her with respect for *catching* Lord Needham before he'd even settled in. The gowns that she and Katie had made, while simple in design and not exactly stylish, were attractive enough for a country ball.

So, what was it, then?

"I'm looking forward to it," she forced herself to say.

He gave a bark of laughter. "What a little liar you are."

"I am not." But her denial lacked conviction even to her own ears.

"Yes, you are. Is it the ball itself, or the announcement I will make during it?"

"My mother said you will seat forty people for dinner." Phoebe cut him a quick glance, and he nodded. "It has been several years since I've even attended a party or dance of any size, my lord. To become the focus of all those people at a dinner table will be nerve-wracking."

"Actually, I'd planned to make the announcement right before supper—not during dinner."

"Oh," she said. "I understand you've invited everyone in this county and the next, so that should be quite an audience. Er, may I ask why you've decided to do it that way?"

"If I said something at dinner, then I'd be limited to only one dance with my betrothed during the ball. This way, I can get two dances with you and *then* make the announcement."

She frowned. "Is that really true?"

"It is what Mr. Dixon has told me and I turn to him for all my etiquette questions."

Phoebe snorted. "I don't believe *that* for a moment."

"What? You don't believe I have questions about etiquette?"

"I suspect you are more than aware of general etiquette, my lord." She gave him a wry smile. "No matter how much you like to behave otherwise. And if you had questions, you would make up your own mind."

He gave a delighted laugh. "You know me so well already."

She ignored him and continued with her thought, "And if Mr. Dixon told you that rubbish—about when to make the announcement and how that would dictate the number of dances you could have with me—then I don't think much of his knowledge of etiquette. As the gentleman hosting the ball, you should have only one dance with any lady."

"Even my betrothed?"

"Especially with your betrothed."

The tunnel-like path opened into a small glade that bordered the tiny stream. Several towering trees grew along a sharp bend in the river that had created a deep, swirling swimming hole.

Phoebe always experienced a sense of deep, quiet peace when she came there.

"It has the feel of an ancient forest. One almost expects to see faeries slipping between the trees."

Lord Needham was surveying the glittering river and overhanging trees with an appreciative expression. She wouldn't have expected such a man to surrender to whimsy.

His disconcertingly pale eyes settled on her shoulder and widened. "You've got a, er, butterfly?" He pointed to her right side.

Phoebe turned to find a bright pink and yellow moth with enormous eyes that seemed to be looking at her.

"It is an elephant hawk moth," she said. "Normally they are nocturnal, but I suppose it is shady enough under the tree canopy to have fooled him."

As if the creature knew it was being talked about, it fluffed up its wings and twitched its antennae.

"Good Lord. It's just sitting there."

A second moth fluttered up and hovered over the first, which turned and gave it an almost irritated look. The second moth disregarded the dirty glance and landed right next to the first and then both creatures stared at her.

Phoebe smiled and turned back to the viscount. "They like me," she said, her face heating at the foolish announcement.

"Obviously."

"I appear to have some sort of attraction for moths and butterflies." As if to lend veracity to her claim, something fluttered around her other shoulder and then a meadow brown landed.

Lord Needham shook his head in wonder. "I have never seen such a thing."

"I asked a gentleman who came collecting the poor creatures a few years ago, and he said butterflies are known for being attracted to particular people, although nobody knows why."

A jackdaw in the tree overhead made a distinctive *pew pew pew* cry and all three insects fluttered away, no doubt searching for cover from one of their chief feathered predators.

"Fickle friends," he said.

"Wise friends," she corrected.

He looked around him with an appraising eye. "That seems an excellent swimming hole—besides being a favorite haunt of pink moths. Has your family made use of it?"

"We used to swim here often. When we were children."

"Oh? You came here even when you lived at Wych House?"

"No, I meant after we moved into Queen's Bower."

"Ah. And that was what, six years ago?"

"Yes."

"You would have been fourteen, am I correct?"

Phoebe didn't know why she was surprised that he knew her age. Perhaps because she knew so little about him. But then, she lacked his money, power, and resources to gather information and had only herself.

"How old are you, my lord?" It was rude to ask such a question but asking questions—rude or otherwise—seemed like a matter of survival with this man.

"How old do you think I am?" he countered.

She could hardly pass up such an invitation to study his face, staring directly at him rather than looking only in furtive snatches.

Like her, his skin was tanned and the lines radiating from the corners of his eyes said he'd spent time squinting against the sun.

A deep groove ran from the right side of his nose to the corner of his lips, the side of his mouth that usually pulled up when he gave the barely there smirk that he was so fond of making.

Although it was only midday, she could see fascinating signs of fresh growth and realized he'd need to shave twice daily to maintain his grooming. His glossy brown hair glinted at the temples, and she noticed for the first time that some of the hair there was a bit of silver. Goodness!

Her eyes met his, the unusual light gray of his irises even more distinctive as his pupils narrowed against the light.

He cocked one brow. "Well?"

"I am bad at guessing such things."

"Coward," he taunted.

"Fine. I think you are five and forty."

He threw back his head and laughed, his response confounding her yet again. When he stopped laughing, he looked at her with blatant appreciation, making her more confused than ever.

"Have you thought about me after that kiss in the library, Lady Phoebe?" he asked, his nostrils flaring slightly.

Her breathing instantly became labored. "I-I beg your pardon?"

"You heard me. And you know what I meant."

She did. Oh yes, she did.

"Of course, I've thought of you," she said, her voice stupidly high and squeaky. She cleared her throat and tried for a more bored, sophisticated tone. "I could hardly *not* think of you."

"What kinds of things did you think about me?"

"I—" Her voice cracked, and she cleared her throat yet again.

"Naughty things? Wicked things?"

"No!" she all but shouted, her face scalding.

He grinned. "Then what kind of things?"

"I—I don't know—I daresay the same type of thing anyone would think. Probably not much different from what *you* thought."

"I somehow doubt that." His voice was even lower than usual, velvet and silk together. "Although I should be very, very pleased if you had."

Phoebe wanted, with every fiber of her being, to ask him what he'd thought about her.

What could he possibly think about such a plain, average, unsophisticated woman like herself? The only thing Phoebe had that could possibly appeal to a man like Needham was her threadbare rank.

He closed the distance between them with one long stride, standing close enough that their bodies almost touched. He leaned down and kissed her, a closed-mouth press of warm, soft lips, the exhalation of his breath on her face feathery.

"I thought about kissing you," he said when he pulled away.

Phoebe had to clench her hands into fists to keep from grabbing his coat and yanking him closer again.

His pupils swelled, the black swallowing the fascinating silver of his pupil. "Do you want more, Lady Phoebe?"

God save her; she nodded.

Again, he kissed her with an almost frustrating gentleness, but this time he followed up his chaste peck with something far more shocking and traced the seam of her lips with the slick, pointed tip of his tongue.

Phoebe heard herself make the most piteous little whimpering sound but couldn't bring herself to care.

"Open for me," he murmured against her mouth. "I want to taste you again." He gently sucked on her lower lip.

Phoebe opened, and he stroked into her, his movements rhythmic, invasive, mesmerizing.

His hands slid around her waist and he pulled her closer, probing deeper, his tongue hot and velvety. He caressed her with increasingly insistent strokes, his hands sliding higher and tightening around her ribcage, his thumbs tauntingly close to the undersides of the breasts.

Phoebe arched her back to chase his elusive touch, not realizing what she was doing until the pebbled tips of her breasts rubbed against the smooth superfine of his coat and the hard body beneath.

She gave a frustrated whimper when his hands moved lower and away from her aching breasts, down and down, until he was gripping her hips, strong fingers splaying over her buttocks, digging into her flesh, pulling her tight against his body.

He made a noise that started off a groan and turned into a deep, rumbling laugh. "My God," he muttered, as if struck, ceasing his tantalizing stroking.

Frustrated by his lack of movement, Phoebe stood up on her toes and boldly mimicked his actions of a moment earlier, running her tongue along his lower lip.

Without prompting, he opened to her.

Phoebe didn't hesitate to probe deeper and explore his lips, teeth, and even the roof of his mouth, astounded by how such a strange activity could be so pleasurable.

When she flicked over his tongue, it was like a prod to a bull, galvanizing him into action.

He growled, tilted his head, and captured her mouth, his knee nudging at the juncture of her legs.

Shock reverberated through her body at his silent demand, but—more shocking still—Phoebe didn't hesitate to spread her thighs for his invasion.

She was distantly aware of his fingers, strong and insistent, digging into her bottom and lifting her until she was astride his leg, the swollen, slick petals of her sex rubbing against his thigh.

"Yes," he muttered, and then enclosed her in his powerful arms and claimed her mouth yet again.

An exquisite tension built inside her body, ratcheting tighter and tighter, until she began to shake, to come undone, to—

"Siiiiiillaaaaaaaaaaaaas!"

Forgetting their tangled tongues, Phoebe screamed and then slammed her jaws shut.

***

Paul jerked back at the sharp pain, his eyes watering and burning. "Goddammit!" he lisped.

The girl looked up at him, tears leaking from her wide eyes. She covered her mouth with her hand. "I'm thorry—tho thorry, my lord."

Paul gave a half laugh and half gasp and turned away to collect himself.

Lord, he'd not done such unsubtle groping and grinding since he'd been a boy; he deserved to have his tongue bitten.

He surreptitiously adjusted his throbbing erection in his breeches before turning back to her.

That's when he saw Viscount Bellamy standing beside a tree not far away, his blue eyes shrewd and knowing in his boyish face.

Paul *knew* in that moment that the cheeky little cockerel must have purposely followed them.

Right before his eyes, the young nobleman's haughty, accusing expression shifted into one of angelic innocence.

In fact, he looked *so* supremely innocent that Paul would later wonder if he had only imagined that initial, almost cynical, expression.

"Hallo, Pheeb. Whatever are you doing here?" Viscount Bellamy asked, turning his hyacinth-blue gaze on Paul. "And Lord Needham, too." He glanced around in wide-eyed surprise, giving a performance that was good enough for Drury Lane. "I thought I was all alone out here."

His red-faced sister squirmed, looking anywhere but at Paul.

"Have you seen Silas?" the boy asked.

"Thighlas?" Paul grimaced and tried again. "*Silas?*"

"Yes, Silas. My squirrel. He must have seen you leave the house and followed you."

Like some other creature we both know, Paul could have said.

"Oh, Doddy," his sister chided. "You and that dratted rodent."

The boy was obviously accustomed to being scolded by his elder sisters and ignored her. Instead, he tilted his chin at the horses. "That's a slapping bay you bought my sister."

"Thank you, Lord Bellamy."

"Call me Doddy," he said expansively.

Paul had to bite back a smile.

Doddy gave him an ingratiating grin that didn't quiet meet his blue eyes. "We're going to be brothers, after all, aren't we?"

"I'm honored, Doddy. You must call me Paul."

The young lord approached the grazing horses with such studied casualness that Paul couldn't help but be amused, suddenly recalling back to when he'd been horse-mad—right before he discovered the more fascinating appeal of the female sex.

"He's a beauty," Doddy said, not taking his eyes from Coal, who was cropping grass, but tensed as the boy drew closer. "Do you stud him?"

"This will be his first year," Paul said.

He considered warning the boy about Coal's temperamental ways, but suspected Doddy knew his way around horses, even though the earl had sold off all his, so he said nothing.

Doddy made a clucking sound and held out the flat of his hand, his stance relaxed and confident. Coal gave him a hard stare, ripped out another mouthful of grass, and then took a few steps toward the outstretched hand, until he could rub an ear against it.

Doddy grinned, his fingers going to that spot behind Coal's ear that would make a horse your faithful slave. The big stallion's jaws froze in mid-chew and his eyes drifted half-way shut.

"That's a boy, eh?" Doddy gave Paul a look of triumph. "He's a regular lad, isn't he?"

Paul couldn't help smiling. "That he is.

Doddy glanced around the clearing as he continued his equine massage. "I say, Pheeb, were you about to shuck your kit and go for a swim?"

"Doddy!"

He winced. "Lord, what are you screeching about?" He turned to Paul. "My sisters are usually at the swimming hole all summer, as thick as flies to a pudding," he explained, not caring how his confession was affecting his sister.

He paused his scratching of Coal. "It's wretched hot—are you going for a dip?" he asked, looking like it wouldn't take much to persuade him.

Paul looked at Lady Phoebe's scarlet, horrified face and had to fight a smile. "Your sister was just showing me the sights. But perhaps another time."

Right then, a butterfly fluttered toward the red-faced woman and then, piquantly, landed on top of her hat.

Doddy laughed and pointed at her. "You've got one of your friends on your hat, Pheeb—a speckled wood, I think."

Lady Phoebe glared silently.

Undaunted, her brother asked, "Where you takin' him, Pheeb?"

"Somewhere else," she hissed, giving him a narrow-eyed look that said she knew he'd been spying. "You'd better go find Silas, hadn't you?"

He kicked up a little puff of dust with the toe of his scuffed boot. "Aw, Pheeb."

"Shoo, Doddy."

The lad shoved his hands into the pockets of his grubby breeches and gave Paul a manly nod. "Awright then... Paul."

Paul struggled to bite back a grin. "Awright, Doddy."

They watched the boy meander off before Phoebe turned toward her horse.

"I think you hurt his feelings," Paul said lightly.

"That's unlikely. He's a little pest who likes to listen at doors and spy."

Well, he certainly got an eyeful today.

Paul closed the distance between them to help her mount, waiting for her to acknowledge him. But she continued to stare at the toes of her boot, unwilling to look at him, the tips of her ears a bright pink.

He slid his hands around her waist, easily lifting her soft, curvy body into the saddle. "It's a good thing he came along."

That got her attention. "Why?" she said, finally turning her gaze on him.

He wrapped his hand around the supple leather of her riding boot, holding her lightly as he met her wide-eyed stare.

Paul tightened his grip slightly and slid his hand up the warm, smooth leather to her calf, his nostrils flaring at the confusion and desire in her innocent eyes.

Bloody hell, but she was a sensual little beast! He couldn't *wait* to get her beneath him.

Or on top of him.

At that thought, his fertile imagination quickly conjured up an image of her skin rosy and glistening with sweat, thighs spread and astride his hips wearing nothing *but* her boots.

He released her with reluctance.

"Why do you think it was a good thing Doddy came along?" she persisted, sounding a bit hurt.

"I'm not saying your brother's appearance was good for my sake," he said, surreptitiously adjusting the rampant cockstand in his leathers. "But it was certainly good for your reputation."

Chapter Eleven

Katie stood on a stepstool while Phoebe finished pinning up the hem.

"I cannot believe you left this so late," the countess complained—not for the first time—as she paced back and forth. "You told me you finished ages ago."

"I did finish it," Phoebe reminded her. "But you said it was too long." Which was why Phoebe was rehemming her sister's gown.

The countess stopped pacing, tilted her head at the section Phoebe was pinning, and said, "That is crooked, Phoebe."

Phoebe had to bite her tongue to keep from yelling. Instead, she removed the last half-dozen pins and started over.

Her mother resumed her pacing and complaining.

Phoebe listened to her with only half her mind, the other half on all the tasks that still needed doing before her parents left Queen's Bower.

Most of the items on the list were chores her mother should do—like making arrangements for the servants who would remain at Queen's Bower to draw upon credit at the village shops. But the countess refused to lift a finger when it came to domestic matters.

In addition to Phoebe's long list, there had been the daily visits from her betrothed to contend with.

Sometimes Lord Needham merely stayed for tea, sometimes they went for a ride.

He did not kiss her again. Indeed, except for lifting her on and off her horse, he barely touched her.

Nor did they discuss anything of any importance—like the woman and child he'd told her would move into the house the day after the ball.

Instead, Needham had asked her many questions about the area. Not just about Little Sissingdon, but about the people who lived there. About farming and the village businesses and, most especially, about Wych House.

Phoebe had once again wrongly assumed that a city-dwelling merchant would care nothing about rural life or farming and she was pleasantly surprised by how knowledgeable he was about both.

It shamed her to admit it, but Wych House and the surrounding businesses, farms, and families were getting a far better landlord than her father had ever been.

The sound of carriage wheels on the drive pulled her from her thoughts and she glanced up from the infernal hemming.

"Who is it, Mama?" she asked.

Lady Addiscombe went to look out the window, which was open to take advantage of the lovely breeze. "I don't know. It looks like a job carriage."

Phoebe put in the last of the pins and stood, her back and knees aching from so long crawling around on the floor.

She joined her mother at the window, Katie right behind her.

"Those are the prettiest boxes I've ever seen," Katie breathed as the servant or deliveryman pulled out box after box, each of them a dusty pink with wide cream ribbon

He had a veritable mountain in his arms by the time he turned and headed for the house.

Katie was at the sitting room door before her mother could stop her.

"Katie!" the countess called after her. "You come back here immed—" she broke off and scowled. "Oh, that *hoyden*! Why do I bother?" she asked petulantly.

Phoebe ignored her mother and followed her sister—albeit at a more decorous pace.

When she reached the small entry hall, Mr. and Mrs. Park were each carrying several boxes, as was Katie.

The delivery driver was hovering, and Phoebe smiled at him. "If you will wait just a moment, I shall give you something for your efforts."

"No, my lady—I was instructed to deny any gratuity, respectfully, of course. All my expenses are paid. I was to give this to Lady Phoebe Bellamy." He held out an expensive-looking envelope with a familiar crest—one she had seen for the first time on the ball invitation from Needham.

"Thank you."

The man pulled his forelock and left.

"Oh, Pheeb! Who is it from?" Katie demanded, bouncing up and down amusingly.

"I don't know," she lied, her face heating. She turned to the servants. "Could you bring those boxes up to the sitting room, please?"

The Parks headed up the stairs, with Katie fluttering behind them.

Phoebe waited until everyone had gone up before breaking the seal and opening the letter.

Dear Lady Phoebe:
I daresay it is unspeakably rude behavior to provide one's betrothed with a ball gown."
Phoebe's face heated, even though there was nobody in the vestibule except *her.*
"I hope I've mitigated my breech of etiquette by asking Doddy's help in the plan. Surely, if your brother has approved the gifts for his sisters, it can't be terribly wrong? Or perhaps that compounded it? In any event, they are yours to wear or not wear, as you choose.
Your servant,
Paul Needham"

Phoebe folded up the expensive paper, her heart pounding with excitement. A new ball gown? Chosen by a *man*? How scandalous!

"I hope it is all right, Pheeb."

Phoebe turned to see Doddy, hands shoved into his pockets, slouched against the door, his expression anxious. "I helped fetch the sizes for the maid he sent and told him your favorite colors," he confessed.

"Of course, you did right." She smiled. "Under normal circumstances, our father would have provided our gowns, but..." Phoebe shrugged.

Doddy, however, wasn't so forgiving. "It was dashed cheese-paring of Papa to make you sew your own gowns after he went to London and kitted himself out!"

Phoebe flinched at his flash of anger. "Oh, Doddy! Please tell me you didn't tell Lord Needham that?"

He scuffed a shoe on the marble floor. "I might have."

He looked so anxious Phoebe couldn't bear to scold him.

Instead, she mortified him by ruffling his hair. "Well, thank you. I'm sure Katie will be over the moon." She hesitated and then asked, "So, what color did you tell the maid was my favorite?"

"Brown."

Phoebe's jaw dropped.

Doddy grinned. "You're such a pea goose. I told her pink." He pulled a face to show what he thought about that color.

"That's perfect, Doddy. What about Katie?"

"Green—that's right, isn't it?"

Katie's loud shriek of delight floated down from upstairs.

"It sounds like it," Phoebe said.

They both laughed.

"I'd better get up there and make sure she isn't overcome with emotion," Phoebe said. "Are you coming?"

"Lord, no," he scoffed. "Girl things."

***

Although Lord Needham offered to send his carriage to bring her family to the ball, Phoebe was grateful when her father exerted himself enough to have the family coach—long buried in the carriage house at Queen's Bower, cleaned and polished to a shine.

She was not so pleased when she discovered he had purchased a team of horses rather than renting job cattle. But it was hardly her place to scold her father for expenditures that seemed to grow by leaps and bounds whenever she turned around.

Besides, not only did she have no power over her parents' profligacy, but tonight was the last night she'd see them or her sister for some time and she didn't want to spoil things by thinking about unpleasantness. It was a shame that Doddy wasn't there tonight, but then going to a ball was his idea of a nightmare.

"That is quite a charming necklace Needham sent over," her father said, his amused gaze flickering to their mother, who'd been extremely, vocally, mortified by Needham's gifts.

She had wanted to forbid the girls wearing them, but, for once, her father had put his foot down.

"Needham will be her husband in three and a half days, my dear. Let us not stand on pointless ceremony," the earl had chided.

Katie and Phoebe had fled the room after that, leaving their parents to pull each other to pieces in private.

But she was grateful to her father, for once.

Katie was positively breathtaking in a muslin gown of pale, pale green that had been cut higher in the bodice for a younger woman.

Phoebe had loaned her sister her own pearls for the occasion, as Needham had sent her a magnificent parure. It was a lovely set made of delicate gold filigree with gorgeous—and *large*—sparkling diamonds.

As an unmarried lady, Phoebe could not wear the tiara, of course, but the necklace, bracelet, and earbobs were stunning with her gown, which was a rosy-pink silk that had obviously been designed for a woman, rather than a girl in her first Season.

Needham had also been thoughtful enough to send cream kid leather opera gloves and matching slippers, both of which were far more luxurious than any Phoebe had ever possessed.

Her new maid wouldn't be arriving until tomorrow, so Katie and Phoebe had enjoyed doing each other's hair.

Katie had worked wonders with Phoebe's boisterous chestnut curls, using the curling tongs to straighten the corkscrews and fashion a smooth chignon that made Phoebe's naturally round face appear slimmer and gave her cheekbones.

Phoebe felt not only stylish and attractive, but like a princess.

And it was all thanks to a man she had done nothing but insult and criticize.

What he had done—sending the gowns—had been thoughtful and kind. Neither of their parents had ever done even half so much for them before.

If not for the presence of Mrs. Ellen Kettering at Wych House, Phoebe would have felt optimistic and excited about her marriage.

***

Paul returned Sir Thomas Lowery's vapid daughter to her mother and nodded and smiled his way across the ballroom.

He had left the next set intentionally free—even though it would doubtless scandalize all the hopeful mamas, if not their daughters—ostensibly to check with his housekeeper and butler on any matters that might have come up before the supper dance.

This was not his first ball, by any means, but it was the first one he'd hosted and he had to admit that doing the pretty with two hundred guests was bloody exhausting. Thank God for Dixon, who was making the evening bearable.

The dinner party, in comparison, had been quite small, with only forty in attendance.

Paul had allowed Dixon—experienced in such matters—to draw up the list of guests.

Since he'd also allowed Dixon to arrange the seating chart, Paul found himself seated between Lady Addiscombe and Lady Lowery, Sir Thomas's wife.

As Paul had no wife to sit at the foot, he had given the position of honor to the Dowager Viscountess Daimler, a widowed lady who'd accompanied her seventeen-year-old granddaughter—a young lady who was not yet out—to the ball.

Judging by the frosty way Lady Addiscombe had behaved throughout dinner—barely speaking to him—she would never be a frequent visitor to Wych House, which was just fine with Paul.

As irksome as the countess's snobbery was, the earl's shallow *bonhomie* grated on Paul more.

Humboldt, the Bow Street Runner who was gathering information on the various projects Paul was involved in—including the action in common recovery with Addiscombe—said the earl was already dipping deep at several exclusive gambling hells in London.

Paul wasn't surprised to hear his prospective father-in-law was quickly wasting the money from the lease to accumulate new bills rather than pay old ones.

As much as Paul was disgusted by his prospective in-laws, he was delighted by his bride-to-be.

Lady Phoebe wore the gown he'd selected, and she looked vibrant and lovely. Paul had chosen the pattern and rosy-pink fabric himself and had allowed the London modiste—Mademoiselle Sonia—to design the gown for Lady Katherine.

He'd not told Lady Phoebe yet, but he'd commissioned a wardrobe from Mademoiselle Sonia. His new wife could go shopping for whatever she wanted after they'd married, but he suspected that she desperately needed clothing *now*.

Although her younger sister was a beauty in the making, Paul found he preferred Phoebe's sweet curves and ripe sensuality to Katie's more classical beauty and willowy elegance.

Indeed, as Paul looked out over the assembled guests, there was no other woman he found even half as attractive as Lady Phoebe.

While Sir Thomas's twin daughters were certainly more traditionally beautiful with their pale English complexions and doll-like blue eyes, he found Phoebe's tanned, healthy glow and sparkling hazel eyes far more intriguing.

He had opened the ball with her, a selection that hadn't been unusual given that Phoebe held the highest ranking among the unmarried ladies.

Because the opening set was a country dance, he'd barely talked with her beyond saying, "You look lovely."

She had flushed and then, the next time they'd been near each other, she'd thanked him quietly on behalf of her and her sister.

Now Paul would have to wait for the supper waltz to talk to her further.

In the interim, he decided to get a bit of fresh air and slipped out of the warm ballroom onto the terrace. There were couples clustered here and there among the pretty lanterns Dixon had contrived to have scattered about.

Paul was just about to sit for a few moments when he saw a flicker of familiar pink disappear behind an enormous old rose bush that sheltered a small bench.

Curious, he wandered closer to the rose arbor and heard a very familiar voice before he saw the speaker herself.

"—and I don't appreciate being threatened with inappropriate behavior, Sebastian. If you don't tell me what you want right now, I am leaving," Phoebe said, her voice strained and taut.

"Ah, don't be that way, darling," a male voice—Sebastian's, Paul assumed—said in a wheedling tone that was more than a bit slurred.

"Please address me with respect, Sebastian."

"I *do* respect you. And I miss you, too—you have no idea how much I miss you, Phoebe. If only you'd been a bit more understanding, you and I could be—"

"Is this what you wanted to say to me?" Phoebe broke in. "You are married, Sebastian, and your wife has given you one son and is with child again. You are exposing her to ridicule and embarrassment by behaving this way. Little Sissingdon is *not* London, where such behavior will be tolerated."

"Look here! I don't—"

"I believe you have been drinking, Sebastian."

"Don't be such a shrew, Phoebe. I just wanted to talk to you. You look nice—very nice. I daresay life will be better now that Lord Moneybags has taken your family's house and I—"

"Please don't refer to Lord Needham that way. And what he does with my family's home is none of your concern."

"Don't speak to me that way." The man's voice had gone from cajoling and sulking to angry. "You should be glad I am even interested in talking to you."

Paul scowled; it was time to step in and put an end to this.

He strode toward the pair, but Phoebe's derisive laughter stopped him.

"I'm sorry I ever even gave you a second of my time, Sebastian. I pity your poor wife. You've been married not even two years, and I heard you've pestered one of your maids into quitting. And you think I should be grateful for attention from a man who forces himself on powerless servants?"

"You bloody well should! You're a plain, dumpy, sharp-tongued harpy who should be grateful that any man would want to—"

Paul surged around the rosebush.

The sight of Phoebe cringing away from a man at least eight inches taller than her—who was grabbing for her—was enough to detonate an explosion in his head.

Any thoughts of handling the matter with civility fled instantly, and Paul lunged.

***

One moment Sebastian's fingers were digging into Phoebe's upper arms like grappling hooks and the next he was just... gone.

Phoebe's head swiveled around and she gawped to see Lord Needham holding Sebastian up *off his feet* and shaking him as if he were a limp rag.

"I don't like drunken bounders who insult women, Lowery." His voice was a low, menacing rumble. "And I especially don't like them doing it at *my* house and *to my guests*. You're going to head directly to the cloakroom, fetch your hat and coat, and be gone in less than five minutes or I shall make you regret ever stepping foot on my property. Is that understood?"

Sebastian made a choking noise.

"What's that?"

"I think he cannot speak, my lord," Phoebe said, more than a little concerned by the way Sebastian's face was turning purple.

Lord Needham turned to her, not relaxing his grip. "Are you hurt?"

"No, I am fine. Really, he did not hurt me and I would have dispatched him myself in a few moments."

"I believe you," Lord Needham said, "but that doesn't make his behavior acceptable."

"No, it doesn't. But I think he might lose consciousness if you don't release him sooner rather than later."

Needham glanced at the younger man and let him go, making no attempt to catch him when he slid to the grass.

"Five minutes," he said, glaring down at Sebastian's heaving body.

He then turned to Phoebe and offered his arm. "My lady?"

Phoebe cast a glance at Sebastian and decided he would survive. She then had to suppress the urge to kick him. If she'd been wearing her sturdy boots, she might have, but she had on only thin slippers.

She laid her hand on Needham's meaty forearm, and he guided her a few feet away before stopping.

"You've lost a hairpin—or two," he said.

Phoebe opened her reticule. "I have extra. Can you mend it? I cannot see to do it and going inside looking disheveled is not something I wish to do."

He nodded, his eyes still on her hair. "I am better at taking them out than putting them in, but I can probably do well enough to last until you can get to the ladies' retiring room.

Phoebe's jaw sagged.

He smiled faintly and held out his hand.

Phoebe shook herself and handed him one pin, and then stood motionless as he came close enough to repair her hair. She could smell his cologne—one of the most intoxicating scents she'd ever smelled—and feel the heat radiating off his massive body. He was so *big* that she was, once again, eye level with the buttons on his coat, which fit him like a glove.

"Thank you for helping me," she said, as his fingers moved with surprising gentleness.

"I'm sorry it was necessary. I should have noticed he was drinking earlier—or one of the servants should have."

"There are many people here tonight. It is hard to watch everyone."

He held out his hand, and Phoebe gave him another pin.

Once he'd placed the pin, he stepped back and nodded. "It will do, but I daresay it won't hold long. I probably could have done a better job if I weren't so concerned about sticking you in the head."

She chuckled. "And I appreciate that."

"Are you sure you're all right, my lady?" he asked quietly.

"Yes, I am fine." She frowned, sighed, and then added, "We were briefly betrothed, and it ended badly. You probably think me mutton-headed to come out here with him, alone, but I saw that he'd had too much to drink, and he was becoming unmanageable, so it seemed preferable to a scene. I never expected that he would attack me." She cut him a quick, embarrassed look. "He usually ignores me when we encounter each other. I thought maybe we could, er, bury the hatchet if I allowed him to talk, but he had other things in mind than apologizing."

He took a step closer, and she had to crane her neck to look up. "I daresay he has regretted that you ended your betrothal."

Phoebe couldn't help snorting at that optimistic assessment. "I doubt that. The only reason he ever wanted to marry me was to further his social connections." Phoebe could have added that he'd tried to court her elder sisters, but they'd been too intelligent to have him. But that was something that still shamed her, so she kept her tongue behind her teeth.

Phoebe paused and then asked, "How do you know I was the one who ended it?"

He shrugged. "People like to talk."

"Goodness! People must be desperate for conversation if they told you about a betrothal that lasted less than a month three years ago."

He merely smiled and said, "You look beautiful dressed in your finery, Lady Phoebe." Even in the low light of colored lantern she saw his pupils swell. "But then you are an attractive and sensual woman without fine gowns and jewels."

Phoebe's lips parted, but she could think of nothing to say to such a lovely compliment—from a man who did not appear to make them lightly.

He chuckled softly. "You look so surprised. Haven't I made it clear that I find you desirable?" He slid a hand around her neck, cradled the back of her head, and then he kissed her.

And kissed her.

When he finally released her, Phoebe's body—which had tensed with fear when she had been with Sebastian—was now so relaxed that she sagged against him.

He steadied her with his huge, gentle hands and his mouth flexed into a wry smile. "I'd better take you back inside before I compromise you at my own ball."

Chapter Twelve

Phoebe had only vague recollections of anything that transpired after their wits-obliterating kiss in his garden.

Immediately afterward, Needham escorted her into the ballroom and stood by her side in front of two hundred and fifty faces that blurred in front of her.

Phoebe smiled dazedly while words like *honored* and *my wife* echoed around her. When she heard clapping, she realized the world now knew she was betrothed and there was no going back on her decision, if there ever had been.

"You are exhausted, my lady. You need to go home and get a good night's sleep and some rest," Needham murmured during the supper waltz—yet another activity he carried out with grace and ease while she was as stiff as a plank of wood in his arms.

Phoebe didn't bother to deny it; she *was* exhausted. Not only because of all the work she'd done over the past few weeks to get the house ready for her family's departure, but because of all the worry.

That was now over; her course had been set and there was no changing it. Relief joined fatigue and exhaustion.

"You can slip out early after supper," Lord Needham said as he danced her around the enormous ballroom, his big body moving with remarkable grace.

Guilt joined the other emotions swirling inside her. It was hardly fair to abandon her betrothed at their ball, was it?

"Oh, I can stay. I'm not that—"

"I do not want you ill on our wedding day because you've worked yourself to the bone," he said, his tone gentle but firm.

He met her startled expression with a knowing look. "I know you have been busy day and night seeing to your family's arrangements. There are still a few days left, and I doubt you'll be sitting idle. But I want you to get some rest tonight. I shall make your excuses to our guests."

Phoebe stared up into his silver-gray gaze, suddenly speechless.

Nobody had ever worried that she was overtaxing herself. She was strong, sturdy Phoebe—inexhaustible, unflappable, and as stout as a draught horse—the one who kept their family fed, clothed, and comfortable.

Lord Needham's concern created intense and conflicting emotions.

On one hand, it was a relief to allow somebody else to shoulder her burdens.

On the other, she felt a faint chill at the realization that what was a firm suggestion from Lord Needham tonight—which she might disregard if she chose to—in a few days would be a husband's command.

Phoebe was still pondering those thoughts the following morning when she woke at eight o'clock—rather than her usual seven—even though she had not come home until after one.

Unable to go back to sleep, Phoebe rose and went down to the kitchen.

Over the years she'd got into the habit of enjoying a cup of tea and discussing household matters with their housekeeper/cook, Mrs. Parks.

Mr. and Mrs. Park sprang to their feet when Phoebe entered, something they never would have done before learning of her betrothal.

For years now, Mrs. Parks had treated her more like a daughter, sitting with her feet up and complaining while Phoebe and Maisy, their only maid, helped her peel potatoes or knead dough.

All that had changed.

"Oh, you're awake, my lady," the housekeeper said now, visibly ill at ease. "I'm sorry I didn't send Maisy up with your hot water. I thought you'd be sleeping in."

"That is fine. The cool water was bracing." She smiled and nodded at Mr. Parks, who pulled his forelock, which he'd never done before.

"Nobody else is awake yet?" Phoebe asked when the two stood looking awkward.

"Only Master Doddy, but he's gone to the vicar for his last day of lessons."

Phoebe nodded; she'd forgotten all about that. "I wanted to remind you that my new abigail will arrive today," Phoebe said.

"Aye, my lady," Parks said, "I'll be there to collect her."

"After I have my breakfast, I shall want to resume packing up my sisters' rooms, Mrs. Parks. Did the additional holland covers arrive?"

"Yes, my lady. Maisy and I shall see to that, and I've got three more girls coming from the village to do a last cleaning before we cover everything."

Phoebe hovered for a moment, wondering if she should stay and eat with them, as she normally did. Based on the way they were both eying her—anxiously—it was probably better that she let them be.

"Please have Maisy bring a tray with tea and toast to the sitting room, Mrs. Parks. I shall have a working breakfast and finish the last of my correspondence."

Mrs. Parks dropped a curtsy. "Very good, my lady."

Phoebe had debated for weeks whether to tell her sisters about her upcoming nuptials.

In the end, she had decided *not* to tell Hy and Selina about her marriage because she knew Selina would be horrified and would think—rightly so—that Phoebe was sacrificing herself.

Besides sparing her sisters any guilt on the subject, Phoebe also knew their mother would never agree to bring Aurelia, Selina, and Hy back for her wedding.

When she had—foolishly—mentioned inviting her sisters to Wych House to attend the ceremony, her mother had given a bitter bark of laughter and said, "If you expect anyone in this family to celebrate such a union, you are deluded."

The words had felt like a slap, and Phoebe had needed to clamp her jaws shut to keep from saying something she knew she'd regret.

And so she had postponed telling any of them about the impending marriage. But today she would write Aurelia a letter. It just felt wrong to get married without sharing the news with *any* of her elder sisters. Besides, by the time Aurelia received the letter, it would be far too late for her to talk Phoebe out of her decision.

Half an hour later Phoebe felt a strange sort of lightness and relief once she put the sealing wafer on Aurelia's letter—as if her marriage was now *real* because she had told her sister about it, even though Aurelia wouldn't read her actual words for days, yet.

Reinvigorated, she put all thoughts of family and her wedding out of her mind and turned her attention toward the daunting pile of dunning letters and bills that had accumulated in the past month.

It was almost one o'clock by the time she finished the last bill, and neither Katie nor their mother had emerged from their rooms.

Phoebe knew the earl was in his study, so she took her letters to him to frank rather than leave them on the salver.

Her father was staring at a letter when she entered. He looked up, distracted, and then forced a smile and folded up the paper. "Yes, my dear?"

"I have to go to the village, so I will mail these—and anything else you might have." She handed him the letters to sign.

He flipped through the letters, grimacing at the number of bills, and then set the whole stack aside on his desk rather than franking them. "I trust you've arranged for the postponement of these?" he asked, gesturing at the bills.

"Yes," she admitted. "But I don't think we can expect them to wait much longer." Phoebe wanted to grab him and shake him; he *had* the money to pay for everything. Why wouldn't he simply do so?

Yet again, she swallowed her words and frustration. She had no power to do anything but beg for more time from their creditors.

"I shall see to them all next month," he promised, just like he always did.

Phoebe sighed and turned to go, but her father's voice stopped her.

"You've only two days left as an unmarried lady."

Phoebe wasn't sure what his point was, but she smiled and said, "Indeed, the day has approached quickly."

"It pleases me to think that Wych House will have a Bellamy for its mistress."

Phoebe was touched by her father's admission. "I shall do my best to care for the house until my brother comes of age and brings his own wife to oversee it."

Something flickered across her father's handsome face and she swore it looked like shame, but it was gone in a flash. "I'm sure you shall, my dear. I'm sure you shall."

Phoebe put on a light cloak and bonnet and went down to the kitchen, where she found Mrs. Park and Maisy. The housekeeper had dismantled the closed oven that was her pride and joy, and Maisy was polishing its various pieces.

Both women leapt to her feet when Phoebe entered the kitchen.

"Yes, my lady?" Mrs. Parks asked.

"I'm going to see Nanny on my way to the village. Do we have any clotted cream left? I thought she might like a little to go with scones and her plum preserves."

"Aye, my lady. The larder is full to overflowing these days," she muttered, and then realized what she'd said—and to whom she'd said it—and flushed and looked away. "Go fetch one of those jars from the still room, Maisy."

They stood in uncomfortable silence as they waited.

Phoebe didn't know whether the servants were odd with her because she was soon to marry one of Britain's richest men, or if they were ashamed that she was the sort of woman who would marry a man who would openly keep his mistress under his roof—because she was *positive* that at least the Parks knew that bit of information, if it hadn't yet leaked out to the rest of the village.

Whatever their reasons, Phoebe could think of nothing to say that would make relations easier.

"Thank you," she said to Maisy when the girl brought the small jar of cream.

Phoebe was passing through the entry hall with her basket of delicacies when Doddy came thumping down the stairs

"Where are you going, Pheeb?"

"To Nanny's."

"Lord! Take me with you," he implored. "Mama has gone stark staring mad and is trying to force me into that new toggery that just came from the tailor. She says I need to make sure it fits well enough for the wedding. She won't listen to sense and will have me looking like a right gabby if I'm not careful."

"Where is your wretched squirrel?"

"Upstairs, sleeping."

She narrowed her eyes.

Doddy crossed his heart. "I swear."

"Fine, come along. But no foot-dragging or other shenanigans."

He muttered something she couldn't hear.

"I beg your pardon?"

"I didn't say anything."

"Dauntry? You come back here this minute!" Their mother's voice echoed down the stairs.

Doddy grabbed Phoebe's hand and pulled her out the door.

The sky was cloudy and there was an unexpectedly cool breeze, making Phoebe glad for the cloak. She hoped they could run her errands without getting caught in a deluge.

"How was your last day with the vicar?" Phoebe asked.

"It was dashed uncomfortable—I thought the old fellow was going to start weeping all over me."

Phoebe laughed. "I daresay he will miss you."

"That's what *he* said, although I don't know why he should." Doddy scratched his wild blond curls, reminding Phoebe that she needed to give him a haircut before the wedding. *That* would not be easy.

Phoebe didn't bother trying to explain to her little brother just how charming and full of life and intelligence he was—he wouldn't listen to her—or that *she, too,* would miss him dearly.

"I thought being sent to a crammer was bad, but I'll be happy when this stupid wedding is over," Doddy muttered.

Phoebe gave a scandalized laugh, and his face flushed.

"I didn't mean it that way," he muttered. "I just mean that Mama has been positively savage about trussing me up in finery."

"You only have to stand and watch, not actually take part," she reminded him.

It would be Phoebe standing in front of God and vowing to love, honor, and obey a relative stranger for the rest of her life.

"Yes, there's that to be thankful for," Doddy agreed with a look of relief.

Phoebe ruffled his hair. "You'll come and do the pretty, eat a wonderful meal at Wych House, and then you'll be off to a whole new life. I'll wager that you won't even miss your poor old sister."

When he didn't answer she looked over in time to see him brush a hand across his cheek.

"Don't be daft, Pheeb."

He strode on ahead, not speaking for some moments before tossing over his shoulder, "I have enough money to buy us some of those boiled sweets that look just like raspberries from Burton's. May we pop in for just a minute?"

She smiled; one minute Doddy was a young man, the next a little boy. "Of course."

But by the time they'd had tea with Nanny—and Phoebe had thoroughly described every detail of her very plain wedding gown—the clouds from earlier had darkened ominously.

"Perhaps we should forget about going to Burton's today, Doddy," she said once they'd left Nanny's cottage.

"Oh, come on, Pheeb. Since when were you afraid of a little rain? Besides, we've only a few days left before you'll be a respectable old married lady and too grand to go knocking about with your scrub of a brother." His expression was genuinely regretful, and it plucked at her heartstrings because he was probably right.

"Very well. But if it pours, you know the field will flood. You shall have to pick me up and carry me so I don't get my feet muddy."

He laughed and ran toward the village. "I'll race you!"

***

Paul was examining the small wooden case of watercolors Lucy had just handed him when the shop bell rang and a flurry of activity sounded near the door.

"Ah, Lord Bellamy, Lady Phoebe, what a pleasure to see you. Why, you're like two drowned rats." Mr. Burton's voice shook with comfortable amusement rather than reverence at the local gentry.

"It's my wretched brother's fault," said a voice Paul knew well. "He had to have some of your boiled sweets."

"Let me bring you a cloth to dry off, my lady. I'll return in a trice."

"Oooh, Pheeb, look at this—he's got lemon, too." Doddy's youthful voice rang out through the store.

"I shall expect to get one of those before you gobble them all, you little monster."

Paul heard the jingle of coins. "I've only got enough for five."

"Excellent—that takes care of me, but what are you going to eat?"

"Aww, Pheeb."

"Might I have it, Papa?"

Paul turned to Lucy, who was looking from the painting set to Paul.

He smiled. "Of course, you may, poppet."

"I really have looked everywhere for the set you gave me for my birthday. But Mama says it must be in a box we left in London." Lucy bit her lip. "I don't like to waste—"

"Shh, you'll not waste anything, love. You'll find the other paints later and use them, too." Paul took the box of paints and led Lucy toward the counter. "Come along. There are some people I want you to meet."

Part of him demanded to know what the hell he was doing introducing his baseborn daughter to Phoebe and her brother in public.

But another part—the proud and prickly part—was disgusted that he would hesitate to introduce Lucy wherever, and to whomever, the hell he pleased. After all, he'd paid a pretty penny to marry into the Bellamy family; *he* was not the one coming to the marriage hat in hand.

Besides, now that Ellen and Lucy had moved into Wych House, the news of who they were was likely already burning its way through the neighborhood. He might as well get used to the difficulties he'd created.

"Hello Lady Phoebe, Doddy."

The soggy siblings swung away from the glass-topped sweet cabinet, over which they'd both been bent like little children.

Paul watched with avidity as his wife-to-be gave him a guarded, but pleasant smile and then looked at Lucy, her smooth brow wrinkling for a moment before her eyes widened and her soft, plump cheeks lit up like fireworks at Vauxhall Gardens.

The door to the Burtons' private apartment swung open and the jovial shopkeeper stepped out with a towel.

"The Missus only has this one, my lady. The others were out on the line—"

Burton saw Paul and stopped in his tracks, his eyes darting from the Bellamy siblings to Paul and Lucy and then back again to the brother and sister, his attention settling on Lady Phoebe. Burton's eyes went so round behind his spectacles that Paul knew the man was aware of *who Lucy* was.

And if one person in the village knew the truth, that meant others did, too.

Well, it had been bound to happen eventually, so no use crying over it.

"Thank you, Mr. Burton," Lady Phoebe said, taking the proffered towel and turning back to Paul, her expression unreadable.

Paul gave Phoebe a slight smile. "Lady Phoebe, Lord Bellamy, allow me to introduce my daughter, Lucy."

Doddy blinked. "Oh, I say, hallo." The lad looked surprised, but not shocked, which told Paul that he probably thought Paul was a widower and nobody had bothered to tell him.

The boy gave a bow of such smooth sophistication that Paul supposed the action must have been bred into his very bones. "It's a pleasure to meet you, Miss Needham."

Lucy's cheeks colored becomingly, and she dropped a rather shaky curtsey. "The pleasure is mine, my lord."

Doddy grinned down at her. "None of that *my lording* if we're to be—" He stopped and cut his sister a glance while scratching his water-darkened curls. "Dash it, Pheeb. Will she be my sister-in-law or"—he flashed a comical look of dismay. "Good Lord, Pheeb! Does this make me an uncle?"

Lady Phoebe dried her face with the towel. "You will be a step uncle and I shall be a step mama. But perhaps we can dispense with such tedious titles and merely be Phoebe and Doddy."

She smiled at Lucy, and Paul felt a tightening in his chest at her genuinely friendly expression. She was not the type, it seemed, to be punitive toward a child, although he supposed this might be part of her polished façade. After all, like her brother, her manners were probably as deeply a part of her as her hazel eyes or curvaceous body.

Lucy's pale face suffused with pink at the friendly gesture. "I am happy you are marrying my Papa." The look she cut the young boy was nothing short of adoring, making Paul realize that Doddy was the kind of fine-boned, angelic-looking specimen girls of all ages couldn't help fawning over.

Any pleasure Paul had been feeling at how well this meeting was going dimmed. It would not do for Lucy to develop an infatuation for the unattainable young lord. The earl and countess had been willing to sacrifice one of their daughters to a crude animal like Paul; they would hardly sacrifice their scion to his illegitimate offspring.

Phoebe smiled. "Thank you, Lucy. I am pleased that I will soon have a new stepdaughter—although I daresay I shall think of you more like a sister." She handed the towel to her brother and peered at the box in Paul's hand. "I did not know you were a painter, Lord Needham?"

Lucy laughed. "Those are my paints, Lady—er, I mean Phoebe."

"Lucy is a talented painter," Paul said, not exaggerating.

"Oh, Papa." Lucy squirmed with embarrassment and said to Lady Phoebe, "I'm not sure if they *really* are any good or if Papa only says they are because he loves me."

"I think your Papa is very honest and plain-spoken and would tell you how he really felt."

Paul smiled at his daughter. "Lady Phoebe is correct, Lucy. I *am* plain-spoken and honest and I say you are a genuine artist."

Lucy's flush deepened, her expression something between pride and mortification.

"What are you going to paint?" Doddy asked.

"There's a rather lovely yellow bird—I'm afraid I don't know the type. Papa has sent for a guide to birds, but it hasn't arrived yet."

"Bright yellow?" Doddy asked.

Lucy nodded.

"That's a male yellowhammer."

"Doddy is the family bird expert," Phoebe explained.

He gave his sister a scoffing look. "It hardly takes much expertise to identify a yellowhammer." He turned back to Lucy. "Next spring, they'll nest in the wyches to have babies."

"If Doddy doesn't steal the eggs first."

The boy flushed. "Dash it, Pheeb, I've not done that for ages."

"A whole two years."

Lucy watched this sibling exchange with a rapt yearning that made Paul feel a deep wrenching inside. She was such a social child that it had pained him to take her away from the few friends she'd had in London. She was the sort who would have loved having lots of brothers and sisters.

Paul's own relationship with his brother Gideon—his only sibling—had been nothing like that between the two Bellamy offspring.

Indeed, by the time Paul was Doddy's age, he and Gideon had hated each other's guts.

Burton was loitering nearby, his eyes flickering between the assembled customers more rapidly than a bluebottle fly. "A proper summer storm out there," he said when he noticed Paul looking at him.

Paul set the paint box on the counter and then gestured to the sweet case. "A bag of boiled sweets, mixed, please."

"Two raspberries and three lemons while you're in there, Mr. Burton," Doddy said, pulling out coins and several pieces of lint, an agate, and a cobnut. He saw Paul looking at the nut and gave him a sheepish smile. "It's for my squirrel."

"You have a pet squirrel?" Lucy asked, her eyes round with awe.

"Well, I don't know if he's a pet—Silas is his own squirrel, but he lives with me." Doddy gave his sister a narrow-eyed look. "Although I do look out for him. But I shan't be able to take care of him now that I'm going away to school." His frown deepened. "And Phoebe and Katie both refuse to take him. I'm sure Hy would do it, but she's not here." He looked genuinely miserable. "I'm not sure what I'll do."

"The little beast belongs out in the woods," Phoebe said.

"Aw, Pheeb."

"I adore squirrels," Lucy said. "My friend Jamie had one, but a lady squirrel." She blushed furiously. "And she had babies. He said I could have one, but then we moved."

Doddy's eyes widened with hope. "I say, perhaps you might—"

Phoebe elbowed him in the ribs.

"Ow! What is it, Pheeb?"

"Do you need somebody to care for Silas?" Paul asked, sparing the boy's side further jabs.

Doddy's smile was like a beam of sunshine. "Yes! He doesn't take much care—he's a very self-sufficient squirrel."

Phoebe gave an unladylike snort.

Lucy took Paul's sleeve. "Oh, Papa, perhaps we might take care of him." She shot Doddy a nervous glance. "Only when you aren't here, of course. When you come back from school, he would like to be with you, I'm sure."

Doddy gave the girl such a glowing smile that Paul suspected female hearts would be breaking all over the county in a few years.

"That's jolly good of you to offer." He gave his sister a smug, triumphant look before turning back. "I can see you're a proper right 'un, Luce."

Lucy looked ready to melt at his feet at having a pet name. She glanced up at Paul. "Oh, please, Papa! Can we take Silas?"

Paul cut his wife-to-be a sly look. "You will need to ask Lady Phoebe, Lucy. After all, she will be mistress of Wych House."

"Please, please, please?" Lucy begged shamelessly, bouncing up and down on her toes.

Phoebe's cheeks were as red as Lucy's as she glared up at Paul. "I can hardly say *no* if you approve, my lord."

Paul grinned down at her and nodded at his daughter. "You may keep him, Lucy."

Phoebe waited until Lucy was done cheering before saying to the girl, "He will steal your things and make a nest in your clothing and generally be a pest."

"He will not!" Doddy said. "At least not if you don't leave your things strewn all about."

Paul cut in before the dispute could grow into a squabble. "Perhaps you might tell Lucy what sort of care he requires?" he suggested, earning another blinding grin.

While Doddy and Lucy discussed Silas, Paul paid for the paint and sweets. He turned to Phoebe when he'd finished. "I'd like to give you a ride home."

Her elegant eyebrows arched. "Oh, did you come in a carriage?"

"You are thinking we are lazy city folk who drive everywhere."

"I was thinking nothing of the sort." But her adorably flustered look told him that was exactly what she'd thought.

"I wouldn't have thought you were so easy to tease, my lady," he said in a low voice.

"And I wouldn't have thought a man grown was nothing but a bigger version of Doddy."

Paul smiled, unabashed by the accusation. "We were going to walk but thought it might rain and so, yes, we took the carriage. There is room for us all."

Phoebe looked out the bit of window that wasn't crowded with Burton's wares and wrinkled her nose in a manner he found far too fetching. "I suppose we had better accept your offer," she muttered so ungraciously, it was difficult not to laugh.

"Papa?"

"Hmm?"

"Doddy says he should bring Silas as soon as possible so that he becomes accustomed to me. May he bring him tomorrow?"

"Yes, it's probably better to bring him tomorrow rather than the day after," he said dryly.

Doddy grinned. "I'd bring him along to the wedding, but he's not got a proper suit, sir."

Lucy thought that was hilarious.

"Thank you for allowing her to keep him," Doddy added, giving him a sheepish smile. "I promise you'll hardly notice he's there."

Lady Phoebe snorted but refrained from commenting.

"Here you are Master Doddy." Burton handed the young lord his pitiful little packet of sweets.

"His lordship is going to give us a ride home," Phoebe said when Doddy peered into the bag, as if hoping there might be more. He looked up at his sister's words.

"Thanks, awfully," he said. "That should stop Pheeb from screeching about getting her boots muddy."

Phoebe gave her brother a long-suffering look that Paul found endearing.

He handed the boy the sack of candies. "Here, these are for you."

Doddy's eyes widened appreciatively as he reached for the bag.

"But doesn't Lucy want any?" Phoebe asked, before her little brother dived into the bag.

"We've got lots," Lucy said dismissively, her eyes still latched on her new hero.

"Smashing," Doddy said, offering around and the bag to everyone before reaching into it with a grubby hand and pulling out two pieces and stuffing them into his mouth. With his cheeks stuffed with boiled sweets, he bore more than a passing resemblance to his squirrel.

"I don't suppose you brought that bang-up yellow bounder I saw you tooling about?" he asked Paul thickly.

"No. And lucky for you, I didn't, or you'd be clinging to the rumble in the rain," Paul said.

The boy didn't look displeased by that vision.

"Don't worry," Lucy piped up. "Mama convinced us to take her barouche so there will be plenty of room for all four of us."

Her words were the equivalent of somebody breaking wind and the small shop became utterly quiet but for the patter of rain.

Luckily for Paul, the Bellamy siblings possessed that very thing he both envied and despised—good breeding—and Doddy refrained from peppering Lucy with questions.

But the boy's shockingly blue eyes had gone from open and friendly to confused and guarded.

"I'll fetch the carriage," Paul said, escaping the shop like the coward he was.

Chapter Thirteen

L ord Needham and Lucy did all the talking on the short drive from Burton's to Queen's Bower.

Phoebe knew she should make an effort, but the look Doddy had given her—and the questions in his eyes—had rendered her mute with dread.

Phoebe had known that *somebody* eventually would have to tell Doddy about Lucy and her mother living at Wych House, but she had hoped that it wouldn't be up to her.

How in the world could she explain this to her little brother? At not quite fifteen, he was no longer a child, and Phoebe shuddered to imagine what sort of things he would get up to with the other boys now that he was going away to school. But that thought didn't make what she had to tell him *now* any easier.

When the luxurious carriage rolled to a stop, Viscount Needham opened the door before his footman could come around and flip down the steps.

"Thank you for taking us home," Phoebe said. She could see her mother's silhouette in the drawing room window, right before the drapes were pulled shut.

"It was my pleasure," Lord Needham said, handing her out first, while Doddy hopped down behind her.

Her brother nodded briefly at the viscount, said a warm goodbye to Lucy, and then waited for Phoebe and took her arm in an oddly protective gesture.

Phoebe knew it was her imagination, but Doddy seemed to have aged five years on the brief carriage ride.

Not until they were safely inside the house did he whirl on her.

"What in the world did she mean, Pheeb?"

She opened her mouth to point out that the middle of the entry hall wasn't the place for such a discussion, but then their mother appeared at the head of the stairs.

"What was that all about?" she demanded.

"We were at Burton's when it began raining, so his lordship gave us a ride," Doddy said, sounding remarkably grown up.

The countess's eyes narrowed, but she nodded. "Phoebe, your new maid is waiting for you and Mrs. Debenham is here to make the last fitting to your gown."

"Oh! I didn't know she was coming today."

Lady Addiscombe heaved a put-upon sigh. "The wedding is in *two* days, Phoebe," she said, as if that explained everything.

And as if Phoebe didn't already know that.

The countess turned to her son. "Dauntry, your father wishes to speak to you in his study."

Doddy lost the look of sophistication he'd worn only a moment earlier. "Papa wants to speak to *me*?"

"That is what I said," she retorted. "Go now, please."

Doddy gave Phoebe a look that promised her he wasn't finished with the subject by any means and then turned and clumped up the stairs, earning a chastisement from his mother to *walk like a gentleman.*

***

Paul was enjoying a glass of port and reading about George Stephenson's recent patent for a steam engine locomotive when Davis entered the dining room.

"You've a visitor, my lord."

The butler wore the same pained look he'd had once before—when Lady Phoebe had paid her surprise visit.

"Well?" Paul demanded. "Who is it?"

"It is Lord Bellamy, sir."

Paul glanced at the clock and frowned; it was after ten o'clock. He'd not yet got around to the country habit of dining at six. Tonight, it had only been Paul, Dixon, and Lucy since Ella rarely came to meals these days, finding it increasingly difficult to leave her chambers.

"Send a tea tray to the library and I'll see the boy there."

"Of course, my lord."

Why the devil was Doddy calling at this hour of the night? Surely nothing could be wrong with Phoebe or her parents would have sent a servant and not their young son?

Or had the boy changed his mind about the rodent and hadn't been able to wait until tomorrow to tell him? Paul hoped that wasn't the case since Lucy had talked of little but *Silas* throughout dinner.

There was a fire in the library as the room was always damp and cold and it was Paul's practice to retire there after dinner most nights. He threw another two logs onto the glowing embers and, by the time he'd replaced the screen, the door opened and young Doddy, dressed in his dinner clothing, strode into the room.

"Good evening, Doddy," Paul said, gesturing to the chairs in front of the fireplace. "Won't you have a seat?"

"I don't know if I shall wish to sit with you, sir."

Paul's eyebrows shot up at his hostile tone. "Oh?"

"I found out something rather disturbing tonight."

So, this wasn't about the squirrel, then.

"And what was that?" Paul asked.

"Your daughter—Lucy, she is your natural child?"

Paul could see by the bright spots of color streaking Doddy's cheeks that asking such an intimate question was not something he did lightly.

"She is."

"And her mother lives in this house?"

"That is true."

Doddy's well-formed jaw moved from side to side, his agitation almost palpable.

Paul felt a pang of guilt at being the source of the boy's unhappiness.

Doddy shoved a hand through his pale blond locks—the sort of wavy tresses that poets were supposed to have—turned and strode toward the door. He stopped before he reached it, spun, and came striding back to Paul.

He met Paul's gaze directly. "I must tell you, sir, that I confronted my father with what I'd heard today at Burton's. When I expressed my displeasure that he should have allowed Phoebe to become betrothed to a man who would have his mistress living in the *very same* house as my sister, he told me she knew of the arrangement."

"Yes, she knows."

Doddy clenched his jaws. "This is—I—" He sucked in a huge breath and then expelled it noisily.

"Have a seat, Doddy," Paul said.

Doddy hesitated a second, but then gracelessly collapsed into the chair. "Please tell me there is some explanation for this?"

"The woman in question is no longer my mistress," Paul said.

Doddy didn't look appeased.

"And she is dying."

The boy opened his mouth, but no words came out.

Paul continued, "My options were to leave my daughter with a severely ill woman; take her away from her dying mother; or to bring both here to live with me. Because I am selfish and wish to have Lucy with me, I chose the third option. I am aware it is unorthodox behavior, but then I am not an orthodox man."

Doddy gazed at him; his blue eyes filled with uncertainty.

"I understand your reaction," Paul said. "I would have expected your father to take a similar position, but he did not."

The boy snorted and shoved his hand through his hair yet again, his fingers trembling slightly this time. "No, Papa would allow nothing to come between himself and his own pleasure." His cheeks went scarlet at that disclosure. "I shouldn't say that," he muttered.

"You are only saying what is widely known," Paul said.

"More's the pity."

As a man who'd grown up with a father bent on his own will to the exclusion of all else, Paul couldn't have agreed more.

The library door opened, and a maid entered with a laden tray.

Doddy stood.

"Stay and have tea with me," Paul said.

For a moment, he thought the boy would say *no*, but he sank back down into his chair.

"Thank you, Mary," Paul said to the maid. "You may leave the tray and I shall do the honors." He smiled at Doddy's surprised look. "I'm quite a hand at managing a tea tray."

Doddy smiled slightly, still visibly ill at ease.

Once the maid was gone, Paul went through the familiar ritual of making tea, although it *had* been some time since he'd last done so.

He glanced up at the boy and found him watching. "I daresay you never have to manage for yourself with all those sisters?"

"No, that is true."

"You'll need to become handy at this now that you'll be going away to school and fagging for some demanding sixth-form boy."

"Is that how you learned?" Doddy asked.

"It was, indeed. How do you like it?"

"Light with one sugar, please."

"I shall let you help yourself to my pastry cook's masterpieces," he said when he saw the lad staring yearningly at the pastries. When he took only two, Paul teased, "Come, come—don't leave them all for me to eat."

Finally, the boy grinned, the first natural expression he'd exhibited since entering the room.

"Where did you go to school, sir?" Doddy asked, brushing his sugar-encrusted fingers on his napkin.

"I'm a Harrovian—your mortal enemy."

Doddy laughed. "Well, not for a few months yet."

"Are you looking forward to it?" Paul asked.

"I always wanted to go, but now…" Doddy shrugged.

"You're worried about your sisters?"

"Yes."

It was unnerving how badly he wanted to tell the boy across from the truth about Ellen and Lucy. But it would be unwise to share the secret, even if it were Paul's to tell, and it was not.

Still, he could reassure Doddy—at least to the extent it was possible.

"I know this is not an ideal arrangement and regret any embarrassment I may cause or have caused your sister. Short of sending Lucy and her mother away, I shall do everything in my power to ensure that Lady Phoebe—and our neighbors—are aware of the value I place upon her and our marriage."

Doddy nodded, suddenly looking like the uncertain fifteen-year-old he was. "I probably should have spoken to Phoebe before coming to you." He gave a soft snort. "She'll be angry with me when she learns I've interfered in her affairs."

"I doubt that—she'll likely be flattered that you care."

"My sisters think of me as a little boy to be coddled and sheltered," he said, once again sounding more mature than his years. "They think I was never aware of the muddle my father made of things. Their only concern has always been to preserve my birthright." He gave a cynical laugh. "As if inheriting Wych House is more important to me than they are."

Paul felt a sharp twinge at the lad's words.

Before he could speak—although he wasn't sure what to say—Doddy went on, "I'm very grateful to you for leasing the house and putting so much care into it. Phoebe explained to me that you are spending far more than most tenants would ever do and I appreciate it, as I will eventually be the beneficiary. Without you, I doubt there would be a house left, as I'm sure my father would conceive of some way to break it up or sell it."

Paul could only nod, the sharp taste of bile flooding his mouth.

It was becoming less and less appealing to contemplate taking this charming lad's patrimony from him.

But Doddy was right; if Paul didn't take Wych House, the earl would always find another partner to his crooked deception.

Suddenly, that argument was no longer good enough to make Paul feel right about what he was doing.

***

"You did *what?*" Phoebe demanded.

"Oh, leave off screeching at me, Pheeb! I know I blundered in and should have talked to you first, but I was just so blood—er, so *mad* when I learned what Papa allowed to happen to you." His cheeks streaked with mortification at having to discuss such a subject with a sister.

"You needn't be angry at anyone," she assured him, not entirely truthfully. She was still more than a little irked at her father, too. As for Lord Needham? Well, she tried not to think about that.

"I hated being the last to know."

"Well, you're probably not the *last* to know," she said lamely.

He snorted. "So you've known since his call here all those weeks ago?"

"Yes," she admitted. "But I think the truth only came out in the village after the ball—when Lucy and her mother arrived at Wych House."

His expression turned grim at her admission. "And we are going to leave right after the wedding and leave you to face our neighbors' reactions all by yourself."

"I don't think it will be as bad as you fear, Doddy. Most of those who might act scandalized would probably have foisted their daughter or sister off on Needham without hesitation."

"I daresay you're right," he admitted, cutting her a look of concern. "For my part I don't think any the worse of you for marrying him, Pheeb." He heaved a sigh. "Dash it, but I *like* the man for all that he's done such a boggle-headed thing."

"I like him, too," she admitted, surprised to discover it was the truth.

Was engaging in trade vulgar? Undoubtedly. Was he abrupt and dismissive of convention? He seemed to revel in it.

On the other side of the coin, he could also be thoughtful and kind—as he'd shown with the ball gowns and his handling of Sebastian—and his lack of artifice was, in its own way, charming.

And then there was the wildly sensual effect he had on her person. Not that anyone needed to know that.

So, yes, she liked him. But was that enough to spend her life with him?

"Are you sure this is the right decision, Pheeb?" Doddy asked, his brow furrowed with worry.

Phoebe forced herself to smile, even though his question was one she asked herself hourly.

"It is the perfect decision, Doddy."

Maybe not for me, she might have added, *but for all the people I care about.*

Chapter Fourteen

Phoebe was well-aware that it was highly unorthodox for a groom to arrange a wedding rather than the bride's family—especially when the bride's parents lived only a few miles away.

She wasn't sure if Lord Needham had taken charge because the countess had been determined not to lift a finger, or because he enjoyed exercising control over every part of his life. She suspected it was a bit of both.

Rather than be offended that he'd not consulted Phoebe on the arrangements, she was relieved to leave everything in his, or, more accurately, Mr. Dixon's, capable hands.

Dixon, the youngest son of Viscount Cowper, had worked for Lord Needham for almost five years. He'd arrived at Wych House before Needham and had stayed while his employer traveled around the country on business matters. As a result, Mr. Dixon was quite well known in the village.

Not only was Mr. Dixon as handsome as an angel, but he was charming, elegant, and personable. In fact, he was exactly the sort of younger son that Phoebe might have married if her father had not been a gambler.

In addition to managing many of his lordship's responsibilities in the House of Lords—such as drafting speeches and researching various legislation—Dixon also oversaw the myriad repairs and improvements taking place in both Wych House and on the tenant properties. He was liked by everyone he met and was, by all accounts, quite a wizard of organization.

He'd certainly worked magic in the tiny family chapel at Wych House, which gleamed from its ancient flagstone floor to its glowing wooden pews to the glittering stained-glass windows. It was also positively bursting with fresh flowers, including Phoebe's personal favorites, peonies.

The wedding breakfast also took place at Wych House and was larger than Phoebe had expected.

Besides the bridal couple and Phoebe's family, there were the vicar and his wife, Sir Thomas and Lady Lowery, Dowager Viscountess Daimler and her granddaughter, Lucy, a man named Harold Twickham, who appeared to be an uncle of sorts to Lord Needham, and four couples who were longtime acquaintances of her father and who had obviously been invited to lend legitimacy to the proceedings.

The guest list was, Phoebe knew, the work of Mr. Dixon. He would have known that a family-only wedding in the middle of the Season would have caused suspicion that the couple had something to hide, and so he had asked both Phoebe's parents about other guests they might invite.

The countess had refused to offer any names for the wedding list, a reaction which had made Phoebe so angry that she'd barely been able to speak to her mother for a week.

Fortunately, the earl had been eager to show his approval for the union and had contacted four friends he'd known for years. One of them was the Duke of Westmoreland, and the other three were almost equally grandly titled. Their presence, along with their wives—none of whom looked especially pleased to be there—was tacit approval of the marriage.

So, if Phoebe and her husband ever went to London, they would probably not receive the cut direct from most of the *haute ton* because of a havey-cavey wedding.

The ceremony itself passed in a blur, and the wedding breakfast wasn't much clearer.

The Duke of Westmoreland sat on Phoebe's right and the Marquess of Brough on her left. Both men were polite and kept the conversation moving along, which was just as well because Phoebe hadn't been able to think about anything, or anyone, other than the man sitting at the opposite end of the table.

Her husband.

And every time she'd stolen a glance at him, he'd been watching her while still holding up the conversation he was having with the Duchess of Westmoreland while Phoebe's mother, on his other side, seemed determined to ignore him.

As the day dragged on through toasts and speeches and several hours of lounging and eating, Phoebe was increasingly torn between dreadful anticipation of the evening ahead and a strong desire to run from the house and never return.

Try as she might, she couldn't banish the last words her mother had spoken to her that morning before she'd left Queen's Bower.

"As much as it disgusts me, I feel it is my duty to warn you about tonight, Phoebe."

Phoebe wished that she could have told her mother that she *didn't* want to know what would happen, but she could not make herself say the words. After all, who else was there to tell her anything?

So, instead, she'd listened with dread and mortification.

"Your husband-to-be is a vulgar, base beast."

Phoebe had opened her mouth to demur, but her mother hadn't been in the mood to listen.

"The mere presence of that vile *woman* in his house and that"—her face had contorted with revulsion as she spat out the next words—"*obscenity* of a daughter—"

"Mama, she is only a child," Phoebe had murmured, distressed by the direction her mother's conversation had taken.

Lady Addiscombe had made a distinctly *un*ladylike sound at that, but at least she had returned to the point.

"The *deed* itself will hurt a great deal and there will be blood. The first time is the worst, but it is always painful." She'd looked at Phoebe and frowned. "Given your disparate sizes and his immense, er, bulk, it may be wise to take a drop or two of this." She had pressed a small glass vial into her hand.

"But, what is—"

"Laudanum, my dear. Take it in a glass of wine—perhaps even two glasses—and ensure there are no gaps in the drapes that might allow in any stray light."

"Why do the drapes matter?"

"So you don't have to *watch him do it!*" the countess had hissed.

Phoebe had slumped back at that point, unable to do more than listen.

"During the act, you must put your mind on other matters." The countess had brightened a little. "Think about drawing up a linen inventory, which will be one of your most pressing tasks once you've become mistress of Wych House. That shall make the unpleasantness pass most speedily. If you are fortunate, you shan't be bothered above a few times a year. Just pray for an heir, my dear. Pray hard."

That conversation had stayed with her through the wedding, the endless breakfast, and the hours afterward, making her tenser with each minute that passed.

Her family had been the last to depart and it had been tearful—at least on Phoebe and Katie's parts—as they'd said their goodbyes. Doddy and Katie would leave Queen's Bower the next morning, so it was the last time Phoebe would see her siblings for months. Although she'd known that for days, the reality of it had struck her painfully hard.

Needham had shown her to her chambers and suggested that she rest before supper, which would be served in their chambers.

That had been two hours ago.

Phoebe had bathed, dressed, dismissed her maid for the night, and then paced. She was still pacing.

She swallowed down her incipient hysteria, only vaguely aware of the luxurious fabrics and wall hangings that graced the vast suite of rooms.

Her chambers had been freshly refurbished in a palate of rose-pink, cream, and beige. They were the most elegant, opulent rooms she had ever stepped foot in. Phoebe wondered if her husband had had any hand in the selection of the colors or if this, too, was the work of Dixon.

Whoever had overseen the decoration had outdone themselves and the array of silks, satins, and velvets in various shades of pink was sumptuous and soothing.

A veritable feast of fruits, nuts, cold meats, and tempting pastries had been laid out in her private sitting room, where a lovely table with crisp linen and sparkling silver and plate was ready and waiting for their supper.

None of that was enough to distract Phoebe from what was about to begin in— she glanced at the ormolu clock on the mantel—three minutes.

She squeezed her hands together to keep them from shaking and walked another circuit of the room, giving herself a mental lecture.

You enjoyed all three kisses. He has never hurt or frightened you. He has never—

The connecting door between the two rooms opened, and Lord Needham entered the room.

Phoebe knew vaguely that she was staring, open-mouthed, but could not help herself.

He wore only a dull pewter banyan that swathed him from shoulders to mid-calves and made him appear positively monolithic.

Naked! He is naked beneath his robe! her mind shrieked, as if she'd not already discerned as much.

Phoebe wasn't the only one staring.

Lord Needham strode toward her with the loose-limbed grace that always surprised her in a man so large. He didn't stop until he was mere inches away, close enough that she needed to crane her neck. His delicious cologne wafted toward her and tickled her nostrils, and the skin over his jaw was so smooth that he must have just shaved.

Although they weren't touching, she felt heat radiating from his body.

"Are you frightened?" he asked in a low rumble.

Why lie? "Yes."

His thin, harsh-looking mouth softened with a faint smile. "You have nothing to fear from me, Phoebe. Especially not in the bedchamber."

She swallowed at the sound of her name on his tongue. Why did it sound so much more intimate without the honorific in front of it? So much more... naked?

Naked. She really needed to stop thinking that word.

Phoebe couldn't seem to stop swallowing, nor could she look away from his riveting gaze.

She had never known anyone with gray eyes before—not true gray, like Needham's. The strangely colorless shards reminded her of the slate clouds right before a freezing rain or snowstorm. They stood out in his deeply tanned face and were striking when paired with his dark brown hair and black eyelashes.

How had she ever thought he was ugly? True, he was all harsh lines and stark angles—pure masculinity without a touch of softness—but in no way could he rightly be called *ugly*.

Needham tilted his chin toward the food and drink. "Did you have a glass of wine or anything to eat? I noticed you had little earlier today."

He'd noticed that?

The thought of him noticing such a minor, insignificant matter made Phoebe's stomach—already a mess—pitch and clench, as if she were on the bridge of a ship.

Why would he notice such a thing? Why did he—

"Phoebe?"

She blinked up at him in confusion. *Oh. He was waiting for an answer.*

"No, I, er, I'm not hungry."

"Wine?"

Again, she swallowed, as if testing her ability to do so. Yes, she could swallow, but she doubted she could *keep* anything down.

"I'd better not."

He clucked his tongue. "You poor darling."

Something about his pity made her bristle. "It is not my fault that I know nothing at all about such... *things*. Indeed, I daresay you would be angry if I *weren't* ignorant," she retorted.

"There is the slightly acerbic Phoebe I know," he said, a faint curve to his lips.

A slightly hysterical laugh bubbled up inside her. "You enjoy it when I'm rude to you, don't you? How singular."

"I like your fire. I liked it that day on the road when you glared up at me. I liked it when you came to this house and told me I had better marry you instead—"

She gasped. "I never did!"

He grinned, the expression so unexpected it knocked the air from her lungs. "Aye, you know you did."

"Well, not in so many words. It was you who offered marriage as a condition if you'll recall."

"Mmm-hmm." His gaze, suddenly darker, flickered over her as he stepped close enough that she could feel him. "As to your other comment—that I would be angry if you weren't innocent? I would not have been angry, but I would have been disappointed."

His nostrils flared in a way that made her thighs clench.

"I will enjoy teaching you about the pleasure your body is capable of experiencing." He paused, his eyes flickering over her, his jaw flexing. "And bestowing."

Phoebe stared up at him like a gapeseed, jolting when his big, warm hand slid around her waist.

"Shhh, love," he murmured, lowering his mouth over hers slowly enough that Phoebe could have backed away if she'd wanted to avoid him.

But, as nervous as she was, the last thing she wanted to do was avoid him.

Indeed, Phoebe had been dreaming about the feel of his firm lips and slick, clever tongue repeatedly since that day in the woods, wondering what might have happened if Doddy hadn't interrupted them.

The touch of hard muscle against her tender flesh was electric, and Phoebe shivered and opened her lips wider for his kiss.

"Mmmm," he hummed against her mouth, sliding his hand around the back of her head, clasping her firmly while he plundered her with increasing heat and passion.

Only when they were both breathing heavily did he pull away.

"Look at me, Phoebe."

Phoebe opened her eyes to find his face only a few inches away, his body almost bent in half.

"That looks most uncomfortable."

He smiled and the skin around his eyes crinkled in a way she'd not noticed before. "I must admit I am no longer as young and limber as I once was."

He straightened to his full height, grimacing. By doing so, he put a great deal of distance between them. Had he always been so very, very tall?

"How tall are you?" she asked in a breathy voice that irked her.

"Perhaps an inch over six feet. And you?"

"Five feet and one-half inch." She pulled a face. "I'd always hoped to grow a little more, but I think the time for that has passed."

"I think you are perfect, just as you are."

Phoebe's cheeks heated. "You will make me look like a short, squat tomato if you continue to say such things, my lord."

"Won't you say my name?" he asked.

Paul. It was a short, easily pronounced name, and yet she found she couldn't make her lips form the word.

All she could do was stare.

He chuckled softly. "Perhaps later." He took her hand and pressed his lips into her palm.

Phoebe whimpered at the sensual gesture, and his pupils flared, swallowing the icy gray iris.

"Shall I ring for supper?" he asked a moment later, releasing her hand.

The thought of food made her feel bilious. "Are—are you hungry?"

"Not for food."

Yet again, her jaw sagged.

"The choice is yours, Phoebe; I can ring for food or we can go to bed."

Her gaze darted to the windows. "Bed?" she asked, her voice a high-pitched squeak. "But it is still daylight."

"Yes."

The thought of eating or drinking anything made her feel sick.

But the thought of *bed...*

Phoebe shook so badly she felt like she was in a carriage traveling down an especially rutted, pitted road.

She threaded her trembling fingers together and inhaled deeply before letting it out and saying, "Bed, please."

His eyebrows lifted in surprise.

"I would like to get it over with," she blurted.

His eyes widened slightly, and then he laughed. A deep belly laugh.

At her.

"No, don't get angry," he said, catching her upper arm when she would have turned away.

Instead, he drew her closer.

"I wasn't laughing *at* you, but at the situation and how badly I am managing it."

"Y-you?"

"Yes, I should be putting you at ease, not making you shake like a leaf in a high wind." He smiled down at her, the expression rueful and kind, and slid a hand behind her neck, which he gently massaged. "You are very tense and stiff."

His strong fingers worked instant magic on her muscles and a mortifying half-grunt, half-moan slipped from her mouth as her body turned to jelly.

"The last thing in the world I want is to *just get it over with,*" he said, stroking her jaw and throat with one hand, continuing his mesmerizing rubbing of her neck and shoulders with the other. "I have been looking forward to this night a great deal."

Her eyelids fluttered as his words penetrated the haze of bliss. "You have?" She swallowed. "But I am so..."

"So?"

Phoebe sighed when his massaging fingers stilled. "So ignorant." She blinked up at him, wishing he would step in and save her, but he just waited patiently for her to finish her thought.

"I know nothing—not what will happen, or—or anything about—" Her breathing became more labored with every word she spoke and yet her lungs were oddly starved for air.

Shut up, Phoebe. Just shut up, she told herself.

But she couldn't stop babbling. "Er, I mean I know what will occur in the most general sense, but when it comes to what to do to p-please you or—"

"Shhh." He kissed her forehead and his fingers resumed their caressing.

Phoebe bit her lower lip to contain a whimper of pleasure; she never would have believed that even the base of her skull had muscles.

"You don't need to think about any of that right now. The only thing you need to do is relax. Hmm?"

Phoebe made a soft sound of assent; all she could manage at that moment.

Needham pulled away and took her hand, leading her toward the massive four-poster bed. "Just relax and let me undress you."

The words were like being doused with freezing water. "Undress me?" she shrieked.

He winced.

"I'm sorry," she said in a more modulated tone. "But w-will you extinguish the candles first?"

He shook his head.

"Oh. But—but why do you need to see me?"

"I don't need to; I *want* to. I want us to be skin to skin."

Skin to skin.

There were the wickedest words she had ever heard.

He gave her another unexpectedly kind smile. "Perhaps I should undress first? Have you seen a naked man before, Phoebe?"

Phoebe tried to gasp and speak at the same time, and it was not successful.

She choked on the word *no* and then kept on choking.

Lord Needham disappeared for a moment while she struggled to catch her breath.

He reappeared holding a glass of water. "Here."

She snatched the glass and took little sips between coughs.

"Thank you," she said in a raspy voice several mortifying moments later.

Phoebe thrust the empty glass at him.

He set it down and then turned to her. "I daresay your mother told you I would sneak into your room in darkness, do my business, and then leave?"

"Yes."

"It will not be that way." He cupped her jaw, an odd, almost soft, expression flickering across his face.

Without realizing what she was doing, Phoebe nuzzled her cheek into his warm palm.

His nostrils flared and his hand tightened slightly before relaxing again. "I want us to be lovers, Phoebe—to enjoy each other's bodies while we make a child. I don't think I am mistaken in believing that you have enjoyed our kisses and like it when we touch?" He held her gaze until she nodded.

"I find you lovely and desirable." He stroked her cheek. "And I adore your blushes."

Phoebe was so hot she was amazed she didn't melt into a puddle.

"I would like us to conduct our marriage in a way that will bring the most pleasure to both of us. I know our backgrounds are very different, but I believe we could get along nicely with a little effort. Wouldn't it be better to be lovers than polite strangers?"

That word again: *lovers*. Just hearing it was enough to send disturbing flutters through her entire body.

She saw he was waiting for an answer and nodded.

He smiled and caressed her cheek once more before lowering his hand.

Phoebe immediately missed him, and it was all she could do not to grab his wrist and yank him back.

"I take it by your response a moment ago that you have not seen a naked, aroused man before?"

She shook her head vigorously. "No."

"People fear the unknown," he said.

Phoebe knew what he meant and agreed with him. In principle.

This, however, was very far from principle. This was real. Phoebe hadn't thought she'd have to see him naked, *ever*. Well, other than his face and hands.

Nor had she expected to show *him* more than that. There were parts of her own body that Phoebe had never seen.

So, no, she'd not expected those things.

But she had to admit to a certain twinge of... curiosity.

"Phoebe?"

Her head jerked up, and she met his gaze.

"I'm going to undress, Phoebe."

She looked up into his patient, questioning eyes and nodded.

He pulled the sash and shrugged the heavy silk robe from his shoulders.

Phoebe couldn't help it; she squeezed her eyes shut. "I'm sorry," she gasped, her voice such a quavering squeak it shamed her.

"You have nothing to be sorry for." He sounded amused rather than angry. "Keep your eyes closed if it helps."

"I think... maybe, yes. Just for a moment."

"I'm going to undress you now."

She gulped and nodded.

Although his hands were big, his fingers were nimble and moved with confident haste to unfasten the buttons on her dressing gown.

"This is a pretty gown," he commented, lifting it from her shoulders to expose the matching night rail beneath. He traced a finger over the openwork that bordered the neckline. "Is this your needlework?"

Phoebe forced her eyes open, feeling foolish at hiding from his gaze. She was, after all, a woman grown.

The first thing that confronted her was a broad expanse of chiseled male chest, slabs of muscles liberally dusted with dark hair.

And a nipple. A tiny male nipple.

She made a mouselike squeak and craned her head back.

His face was turned to the side, his harsh, rather brutal profile toward her as he looked at the dressing gown he'd removed and held in his hands.

His profile looked like something one might find on an ancient coin. There was a barbaric appeal in features that were so chiseled and hard.

He turned to look at her, and Phoebe realized she'd not answered his question.

"Er, no, it is Katie's needlework."

He cocked an eyebrow at that. "That… surprises me."

"Because she is such a hoyden?" Phoebe guessed.

"I wouldn't say *hoyden*, but she doesn't seem like the sort to sit still long enough to stitch anything."

"It is a challenge to get her to finish her projects," Phoebe admitted.

The night rail had come from Katie's own trousseau chest. Her sister had generously offered it up to Phoebe without hesitation, saying, "I probably have years—if ever—before I shall need the contents of a wedding chest."

Although the gown was pretty, it was fussier than Phoebe liked. Yet the high neck and long sleeves had made it feel like the *safest* choice for tonight.

Lord Needham worked his way down and down. Rather than stop when he reached her waist—at which point she could have stepped out of the gown—he kept going, dropping to his haunches to reach the buttons that ran all the way to the floor.

Phoebe clutched the gaping edges of the gown and pulled them closed around her chest as she stared down at him

But he paid her no mind and continued his labor until he reached the very last button. Only then did he look up at her.

Phoebe schooled herself not to look below his face—even though she could see something disturbingly large thrusting and bobbing on the edge of her vision.

He parted the two halves of the gown, exposing from her feet to her hips. The sound he made—an almost primitive grunt of desire—sent warmth flooding to her tightly clenched thighs.

"You are lovely," he said, his gaze almost reverent as he lightly caressed her legs. His hands closed around her hips, his fingers almost spanning her as he moved her back a step, until she was at arm's length, her lower back just touching the high mattress.

"Climb up on the bed, Phoebe." She hesitated and he nodded, as if she'd asked for encouragement. "Go on."

She clutched her gown closed and used the elegant gryphon shaped bed ladder to scale the massive bed.

Only when she sat on the mattress did she realize how that brought her pelvis almost even with his head.

Phoebe gasped, but, thankfully, didn't descend into another coughing fit, and drew her knees tightly together, holding the gown closed with one hand and trying to pull the material over her exposed legs with the other.

His hands closed around her ankles like warm manacles and he lowered slowly from his haunches to his knees, grimacing a little when they hit the carpet.

"Relax your legs," he said.

Phoebe's brain struggled to comprehend just what he was planning and questions bounced around inside her head:

Why should she relax her legs?

Did it hurt his knees to kneel?

At least the carpet beside the bed was unusually plush.

What was he doing with—

He smiled up at her. "If you relax, I promise I shall make it good for you, Phoebe."

Her legs turned to water at the confident command in his voice.

"Good girl," he murmured, lifting one of her legs and hooking her knee over his shoulder.

"Oh!" she gasped.

His eyes were no longer a silvery gray, but almost black. His expression was one of hungry anticipation as he positioned her other leg in the same way.

Phoebe had never imagined a man would ever look at her with such naked desire.

She could scarcely believe that she was sitting on a bed, all but naked, with her thighs on a man's shoulders. This was nothing like what her mother had told her.

She felt lightheaded, as if she'd left her body and was watching the shocking events from somebody else's vantage point.

And then he leaned forward, and she *felt* him—the heat of his damp breath on her thighs, which his broad shoulders nudged wider as he pushed closer.

Phoebe gave another soft gasp when he looped his arms around her thighs and stroked the tangle of dark curls that covered her sex.

His caresses were gentle but firm and made her intensely aware of the heaviness in her womb and the delicious lethargy that was spreading through the rest of her body.

His movements were so certain, so matter-of-fact, that it seemed silly to feel shocked by what had initially seemed to be outrageous behavior.

Perhaps what he was doing wasn't so unusual, after all?

Although she had touched herself on more than one occasion—certainly more often lately, since that first kiss with Needham—she'd only done so under cover of darkness, her actions quick, guilty, and furtive.

Phoebe knew she should have been embarrassed by the way Needham was staring at her in such open admiration, murmuring quiet words of praise like *pretty* and *sweet* and *soft*. But instead of shame, she felt warm and safe and… cherished.

Even when his big fingers gently parted her lower lips and exposed that most private part of her to his gaze—something even *she* had never seen before—Phoebe lay relaxed and open.

He sucked in a breath, his gaze darkening further. "So beautiful and wet." He swallowed convulsively; his face taut as he stroked his fingers through her slickness.

Phoebe's own breathing grew ragged as she watched and waited to see what he'd do next.

He shrugged his shoulders, and the action pulled her closer still, until his hot breath fanned over the delicate petals of her sex, causing her inner muscles to clench, an action that sent ripples of pleasure cascading through her body.

"My God," he muttered, the words sounding as if they'd been forced from his lungs.

He spread her wider with his fingers and then lowered his mouth over her.

And that's when Phoebe stopped thinking entirely.

***

Paul knew he was a brute to behave so vulgarly with a virgin, but *hell and damnation,* her cunt tasted sweet! And her lush little body was so damned responsive that he hadn't been this excited by a woman in years and years.

Staring at her swollen pink petals and tiny bud had almost unhinged him; he wanted to *consume* her.

He'd never had a virgin before and was startled by the effect it seemed to be having on him. Not just his body, but his brain, as well.

He was so bloody aroused by the thought of being inside her that he'd had to milk himself twice today—once when he'd woken hard wanting her, and then again barely an hour ago, after his valet had shaved him.

And here he was again, as hard as an iron rod after just looking at her.

It had been ages since he'd wanted to taste a woman so badly; she was so damned delicious that Paul was beginning to suspect he could bring himself off just by making her orgasm.

It would certainly be a pleasure to try.

Only once before in his life, when he'd been sixteen and fancied himself in love—for the first and only time—had Paul ever bedded a woman who was not a professional.

Paul supposed it was possible that he'd been this excited when he'd made love to Catherine, but the memory was almost two decades old and too hazy to recall clearly.

After Catherine, he'd only ever engaged in sex with his mistresses.

Catherine might not have been a professional, but she had taught him plenty, not the least of which was that it was far better to treat bed sport as just another business transaction.

Just like in business, Paul had always put a great deal of time into choosing his mistresses, and usually kept them for at least a few years before he tired of them and moved on.

He not only made sure they were disease free and had no delusions of marriage, but he'd wanted a certain… compatibility from the women he shared a bed with.

While he liked pretty women as much as the next man, a woman's sensuality was far more important to him than her appearance. The last thing Paul wanted was a cold, unemotional bed partner who didn't want to touch him or be touched—no matter how beautiful she might be.

Just because Paul paid his lovers did not mean they were lacking passion. In fact, the one thing all his mistresses had had in common was a love of sexual pleasure.

Paul had noticed Phoebe's response the first time he'd kissed her and it had been a big part of his impulsive decision to ask her to marry him.

Indeed, her easy acceptance of his mouth between her thighs—an act that would send a great many of her contemporaries running in the opposite direction—told him that his blue-blooded young wife was a sensualist whose lush, womanly body was built for pleasure.

And Paul would give her all the pleasure she could take and more.

While he wanted nothing more than to bury himself to the hilt in her tight heat, he would use the rest of the evening to relax her, if that was what it took.

Tonight was all about Phoebe. Indeed, every night for the foreseeable future would be dedicated to ensuring his young bride enjoyed herself.

While his current behavior was probably shocking her, it was—judging from how wet and engorged her sex was—arousing her as well.

Even if she *had* been ashamed at first, she'd forgotten it and was now as curious as a kitten as she propped herself up on her elbows to watch while he licked and nibbled and teased.

Paul cherished her innocent excitement and wanted to keep her sweetly eager and inquisitive rather than terrify her. The best way to do that would be to flood her with so much pleasure that she'd scarcely remember the slight amount of pain he'd eventually bring her.

He couldn't have been working her for more than a minute or two when her eyelids drooped and her body began to quiver. She whimpered, using his shoulders for leverage and grinding her pelvis against his mouth, demanding more.

Paul gave her what she wanted, sucking her tiny nub between his lips and driving her over the edge into bliss.

Her lush thighs—which were surprisingly muscular from all the walking she did—clamped tight around his head and squeezed his face like an erotic vise as she gave in to her orgasm.

Her eyelids fluttered shut, her arms gave out, and she slumped back as she came apart beneath his mouth and tongue.

When her clitoris became too sensitive for his touch to be pleasurable, Paul moved his attention lower, teasing her entrance with the tip of his tongue, penetrating her gently and shallowly at first.

Paul couldn't see her face as she came back to awareness, but he felt the jolt of astonishment that stiffened her body when she realized what he was doing.

Her hips, which had naturally begun to pulse, eager to take him deeper, froze.

A few seconds later, she pushed up on her elbows, her eyes locking with his as Paul penetrated her as deeply as he was able.

Paul reveled in her expression of utter shock, uncaring of the earthy, animalistic noises he was making as he used his tongue to fuck her. He groaned, intoxicated by the taste of her, laving her faster and deeper, greedy for every drop of her sweet nectar.

Her shock changed to wonder, then to desire, as her eyes glazed over and her hips began to buck and grind, demanding more, more, *more.*

Soon, she was riding his tongue, mouth, and even his chin, chasing her second orgasm with abandon, uncaring of how she looked or sounded. Her body shook and clenched as she came, the waves of her orgasm rippling through her in gradually diminishing spasms, until she was limp.

Paul gave her little bud one last hard suck, earning a sweet little whimper, and then stood with a groan, grimacing when his knees popped at the abuse, no matter how thick the rug.

He paused a moment to enjoy the sight of starchy Lady Phoebe sprawled out on her back, her open nightgown forgotten, full breasts exposed to his greedy gaze, pale skin flushed and passion mottled, legs splayed wide, and her pussy slick and swollen.

Her eyelids lifted lazily, as if they weighed a stone, and the sated, sensual smile she gave him made his balls tighten with anticipation.

Paul hooked his hands beneath her knees and pulled her forward until her arse was hanging just over the edge of the extra-thick mattress.

He'd chosen everything in his wife's chambers—unwilling to leave such an intimate task to Dixon—and he'd taken particular care in the bed he'd selected.

Paul was an engineer—so he thought like one. He knew their one-foot height difference would make some sexual positions challenging, so it had amused him to think of ways that he could service her without permanently damaging his back.

Not only was the bed high enough to merit the gryphon-shaped step ladder, but he'd purchased an extra-thick mattress to bring it up even higher.

As a result of all that foresight, he only needed to bend his knees a little to position the head of his cock at her entrance. The view was superlative, and he hesitated a moment to appreciate the sight of his thick, brutish rod pressing against her tiny pink opening.

Paul was a big man all over, and it would hurt when he took her, but he was determined to follow the pain with pleasure and leave her eager for the next time.

He breeched her slowly, pushing only the crown inside her as he kept his gaze riveted to her face.

Although he knew it was inevitable, Paul hated it when a spasm of pain chased away her expression of sleepy satiation.

"Try to relax your muscles," he urged, penetrating no further. He held her gaze, waiting until her body lost some of its tension before asking, "All right?"

Phoebe nodded, the action hesitant and jerky; she was still scared.

Paul decided that going slowly was a mistake and would only prolong the initial unpleasantness; she'd been right about getting it over with quickly—at least when it came to this first part.

He clenched his jaws and drove himself deep, intensely aware of the fragile barrier he tore through.

Phoebe sucked in a breath and let out a little whimper that squeezed his heart.

She was tight—gloriously so—but it was hard to take much enjoyment in the sensation when his partner was so obviously miserable.

"That was the worst of it," Paul promised her, hoping his words would ease her worries, if not her discomfort. He gently caressed her thighs, hips, and stomach while he waited for her body to adjust.

"I don't understand why I can't make myself relax," she said, visibly distressed.

Indeed, she was as taut as a board, and her inability to control her body just seemed to make her *more* tense.

"This will relax you." He slid his thumb between her swollen lips and massaged the base of her clitoris.

She gasped, stiffening even more at the intimate touch.

"Take a few moments to breathe and become accustomed to me."

A primitive, possessive joy pulsed through his body as he watched her respond to his erotic stroking.

First, her breathing slowed and then her eyelids dropped a little. Finally, her body went slack—all except her exquisitely tight sheath, which began to swell and throb around him.

Beast that he was, Paul savored the knowledge that he was the first man to claim her in a way as old as humankind.

His. She was all his.

Keeping up his erotic caressing, Paul reached up with his other hand and brushed back some strands that had become loose from the thick braid.

He had to smile: he'd been so desperate to get his mouth on her he'd not even taken down her glossy chestnut hair.

Well, plenty of time for that later.

He met her gaze and was pleased that her eyes—while open wide—were no long fearful.

"Are you in pain?"

She shook her head and gave him an adorably shy smile. "No, it doesn't hurt anymore. It wasn't as bad as what I'd been warn—er, told to expect." She blushed furiously talking about the act even while she was spread and pinned beneath him.

Paul thought *warn* was probably exactly the word her mother had used. He shuddered to think what the Countess of Addiscombe had told her poor daughter. Not only did Lady Addiscombe hate Paul, but he couldn't imagine she had too much love for the sexual act, given how much she and the earl despised each other.

He would make sure that was never true for Phoebe.

Paul intensified his stroking and this time her orgasm seemed stronger, her contractions causing them both to gasp, her body squeezing him so hard it was actually painful.

The spasms went on and on and Paul was shaking with need by the time she went limp; he couldn't last much longer.

He slid his hands beneath her thighs and then straightened his knees, standing all the way up. The change in angle lifted her bottom and lower back off the bed, and she gave a breathy laugh as she stared up the length of her body at him.

Paul watched the place where they were joined as he withdrew.

His thick shaft glistened with her juices and it amazed him that he could fit inside her.

He kept watch for any sign of discomfort, using only the tip of his cock, pulsing gently as he stretched her entrance again and again and again.

Good God, she looked gorgeous taking him!

Rather than look apprehensive or pained, her eyes caressed his chest and shoulders and stomach, her expression far more admiring than it ever was when she looked at his face.

Well, Paul thought wryly, *I am no handsome prince, that is certain. I am pleased there is at least part of me that will give her pleasure to look at.*

She was staring at him so intently that she obviously hadn't noticed what an erotic picture she made, her full breasts bouncing with each thrust.

Paul took full advantage of her distraction to gorge on the sight of her, slowly deepening his thrusts, giving her more with each stroke, until she was taking all of him. Her eyes glazed and her mouth went slack, her thighs flexing as she instinctively raised her hips to take him deeper.

She was mesmerizing and Paul watched greedily as her breathing deepened, her eyes closed, and her back arched violently just before she cried out, the sound a low, animal keening that filled the room.

Paul stilled his thrusting to revel in her contractions, her inner muscles squeezing him almost painfully tight.

Every muscle in his body was sore and tired from restraining his need and once the last wave of pleasure eddied from her body, he resumed his thrusting.

He rode her deep and hard—far too hard for a first time, some distant, unheeded part of his mind nagged—almost maddened by the desire to claim and fill her.

This is my wife.

The words startled him; the simplicity of the thought strangely profound.

He'd had a lot of women in his life, but never one the Bible called *the flesh of his flesh.*

His wife.

Paul stared down at her as his hips drummed with increasing savagery, giving her every inch each with each stroke. She met his gaze squarely, her lips parted and her eyes dark as she watched his descent into passion.

Good.

Paul wanted her to see him—to know without a doubt that it was Paul Needham, a brutish, ugly, vulgar cit who was inside her.

The man she belonged to.

Mine.

Paul stared into her eyes as he pumped into her body. Even though he was in her as deeply and intimately as a man could invade a woman, she remained as remote and untouchable as the moon.

There was no affection or love in her eyes as she looked back at him, not that Paul had expected any such thing; he was no fool.

But she blazed with desire for him, and that was an emotion he would happily settle for.

At least for now.

Paul angled his thrusting in such a way that she gasped and arched off the bed, her cool eyes losing focus as he repeatedly grazed the most tender part of her.

It didn't take long before her body tightened around him, squeezing him like a fist.

"Yes," he growled, driving himself deeper. "Come for me," he ordered.

Paul gloried in the small, desperate cry that broke from her pink lips as another orgasm shattered her.

He buried himself to the hilt and then surrendered to his need.

His balls, aching and full, exploded, and his shaft swelled and thickened, filling her with jet after jet of hot seed. Each spasm was wrenching, and it felt like his spine might snap.

She convulsed around him, her own climax milking him of every drop.

For the first time in his life, Paul welcomed the possibility of putting a child inside a woman's belly.

Not just any woman, but my wife.

Another wave of primitive joy pulsed through his body at the thought of Phoebe pregnant and swelling with his baby.

He'd known her for such a short time, yet already he *wanted* her with a fierceness he'd never felt.

A familiar, blissful lassitude rolled through him as the last waves of his orgasm eddied through his body. This time, the bliss felt more than just physical.

God help him for even thinking such a thought, but the strange euphoria felt almost... spiritual. As if Paul had been dead inside, and Phoebe had woken him.

A thread of unease wormed its way into the elation.

There was no denying that she'd woken some feeling or emotion inside him, but it remained to be seen whether that was something he would feel grateful for as time went on.

Chapter Fifteen

The bed was empty when Phoebe woke up the next morning, the sun streaming through one of the drapes, which somebody—her maid, perhaps—must have opened.

On her nightstand was a cold cup of chocolate, a sight which shocked her. She'd been so heavily asleep that she'd not heard a maid enter the bed chamber.

Phoebe never slept so soundly!

And then memories of the night before flooded her and Phoebe glanced down; yes, she was naked, not wearing even a stitch.

"Oh, goodness," she muttered, raising her hands to her hot cheeks, although there was nobody there to see her mortification.

But her maid would have seen her when she brought the chocolate.

Facing Spragg would be mortifying.

She sighed and dropped her hands; there was no point in wallowing in her embarrassment.

Her dressing gown was draped across the bottom of the bed and she quickly slipped out from beneath the covers and slid her arms into the fine white lawn, her thoughts going back to last night when Lord Needham—her husband—had taken it off her.

Phoebe glanced into her dressing table mirror and gaped at her reflection.

She'd forgotten that he'd taken her hair down… after. After they'd consummated their marriage.

Phoebe had dozed for a while, awakening when she'd felt gentle hands in her hair.

She squeezed her eyes shut at the memory of her husband tenderly undoing her plait and then running his fingers through the heavy tresses before arranging them over her in such a way that they'd covered her bare breasts but had left her nipples conspicuously exposed.

When she'd tried to cover them, too, he'd taken her hand and held it.

"You have lovely hair," he'd said, looking at her in that hungry way he had. "And lovely breasts which I've neglected terribly."

"Neglected? What do you mean?"

Then he'd shown her.

Phoebe's head became hot at the memory of what he'd done—and especially how she'd reacted.

If the things he'd done between her thighs had been a revelation, what he'd done with her breasts had left her speechless.

They never felt like that when *she* touched them.

A choked laugh slipped out of her and she forced her eyes open, studying her reflection.

Her hair was a dark curly cloud and her eyes were greener today and sparkled. And of course her face was flushed a rosy pink.

She sighed and strode to the servant pull. Everyone in the house knew what had happened in this room last night, so there was no reason to be missish about it.

By the time Spragg opened the door a few minutes later Phoebe had tamed and plaited her hair into a thick rope and her flush had subsided.

One look at the smiling maid brought the blood flooding back to her cheeks.

"His lordship said you'd want a bath, my lady," Spragg said before Phoebe started babbling. "And there is a breakfast tray on its way up even as we speak."

"Oh." She blinked at that. Baths at Queen's Bower were once weekly occasions that took place in the kitchen behind a screen. To have one in one's own room? And with breakfast, too? What decadence and luxury!

She saw the maid was waiting for a response and smiled. "That sounds delightful." Something occurred to her. "Did you bring up the chocolate, Spragg?"

"No, that was his lordship."

"Oh," she said, too startled to come up with anything better.

"You needn't worry that you missed it, my lady. His lordship instructed Cook to have a fresh pot on your tray."

Why did that make Phoebe feel like crying?

***

Paul and Dixon were going through the accounts for his recently acquired copper mine when there was a light knock on the door.

"Come in," Paul called.

The door opened and Phoebe hovered on the threshold. "I hope I'm not interrupting?"

Paul stood, took off his spectacles, and strode toward her. "Not at all. Come in and have a seat." He turned to Dixon. "This is a good time to take a break. Go ahead and send word that we'll be wanting at least ten more men at Middleton."

"Very good, my lord." Dixon bowed to Phoebe, who—Paul couldn't help noticing—blushed wildly.

Paul bit back a smile at her shy, mortified expression. No doubt she was wondering if everyone was looking at her and imagining what had happened last night in her bed.

That's certainly what Paul was thinking. In fact, just recalling the prior evening was enough to make him hard.

Yes, he was well and truly smitten.

Once the door closed behind Dixon, he took the seat nearest Phoebe and asked, "How are you this morning?"

She pinkened delightfully and lowered her gaze. "I'm well, thank you. And thank you also for the bath, breakfast in bed, and the chocolate—which Spragg tells me you delivered personally."

"I thought you might enjoy a relaxed morning."

"That was exceptionally considerate of you. How did you know I adore chocolate?"

"Does anyone *not* adore chocolate?"

She laughed. "Well, thank you, again."

Paul leaned toward her and took her hand and Phoebe tensed at the gesture; no doubt she believed that any display of affection outside the bedroom was both vulgar and common.

Well, that was too bad; she would need to become accustomed to such things because he felt compelled to touch her, even if it was only her hand.

"I hope I am always considerate of your desires. Was there something in particular you wanted to talk about? Or did you just come to thank your considerate husband?" he teased.

"No, I wanted to ask something."

She withdrew her hand from his.

"Yes?"

"I rode over to Queen's Bower a little while ago."

"Ah, yes. Your father told me yesterday that he, the countess, and Katie will travel together to Bath while Doddy heads off on a solo journey."

Paul had been displeased to discover that the earl had accepted an invitation to the Regent's house, Oatlands. Apparently Prinny had been delighted to discover his old card partner was once again back in circulation.

Paul could practically hear his father-in-law's gaming debts accumulating.

"Did you catch them before they left?" Paul asked.

"Yes, but that wasn't why I went over. There were still a few things that needed doing before the housekeeper and her husband left for their holiday."

"Doddy said you'd been working yourself to exhaustion taking care of everything." *That* was something she would no longer be doing—acting as her parents' housekeeper/bailiff/butler/secretary/et cetera.

"Did he?" she asked, looking surprised. "I didn't think my brother ever paid attention to such things."

Paul thought the young man gave a great deal of thought to all his sisters and their welfare.

"But it wasn't the visit I wished to talk about," she said. "It was that groom— Carthage, I believe his name is. He said you'd instructed him to ride with me?"

"Yes, that is correct. Carthage is your personal groom, although if he is not available any of the grooms will accompany you when you ride." Paul's eyes narrowed. "Why do you ask? Was Carthage disrespectful or—"

"No, of course not. He was fine. It's just that I don't need anyone to accompany me on my rides."

He smiled faintly. "I may not be up to snuff on my etiquette, my dear, but I know that ladies of quality do not ride unaccompanied."

"Perhaps that is true in London or—or elsewhere, but here, where I have lived my entire life, that is hardly necessary."

"I would prefer you do not ride unaccompanied."

Her expressive eyebrows descended. "But I would prefer *not* to have a groom with me."

"Then I shall be overjoyed to ride with you."

She huffed. "I would, of course, enjoy riding with you, but you will not be available every time I wish to go."

"True. And that is when you will take Carthage or one of the others."

Paul could practically hear her teeth grinding. He could only imagine her response when she learned his position on going for long walks unattended.

But one thing at a time.

"We none of us used a groom when I lived at Queen's Bower," she said.

"You didn't have horses," he pointed out gently.

"Yes, but even when we did—years ago—we didn't always take a groom."

"I daresay that was more a function of economy rather than desire. In fact, I know it was because your mother who made a point to say that she hoped I would curb your solitary excursions."

In fact, that had been one of the few things the countess had said to him. Of course, she'd couched it rather more rudely than Paul had just described it.

Phoebe's jaw flexed. "She said that?"

Paul nodded.

Phoebe's eyes, usually so cool and clear, looked stormy and he couldn't tell if that was for him or for her mother.

"Regardless of what your mother said I would have insisted on a groom for your own safety, Phoebe, not because I wish to constrain you in any way."

Paul was fascinated by the play of emotions that flickered across her face.

His Phoebe had enjoyed an unusual degree of liberty for a young, gently-bred woman—likely due to all the responsibilities she'd shouldered for her family—so this would be a change for her.

Paul would never have guessed that something so minor as riding with a groom—which every woman of quality did—would cause such heartburn.

He studied her unhappy expression and decided he might as well tell her the other reason for his requirement, although he'd hoped not to have to broach such a grim matter with his brand-new wife on their first day of marriage.

"Propriety isn't the only reason I want you to ride with a groom. There is something you should know about my business," Paul said, keeping his words and tone mild so as not to terrify her. "I have enemies, people who have tried to hurt me."

"People try to hurt you?" she repeated, visibly stunned.

"Sometimes. Usually, they will just cause problems at one of my mines, factories, or mills. But recently I've had people who've waited outside my houses or businesses to, er, engage me."

He didn't tell her that one man had tried to engage him with a six-inch knife.

"Because you are my wife, you, too, might become a target for discontent."

Her brow furrowed as she struggled to absorb that. "But you don't own any business *here*."

"Unfortunately, the attacks haven't just happened in places where I own and operate a business."

"If any stranger came to Little Sissingdon they would be noticed immediately—it would be difficult for somebody to attack either one of us, here."

Paul thought her charmingly naïve but kept that observation to himself.

"I'm sure that is true," he said. "But I will be happier if you have a large groom accompanying you wherever you go."

He could see that wasn't the answer she wanted, but he would not be moved from his position.

When she merely sat and stewed, Paul changed the subject. "Did you see your family before they left today?"

"I already told you that I saw them," she snapped. Her cheeks darkened even more—probably at her rude tone—and she composed her features into a cool, bland smile. "Thank you so much for sending Doddy in your post chaise. He is far more excited about riding behind your *slapping* team than he is about spending a summer with a crammer."

"Yes, he told me much the same thing. He was elated that I keep several changes of horses on that road. He will have the enjoyment of my *slapping* cattle for his entire journey."

"Do you keep a lot of horses at posting inns."

"Only on the routes I take frequently."

"How often do you travel?"

"Once or twice a month, more often when the venture is newer or uncertain."

And even more often when there were acts of sabotage to contend with.

"New ventures? Does that mean you have something other than, er, iron works and coal mines?"

He smiled at both her naïve question and gentle flush; proper ladies did not talk about something as vulgar as trade.

"My father began with coal mines and several foundries and I expanded those holdings greatly. But—as the old maxim goes—it isn't wise to keep all one's eggs in the same basket so I've invested in other areas."

"Such as?" she asked, looking genuinely interested.

"Two copper mines, a lead mine, a shipbuilding operation in Bristol, a farm equipment manufactory, several potteries, glassworks, brickworks, and most recently two textile mills in Nottingham."

"My goodness," she murmured. "I had no idea that people could learn how to do so many different things."

"I actually know very little about mills, potteries, or brickworks so I have people who are far more knowledgeable and skilled than I am to manage each of those."

"Will I stay here when you go on these trips?"

"I will want you with me when I travel."

"You will?"

"Is that so surprising?" he asked.

Her expression said it was. "What would I do on your trips."

"I own houses in the places where I do a great deal of business. While they are all well-run, they are crying out for a mistress's touch."

She perked up at that news. "Are these in towns or the country?"

"Mostly in large cities." He smiled at her obvious enthusiasm. "I must warn you that most of those places are not glamorous."

She scowled. "You think that is all that interests me? Glamor?"

Paul avoided that loaded question, choosing to answer the one she'd asked before it. "As for what you would do on these visits? I will be expected to do more entertaining now that I am married. In the past I've only ever given dinners for other businessmen, but now I should host balls and other functions."

She swallowed and he could almost read her thoughts—that she would be entertaining people who would all be far beneath her socially. And she would be right. The people he knew in Leeds, Manchester, Bristol, Nottingham, and Liverpool were all from the merchant class.

Some imp prodded him to say, "Don't worry, most of them speak intelligibly although you will be exposed to much regional dialect from the servants."

She opened her mouth, doubtless to retort, when she saw that he was smiling. She flashed him a smile of her own—a wry one. "You believe I am high in the instep, don't you?"

"Aren't you? I recall the way you regarded me the first, second, and even third time we met. I also recall overhearing the words *vile, hideous, encroaching cit* from your pretty mouth. As amusing as I find the sobriquet, it is not something you will want to say when you are presiding over my table."

Her cheeks burst into flame. "You will never forgive that, will you?"

"There is nothing to forgive," he said. "Indeed, I'm grateful to know your true opinion of me."

She gave an exasperated groan. "You have no idea how much I regret ever saying those words. It shames me that I could say such an ignorant thing." She faced him squarely, looking him dead in the eyes in the way Paul found so engaging. "I can admit I was wrong, my lord."

She inhaled deeply and then continued, speaking quickly, as if to get it all out in a hurry. "I hope I am not the sort of person who will lift my nose at the very thing— your businesses, for example—that make it possible to live in this house and have baths delivered to my exceptionally opulent chambers and send my little brother to school and my mother on a luxurious repairing lease in Bath, and who knows what else. All I can do is tell you that I will do better in the future. Oh, and I can apologize for my parents," she added. "Because they will probably continue to treat you the same way."

"You mean as if I were a milch cow?"

She frowned. "I am not familiar with that term, but I can guess the meaning— that you are an easy source of money?"

He nodded.

"I'm mortified by their behavior." She dropped her gaze to her fingers, which were laced so tightly the knuckles were white. "I am grateful to you—"

"*That* is one emotion I ask you to spare me," he said, not heatedly, but firmly.

"Gratitude? But what is wrong with that?"

"You need not be grateful for what I feel duty bound to provide for my wife and family, Phoebe. Are you grateful to your siblings for the things they do for you?"

She paused a moment, her expression reflective. "I'm grateful, but I doubt that I actually thank them. At least not in words."

"Good. You may do the same with me." He paused and then added with a faint smirk "But if your mother ever decides to express gratitude, please send her to me immediately."

She gave a startled laugh. "I shall do so—and perhaps sell tickets to the event.

It was Paul's turn to chuckle. He eyed her appreciatively. "I enjoy your ready wit and the sharp edge of your tongue far more than I would ever enjoy your gratitude."

Again, her cheeks darkened. "You are a strange man."

"Undoubtedly," he agreed, making her smile.

She stood and Paul joined her, walking her toward the door. "So, all is well then, Phoebe? You are not angry with me for requiring you to take a footman with you?"

She hesitated only a second before saying, "No, not angry. It is just something new. I will become accustomed to it, in time."

***

Phoebe left her husband's study feeling as if she'd just been cleverly outwitted—even though Needham had done nothing sly at all but had directly ordered her to ride with a groom.

Phoebe had been obedient to her parents' wishes and demands all her life, so part of her was resigned to the fact she was now under the dominion of a new master.

She was her husband's property as much as the carpet under his feet or the hounds in his kennel.

Life with her father had taught Phoebe that men made the decisions and women lived with the results, so she was a bit surprised how disgruntled she was by Needham's order today.

After all, compared to what the earl had wreaked on his family—destitution and social ignominy—requiring Phoebe to take a groom with her when she went riding was hardly abusive or oppressive. Indeed, his request was entirely proper and was the same as any *ton* chaperone or parent would make.

Perhaps the real reason you are so irked is because Needham—a man from the merchant class—needed to curb your improper behavior? a voice in her head whispered.

Could that be it? Could she really be so snobbish and—

"My lady?"

Phoebe turned at the sound of the childish voice, a smile coming naturally to her lips when she saw her pretty stepdaughter.

"Hallo, Lucy. I thought we'd agreed you'd call me Phoebe?"

Lucy's cheeks pinkened. "I thought you might have forgotten… Phoebe."

"I didn't get much chance to talk to you yesterday. Did you enjoy the wedding?"

Lucy had confided to Phoebe the day before the wedding that it would be the first ceremony she'd been allowed to attend, not surprising as she was only thirteen.

"It was lovely," she said, her huge blue eyes sparkling. "The chapel looked so beautiful with all those flowers—what were they called, again?"

"Peonies. They are my favorite."

"That is what Papa said."

Phoebe had forgotten to ask Needham last night how he'd known they were her favorite. Of course, they'd been engaged in far more riveting activities…

"—to see her?"

"I'm sorry?" Phoebe said, ashamed that she'd been fantasizing about last night instead of listening.

"Mama wonders if you will come to see her? She would like to have tea with you." Lucy paused, her brow creasing with concern. "She said that I should be sure to tell you that she will understand if you are too busy."

Phoebe knew what that message meant: the woman was offering Phoebe a convenient excuse to avoid the visit.

Indecision, anger, shame, and a half dozen other emotions seethed and whirled inside her. Phoebe gritted her teeth; how dare Needham place her in such an intolerable position!

Phoebe quashed that ugly line of thinking immediately.

After all, she had entered this marriage with open eyes. Her choices were simple: accept an offer to tea with the woman or appear churlish in front of a child.

She sighed. Why not have tea with her husband's mistress—or ex-mistress, if he was to be believed? After all, the woman already lived in her house.

Or perhaps it is you *who live in* her *house.*

Phoebe ignored the unhelpful thought.

One look at Lucy's innocent expression was enough to smother the angry, jealous flames that had flared in her belly.

She forced a smile. "Of course, I'll have tea with her, Lucy."

Lucy's answering smile was blinding. "Oh, Mama will be so delighted. You see, she has had no visitors except me and Papa."

So, Needham visits her?

Her smile began to crumble around the edges. "Er, you are in the east wing?"

"Yes. It is lovely. Papa has made it so comfortable." Lucy turned and headed toward the east wing, where Phoebe's great aunt Dorothy had lived for many years.

Although nobody had mentioned that Ellen Kettering and her daughter lived in that portion of the house, Phoebe had assumed as much for two reasons.

One, because it was the only self-contained area and possessed a tiny kitchen where her great aunt's maid and caretaker had prepared all her meals.

And two, because her housekeeper, Mrs. Nutter, had conspicuously left out the east wing when she'd given her a tour of all the recent improvements.

Phoebe wasn't surprised the servants knew who she was; they'd have known before the townsfolk.

When Phoebe turned to go up the main staircase Lucy took her hand and pulled her toward the lower gallery. "There is a quicker way through here," she said, cutting her an impish look.

"Ah, you've found the hidden stairway, have you?"

"You know about it?"

"I grew up here, remember?"

"Oh, that's true—I keep forgetting that. So, Doddy knows about the stairs, too."

Judging by the star-struck look in her eyes Phoebe's most important attribute was her relationship to Doddy. She was accustomed to seeing young girls moon over her gorgeous brother but did hope Lucy's infatuation wouldn't last. The countess might have allowed her dowdy second youngest daughter to marry a wealthy ironmonger, but she would never countenance her son marrying his illegitimate daughter.

"How is Silas settling in?" she couldn't help asking.

Lucy grinned. "He took to me right away. Doddy said he's never seen Silas like anyone as much as he likes me."

Phoebe smiled; Doddy was no fool. He'd found a loving caretaker for his mischievous pet and was clearly determined to keep her.

Once they'd passed through the south corridor Lucy stopped and pushed the panel that exposed the narrow staircase.

The strange little stairwell now smelled like beeswax rather than rot, as it had when she'd been a child. Somebody had lighted candles in sconces all the way up the twisty stairs so they were no longer grim and scary.

"This looks much nicer now," Phoebe said. "Back when I lived here it was dark and filled with cobwebs since nobody used it."

"Are you glad to be living here again?" Lucy asked.

Was she?

Phoebe couldn't decide.

On the one hand, Wych House had never looked so prosperous.

On the other, she was a bit nostalgic for the house that lived in her memories, no matter that it had been shabby and often uncomfortable.

"I'm glad to be living here with *you*," she said when she saw Lucy was waiting. That was true enough—the little girl was charming.

If only it was just Lucy who lived with them.

"And Silas, too?" Lucy asked, looking hopeful.

Phoebe had to laugh at that. "Yes, it's just like home with Silas here."

Lucy stopped in front of a door near the end of the corridor and opened it without knocking.

Phoebe had believed her new chambers were beautiful and delicate, but never before had Phoebe seen such a... heavenly room.

There was almost no color but for a few hints of gilt on some of the wood. All the carpets, hangings, and furniture were varying shades of white and cream and the windows were covered with filmy gossamer fabric that filtered the bright sunlight into something softer.

Phoebe felt like she was on a cloud.

The woman occupying the feminine bower was the most elegant item in the room.

Ellen Kettering was exquisitely beautiful, and painfully fragile, as she reclined on a chaise longue, her tall, shapely body swathed in a dressing gown of blush colored silk. Her hair, a pure cornsilk blond, was artfully arranged to appear as if she'd just tumbled from the arms of a lover.

Her huge eyes were celestial blue and fringed with darker lashes.

Phoebe at first thought Mrs. Kettering had painted her cheeks but realized as she came closer that the fetching spots of pink were signs of her illness, not the result of cosmetics.

A knife twisted in her belly at the sight of so much female beauty. So, this woman had lain with Needham—had done the things with him that he had done to Phoebe last night. And Lucy was walking, talking proof of their former union.

Phoebe should have guessed she'd be beautiful—Lucy was a surpassingly lovely child—but it hurt to realize just *how* lovely Needham's prior mistress was.

"I brought her to you, Mama," Lucy announced proudly, breaking the silence that had formed while the two women had taken each other's measures.

"Thank you so much for coming," Phoebe's hostess said in a melodic, low voice that was every bit as lovely as her person.

Try as she might, Phoebe couldn't hear even the faintest touch of Yorkshire brogue in her words. Indeed, this woman could have passed for somebody of Phoebe's class.

The thought was startling—a mistress who sounded like a lady?

Phoebe forced a smile and inclined her head. "Thank you for inviting me, Mrs. Kettering."

An older woman, garbed in a dark, sensibly cut bombazine gown bustled into the room, her eyes narrowing when she saw Phoebe.

"My lady." She dropped a perfunctory curtsey.

"This is Mrs. Peacham, Lady Needham. She has been with me for so long I don't remember life without her."

The harsh featured servant ignored her mistress's praise. "You won't overtire yourself, Miss Ellen?"

Mrs. Kettering patted the older woman's hand. "No, Peachy, I shall be a good girl. I only wanted to make Lady Needham's acquaintance."

Mrs. Peacham shot a direct, speaking look at Phoebe.

"I shan't stay long," Phoebe assured her.

The older woman gave her a curt nod and turned to her charge. "I'll bring in your tea." She curtsied again to Phoebe and returned through the door she'd emerged from.

"Lucy, darling, perhaps you might give Lady Needham and myself some time to become acquainted?"

Lucy cut Phoebe a hesitant glance. For the first time, Phoebe wondered just what the girl thought about all this. She was old enough to know the arrangement was unorthodox. Poor Lucy.

Phoebe smiled at her. "I can find my way back."

"I shall take Silas out for his afternoon walk, then."

Ellen Kettering's face was full of pride and love as she watched her daughter leave.

When the door shut behind her, she turned to Phoebe. "I thought we might speak more plainly without Lucy here."

"She is a clever, delightful girl."

Mrs. Kettering's cheeks flushed with pleasure rather than illness. "Thank you. I am naturally prejudiced in her favor." She shifted on her cushions slightly and a grimace of pain briefly distorted her features.

"Is now a bad time, Mrs. Kettering?" Phoebe asked.

The other woman gave a wry smile. "I'm afraid there are no good days, but this is certainly one of the better ones." She lifted an exquisite lace handkerchief to her mouth and coughed so hard it hurt Phoebe just to hear it. "I apologize," she said, her voice raw and hoarse.

The door opened and Mrs. Peacham entered with the tea tray.

"Will you do the honors, my lady?" Mrs. Kettering asked.

"Of course."

The servant set down the tray and then hovered uncertainly.

"Thank you, Peachy, that will be all," she said, her voice firm.

The older woman hesitated, said, "Don't tire yourself," and then she stomped from the room, closing the door with a decisive *click*.

Mrs. Kettering gave Phoebe a humorous look. "She still believes I am five."

"Our old nurse is the same way," Phoebe admitted, busying herself with the tea and grateful to have something to do.

"She is right that I become tired quickly, so I hope you will forgive me if I speak my piece rather bluntly."

Phoebe glanced up from the tea strainer. "Please do."

Mrs. Kettering smiled and the expression seemed genuine. "Paul said you were direct."

The jealousy that seemed to be on constant simmer in her belly bubbled up at this proof of her husband's continuing intimacy with his mistress.

"I know you probably hate me," Mrs. Kettering said.

Phoebe blinked at the shocking statement and opened her mouth but couldn't think how to respond.

Mrs. Kettering chuckled. "That was gauche of me, but I know it is what I would feel in your position. And I wanted you to know I don't blame you."

"How do you like your tea?" Phoebe asked, shaken by the other woman's too accurate assessment.

"White with two sugars, please. No pastries or biscuits for me," she added when Phoebe gestured to the tray.

"Thank you," she said, taking her cup and saucer.

She waited until Phoebe had served herself before speaking. "I wanted to congratulate you on your marriage. I don't think I have ever seen Paul look more... satisfied."

Phoebe was once again uncertain of what to say.

"Second, I wanted to apologize for my presence here." Her cheeks darkened slightly. "I am ashamed to be here. I daresay it won't matter when I tell you this, but I promise you, I would not be here if not for my health."

Phoebe struggled to absorb everything she was saying.

Mrs. Kettering continued when she didn't respond. "I am only here for my daughter's sake. We have always been close and to send her away during this difficult time would have crushed her."

Another fit of coughing wracked her slender form and this time when her hand came away Phoebe saw blood on the lace.

A flare of pity warred with the jealousy Phoebe was still struggling to suppress.

Phoebe was no stranger to consumption—her sister Hy's dear friend Charles Maitland had died from it—and she knew blood was an indicator that Mrs. Kettering was very sick indeed.

When she caught her breath, she continued, "I know you have every reason to hate and despise me." Desperation and fear spasmed across Mrs. Kettering's beautiful face. "But I beg of you, my lady, please don't allow your dislike of me to influence how you treat Lucy when I'm gone. I"—she chewed her lip for a moment and then sighed and met Phoebe's gaze. "That is something that eats away at me day and night, my fear for her future and her relationship with her father."

Phoebe set down her tea and stared for a moment at her untouched macaroon before looking up at the other woman.

"Lord Needham is correct in that I do value plain speaking. You are right when you say your presence here is beyond mortifying to me. Intellectually I understand why you are here, but emotionally it is... difficult. That said, I like to think I am humane and kind and would never punish a child for an adult's behavior. Also, I find Lucy to be a charming, intelligent child with lovely manners and I enjoy being around her."

That was all true; if not for Lucy's relationship with this woman and Needham, she would be thrilled to have her living with them.

"Please be assured that I will treat her with the same care and consideration as I have my younger siblings."

Mrs. Kettering's relief was visible in both her face and posture. "Thank you, my lady. That is... well, my worry for her has been a crushing weight upon me."

"I can imagine," Phoebe said, picking up her cup and saucer and taking a sip. "I should also keep in mind that Needham would not allow her to be illtreated by anyone—wife or otherwise."

Mrs. Kettering smiled. "You are right, of course. He is fiercely protective of her. As he will be of your children."

It was Phoebe's turn to blush wildly.

Mrs. Kettering set down her cup and saucer. "Thank you for coming today, my lady. I will not impose on you again now that we have an understanding."

Phoebe was relieved to hear it.

As pleasant and charming as Mrs. Kettering had turned out to be, their meeting was one she never hoped to repeat.

Chapter Sixteen

Paul had wondered at dinner if something was bothering his wife.

He had waited for her to broach the subject afterward, when they had retired to the library—he to plow through the never-ending paperwork and Phoebe to write letters—but the evening had passed in companionable silence so he'd assumed she was fine.

Or so he thought until he entered her chambers.

She was sitting up in bed, an opened book in her lap, wearing a gown remarkably like the one she'd worn last night—long sleeved with a boggling number of buttons.

Paul made a mental note to send a message to Mademoiselle Sonia and have her make several nightgowns that were more to his taste. Or perhaps he might get one from the modiste who lived in the village—Mrs. Dettingham, or something like that. Surely a night rail was an acceptable gift from a husband to his wife?

He knew she would be too sore tonight and had no intention of mounting her, but he wanted to accustom her to having him in her bed every night, all night.

Paul met her gaze—once again stormy—turned on his heel and went back in his room. When he returned, she was sitting up, book closed, her brow furrowed.

He raised his hands to show what he held: a bottle of wine and two glasses. It took only a few moments to pour two glasses of delicious claret.

Paul gestured to the sitting area in front of the dormant fireplace. "Come and sit with me for a moment."

She hesitated, scowled, and then shoved back the blankets.

By the time she came to sit with him she'd wrapped a thick dressing gown around her copious nightgown and wore big woolly slippers.

If she believed such concealing clothing rendered her unattractive to him, she was dead wrong.

When Paul thought about all the seductive clothing his various mistresses had worn over the years to tempt and tantalize him, he had to smile. If they'd only known that flannel and wool aroused him as quickly as silk and lace, they could have been warm and cozy.

"What is bothering you, my dear?"

"Nothing." She took a sip of wine and then frowned, as if she were drinking bilge water rather than an expensive claret.

"Is it not to your liking? I can ring for something else."

"No, it is fine."

They sipped their wine and the moments slipped past, the clock on the mantel softly marking the seconds.

"I met Mrs. Kettering today."

Ah, here it is.

"I see."

"Lucy brought me to her because she wanted to meet me," she hastily added, as if he would suspect her of seeking the other woman out.

"I assumed it was something of that nature."

When she didn't speak, he asked. "Was Ellen rude or discourteous to you?"

"No, quite the opposite. She was gracious and very solicitous and congratulatory." Phoebe looked more perplexed with each word she uttered.

"You are upset because she was too… kind?"

"Of course, I'm not upset that she was *kind*," she snapped, showing that fire Paul so enjoyed. "I'm just so"—she broke off with a growl of annoyance—"I'm so confused and angry and"—she flung up her hands—"I don't know what I am. Lots of things," she added sullenly.

Why was Paul surprised by her unhappiness on this subject? He really was an insensitive brute to think she could adjust to this situation without any anguish. He wished he could tell her everything, but… He simply could not. Not yet. Not until he trusted her.

But at least he could tell her something.

"What Ellen and I had was a long time ago, Phoebe." That, at least, was true. "I ceased to think of her"—he struggled for a word that wouldn't offend her—"er, romantically, over a decade ago." Again, true. "There are two reasons she is here—she is dying and Lucy would be devastated to be separated from her and I do not wish to be apart from Lucy." He leaned toward her. "But I will not be going to her bed."

"I know that!" she retorted with more than a little heat. "And I know she is very ill. And I believe that she is only agreeing to this because of Lucy. But it still bothers me and I feel petty for allowing it to bother me."

"I think those feelings are normal, Phoebe," he said dryly. "It is, after all, an unfortunate situation."

She made a noise of profound exasperation and glared at him.

Paul met her angry gaze. "Come and sit on my lap."

Her eyes widened in shock.

"Please?"

She frowned and chewed her lip as she considered his request.

He wouldn't force her, and he was patient.

After a long moment, she stood and came to him, glancing down uncertainly.

Paul took her hand and gently tugged until she lowered her deliciously plump bottom onto his thighs. He shifted her until he was cradling her with one arm, and then tilted her chin until she met his gaze.

"There. This is much nicer," he said.

"I've never sat on anyone's lap before."

"Then you must make up for lost time with me."

She gave a breathy, nervous laugh. "Am I not heavy?"

"No. You are perfect." He kissed her very kissable lips, lightly and gently at first, teasing her tongue and luring her deeper into his mouth until *she* became the aggressor.

She started off shyly but, as was her way, soon took charge of the situation, shifting on his lap until she was facing him, her fleshy arse grinding against his erection and tormenting him delightfully.

Paul opened wider to her and allowed her to pull him lower, her fingers digging insistently into his shoulders while she probed him deeper and deeper with her tongue, nipping and sucking.

Her efforts were clumsy, but ardent, and it was absolutely the most erotic kiss in his life.

Because they both needed to breathe, Paul eventually sat back, reluctantly breaking their connection.

She whimpered, her lips chasing his.

Paul's control was already straining at its tether and it was a struggle to recall that he could not take her tonight.

His imagination—vivid where Phoebe was concerned—was picturing her straddled over him, the ugly nightgown on the floor, and Paul's hard, leaking cock forcing its way into her tight passage.

To make matters even worse, her eyes were heavy with arousal tonight, rather than worry or fear.

But Paul saw something else beneath her lust filled gaze: exhaustion.

That was enough for him to leash his raging desire.

"You are tired, Phoebe," he murmured, brushing a curl back from her brow.

"A little."

"It has been a hectic month. Tonight, we will sleep."

She hesitated, but then nodded.

Paul eyes flickered over the layers of clothing. "But I want you out of all this flannel, first."

That earned a laugh out of her. "It is not flannel."

"It isn't?" he teased, tugging open the sash of her dressing gown and then starting on the interminable buttons of her night rail.

Unlike last night, he would only undo enough of the tiny buttons to remove the dreadful garment.

"It looks like flannel to me."

"How can you be a mill owner and not know the difference between flannel and cotton?"

"Are they not the same?" he asked, feigning ignorance.

"No! Of course, they—" She gave him a suspicious look. "You are funning me—you know the difference."

"Up," he said, lifting her by the waist and then easily stripping her once she was standing.

He smiled down at her, amused when her entire body blushed. "Get in bed and I will extinguish the candles."

She turned and scampered quickly, her bottom bouncing in a way that was truly magnificent. When she reached the bed, she covered herself up to the neck, clasped the blankets to her chest, and sat back against the pile of cushions, her eyes wide and watchful, as if she were watching a play.

Paul shrugged off his own robe because that was something else that she needed to become accustomed to: his naked body.

Although she turned a fiery red, she didn't close her eyes. Instead, she allowed her gaze to roam over him—but took only brief, jerky glances at his obvious arousal.

Progress.

Paul strode around the room, snuffing candles.

Once it was dark, he climbed into bed and turned on his side to face her. "Come here," he murmured softly, reaching out to bring her closer, until he was the larger spoon to her much smaller one.

She was only stiff for a moment before relaxing and snuggling up against him.

Paul lowered his nose to her hair—once again plaited and bound—and inhaled deeply. She smelled of lavender, fresh grass, and the outdoors. No wonder butterflies were attracted to her.

Just like last night—after Paul had stimulated her to orgasm by touching and sucking only her breasts and nipples—she fell asleep in a laughably short time.

Paul had hardened instantly when their naked bodies pressed together and his cock was still throbbing against the satiny skin of her back

He sighed. It would be a long, uneventful night for his prick and probably a sleepless night for the rest of him.

***

Phoebe wasn't surprised to find the bed empty when she woke the following morning because she'd been awake when her husband took his leave of her at only five-thirty.

What he did so early in the morning Phoebe did not know.

She had watched him from beneath her lashes, amused and touched when he'd made an obvious effort to collect his robe and slippers and tiptoe from the room without waking her.

Once the door had shut, she had drifted into a light doze, waking again an hour later at six-thirty, which was still far earlier than Spragg came to her.

Rather than get out of bed, she luxuriated, recalling last night.

Her husband's answer about Ellen Kettering had been as comforting as it was possible for such an answer to be on such a volatile subject.

The woman *had* been kind. She was also exceedingly lovely—fair, shaped like an hourglass, and perfect—a fact which had niggled at her like burr, the jealousy she had already felt even more corrosive now that she could put a face to the name.

And it *was* jealousy.

Phoebe knew that she should feel shame more sharply—as her mother did—but she didn't. Instead, it ate at her to think that her husband—a man whom Phoebe had despised only a month ago but was now strangely possessive about—had known such a beautiful lover.

It was painful to imagine what he must think of Phoebe after having a mistress who looked like Mrs. Kettering.

Oh, Phoebe knew she was not *ugly*, but neither was she beautiful. The best she could hope for was apple-cheeked wholesomeness.

As for Needham and her rapidly changing feelings toward him?

Phoebe could no longer remember why she'd ever thought him ugly, vulgar, or inferior in any way.

She had always believed that Sebastian Lowery's slender, handsome, and elegant person was the epitome of masculine perfection.

And yet when she thought about the last time that she'd seen him—the evening of Needham's ball—all she could remember was how weak, sulky, and petulant he'd looked while Needham had held him by the neck, like an adult cat held a kitten.

Phoebe smiled to herself at that analogy.

Sometime over the past weeks she had come to admire Needham's physical strength rather than see his big body as proof of his lack of gentility.

Yet as big and powerful as he was, Needham was no bully. Not like Sebastian, who was self-centered and manipulative enough to think it was his right as a wealthy man to prey on powerless servants.

Was Needham domineering?

Absolutely.

Dictatorial and controlling?

Yes to both and he would probably become even more so as he aged.

But he did not engage in the sort of mental and emotional cruelty that Sebastian had shown himself capable of.

Thus far in their dealings he had been nothing but honest to her.

Paul Needham would give you the word with the bark on it. That might be uncomfortable, but at least a person knew where they stood.

A month ago, Phoebe had found such behavior offensive, abrasive, and uncouth. Now, suddenly, she respected it.

Things were changing so quickly it made her feel dizzy sometimes.

But although she felt uncertain and tentative in so many ways, she could not say she was unhappy.

She missed her family, of course, but it was, she hated to admit, a relief not to be the one who always had to tell one of her siblings *no* because their meager budget would not stretch to cover something they wanted.

She was elated that she no longer needed to pinch pennies to make sure her family could pay its butcher bill, or that she had to demean herself and beg the roofer for more time to pay the bill.

There were, she saw quite suddenly and plainly, a hundred other small unpleasantries she had grown accustomed to shouldering for her family over the years. All were things her mother or father should have done, but which they'd relegated to their children because they were so absorbed in themselves and their hatred for each other.

Phoebe had only been married a few days but already she knew that her husband would never taunt her the way her father did her mother.

Nor would he leave her to shoulder all the burdens.

Indeed, Needham was far more likely to take on too much and leave her with nothing at all to do.

Which was why Phoebe was looking forward to meeting with her new housekeeper, Mrs. Nutter, so she could demonstrate her worth to her new husband by ensuring that his household ran smoothly.

Already Phoebe had noticed areas where she could make her husband's life more comfortable.

Last night in the library she had noticed that he needed a better lamp beside his desk because he'd been squinting at his paperwork. His chair needed fresh horsehair in the sagging seat and the drapes needed to be replaced.

Those were the sorts of things that Phoebe had noticed after only one day.

She knew there would be much, much more she could do for him.

And while Needham had made haste to get part of the house ready for occupation, there were still dozens of rooms that hadn't been touched yet.

When Phoebe thought about his *other* houses—she had been afraid to ask Needham how many—her task began to look quite overwhelming.

His name is Paul, you had better become accustomed to saying it.

"Paul," she whispered, and then blushed, even though she was alone.

What was wrong with her to be so silly? He had done unspeakably intimate things to her and yet she became hot and shy just thinking his Christian name.

Now that Phoebe thought about it, she had never once heard her mother say her father's first name. Indeed, the only reason she knew it was Geoffrey is because it was inscribed on the family crypt, along with an open-ended date.

Now that Phoebe was married, she had a difficult time believing that her parents had ever done the things she and Needham—*Paul*—had done on their wedding night.

Phoebe hastily shoved away her wicked thoughts and rang for her maid to dress her.

The morning sped by and after nuncheon, she decided to nip into the village to purchase a fresh bottle of Hungary Water as she'd been using the dregs of her current bottle for ages.

She went to fetch her hat and lightest cloak and found Spragg in her dressing room.

"I am going to fetch something at Burton's," she said as she checked her hair in the mirror. "Do you need anything?"

"Oh—are you going now, my lady?"

"Yes. Why?"

"I was meaning to go myself, my lady. Might I come along."

Phoebe had wanted to have some time alone as she'd been closeted with servants all morning. But she smiled. "I'd be glad of your company."

After returning from town, Phoebe decided to finish a letter she'd begun to Aurelia last night but hadn't completed.

She knew Needham wasn't using the library because she'd seen him ride out with his bailiff just before nuncheon and one of the footmen informed her that he'd not yet returned.

But when she opened the door, she found a guinea gold head bent over her husband's desk.

"I'm sorry," she said when Mr. Dixon shot to his feet. "I didn't mean to interrupt."

"Please, my lady, it is no interruption at all. And if it were, it would be a pleasant one."

He shoved a hand through his hair and glared down at the desk so fiercely she couldn't help laughing.

"What is vexing you?" she asked, going over to the small secretary desk she'd claimed for herself and removing her half-written letter from beneath the blotter.

"I'm trying to decipher this gentleman's handwriting and believe it would be easier to read Mandarin." He cut her a rueful, pleading look. "I don't want to impose—but are you any good at all at deciphering mysteries?"

She set her letter aside. "As a matter of fact, I've spent the last few years helping to tutor my young brother. His pet squirrel has tidier penmanship."

Mr. Dixon laughed, the expression rendering him near angelic. Goodness but he was a beautiful, personable young man.

As the younger son of a well-respected viscount, Mr. Dixon was the sort of man that Phoebe might have met and married if she'd ever had the chance to have a Season and attend proper *ton* parties.

"Would you mind having a look at it?" he asked.

She smiled. "Of course."

"Here," he said when she came to the desk, "You take the chair, I shall hover hopefully."

Phoebe laughed and sat, studying the letter in question. After a moment, she said, "Oh, dear."

He made a triumphant sound. "Isn't it dreadful? I would have merely sent a response letting him know it was unreadable, but time is of the essence."

"Hmm, well, let me see… I believe this word here is"—she squinted—"could this be *cylinder*?"

He leaned over her shoulder. "By Jove! It is."

"This one next to it, I'm afraid it makes no sense to me—it looks like *piston*?"

"*How* did I not see that?" he demanded.

"Do you know that word?" she asked doubtfully.

"Yes, it is a mechanical term that is not generally known. But that sentence now makes perfect sense." He grinned down at her and held out a hand to help her up. "You have been invalua—"

The door to the library opened and her husband entered the room with another man on his heels.

When Needham saw them at the desk, there was the slightest hitch in his step and his gray gaze flickered between Phoebe and Mr. Dixon.

Mr. Dixon released her hand and turned to his employer. "Lady Needham has just helped to decipher that wretched letter from Mr. Watt, sir. He is confident the bore angle is correct for both the cylinder and piston."

Needham nodded, his eyes hooded. "Indeed. You are very clever, my dear, and you have saved us a great deal of expense with your translation. I, personally, could make nothing of it."

Phoebe smiled and stepped away from both the desk and Mr. Dixon. "I'll just fetch my letter and leave you to your business," she said.

Part of her had hoped that her husband would tell her she could stay, but he merely nodded and watched her, his gaze brooding.

***

Paul listened to Dixon and Joe Charm, his bailiff, debate the merits of seeding some pasture or other, his mind on the scene he'd interrupted upon entering the library.

Or, more precisely, on his *reaction* to the scene, which had been visceral.

And more than a little disturbing.

Paul liked Dixon—and what is more, he trusted him. He had always realized, in a vague sort of way, that the younger man was handsome. But not until he'd seen the way his wife blushed and dropped her gaze at dinner last night had he realized just how attractive Dixon was to members of the opposite sex.

Nobody would ever call Paul attractive—not even those few who loved him.

As a younger man, he had been downright ugly. Thankfully, he had grown into his prominent nose and big frame over the years, but he was no fool; he knew exactly why women agreed to warm his bed and why aristocratic men invited him to join their exclusive clubs: money.

It was the same reason that Phoebe had married him and her parents had allowed what was, for their daughter, a devastating step down socially.

For years Paul had avoided matchmaking parents, but then Lady Phoebe Bellamy had marched into his life. While he had teased her with the threat of marrying her lovely sister, the thought had never truly taken hold in his mind.

No, the only woman who'd tempted him in twenty years had been Lady Phoebe.

Paul knew that physically, at least, his wife was ordinary. And yet he was more enamored of her after barely a month than he'd ever been of any of his mistresses.

It had been two decades since he had last experienced the sharp, searing jealousy that had cut through him when he'd seen Dixon standing close to his wife and holding her hand.

The last time he'd felt so powerfully had been over a woman named Christina Bower. The man in question had been his brother Gideon, who had always coveted everything Paul had, and had done an excellent job of taking most of it.

Gideon had—effortlessly—taken Christina and then laughingly thrown the poor, confused girl aside once he'd had her.

"You may be the heir, Paul, but when it comes to everything else in life, I will beat you every time," Gideon had taunted even after Paul had tracked him down and beaten him to a pulp.

Not surprisingly, gut-churning jealousy was every bit as unpleasant now as it had been way back then.

But this time, Paul's jealousy was irrational.

Dixon was *not* Gideon and Phoebe was not a poor, ignorant village lass bedazzled by the local lord's wealthy sons.

But rationality meant nothing to him right now. He had wanted to smash Dixon's face when he'd see him smiling down at his wife, who had been turned up toward him like a flower seeking the sun.

Paul wanted to smash Dixon's face just thinking about it.

He wanted to smash his *own* face even more for acting like such a gudgeon.

"—once his lordship acquires the new land it would make sense to do that. Do you agree, my lord?"

Paul looked up from his fuming to find both men looking at him, curious and waiting.

"Yes, that is fine," he said, having no idea what he was agreeing to.

***

That night Phoebe wore yet another prim, buttoned down nightgown, this one almost identical to the last two, but in pale blue.

Unlike last night, however, she smiled up at Paul as he entered her room, her innocent, welcoming expression telling him that she had no notion of the irrational stew of possessiveness and jealousy churning inside him.

She had not noticed his mood at dinner either, when she and Dixon had chatted like old friends, discussing the many connections they shared—like Dixon's grandmother and Lady Phoebe's great aunt, both of whom had apparently been friends a half century ago.

By the time the meal was over, Paul had begun to accept that he'd inflicted a gross and repellent injustice on his wife by marrying her.

Not only was he fifteen years her senior, but he was also a product of the merchant class who still engaged in business, and was an ugly, hulking monster to boot!

Dixon, on the other hand, was the sort of storybook prince girls dreamed about. With his guinea gold locks and perfect features he was the epitome of male beauty. He was also cultured and courtly.

He was everything that Paul Needham was *not*.

Paul also knew that the younger man was far too decent and gentlemanly to strip his virgin bride naked and bury his tongue in her cunt on her wedding night.

No, Dixon would, like the rest of his aristocratic breed, save such debauchery for his mistress.

If Paul had possessed even an ounce of decency, he would have introduced Phoebe to Dixon the same day that she had come to beg him not to marry any of her sisters.

But he had not done that.

Instead, he had been unspeakably selfish and snatched her up for himself.

And now she belonged to *him*, by God.

And neither Dixon nor any other effete aristocratic fop could have her.

So, that was his mood when he entered his wife's chambers.

"Get undressed," he ordered quietly, snuffing the candles and darkening the room before disrobing.

Because suddenly, *Paul* was the one who craved darkness. And *Paul* was the one who didn't want her to look at him.

When he climbed into bed, she was lying motionless, all the way on the opposite side of the bed.

You should leave her be and just go to sleep. Things will look better tomorrow.

Paul's fists clenched in frustration.

Yes, that is what he *should* do. A man should not make love to a woman—especially an inexperienced one like Phoebe—when he was angry.

"Have I done something to displease you?" She spoke in a small voice that was unlike her normal confident tone.

Paul felt like an ignorant clodpole for scaring her, but he couldn't seem to stop himself.

"You have not done anything to displease me," he said coolly and quietly.

It wasn't a lie—*she* hadn't displeased him. He was displeased with himself and despised the emotions roiling in his belly. Jealousy was for young hot-heads, not mature men.

His own emotions shamed him.

But the shame wasn't enough to keep him from wanting her.

Or taking her.

Paul pushed back the covers and found her body in the darkness.

As badly as he wanted to rip her gown in half, he merely raised it above her waist, spread her thighs, and readied her body for his, taking his time and using his lips and fingers, bringing her climax after climax before he finally climbed on top of her and surrendered to his own desires.

Paul was not so lost to decency as to breed her more than once a night—at least not yet—even though he wanted her again almost immediately after.

Instead, he lowered the hem of her gown, covered her with the blanket, and spooned her.

"Good night, Phoebe," he murmured into her fragrant hair.

She yawned, apparently exhausted by all her orgasms. "Good night, my lord."

She quickly passed into a heavy sleep while Paul lay staring at the darkness, his lips and tongue numb from use, his cock once again hard, his need for her unassuaged.

How was that even possible?

He was a man of science. Surely logic—dutifully and rigidly applied—could tell him why he wanted her so badly and why had he become so jealous over nothing?

Because *that* was a problem that needed solving. A man could not burn so hot for a woman indefinitely. At least not without burning himself up in the process.

Many hours later, as the gray light of dawn sliced through a gap in the drapes, Paul was still no closer to finding an answer to his questions.

Chapter Seventeen

Three days later the storm broke.

"The acts of sabotage have spread, my lord," Dixon said, handing Paul a letter that had arrived with that morning's mail. "It's not only the new ovens that have suffered damage; now the older ones are being attacked. The ten men you sent will not be enough to protect all the areas."

Paul knew that, of course—and so did the man behind the vandalism: his brother Gideon, although he had no solid evidence to that effect.

His vision wavered with sudden fury at the unwanted, but not unexpected, news that Gideon had expanded his battlefronts.

He looked at his secretary. "And does Bateman say whether any suspects have been detained or questioned?"

Dixon looked unhappy at the question, as if *he* were the one at fault. "He says the magistrate has talked to over a dozen different men, but all have witnesses."

Of course they would, because it wouldn't be just one man responsible for the acts; they would take turns. Paul knew there were at least three of them, not including his brother—Gideon would mastermind the plan but never get his hands dirty with any actual vandalism. No, Gideon was too clever for that. His tools—the men he employed to do his dirty work—were not necessarily stupid, but they *were* desperate.

Unlike his brother, these men were impoverished with nobody to rescue them if they came to trouble.

Gideon knew that no matter what crime or mischief he got up to, Paul would make sure he never went to gaol.

"Do you want to arrange for more men, my lord?" Dixon asked, clearly uncomfortable with Paul's seething silence.

"Not yet. What I shall need to do is—"

The door to the library flew open hard enough to crack against the wall. A fury stood in the open doorway.

"Is it true that I may not even take *walks* without a gaoler to attend me?" Phoebe demanded, her hazel eyes flashing.

Paul, who had already stood, turned to Dixon. "Leave us," he ordered quietly. "Take the rest of the afternoon for yourself. We can attend to this later, after dinner."

"Of course, my lord." Dixon scuttled toward the door, dropping a graceful, if speedy, bow. "My lady."

Phoebe ignored him, her chest heaving.

"Won't you have a seat?" Paul said when Dixon shut the door behind him.

"I don't want to sit! I want to take a walk to the village without my maid insisting on attending me. And how *dare* you give her orders behind my back?"

The hot anger that had been straining at the leash only moments before suddenly turned ice cold.

"How *dare* I?" Paul repeated softly.

***

Phoebe wished she could take the hasty words back as soon as they left her mouth.

And that was *before* she saw the effect they had on her husband. He was always an intimidating man—even when he was in a pleasant mood—but right then he was positively terrifying. How he was able to be *more* frightening when he was quiet was a mystery.

While Phoebe could not turn back the clock, she could compose herself and not come across as an irrational female, which she could *see* he was thinking, and which would allow him to dismiss her concerns as hysterical.

"Please, have a seat," he said again, gesturing to the chair in front of his desk.

Phoebe sat, but only because courtesy kept him from doing so while she was still standing.

"Let me address your second concern, about me *daring* to give orders to your maid. She is a servant in my house, a domestic in my employ, I feel that gives me the right to give her orders." His pupils were so small they appeared non-existent. Was it possible for a person's eyes to actually change shades? Because right then, Needham's irises seemed to have been leached of all color.

Phoebe bit her lip to keep from saying something she would almost certainly regret.

"As to walking unaccompanied. I'd hoped I'd made it clear a few mornings ago, when we discussed taking your groom on—"

"But that is a *ride*, I am merely wishing to walk."

His eyes, impossibly, became even frostier. "May I finish my answer?"

"I apologize for interrupting you," she said, needing to force the words out. "Please continue."

"You may walk anywhere in the park or gardens, which are quite extensive, without taking somebody with you. But yes, when you leave the grounds, you will not go unattended."

She struggled with her temper, torn between wanting to make him understand and wishing to shout accusations.

"I take great pleasure in walking," she forced out, every bit as quietly as he was talking. "I often walk for miles—which is more than Spragg or any of the other maids would find enjoyable. Not only that, but—" Phoebe broke off, not sure how to explain the next part.

Needham merely waited, his expression unreadable.

"I need privacy, my lord. And if I have a maid with me, I feel compelled to accommodate my pace and be sociable."

"Have you conversed with Carthage on your morning rides these past few days?"

"Not in general. He usually rides behind me at a slight distance." At first that had felt odd, but she'd been pleasantly surprised by how quickly she forgot that he was even with her.

Not that she wanted to admit that to her husband.

"Can you not instruct your maid to walk behind you?"

It was so *reasonable* a solution, and yet…

"That still would not address the issue of their fatigue."

"I daresay it is possible to find somebody, not objectionable to you, who is a great walker and could be available to you at all times."

She laughed, but then realized he was not speaking in jest. "You would actually engage a servant just to *walk* with me?"

"Yes."

"But—but would that not be a great expense just so I would have somebody to go for a walk? I don't even go every day, sometimes I only walk a few times a week. What would the person do the rest of the time?"

"If it gives you pleasure, then it is money well spent. As for what they would do the rest of the time, that is immaterial as long as they are easily and conveniently at hand when you want them."

Phoebe was left utterly speechless as she took in his implacable expression.

She had known he was a very wealthy man—indeed, she had seen proof of it—but to hire a person whose only duty was to await their employer's beck and call was just—

Her eyes snapped up to his face and she said, "Just like a mistress."

Yet again she wished she could take the words back.

And then crawl under a rock.

His eyebrows arched and the sardonic expression on his face was like a spur digging into her side, driving her onward to greater folly.

"Well, isn't that how men arrange things with their m-mistresses?" she demanded, sounding breathy rather than sophisticated and jaded, as she had hoped.

His lips curved into a faint smile—an expression that inexplicably made her face burn.

Phoebe opened her mouth to retract her comment, but she was not quick enough.

"What an unconventional wife you are turning out to be. I seem to recall you telling me not long ago that *decent* women did not wish to discuss or even acknowledge such subjects And yet here you are asking me how I structure my amorous liaisons with my mistress."

Her belly pitched at was essentially an admission that he *had* a mistress and Phoebe struggled for something to say.

"As a matter of fact, it is a remarkably similar situation," Needham said. "Your walking companion would be engaged for one task, and one task only: to service your need and give you pleasure whenever and as often as you demanded it."

The air positively crackled between them at the evocative words *service, need,* and *pleasure.*

Images and even physical sensations from the last few nights assaulted her. But this time, she imagined him engaging in those same *services* with some other, nameless woman who was, in her too fertile imagination, more beautiful and infinitely more skilled than Phoebe.

She shot to her feet.

He rose with her and strode from behind his desk, not stopping until he was directly in front of her.

Phoebe glared at a button on his coat.

As he did so often, he took her chin in his warm, strong fingers and tilted her face until she had to look at him.

He caressed her chin and cheek with light, almost thoughtful, stroking, his pale gray gaze slowly darkening the longer he looked at her.

Phoebe's body quickly—and very inconveniently—tightened under his stare.

She had to say something or she'd collapse at his feet in a blithering heap. "I do not want you to engage a *walker companion* for me. Please," she added to soften the sharp tone.

"Very well," he said, capitulating with surprising ease. "But you will still take somebody on your walks with you."

She swallowed down her angry, rebellious words. What he didn't know, wouldn't hurt him.

He slid his palm around the curve of her jaw, his lips *almost* curving into a smile. "I would ask that you obey my wishes, Phoebe. Please don't turn me into your gaoler."

Phoebe had to bite her tongue to keep down any one of a half dozen retorts. Instead, she turned away abruptly, both satisfied and disappointed when he made no attempt to detain her.

Indeed, he was at the door in a few long strides, and opened it without comment.

Phoebe made it to her room, which was, blessedly, empty of Spragg, before she gave vent to her emotions.

A pillow was the innocent recipient of her temper.

When she had calmed, it wasn't because she'd resigned herself to obedience.

But rather because her mind was busying itself with ways in which she might contravene the spirit of his command, if not the actual substance.

Chapter Eighteen

It was immediately clear that Phoebe had retreated not to surrender, but to regroup and then launch a fresh offensive, this one an entirely different sort of campaign.

This time she didn't attack alone. Instead, she involved the willing—albeit unwitting—Mr. Dixon as her co-combatant.

The first skirmish took place two days later at the Prince and Weasel—affectionally called The Weasel by the locals.

The Weasel was the tiny inn that served as a gathering place in Little Sissingdon when Burton's Mercantile was not convenient.

Paul knew that Phoebe had gone riding both days, each time with Carthage, and had taken two walks, one with Lucy as a companion and the other with Spragg, her rather phlegmatic maid.

Foolishly, Paul had believed his wife had seen the wisdom of his request and that the matter was settled.

Her behavior, which had been unusually mild and compliant, should have been the warning shot over his bow.

Paul had gone to her bedroom and made love to her both nights and she had responded just as eagerly and charmingly to his overtures as ever.

Although she still took up far too much of Paul's mental energy during the day, he was half-way to believing that perhaps his desire for her might not blossom into full-blown obsession after all.

Indeed, he was patting himself on the back—metaphorically speaking—on having tamed his inconvenient, uncomfortable passions as easily as he had tamed his headstrong wife.

In other words, he was a victim of his own hubris. A line from a poem he'd read a few years ago came back to him, "*My name is Ozymandias, king of kings; Look on my works, ye Mighty, and despair!*"

Rather than despair, however, the sight that met Paul at The Weasel filled him with intense aggravation, jealousy, and a certain grudging respect.

"Oh, look," his wife said to Mr. Dixon, with whom she was sitting, in an overly cheerful voice that carried across the small room, "There is Needham, now. We may consult him on the matter."

Mr. Dixon had the decency to look flustered as he stood.

"Good afternoon, my lord."

"Good afternoon, Dixon, my lady." Paul stripped off his gloves and dipped his chin toward their table, which was filled with evidence of tea and scones that had been greatly enjoyed. "May I join you?"

Dixon all but leapt to procure another chair, banging into Mr. Thomas, the innkeeper, who'd already gone into action upon seeing not only the local lord, but also his landlord now that Paul was in the process of purchasing the land the Earl of Addiscombe had sold off a few years earlier.

Paul tossed his gloves into his hat and handed both to Thomas without taking his gaze off his wife, who was smiling at him and looking exactly like a cat who'd been at the cream pot.

"A pint of your homebrew, if you please, Mr. Thomas."

"Right away, my lord."

Dixon hesitated, his hand on the chair back, his posture shrieking uncertainty.

Again, Paul didn't take his eyes from his wife while he spoke to the man, "I've left a draft of the letter to Bateman on your desk, Mr. Dixon. Perhaps you might have time to finish recopying it and get it on its way before dinner. I shall escort my wife back to Wych House."

Dixon couldn't have left quicker if he'd been launched from a cannon.

Phoebe no longer appeared triumphant, but almost... sulky, although he suspected the uninitiated wouldn't recognize the subtle hints of her displeasure.

"What was it you wished to ask me, my dear?" he asked mildly, nodding his thanks to the innkeeper when he set down his pint.

"Anything else for you, my lady?"

Phoebe bestowed a glowing smile on the innkeeper. "No, I am quite unable to eat another bite. Please do pass my compliments to Mrs. Thomas, and also my enduring hope that she will one day share her secret recipe with me."

"She won't even tell me, Lady Phoeb—er, I mean Lady Needham." Thomas chuckled uneasily, clearly sensing something in the atmosphere. Or, more likely, he had watched the new viscountess and the viscount's handsome secretary and wondered what was in the works.

As had the people who were occupying every single one of the other tables. Quite a crowd for this time of day, Paul would imagine.

"Thank you, that will be all," Paul said, when the innkeeper hovered uncertainly.

"You were going to tell me what I should look at," he reminded his wife.

Ever conscious of appearances, Phoebe smiled and slid a book of fabric swatches across the table. "I thought the dull gold would do nicely for the library."

Paul glanced down at the swatch in question, unsurprised that it was lovely and exactly the sort of thing he approved of.

"I like it," he said, amused by the coincidence. He, too, had been in town looking at swatches at the tiny millinery shop owned and operated by Mrs. Debenham. While she'd not had exactly what Paul had in mind, he had found three bolts of material that had pleased him very much. And which had shocked the middle-aged dressmaker to her toes. Apparently using expensive silk netting for anything but overdresses had never occurred to the woman.

"You want me to make a n-nightgown?" she had repeated, uncertainly.

Paul smiled at the memory.

"What is so amusing, my lord?" Phoebe asked him.

"I am pleased you are taking charge of the refurbishment as I found Mrs. Nutter's choices rather pedestrian. Your taste is exquisite."

She flushed at his compliment, clearly not expecting it.

"I take it that Mr. Dixon also possesses some insight into the matter of draperies?"

Her expression said *this* was more what she'd believed he would say.

"His father's house—Brookhurst—is consider one of the finest examples of the Early Baroque style. He will have grown up accustomed to living in a house that is graciously and elegantly appointed."

Unlike you, was the thrust of her comment.

"What does that mean, exactly?"

"What does what mean?"

"Early Baroque."

"You want to know what Early Baroque is?" she repeated.

"Yes—when was that? What years? How is it different from, say—well, is there a Middle Baroque?"

She was flustered and desperately tried to hide it. "Surely you don't wish to discuss architecture. Such information can be of no use to you."

Paul almost stood and clapped at her impressive rebound—from breathlessly flustered to throwing a proper facer in less than a few seconds—which effectively put him in his place.

Paul's place being far from a gentleman of Dixon's character and breeding.

His new wife was a scrapper for all that she was such a small thing.

"I am always hoping to better myself, my dear. And I believe all knowledge is worth having."

She squinted slightly, as if peering through a fog—certain there was something obscured within it.

Paul smiled mildly, presenting the very picture of an encroaching cit who was eager to learn from his betters.

"There is a book on the subject in the library," she said, once again finding her feet. "I shall fetch it for you. I daresay it will do a more creditable job on the subject than I could."

Oh, his Phoebe. What a treasure.

It was at that moment that Paul suspected he was falling in love.

***

A few days after the exchange in The Weasel Paul was riding back from one of the abandoned outbuildings on yet another parcel of land he'd contracted to purchase.

As Twickham had predicted, the man who'd bought the bulk of the Earl of Addiscombe's unentailed thirty-two thousand acres had become badly dipped thanks to several ill-advised investments on the Exchange and was in a burning hurry to sell.

Fortunately for Paul—not so fortunately for the seller—there were few buyers, so Paul had used that fact to drive the asking price—already much reduced—down by more than twelve percent.

While the property had cost him considerably more than a song, it had still been the best land bargain he'd made in fifteen years.

Twickham was working on acquiring the remaining two properties that Addiscombe had sold.

Paul hardly needed them—he had plenty of land on which to build his new house, if that is what he decided to do—but he had developed something of a mania to stitch the once-grand property back together.

He'd also developed a mania to figure out what his wife's next offensive would be.

And Paul had no doubt that is exactly what she was doing: scheming and planning.

Phoebe should never, ever gamble. If her father's countenance at the card table was as transparent as his daughter's, it was no wonder that he'd lost his fortune.

Already Paul could read her expressions like a book. For instance, he knew she was at her most devious when she appeared most docile and submissive, two things she most certainly was *not*.

Paul almost felt bad for her. She was new at campaigning while he was a scarred, grizzled veteran.

So that is why when he saw two figures on the abandoned, weed-filled stretch of road he wasn't surprised that one of them wore a charming emerald green habit.

Paul kept his distance until the couple turned off the road into a small cluster of trees and then he urged Coal into a gallop. When he came to the spot where they'd turned off, he saw there was a faint trail through the foliage.

"It is time to advance, my lad," Paul murmured to his horse.

It was almost as if Coal knew to be quiet, his huge hooves scarcely making a sound as he picked his way down the overgrown trail.

Paul heard them before he saw them—laughing and talking.

Their horses were loosely tethered a short distance from a tiny derelict cottage.

At first, Paul's secretary was leaning so close to Paul's wife that he didn't see her much smaller body.

Fear struck him sharply, like a knife in his belly.

Please God, don't let this be like Gideon and Catherine. Please don't—

His wife's voice came from somewhere behind Dixon: "Yes, yes—just a bit harder. That's almost perfect," she said, her tone… exultant.

Just then Coal clipped a stone with his hoof and sent it bouncing.

When Dixon turned around to face him Paul became almost dizzy with relief at the sight of Phoebe—fully clothed. She was crouching and poking a length of wire around in the keyhole while Dixon fiddled with the handle.

"Good afternoon, my lord," Dixon said, his fair cheeks flushing.

Paul didn't trust his voice yet, so he merely looked from one to the other, before allowing his gaze to settle on Dixon.

"Her ladyship says the structure is cool enough and the temperature stable enough, to store perishables," Dixon offered.

"That is very interesting," he said in a flat tone.

Dixon's fair skin was almost as red as Phoebe's. Indeed, the two had a similar look—all aquiline elegance and breeding—and could have passed for siblings.

Paul only had to look at the other man for a moment before Dixon cleared his throat. "Er, actually, my lord, I am pleased you came along. I just remembered a letter to Mr. Brindle that needs to go out with the last mail. I would hate to rush Lady Needham on her way. But now, as you are here, perhaps you might escort her back to Wych House."

"I would be happy to do so."

An uncomfortable silence fell over the small clearing as Mr. Dixon hastened to mount his horse, his foot slipping twice before he was finally astride.

"I shall see you at dinner, my lord, my lady." He inclined his head and urged his horse into a canter.

Paul turned to his wife.

Her face was also red and her eyes were throwing sparks. "That was excessively rude," she growled. Yes, it was definitely a growl.

"Where is your groom?" Paul asked.

She blinked, clearly startled by the question. "I do not need him; I was with Mr. Dixon."

"I think you must know that it is improper for a newly married young woman to go off on extensive jaunts with an attractive young man."

"Oh, is he attractive? I hadn't noticed."

"You can rest assured that the people at The Prince and Weasel noticed."

She flushed, her mouth tightening before she turned her back on him and began untying her horse's reins from the post.

Paul waited until she realized there was no way for her to mount.

Once she did, she spun around, her eyes throwing sparks.

"What is the matter, my lord? Are you afraid your employee will lose control and ravish me?"

Paul smiled coldly. "Perhaps it was not Mr. Dixon's self-control I am worried about, my dear."

**

Phoebe's hand flew before she even knew it had moved and she struck his face hard enough to make his head snap to the side and send his hat flying.

She gasped and stared at her hand, as if it were some stranger that had acted of its own volition.

Phoebe looked from her stinging palm to her husband. He wore the faint smile and hooded gaze she now knew hid a hot, smoldering anger.

He bent and picked up his hat, dusting it lightly before setting it on his head.

He picked up the reins she had dropped when she'd assaulted him.

Because that was exactly what she had done: assaulted him.

"I'm—I'm sorry," she said, her voice shaky. "I shouldn't have done that. I've never struck anyone before."

"Well, you shan't be able to say that again, shall you?" he asked, dark humor glinting in his icy gaze.

Any remorse she'd felt dissipated. "You think this is amusing? It entertains you to make filthy assumptions about my behavior?"

"I think your reaction is amusing."

"How dare you say such an odious thing to me?"

He looped the reins over Brandy's neck. "Because I *am* odious, my dear."

"So, you vent your spleen on me, even though I have done nothing to deserve it?

He turned to her and gave her a steady look. "Is that true? You are blameless?"

Phoebe's face flushed. "Just because you are a slave to your baser passions does not mean the rest of us are the same," she shot back at him.

Now *where* had that come from?

He smiled.

"What?"

"It sounds as though you've been thinking about my baser passions." Needham took a step closer. "Is that true?"

When Phoebe tried to step back, she bumped into the old hitching post.

"Tell me about my baser passions, Phoebe."

She shook her head weakly, mesmerized by his gaze. It was bright outside, even under the canopy of trees, making his pupils tiny specks in a field of silver gray.

"No clever answer?" he murmured, cocking his head.

Before she knew what he was doing, he captured her chin and lowered his mouth over hers, holding her gently but firmly and kissing her breathless, not stopping until her pulse threatened to burst from beneath her skin.

When he released her, he gazed down at her with eyes that blazed. "You are playing a dangerous game, Phoebe."

"What game? I'm not—"

He kissed her again, this time harder—almost brutally—his hands dropping to her bottom, which he cupped and then lifted her, holding her in such a way that her spread thighs were forced to balance on his thigh for support.

Phoebe groaned at the exquisite friction, her hips instinctively bucking and grinding, seeking the pleasure he was slowly and surely teaching her to need as much as air or water.

Just when her crisis began to reach its peak, he lowered her abruptly and stepped away, again holding her chin, his gaze no longer hot, but as cold as frost crystals.

"There is something I don't think you understand about me, Phoebe. Or perhaps you've just refused to accept it. But I am, in the main, the sort of man who guards all his possessions—"

She tried to jerk her chin away. "I am *not* your poss—"

He held her more firmly and continued as if she'd never spoken. "Where you are concerned, I am an *exceedingly* jealous man. I don't like it when you have nuncheon with Dixon, just the two of you, flaunting your behavior for all our neighbors to see and speculate about. I don't like it when you flirt and charm him every night at dinner and then answer me in monosyllables. And I don't like it when you go off riding with my handsome young noble secretary—"

"But we didn't *do* anything."

"But you wanted me to *think* you might, didn't you, Phoebe?"

She opened her mouth to lie and deny it, suddenly ashamed that she had hoped to get a response out of him.

But not one this frightening.

Phoebe chewed her lip; what in the world could she say? "I don't—er, I—"

"It doesn't matter," he said coolly. "What matters is that I don't like watching or knowing that Dixon gets to enjoy the pleasure of your company while you deny me. You are mine, Phoebe, mine alone. Mine to enjoy however and whenever I please."

He kissed her ruthlessly, his big hand cradling her head in a firm, unbreakable hold while he plundered her.

Phoebe desperately wanted to resist him—or, better yet, to reject him—but it *hurt* to deny herself the pleasure of his touch.

So, yet again, her resolve melted faster than butter on a scorching hot pan.

She dug her fingers into the thick muscles of his shoulders, kneading him while she thrust her tongue into his mouth, their angry jousting so arousing she couldn't resist rubbing herself against his hard thigh.

Yet *again* it was Needham who ended their kiss, leaving her panting like a dog in heat.

He glared down at her and the possessive fire in his gaze made her knees weak. "I don't wish to share you with Sebastian Lowery or Dixon, or any other handsome young man." He brushed a big, brutish thumb gently over her lower lip, his nostrils flaring. "You are mine, Phoebe. Mine."

It was almost impossible to recall why she was angry with him when he said things like that—and when he looked at her with such unabashed desire—but Phoebe dug deep and mined one last nugget of resistance.

She sneered. "So, if I wish to ride with an old, ugly man you will not forbid it?"

He looked amused. "Let me just say that none of the grooms or footmen I employ are the sort to send a young, impressionable girl's heart pounding."

Phoebe was torn between fury at the way he was treating her as a possession and elation that she had apparently captivated a powerful, intimidating, sophisticated man like Paul Needham.

"You are positively *gothic!*" She wrenched her chin away from his fingers—or at least tried—but he held her in an unbreakable grip. "Let me go!"

"You will go when I say you may," he murmured, and then he claimed her mouth again.

Phoebe resisted his erotic handling for all of three seconds before her traitorous body melted. Her mind raged on for a few seconds longer, but then it, too gave in to his sensual mastery.

I am so lost to him.

That was the last rational thought she had before Paul showed her yet again how her body, and even her mind, belonged to him. His to control and command.

Utterly and completely *his*.

Chapter Nineteen

Paul was standing by the study window when Phoebe came cantering from the direction of the stables, Carthage a proper distance behind her, his huge, barrel-shaped body surprisingly graceful astride the large-boned bay.

His wife had an excellent seat and her shapely little body looked positively edible in her new sapphire blue habit. It was one of the garments he'd ordered from Mademoiselle Sonia. It had arrived several days earlier but Phoebe had refused to open any of the boxes until today.

Paul's lips curved into a smile at her small rebellion.

It amused him when she showed her fire. Especially when she tried to resist him, as she'd done in bed last night.

At dinner, she had—once again—answered his questions in monosyllables while lavishing all her attention on poor Dixon, who'd looked ready to expire from terror.

After enjoying his port and cigarillo with Dixon, Paul had gone to the library, hoping to find her there since it appeared to be a favorite haunt of hers. But the maid he'd spoken to when he rang for tea said the viscountess had gone up to her chambers directly after dinner.

Pouting, he'd assumed—it turned out correctly.

When Paul had gone to her chambers she had lain as still and stiff as a board when he'd climbed onto her bed.

"Do you not feel well, my dear? Shall I leave you to your rest?"

Her jaw had moved side-to-side, her expression mulish. And then she'd lifted her chin, "I am prepared to do my duty."

Paul had laughed at that, which had only made her look more resolved *not* to enjoy herself.

She'd not resisted him when he'd stripped off her nightgown—yet another puritanical gown that she'd insisted on wearing, even though an entire mountain of unopened clothing boxes sat conspicuously in the middle of her dressing room floor, like a gauntlet.

She hadn't tried to cover herself when he'd laid her bare, nor had she made a sound when he'd shrugged off his own robe, feigning disinterest, although her eyes had briefly slid to his erect cock—which he knew she was curious about—before jumping to something over his shoulder.

When he had nudged her soft, creamy thighs apart—or at least tried to, but she'd held them as tightly clenched as a mousetrap—she had reached for candle he'd left burning beside the bed.

"Leave it," he'd ordered.

"I wish for the light *off*."

"I wish for it *on*," he'd replied.

"So I am to have no say in my own bedchamber?"

"Not on that matter."

"I see. What else?"

"I shall tell you as things come up," he'd said, amused by her acerbic tone and stormy expression.

He'd glanced down at something else that had come up—his cock, which was hard and leaking as it jutted out from his hips. His balls had been full and aching all day thinking about their tussle the day before—both at the cottage and last night, in her bed.

His new wife would never know how close she'd come to getting her first rogering in the splendor of the outdoors the day before.

Her willful antics at dinner hadn't diminished his desire for her one iota. Quite the reverse, they'd made him look forward to taming her yet again when he went to her bed.

Her martyrish behavior from the moment he'd opened her door had fed his lust for her even more. Indeed, he'd been so bloody aroused at the sight of her covered from the neck to wrists to ankles that he'd been tempted to toss her gown up over her waist and breed her hard and fast to dull the sharp edge of his need, saving a slow pleasuring for later.

But the way she'd been seething and glaring told him that a fast, hard fuck would be ill advised tonight. His most impressive bed skills were necessary to sooth her ruffled feathers, no matter how amusing he was finding her daily resistance.

It had been a challenge to hold her gaze when what he'd really wanted was to look down to where her tiny pink nub was eagerly thrusting from her dark curls.

While Phoebe's mind might have been angry with him, her body had been primed and begging.

"Open your thighs for me," he'd ordered

Her jaw had firmed and her knees had remained locked.

Their eyes had locked, as well. His no doubt cold and determined, hers mulish and angry.

Paul had been pondering his next response when she gave a growl of annoyance and flung her knees apart, opening her legs *wide*.

"There," she'd snarled. "Is that wide enough, my lord?"

"That is perfect," he'd murmured mildly, giving in to his urge and looking down.

The sight that met his eyes—her prim, puffy lips and the tender pink petals they shielded—had knocked the words from his head.

Any thoughts of taunting or teasing her had fled instantly and he'd fallen on her like the obsessed deviant that he was.

Oh, how he had feasted on his angry young bride!

And how futilely she'd tried to ignore the pleasure building inside her. It had been difficult not to laugh as she'd struggled to remain non-responsive in the face of a full sensual onslaught.

Paul had ravaged her like a man possessed—possessed by *her*—forcing orgasm after orgasm from her sweet little cunt. Just the thought of how she'd swelled and slickened and writhed and begged beneath his mouth and tongue was enough to make him hard again.

She might never love him, but, by God, her body did.

He had given her all the pleasure she could stand—four times she'd climaxed before she'd whimpered that she couldn't do it again. Only then had he entered her, sheathing himself to his root and then riding her to a fifth and final orgasm, that last one shared.

Afterward, she'd been too sated to even notice when he'd turned on his side and wrapped an arm around her, dragging her back against his front, tucking his spent cock into the cleft of her arse, and cupping a generous handful of tit in the palm of one hand.

She had fallen asleep almost immediately, but Paul had been awake for at least an hour afterward.

It hadn't been unpleasant—not like those nights when his mind raced with *ideas* that wouldn't let him sleep even though his body was exhausted.

No, it had been a lazy, dozy experience—in which he'd felt both physically and emotionally sated—and he'd reveled in the moment, for once not wanting or yearning for anything else.

Of course such contentment hadn't been able to last. He'd eventually fallen asleep and woken a few hours later with a ragingly hard cock.

The rigid tension of her body in his arms told Paul that he wasn't the only one conscious of his throbbing prick nestled between her cheeks, pressed snugly against her tight little pucker.

Oh, the thoughts *that* had given him.

But there would be plenty of time to initiate her into the joys of that particular union in the months and years ahead.

Instead, he'd lifted her leg and brought it back over his hip. It was the first time he'd taken her twice in one night. His thick shaft had slid easily into her tight but primed sheath and her body had been warm and pliable in his arms as he'd fucked her with a slow, erotic rhythm.

Mounting a woman from behind like that was one of his favorite positions. It left the front of her body exposed and his hands free to explore. Paul had made the most of the opportunity, teasing her sensitive bud until she'd bucked and ground against him, trapped between his teasing fingers and his probing prick.

There was something about their size difference—Paul so huge and hard and Phoebe so small and soft—that rendered him insatiable for her.

Paul had always been highly sexual. Indeed, it was rare that he was without a mistress, but he'd ended things with Margaret once he'd become betrothed to Phoebe, which had meant he'd gone several weeks without a woman—which might explain why he was so hungry for her all the time.

But he didn't think that was true.

It was Phoebe herself, pure and simple.

Paul was aware that he was being even more domineering, demanding, and dictatorial with his new wife than he normally was with his women. While it was true that he had always liked—no, he *needed*—to control everything and everyone within his orbit, and a great deal that was well beyond it, Paul was even worse with Phoebe.

He had no idea why he was so taken with her.

She wasn't beautiful. Indeed, she was the sort of woman it would be easy to overlook in a *ton* ballroom. She was exceedingly small of stature, but sturdy rather than sylphlike. Her features were pleasingly regular, but nothing out of the common way. She was not especially accomplished—he was probably more proficient at the piano than she was and Lucy was a far better watercolorist.

Given the position of authority that she'd held in her father's household—the only one with common sense, it seemed—she was managing, opinionated, and argumentative. As those were three qualities that Paul possessed in spades, they were destined to lock horns, and one of them would have to lose.

Paul knew which of them it would be.

The only thing he could think that accounted for his wild infatuation was her seeming... untouchability.

It wasn't just that she was a *lady*. He'd fucked plenty of women with titles attached to their names.

No, it was her reserve—her remoteness.

He suspected she'd built a wall of reserve around her heart after that puling twit Lowery had broken her heart—or at least her pride. If there was one thing Paul knew about, it was building walls.

It wasn't that he wanted to smash her defenses—he respected her strength and vitality too much to want to do that—but he most certainly wanted to conquer the reserve she'd placed between them and gentle her to his touch.

Paul wanted—in cruder parlance—to have her eating out of his hand.

He had already accomplished that in their marriage bed and hoped that the power skirmishes over her wandering around the county unattended would soon come to an end, as well.

Last night in bed he had discovered something interesting. Rather than look annoyed when he'd taken her a second time, she had, for the first time he could recall, looked genuinely at peace this morning.

That is when he'd realized that just like him, Phoebe was highly sexual and required frequent release. A well-sated Phoebe was a more tractable Phoebe.

Paul was thrilled that he'd be the one to keep her satisfied.

But while he would allow her a certain degree of latitude when it came to their private lives, when it came to his household, there was only one master, and that was Paul.

He was honest enough with himself to admit he'd probably become *more*, rather than *less* controlling as he got older. Especially on matters like Phoebe's safety.

He was relieved that she'd obeyed him on the matter of a groom both yesterday and today. As invigorating as it was to lock horns with her, he did not enjoy actual conflict. He could think of far better ways to generate passion.

"My lord?"

Paul jolted at the sound of Dixon's voice; he'd forgotten the man was working at the other desk.

Paul turned to his secretary and smiled. "I'm sorry to keep you waiting while I gather wool." *And fantasize about fucking my wife.* "I am ready to go over the day's mail."

Dixon cleared his throat. It was a habit Paul had noticed in this younger man whenever he was in a position to deliver information that he didn't think would please the listener—primarily Paul.

"There were more… incidents."

Paul waited for the rest.

"Three of the new ovens were completely destroyed and another twenty will require a month to repair. Er, that will, naturally, slow the completion of the next batch."

Paul felt a familiar rage building inside his belly and turned away from his secretary so he wouldn't frighten the younger man.

This was the fifth act of sabotage at the Silkstone operation this year, alone.

"And still nobody was apprehended in connection with the vandalism?"

"No, sir."

Not that Paul had any doubts in his mind. But it would have been nice if the local constabulary had exerted themselves.

Still, he knew that was unreasonable of him. They were all related in the area and the local magistrate would be leery of stirring the nest when he would have to live with the results.

"I suppose I had better pay a visit."

"Very good, my lord. I shall make preparations for the journey. When would you like to leave?"

Paul stared sightlessly at the wall of books across from him, his mind working through the details before he spoke.

"Tomorrow," he said, turning to focus his gaze on his employee. "I shan't need you with me."

"Yes, sir. I've plenty to keep me busy here."

"I shall be taking Lady Needham with me so I'll want extra outriders."

Dixon hesitated only a fraction of a second before nodding.

"If you have something to say, please say it."

"Shall I send a message for Mr. Humboldt to accompany you, sir? Perhaps he might bring several of his associates with him?"

Humboldt was a Bow Street Runner who'd guarded Paul in the past and could pass for a groom.

"Yes, that is good thinking. He can guard my wife." Between Humboldt and Carthage she would be well protected if any trouble should arise. "I think Humboldt will be enough for the ride there but send word that four others should follow us up there later in the week."

"Very good, sir."

"What other business was there today?" Paul asked, his mind already on the journey ahead of him and what his wife would say when she learned that she would soon be visiting the very place that produced both Paul and his vulgar cit wealth.

***

"Tomorrow?" Phoebe said, even though she had heard her husband perfectly well.

"Yes." He glanced down at the stack of papers, clearly wishing to get back to them. He had sent word that he wanted to see her immediately after she'd returned from her ride.

So, she had come to him without changing from her habit, her boots dirty and body sweaty, smelling of horse.

"But, what about the dinner party I was to give next Thursday?"

His grimace told her that he'd forgotten about their first function as a married couple.

"I am sorry," he said, sounding it. "You will have to cancel it."

She shrugged and then smiled when he looked surprised. "I wasn't really looking forward to it without any of my family being here. I shall send out messages directly. Er, might I know what has happened?"

"Some issues have arisen at the new property in Leeds—in Middleton, to be precise. I thought I could manage them from here, but my presence is necessary."

"Would it be all right to tell people that you've been called away on a matter of some importance, then."

"Yes, that will do."

"And how long shall we stay?"

"I don't know," he admitted, looking rather harried as he pinched the bridge of his nose above his spectacles. "I'm sorry," he added, although she'd not said anything. "I am not purposely being vague."

"I only ask because I had accepted a few invitations for us for the week after next. I shall just cancel them all."

"That would be best."

Phoebe had left him, then, eager to get on with it.

The rest of the afternoon fled so quickly it had been bedtime before she knew it.

She'd had Spragg prepare her for bed, as usual, vaguely aware that her neck and back felt achy. Not until she'd sent her maid away and crawled into her own bed had she realized how exhausted she was.

She had only intended to close her eyes for a few moments, to rest before Needham came to her. But the next thing she knew, it was morning and Spragg was standing beside the bed.

A quick glance at her husband's pillow showed it was undisturbed.

Phoebe stared for a long moment, even though there was nothing to see. He must have come to her room, found her asleep, and returned to his own bed.

It startled her to realize that she regretted not staying awake for him.

She shook herself and pushed back the blankets; there would be more nights. Many more.

Not until she'd risen and stripped off her nightgown did Phoebe discover that she had started her courses sometime during the night.

So, she was not pregnant.

For some reason, she had the strangest urge to cry.

Chapter Twenty

The Great North Road

Phoebe stared out at the falling gloom, her mind on the rapidly approaching journey's end.

This was the farthest she'd ever been from home—both geographically and temporally—and it was proving more jarring than she would have guessed. She missed everything about home—not just her family, but her routine and the familiar surroundings.

Even though three days had passed, she was still strangely dejected that her courses had begun the morning of their trip.

It astounded her how much she'd hoped to be with child.

Indeed, if somebody would have asked her, six months ago, if she was desperate for children, she would have denied it.

Yes, but six months ago you didn't have proof of your husband's virility living under your very own roof.

The thought shamed her—even though it was only inside her head. Could she really be competitive about such a thing?

She hoped not.

Phoebe wasn't only saddened that she wasn't pregnant, she was also confused and more than a little worried. Was something wrong with her? After all, her mother, her only source of information on pregnancy—a rather reliable one as she'd been in that felicitous state many times herself—had made it sound as if only one episode were required to make a normally fecund female pregnant.

Which begged the question whether Phoebe was even *capable* of becoming pregnant as Paul, it was still difficult to think his name, even in the privacy of her own head—had bred her often—a few times twice on the same evening.

She glanced from under her lashes to where he sat, as usual engaged in poring over inscrutable documents.

He wore spectacles when he needed to read and something about the sight of such a big, powerful man with delicate gold-rimmed spectacles perched on his giant beak of a nose caused a fluttering in her belly. Even the unpleasant cramping she'd been experiencing over the three-day journey—which he had purposely taken more slowly for her sake—couldn't ruin the delicious sensation.

His expression was one of utter concentration and his fascinating mouth—yet another thing that gave her flutterings as she remembered how skilled his stern, thin lips could be—was compressed in a frown of concentration as he compared something on one document with another and then used a stub of pencil to scribble something in the margin.

His lashes were easily as long and thick as Doddy's, except soot black where her brother's were golden. They were almost amusingly delicate and pretty on a face that was decidedly neither of those things.

Was it wanton of her that she had missed him these past three nights? He had engaged two chambers at each of the inns where they had stayed. They'd dined together in private parlors, but after their meals he had excused himself, leaving her to entertain herself until bedtime.

Phoebe was accustomed to having all her sisters and her brother to liven up an evening with card games or other foolishness. Even at Wych House she'd had Lucy to amuse her during the days and Mr. Dixon at dinner, Paul afterward in the library, although they had done very little talking.

She was, she realized with a shock, rather lonely without any social interaction.

Phoebe yearned to ask him what he did when he left after dinner and wished she had the courage to ask if she might join him. Even if he only went somewhere to read, surely they could sit in companionable silence, as they'd done during the carriage ride?

He had been everything that was polite, courteous, and thoughtful on the long days on the road. The carriage itself was wonderfully luxurious and filled with plush rugs and cushions to assure her of every comfort. With four liveried servants and another two outriders, they travelled in a manner which was as grand as any duke's.

The innkeepers had, without fail, rushed out to greet them when they'd stopped each night. Not only was Lord Needham well-known, but he appeared to be well-liked and almost venerated by those they encountered.

It is his money they respect; his wealth is the reason they toad-eat him.

"Did you need something, my dear?" the man she was thinking about and staring at asked, his low baritone shattering the silence.

Phoebe blinked at him, confused.

"You were looking at me as if I were a... puzzle. And not an especially pleasing one."

Predictably, her face heated. "No, I, er, was thinking of something entirely different." She turned to look out the window, the sight beyond the glass depressing in its ugliness. "When will we arrive at Hill House?"

"Shortly," he said, putting his paperwork into his satchel and then rising from his seat just enough to move over to her side. "Scoot over a little," he ordered, when she merely gawked up at him.

Phoebe pushed herself all the way to the corner of the seat. Even so, when he sat beside her his huge body touched hers from calf to shoulder.

He leaned even closer—the heat from his body and the faint lemony scent of his cologne annoyingly intoxicating—and pointed to a hideous sort of tower with smoke puffing out of it. "There is my newest blast furnace."

Phoebe stared at the eyesore, one of many in an area that was riddled with them. What was she supposed to say? How pretty?

"Oh, how... interesting," is what she managed.

He chuckled, his laugh vibrating through her body. "Not attractive, I'll grant you, but extremely productive and lucrative."

The carriage crested a slight rise and she saw evidence of even more industry marring the landscape. But there were also several rows of quaint little cottages some distance off the road, each a bit different, but somehow similar enough to know they'd been built by the same craftsman.

"Are those new?" she asked, scrambling for something to say that wasn't offensive.

"Yes. They are all occupied by people who work for me." He paused and then added, "The company has constructed over two hundred of them in the last five years."

Phoebe's jaw dropped. "Goodness! That seems a great many."

"Yes, but we still need a great many more."

"You must have a lot of workers."

"Thousands."

Phoebe took a moment to consider his answer. Thousands? That was far, far more than she ever would have believed possible. She tried to imagine being responsible for so many employees and simply could not wrap her mind around it. She'd found it daunting to make sure that Mr. and Mrs. Parks and Maisy were paid every month.

"That is a great many people," she finally said, unashamed that she sounded awed. It *was* awe-inspiring.

"Needham Iron provides one-eighth of all British cast iron production."

She heard the pride in his voice and, for once, she understood it and found it touching rather than vulgar.

The carriage slowed and she saw they were nearing a small village.

People stopped what they were doing and turned to watch, others came out of shops and stores and stood as if witnessing visiting royalty.

Phoebe had to twist her body to look at Needham.

His hooded gaze was on her rather than the crowds that were rapidly gathering.

"They have come out to greet you," she said.

His mouth pulled into a smile that was cold. "Paying tribute to a cit."

Phoebe huffed. "You will never forget that, will you?"

Rather than answer, his eyes slid to the window and widened at something. His expression shifted from bored and sleepy to positively savage.

Phoebe followed the path of his glare to three men standing at the edge of the crowd. A woman stood beside them; a baby cradled in her arms. All four scowled as they watched the carriage roll past.

"Who are they?" she asked.

He sat back and stared straight ahead. "Who do you mean?"

"The four people you were glaring at—and who were glaring right back at you."

He shrugged, his shoulder brushing against hers. "There are people who are not happy with what I've done here."

"But, why? If you are building houses and bringing jobs?"

"Some think they are not the right kind of jobs."

"You mean iron work?"

He gestured to the window on the other side.

They had already left the village behind and the road wound between several large structures, all belching various quantities of smoke into the air.

"There are also two potteries, a glassworks, a brickworks, and a rolling mill."

Indeed, it all appeared to be a great hive of industry with people bustling all around the buildings even though it was dusk.

"What is a rolling mill?" she asked.

He gave her a quizzical look.

"What? Why are you looking at me like that?" Phoebe asked.

"Do you really want to know the answer?"

"I wouldn't have asked if I didn't."

He turned to look out the window. "I wouldn't have thought vulgar industry was of any interest to you."

Phoebe then did something she'd only ever done to her two younger siblings. She reached out with her gloved hand and took *his* chin—the way he had done to her so often—and turned his face to hers.

She would have laughed out loud at his shocked expression if she'd not been so peeved.

"The clothing on my back, my brother's schooling, indeed—everything I have comes from your *vulgar industry*. I've said foolish—apparently unforgiveable—things about you and your business in the past. But I am hardly so hypocritical as to reap the rewards yet revile the source of all my comfort. So please, my lord, if you cannot forgive the foolish things I said, perhaps you might strive to at least forget them?"

His brooding stare was almost tangible in its weight. She had, in some way, obviously insulted him again.

Phoebe dropped her hand and began to turn away, only to have her chin seized in response.

"You are right," he said.

Her lips parted in surprise.

He barked a laugh. "You are right to look bumfuzzled, because it is rare that I am in the wrong."

"Or at least rare that you admit it," she retorted.

Merry glints lighted his strange eyes. "I will both forgive and forget—under one condition."

Phoebe rolled her eyes, remembering the last time he'd had *only one condition*.

He nodded, even though she'd not spoken. "Yes, I am a merchant and I always require payment in either coin or like kind."

"Very well, let us bargain. Although I should warn you that I have a good deal of experience with haggling, myself," Phoebe said.

His eyebrows shot up. "Indeed?"

"Oh, yes. Mr. Andrews, the butcher in Little Sissingdon, more than once thought to fob me off with inferior cuts of meat."

He grinned and the rare expression warmed her. "Duly noted."

'What is your condition, my lord?"

"I shall endeavor to forget the past if you will call me by my name. Not in front of others, of course," he hastened to add when she opened her mouth to demur. "But when we are alone." His cold eyes heated. "Especially when we are intimate."

Phoebe raised her hands to her cheeks, the cool kid leather heating quickly upon touching her hot skin. "You do like to make me blush, don't you, my lo—er"—she heaved a sigh—"Paul."

He smiled. "There, that was not so difficult, was it?"

It had actually been *very* difficult, but there was no need to be truthful. "No, it was not."

Before he could respond, the carriage slowed and then turned.

"Ah, we are almost there," he said, again pointing to the window on her side. "There is your first look at Hill House."

***

Paul saw both admiration and relief color her features when she saw Hill House. "Oh, it is quite lovely."

He could see that she'd been dreading some reproduction gothic monstrosity that several industrialists had recently built, complete with turrets and a moat.

"It was built in the 1640s," he said. "Some insist that it was one of Inigo Jones's early projects although there is no proof of that."

Her gaze fastened to the entrance to the house, where the servants awaited the carriage, neatly arranged in one long row to meet their new mistress.

"That is an unusual but lovely entryway," she said.

"It is known as an aedicular doorway, which draws its inspiration from a Roman shrine."

She turned her torso slowly, until she was facing him, "I am impressed."

"Don't be—my knowledge of architecture extends only far enough to understand my houses. I daresay it shall be years before I am fully conversant with Wych House."

She smiled. "By then it shall be Doddy's home and you will be forced to memorize some new property."

Paul's breath caught in his throat at her teasing and something unpleasant uncoiled in his belly. He wondered if his answering smile was as stilted as it felt.

Fortunately, they were at their destination and the carriage came to a halt before she might have noticed.

Paul opened the door before any of the grooms or Phoebe's footman could do so, putting down the steps and then handing her out.

She had an expression on her face that he recognized from the day she had met the servants at Wych House, none of whom had been there when she'd been a girl. It was a gracious, ladylike smile that managed to be pleasant without being *too* friendly.

It was yet another characteristic that was probably bred into her blood and bones. Paul couldn't ape a similar expression if he practiced in front of a looking glass for a year.

The pride that bloomed in his belly as he took in his aristocratic wife both annoyed and amused him. As if he had anything at all to do with her breeding.

He was becoming as big a sycophant as his father had been when it came to aristocrats, albeit only with one particular woman.

Paul turned to find Mrs. Hodge and Norris waiting for him.

"It is a pleasure to see you," he said, speaking truthfully. He'd known both servants for most of his life.

"We've *just* managed to finish the master and mistress chambers yesterday," Mrs. Hodge said, smiling from Paul to Phoebe. "It will be all new and fresh for you, my lady."

Phoebe cut him a startled glance. "How efficient you are, my lord."

Paul tried not to preen.

The next few minutes were taken up with yet another masterful—or should it be mistressful—display of ease and refinement as Phoebe met her new servants, all the way down to the ten-year-old boot boy, who happened to be one of Norris's many nieces and nephews.

"What will it be, my dear? A tour, or a rest first?" he asked.

The tightness around her eyes told him her answer before she spoke. "I will save the tour for tomorrow, when I am fresh. Tea and then a bath, would be lovely," she said, smiling at Mrs. Hodge.

The housekeeper nodded. "Right away, my lady."

"I shall show my wife up to her chambers," Paul said, his nod dismissing both upper servants.

"Thank you for agreeing to postpone the house tour," she murmured as they ascended the staircase. "I never would have imagined that sitting all day could be so fatiguing."

No doubt that was compounded by her courses. Paul had had enough mistresses over the years to know that some women suffered greatly for five days every month. Indeed, Ellen was all but prostrate—even before her illness had worsened.

Paul was wise enough to keep those observations to himself.

"Is this where you grew up?" she asked as he led her to the second-floor landing and turned right.

"Here and at Castleton, which is a house my father had built in Cumberland."

"Do you go there often?"

"It is now occupied by a tenant." No need to explain who that tenant was and why Paul never went there.

Paul opened the door to the chambers that had once belonged to his mother and watched his wife's reaction.

"Oh, it is lovely," she said, her eyes wide as she gazed around at the seafoam green and pale blue room, which looked cool and refreshing, as if it were underwater.

"It was my mother's room," he said as they walked through to the dressing room and then on to the private sitting room. "It hadn't been occupied since her death and was desperately in need of refreshing. I believe the furniture is mostly the same, but all the hangings, carpets, and so forth are newly done."

She looked delighted when she turned to him. "It is beautiful—so cool and restful. It was very thoughtful of you. Thank you."

"It was my pleasure." And it had been, too. Paul wanted to make her happy—to keep her satisfied in every possibly way. Yes, he was a besotted fool for his wife.

There was a light knock on the door and then Spragg entered, accompanied by Charles, Phoebe's personal footman, who was laden down with a trunk of prodigious size.

Paul had advised her to pack for as long as three weeks, but he hoped to have matters in hand long before then.

"Oh, that is not mine," she said when another servant deposited a smaller version of the big portmanteau.

"You may leave it here," Paul said to the servant, and then turned to his wife. "It is yours." He smiled faintly. "A wedding gift from me." *And for me*, he might have added.

Her cheeks colored prettily. "Oh. Thank you."

Just imagining her wearing one of the garments he'd chosen made him hard and he wondered how much longer until her courses were over and he could visit her bed.

Paul had been amused that Phoebe had chosen to use their body servants to communicate such delicate information. Spragg had told Symond—Paul's valet—about her mistress's courses, and then Symond had relayed that information to Paul.

The aristocracy, he knew from experience, disliked embarrassing personal conversations even more than poverty, filth, or discomfort.

Personally, Paul been torn between disappointment that she was not breeding and relief that childbirth—and all its inherent dangers—had been put off for at least another month.

As badly as Paul wanted to see her swollen with his child, he couldn't forgot that his own mother had died in childbed.

Although he'd been told that a woman's size had nothing to do with ease of pregnancy, Paul couldn't help being worried for Phoebe, who was so small he couldn't imagine her having an easy time of it.

Phoebe began to direct her servants on where she wanted things, so Paul left her to her unpacking and went to the bookroom.

He pulled the servant cord and didn't have to wait long until Norris was at the door.

"Has my brother been here recently?" he asked, seeing no point in beating about the bush.

Norris's fiery blush told him the answer before the man could summon words.

"I know he would have made it difficult for you, Norris, so you needn't feel guilty."

Norrish sagged with relief. "Thank you, my lord. I was drafting a letter to you about his visit, but—"

"But you thought a conversation would be easier?"

Norrish grimaced. "Well, perhaps not easier, but less complicated."

Paul sat at his desk and looked at the drawer on the bottom right, which was slightly open when it should have been locked. Inside the drawer was a cashbox. Paul already knew what he would find—nothing—when he opened the lid.

He closed the drawer and looked up at Norris, whose face was puckered with misery.

"I'm sorry, my lord. He was in here less than five minutes—I'm afraid the newest footman didn't know he was not to—"

"Hush," he murmured, feeling guilty for making the older man so anxious.

And furious at his idiot brother for putting Norris in this position.

"Do not punish the new footman, Norris. The poor fellow could not have guessed my own brother wouldn't be allowed into the house. So, when did this take place?"

"Six days ago, my lord."

"He is at his mother's?" Gideon's mother, Susan Temple, owned a lavish, gaudy mansion a mere four miles from Hill House. Paul knew that Norris had at least three family members working for Mrs. Temple.

"He keeps a room there but apparently spends much of his time, er, carousing, and rarely even dines at home."

Paul snorted. That would have displeased her. Gideon was Susan's only child and the light of her existence. The fact that he treated her execrably only seemed to make her love him more.

"Any more vandalism here at Hill House?" he asked.

"Not since you sent the two men to keep watch, my lord."

The men in question were ex-Runners, both of whom Paul employed full-time for a variety of issues.

Norris softly cleared his throat. "There is one more thing."

Paul sighed. "Yes?"

"Dick Whitten's daughter came to call on you. She'd been told you were arriving yesterday. Mrs. Hodge sent her away with a flea in her ear, but she is a bold piece, er, begging your pardon, my lord."

Paul chuckled. "I recall Sabrina quite well. Still cutting up her poor father's peace, I take it?"

"She has aged poor Whitten badly," Norris said in a rare moment of candor. "He'd believed her betrothed to Ned Bateman's son, but"—he shrugged his shoulders.

"Yes, I'd heard that was over. Any idea what she wants from me?"

"She wants a chambermaid position."

"I thought she was working for Mrs. Temple?"

"Er, not any longer, sir."

So, his stepmother had fired the girl, had she? Paul couldn't say he was surprised.

"What are your thoughts about giving her a job?" Paul asked.

"While it is true that she is a handful, Poundstone—Mrs. Temple's butler, you know—said she was good at her job. It is only with the male members of the staff that there was some trouble."

That was a kind assessment. Paul had known Sabrina Whitten all her life. Dick Whitten had always indulged her and now, at seventeen, she was an astoundingly beautiful and willful young woman who believed she could manipulate everyone as easily as she did her father.

Paul often visited Whitten to check on him, bringing a basket of delicacies as he did with all his injured employees, and Sabrina had made it clear the last few times he'd visited their house that she was his for the taking.

Indeed, she'd become so pestersome that Paul had sent one of the servants with the last basket, not wishing to deal with her.

"Why did she leave Mrs. Temple's?"

"There were vague accusations about misplaced items, but Mrs. Temple never laid an information against the girl. It's my belief that she didn't want the girl about when Mr. Gideon came to visit, my lord. "

Paul snorted. He could see the wisdom in that; Sabrina Whitten was appealing enough to tempt a dead man.

"Do you want to hire her—won't she upset the happy balance you have here?"

Norris sighed. "She needs work, my lord. Whitten is in a bad way and I know he worries what will happen to her when he is gone."

Dick Whitten had been a friend of Paul's when they'd both been lads. Later, he'd worked for Paul as a keel bully—one of the men who loaded and unloaded coal— before his leg had been badly crushed in an accident. Paul had given him one of the new cottages and carried him without any rent as well as giving him a quarterly allowance, which he did for any employee who'd been injured while at work.

If Dick managed his money, he should enjoy a comfortable living. But that didn't include taking care of a daughter who liked to live beyond her means.

"I'll go talk to Whitten," Paul said. "In the meantime, hire the girl—so long as Mrs. Hodge does not disapprove," he added, earning a faint smile from the other man. Norris and Hodge were both married to others and yet often reminded Paul of a long-married couple who could read each other's minds.

"What have you heard about the Nott family lately?"

Norris's expression became grim. "*She* came up here demanding that we send word to you that she needed more money."

Paul tried not to scowl. "Why didn't you mention that Lily came here in your last letter?"

"It only happened a few days ago, sir."

The Nott family was comprised of one married brother, Robert; two unmarried brothers, Tom and Nate; and their unmarried sister, Lily, and her out-of-wedlock child.

Paul had made enemies of the Notts when he'd bought the greater part of their property from their father, who'd been deeply in debt to a moneylender in Leeds and had come to Paul begging for help.

He sometimes wondered if Richard Nott had expected Paul to just *give* him the money, because apparently purchasing it at well over market value had not been enough to satisfy the old man or his sons.

Richard Nott drank himself to death, poisoning his sons' minds against Paul in the process.

Although a rich coal seam ran through the corner of their property, the Notts had, over several generations, extracted most of the easily accessible coal using shallow bell pits. By the time Paul bought their land they were barely eking out a living.

After Paul purchased the property he began to mine the seam using a series of adits and had built honeycomb ovens to process the coal into coke.

While it was true that he would get a great deal of money out of the property over time, it required a lot of capital to develop it—more than the Nott family would ever have been able to save or borrow.

If Paul hadn't purchased the land, the Notts would have been forced to sell to somebody else within the next year or two and likely for far less than Paul had paid.

Common sense told Paul that the three brothers—none of whom were employed—were at least some of the vandals his brother Gideon was working with.

While the Notts weren't the most popular family in the area, people would still close ranks around them and it would make it difficult for local officials to investigate.

The men Paul was bringing from London would have both an easier and harder time finding answers. Easier because they had no loyalties at stake and harder because the locals wouldn't be forthcoming.

All in all, it was an explosive situation and Paul did not feel optimistic that it would have a good ending.

And he could thank his brother Gideon for creating most of the trouble.

Chapter Twenty-One

Phoebe quickly discovered that she had nowhere near as much work to do at Hill House as she'd needed to do at poor Wych House.

Thanks to Mrs. Hodge, the house operated as smoothly as a finely made watch.

The housekeeper had worked for Needham's family since before Paul's birth and she was vocal in her affection—near worship—for the current master of the house. In fact, *all* the servants looked positively overjoyed that her husband was visiting.

Mrs. Hodge—over a cozy cup of tea and Cook's divine macaroons—had confided in Phoebe just how *Master Paul* had come to be such a universally beloved employer.

"I've been with Master Paul the longest. In fact, I started off as a housemaid here, working for his father," she said, and then flushed at her declaration, almost as if she were embarrassed to be boasting.

Phoebe thought it charming; her mother and father had never engendered such love and loyalty in their servants.

"You knew his lordship's mother, then," Phoebe said.

"Oh, yes. Mrs. Needham—because this was before his lordship was ennobled—was a lovely woman."

As the housekeeper had already shown Phoebe the small portrait gallery, complete with a full-length portrait of Needham's mother—she knew the housekeeper was not speaking literally. It had been unnerving just how much her husband resembled his mother, both in physical size and appearance. It would be stretching it to call the woman *handsome*.

"She was the second Mrs. Needham," Mrs. Hodge went on. "The first Mrs. Needham, bless her, also died in childbed."

Phoebe swallowed that information like a dry lump of bread that did not want to go down. Suddenly, she wasn't all that remorseful that she wasn't yet pregnant.

"The master was such a good little boy," Mrs. Hodge said, smiling fondly. "He got into mischief, of course, but never in a cruel or destructive way like—er, like so many little boys can be."

Phoebe had trouble picturing her stern, hard-working husband *getting into mischief*. She had envisioned a sober child who did all the sums his tutor assigned and then asked for more.

"The house was so empty and quiet when he went away to school." Mrs. Hodge's mouth puckered, giving Phoebe some idea what she thought about the aristocratic practice of sending young boys away to be schooled.

Phoebe struggled to dredge up the little Needham had shared about his family—which was almost nothing.

"Did his lordship's father remarry after his second wife's death?" Phoebe asked.

Mrs. Hodge jolted and the cup and saucer slipped from her fingers, spilling tea all over her lap. She yelped and leapt to her feet.

"My goodness," Phoebe exclaimed, handing the older woman her table napkin. "Did you burn yourself?"

"No, no, I am fine," she insisted, ineffectually daubing at her gown. "I *do* beg your pardon, how clumsy of me. I don't know what—"

A sharp knock on the door cut her off.

"Yes, come in," Mrs. Hodge called out.

The maid who entered looked startled by the scene. "Er, sorry to disturb you, but Mrs. Temple is here to see her ladyship."

"*What?*" the housekeeper shrieked.

Phoebe winced.

"You didn't tell her the mistress was at home to visitors, did you?" Mrs. Hodge demanded

"I didn't mean to, ma'am, but you know how she is and—"

"Hush!" Mrs. Hodge ordered sharply, looking so pale that Phoebe took her arm.

"You should sit down, Mrs. Hodge." She turned the servant. "Fetch some hartshorn from my maid and bring it back directly."

"Oh, that is not necessary," Mrs. Hodge protested feebly. "I have some in the cabinet."

Sally scurried to where Mrs. Hodge pointed.

"Who is Mrs. Temple, ma'am," Phoebe asked the housekeeper while the girl put a few drops into a glass of water.

"Is the master here, Sally?" Mrs. Hodge asked, ignoring Phoebe's question.

"No, ma'am. He's gone out to the new kilns and shan't be back until just before dinner."

Phoebe's antennae, which had already been twitching at the housekeeper's strange behavior, began to positively vibrate.

"You stay with Mrs. Hodge, Sally. I shall go see this Mrs. Temple."

Mrs. Hodge whimpered. "Oh, I don't think that is such a—"

"What room is she in, Sally?" Phoebe asked.

"I put her in the Rose room, my lady."

Phoebe brushed off the housekeeper's efforts to detain her and strode from the room.

She didn't know what to expect based on her housekeeper's reaction, but it certainly was not the woman she encountered.

Mrs. Temple, whoever she was, was an exceedingly lovely woman in perhaps her mid-fifties. She was dressed in the kick of fashion, although perhaps a bit too flamboyantly, for a morning call in the country.

"Ah, Lady Needham, such a delight to finally meet you," the woman said in a heavy Yorkshire accent.

Finally?

"The honor is mine," Phoebe said coolly. "Won't you have a seat, ma'am?"

"Yes, thank you. You are probably wondering what I'm doing barging in when thee—er, when *you* are not yet receiving callers."

Phoebe *was* wondering about that but was too well bred to say it. "I am pleased that you called," she lied quietly.

Mrs. Temple crowed with delight. "There, now! I knew you'd see it that way. I thought as we were the closest thing to family that we shouldn't stand on ceremony."

"Family?"

Mrs. Temple, who had lovely sky-blue eyes, gave a chuckle that was probably meant to sound indulgent, but came off bitter and angry. "Oh, that naughty Paul did not tell you about his step mama, did he?"

Or at least that is what she thought the woman said as her accent was almost incomprehensible to Phoebe's southern ears.

As Phoebe struggled to decipher the words and then absorb their meaning, the door to the sitting room opened and Norris entered, looking as though he'd sprinted across the house to get there.

"Yes?" Phoebe said when the normally staid butler merely glared at Mrs. Temple.

"You can't protect her from the truth, Daniel." Mrs. Temple smiled triumphantly at the butler, who looked at her with such open loathing it took Phoebe's breath away.

"Please have a tea tray sent up," Phoebe said, effectively putting an end to whatever was transpiring between the two of them.

Norris's expression went from angry to mortified. "Of course, my lady." He cut Mrs. Temple one last stern look before leaving them alone.

"Perhaps you might tell me what this is all about," Phoebe said, using her coolest, yet still polite, tone.

Mrs. Temple laughed. "Oh, no—don't poker up. You were so prettily polite before."

Phoebe waited.

Mrs. Temple sighed and Phoebe saw something of the ravishing girl she must have once been in the petulant gesture.

"I was not the former Lord Needham's wife, but I *am* the mother of his child."

Phoebe's eyes widened. "But I thought the viscount's mother died in—"

"Lord! Not *Paul.*" She gave a raucous laugh that was at odds with her delicate appearance. "No, Gideon is my boy."

The next quarter hour proved to be almost as shocking as the day Paul had come to her parents' sitting room at Queen's Bower.

Mrs. Temple, it turned out, had been a chamber maid in the former Lord Needham's employ. And then she'd become his mistress and borne him three children, only one of whom had survived infancy.

All this had apparently happened while Paul's father had been married to Paul's mother.

Phoebe clutched at the tea tray like a lifeline when it arrived, her mind reeling over what she'd just learned.

"And how old is your son, Mrs. Temple?" she asked as she engaged in the familiar, soothing ritual of preparing tea.

"Oh, do call me Suki! I still think on me mother when I hear *Mrs. Temple*."

Which meant there had never been a *Mister* Temple.

"Gideon was born almost a month before his brother." Mrs. Temple glanced around the sitting room and her expression soured. "But for a flip of the blanket all this would be my Gideon's."

Phoebe's mouth opened, but she couldn't think of what to say.

"Oh, I beg your pardon," Mrs. Temple said, chuckling. "That won't be the sort of thing a lady says at tea, will it?"

Or any other place.

Rather than answer, Phoebe said, "You moved away when your son was born?"

Suki frowned. "'Course not! Why would I?"

Good. God.

Phoebe noticed that her hand hurt and realized she'd been squeezing the handle of the tea strainer so hard it left marks in her skin.

"It was a good thing I stayed," Suki added with a forthright nod. "Why, Paul was just a wee motherless thing. He nursed at my own breast, just like his brother." She smiled fondly. "Those were peaceful times; me holding one at each teat." She clucked her tongue. "Two more different wee'uns you'd never find. My Gideon as delicate and pretty as an angel and Paul such a big, ugly thing."

Phoebe frowned at her crude description—but Mrs. Temple was so lost in the past that she didn't notice.

She was then angry at herself for feeling offended on her husband's behalf when he was clearly bent on following in his father's footsteps when it came to keeping wives and mistresses beneath the same roof.

Which of the housemaids at Wych House had Paul selected to be wetnurse to Phoebe's infant if she were to die in childbed?

"It's in their blood, lass."

Phoebe looked up from her awful thoughts to find Mrs. Temple eyeing her almost kindly.

"I beg your pardon?"

The older woman just smiled at her frosty tone, making Phoebe feel like a squalling toddler.

"Did you see the painting of my Jonathan in the gallery?" she asked.

Phoebe assumed she meant the first Viscount Needham.

"Yes."

"He looked nothing like Paul—and not much like my Gideon, neither."

Phoebe had noticed that Paul's father had been a small, rat-faced man who'd shared almost *no* resemblance with his monstrously huge son.

"There might be no physical resemblance between father and sons, but they're as alike as three peas in a pod when it comes to runnin' about and spreading their seed."

Phoebe gasped and the other woman laughed.

"Oh, I am such a thoughtless vulgar thing, aren't I?" She set down her largely untouched cup of tea and pushed to her feet. "I shouldn't have come, but I wanted to have a look at you. Ellen said you were just a plain dab of a thing but as dignified as a queen."

Phoebe's face heated. Not at being called a plain—she was accustomed to that—but it was unnerving to discover that her husband's mistress was corresponding with her husband's *father's* mistress.

Mrs. Temple heaved a tragic sigh and, once again, made that annoying tongue clucking noise. "Poor Paul."

Poor Paul? What in the world did *that* mean?

Phoebe was dying to know, but she refused to ask.

It turned out she didn't have to.

"Ellen was the love of Paul's life, you know," Suki said, her expression contemplative as she strolled around the room, examining various items as she went. "The way he carried on about Catherine made a person believe there wouldn't be another for him. But then only five years later, Paul was knocked sideways yet again."

It was astonishing how painful those words were, even though Phoebe should have suspected something like that. While she had never seen Paul and Ellen Kettering in the same room, she'd seen him with Lucy often enough and it was clear that he loved her dearly.

"Who was Catherine?" Phoebe asked, before she could stop herself.

Mrs. Temple looked pleased by her interest. "Just a little village tart Paul thought he was in love with." She snorted. "Why, he was barely sixteen at the time. Just like all young lads who fall for the first girl they"—she broke off and grimaced, her humorous gaze on Phoebe's likely horrified face. "Never you mind about Catherine; she's married to the wainwright and has five strapping children. But Ellen, now, *she* is a whole different kettle of fish.

"For a time, I thought Paul might marry her, but he was like his father in that way and would not demean himself by marrying downward. And Ellen was certainly a long step down—at least by then."

Phoebe struggled to follow the woman's vague story, ashamed by how desperately she wanted to know more.

Suki stopped pacing and fingered one of the gold brocade drapes.

"Oh, these are lovely. I'll wager *Hodgey* picked them out, didn't she?" She cut Phoebe a conspiratorial look. "She always did like to behave as if she were mistress of—" She broke off and squinted out the window. "Well! What's *she* doing here?"

Phoebe knew she should just run from the room while the other woman was distracted, but something drew her to Suki's side like her own personal siren luring her toward rocks.

Outside the window a striking red-headed woman was engaged in what looked to be a heated dispute with three male servants.

Mrs. Temple did a bit more clucking. "She's a beauty, just like her ma was."

Phoebe had to agree; even from a distance the woman's loveliness was blinding. "Who is she?"

"That's Lila Nott."

The woman, Lila, held up the bundle in her arms and jerked her chin at the house.

"Is that her child she is waving around so roughly?" Phoebe asked, a sick feeling in her stomach.

"Aye. Poor, wee, fatherless babe."

"How did the father die?" Phoebe asked.

Suki gave her a startled look and then barked a laugh. "He didn't."

Phoebe's face scalded as she took the other woman's meaning.

Lila Nott had seen them in the window and had stopped her ranting. Instead, she was staring, her exquisite features twisted in anger.

Phoebe recalled where she'd seen her before; this was the woman who'd glared at their carriage with so much hostility when they'd first arrived. She had worn a bonnet then, so her distinctive hair had been covered.

"I daresay she's here for more money. It's not like Paul to be so mean."

Phoebe turned to the older woman. "Are you intimating that is my husband's child."

Mrs. Temple's eyes went round with shock and for a moment phoebe thought she would apologize.

But then she burst out laughing.

When she could catch her breath, she met Phoebe's seething gaze and patted her cheek with one lilac scented hand. "Oh, you poor innocent thing. Why, it's a good thing I've come today—although I'll likely get a proper scolding from Paul when he learns of it. That'll be soon as I'm guessing even now Hodgey or Norris will be running to tell him."

"What are you implying about that woman's baby?" Phoebe repeated.

Mrs. Temple gave her a pitying look. "The Needham men are virile, my lady. Lord knows I tamed my Johnny as much as I could, but he still wandered, even at his age. They're just more needful of variety than most other men." She jerked her chin toward the woman who'd gone back to arguing with the servants.

"Mostly Paul is real generous with his by-blows and their mothers. But the Nott boys have been causing problems for him since he bought that land out from under them. That trouble is why Paul is here, I suppose." She snorted and added sourly, "The good Lord knows he never comes home for the pleasure of it."

Suki frowned at whatever she saw on Phoebe's face—likely rage, frustration, and despair.

Predictably, she clucked her tongue. "Oh, you poor, poor child. You can't tame or change men of their sort. They're gods—or leastways kings—to the people here. They can do whatever they want, with nobody to stop them. It's difficult to fault them when the women round here are after them like bitches in heat."

Phoebe flinched, but Suki was too caught up to notice.

"There's a word for doin' things and getting away with it." Mrs. Temple's brow creased. "Imp—something."

"Impunity," Phoebe said quietly.

"Aye, impunity. The Needham men do whatever they like to whoever they like and the people here allow it. The men all work for Paul, so they pull their forelocks and bow while their wives and daughters flock to him like flies to honey. They're made that way and you just need to enjoy what they choose to share with you." Her gaze, suddenly acquisitive, flickered around the room. "And Paul has given you a considerable amount, hasn't he, dearie? Not only has he made you a viscountess, which is more than my Johnny did for me, but I'll wager he was plenty generous with settlements, wasn't he?"

Phoebe had no intention of answering such an impertinent question.

Mrs. Temple looked amused at whatever she saw on Phoebe's face. "Don't fret. You'll get all this" she waved a hand around them—"and plenty of him, too, if Paul's even half as randy as Jonathan was. And all it costs you is to look the other way on occasion."

Phoebe couldn't bear contemplating a future where her husband's mistresses and illegitimate children were everywhere she turned. She had been foolish to believe that it wouldn't hurt to think of him with other women.

Not that she would change what she had done even if such a thing were possible.

As miserable as it would be to endure such a marriage, she could not regret saving her sisters from such a dreadful fate.

Not to mention that you are utterly infatuated with him and can't bear to think of anyone else with him.

Phoebe didn't bother to deny the accusation. Susan Temple had accurately described Paul Needham in one way—he *was* like a king. And while his enormous wealth and power was certainly part of his appeal, it was the man himself Phoebe found irresistible.

Just when had she begun to feel that way about him?

"Well, look at that!" Mrs. Temple's voice startled Phoebe out of her uncomfortable musing. "I've overstayed my welcome and been here almost an hour. I'll show myself out." Mrs. Temple chuckled. "Lord knows I'm familiar enough with this house since I've cleaned every inch of it."

Phoebe didn't bother to answer or walk the woman out—a horrific breech of manners and by far the rudest she'd ever been to a caller—instead she watched the small drama that was still playing out on the lawn.

Lila Nott shouted something at the biggest man, spat on the ground, and then spun on her heel and stormed off.

She was almost to the shrubbery—which is where she must have slipped through—when she stopped and turned.

It was too far away to see her face clearly, but Phoebe knew she was staring at the house.

Staring at her.

Not until she felt a slight tickle on her chin did she reach up. Her hand came away wet; she was crying. What was *wrong* with her? When had she become so emotional? And over what—yet another mistress and illegitimate child?

Stop sniveling! she scolded herself. *You married him with your eyes wide open.*

Yes, she certainly had.

When Phoebe looked up again, the woman and her child were gone.

***

Paul knew there was trouble when Norris *and* Mrs. Hodge met him at the door.

He frowned at them. "What are the two of you doing awake? It is almost three o'clock in the morning and I told you not to wait up for me."

They exchanged nervous glances, but neither seemed eager to speak.

Paul glanced down at his filthy clothing and scowled. "But as you have both seen fit to disobey me, you can heat some water for me and I will take it up to my room."

His butler instantly opened his mouth to argue. "I can bring—"

"No, you cannot," he snapped at Norris. "I've told you more than once that I don't want you hauling buckets or heavy trays up the stairs like a draught animal." He narrowed his eyes, the anger from earlier begin to slip its leash; Norris didn't deserve it, so Paul gritted his teeth and tightened his grip on his temper.

Instead of yelling, he lowered his voice and said, "When I give an order—even if it is for your own health, Norris—I expect to be obeyed."

Norris looked mortified. "Yes, of course, my lord."

"Good. Now help me out of this coat and see that you don't let any more dirt than necessary fall off onto Hodgey's clean floor."

The butler gave a slight smile at Paul's mild attempt at humor.

"So," Paul prodded, while Norris helped him off with his sopping wet, filthy garment. "What disaster happened today?"

He looked at Mrs. Hodge when he asked the question, but she only swallowed.

"Out with it, ma'am. It can hardly be worse the than the day I've endured."

"Mrs. Temple called upon her ladyship."

Paul thought his head might just explode. "*Goddammit!*"

Mrs. Hodge winced at his blasphemy but straightened from her cringing position and glared. "Paul Edward Needham! I taught you better than that."

"I beg your pardon, Hodgey," he muttered, amazed that she could still make him feel guilty even though he was five-and-thirty.

"And Lila Nott was here to see you," Norris blurted, staring down at the ruined coat rather than at Paul.

Paul swore, but under his breath this time. "Is there anything else? Did it rain locusts and toads?"

"I told Sabrina Whitten she could start work today." Hodgey said.

Paul groaned. Well, he'd brought it on himself, hadn't he? "Did she do something already? Break the Sevres vase? Steal the silver? Elope with a footman?"

"Er, no, my lord. But she is increasing."

Paul inhaled deeply and then let it out. "Who is the father?"

Both servants looked at their feet.

"Damna—" he caught the epithet before it came to fruition. "I see," Paul said. "How far along is she?"

Mrs. Hodge said. "Perhaps three months."

"What does that mean? Is she showing?"

"Not unless she makes a point of it," the old woman retorted so tartly that Paul assumed that's exactly what the young hoyden was doing.

"She's afraid you'll send her away, my lord. And she says her father will not last out the summer."

Paul was too bloody weary to contemplate having a visibly pregnant maidservant working in his house, cringing at the rumors that would circulate. "I will talk to her tomorrow."

They both nodded.

He turned toward the corridor that led to the kitchen but heard a throat clear and turned.

This time it was Mrs. Hodge.

"Yes?" he asked in a dangerously quiet voice. "Was there something else you forgot?"

"Your boots, my lord."

He glanced down at them. "I daresay they are ruined. Symond will doubtless scold me for wearing my newer pair."

"They are encrusted with mud, my lord." Mrs. Hodge looked deliberately at the marble floor and he saw that he'd left clumps of slimy, sooty mud.

"Ah. You wish me to take them off, I suppose."

She merely smiled.

Paul sighed and went to sit.

"Perhaps not there, my lord," she hastily said, looking pointedly at the pale-yellow silk on the chair cushion. "Mr. Norris will bring you something else."

Paul had to laugh. No matter how wealthy and powerful he became, Hodgey could always knock him down a few pegs and make him feel like a little boy.

"Yes, ma'am," he said mildly exchanging an amused look with Norris, who opened the cleverly concealed cupboard panel and removed the short wooden stool the footmen often used while waiting up at night.

He set it before Paul and then bent his old back to act as boot jack.

"While your water is heating you can sit and eat the cold supper that Cook prepared just for you," his housekeeper said.

He toed the heel of his boot to help Norris get the wet leather off. Symond would weep at such a thing, but then the boots were already ruined.

"Mmm, potted tongue?" he asked, glancing up hopefully.

His housekeeper chuckled. "Perhaps."

"Did Susan upset Lady Needham, Hodgey?" he asked, her old nickname slipping out naturally. There had been a time in his life when Hodgey had been as close as a mother to him. Not only had she loved and cared for him, making up for Jonathan Needham's cool indifference, but she'd shielded and protected him from Suki Temple's jealous, uneven temper when Paul hadn't been able to protect himself.

"Her ladyship did not appear... happy, my lord."

"How long were they alone together."

"Long enough, and it didn't help that Lila Nott was raising a fuss at the same time."

So, he would have some explaining to do. But not tonight. No, she'd be long asleep at almost three o'clock in the morning and he was simply too weary.

It was not a conversation he was looking forward to having with her.

***

Phoebe sat in front of the mirror and fumed while Spragg arranged her hair.

She'd woken that morning in a happy frame of mind, as she always did, and then recalled why she was alone in her bed: because her lord and master had not returned home until almost three o'clock that morning.

Yesterday, after her visit from Mrs. Temple, she had been prepared to tell her husband that he needn't bother coming to her that night, even though her courses had finished.

But he'd not even given her the courtesy of coming to dinner so that she might treat him with blighting coldness throughout the meal and then reject him afterward.

Two hours before dinner she'd been in her private sitting room writing letter after letter to her sister Aurelia—and throwing each of them away—as she was the sibling Phoebe had always gone to for advice and comfort. But every time she mentioned the meat of the matter—her husband's *amours*—she'd cringed and been unable to carry through describing such a mortifying subject.

And so she'd been in a vile temper when the servant had delivered the message that her husband wouldn't be home for dinner.

"Where is he?" she'd demanded before she could check her temper.

The footman, not her own Andrew, but one of Needham's men, had flinched back from either her question or the heat with which she'd asked it or both.

"Er, Mr. Norris did not tell me that, my lady."

And Phoebe could just imagine why.

So, he'd lasted an entire two weeks before he'd gone to another woman's bed.

Perhaps he didn't wait. Perhaps he already has a mistress-a second one—established in Little Sissingdon?

No, she didn't believe that.

But only because he would not hesitate to tell her as much if it were true. Indeed, he was direct enough, and proud enough of his *seed spreading virility,* to use Mrs. Temple's odious phrase, to want to share the fact with her.

And why not rub her face in it? After all, she'd already accepted the presence of one mistress in her house. There were thirty-seven bedchambers at Wych House—he could fill them all with his women and ill-gotten children.

Phoebe had told herself last night that she was grateful he wouldn't be dining with her or coming to her bed because she'd needed time alone to calm her temper.

But being alone had not helped. Indeed, rather than use the time to reflect on the situation and her powerlessness to effect any changes, she had jealously listened for his return, imagining him tangled in some other woman's arms, bedsheets wrapped around his sweaty, muscular torso.

By the time she'd heard movement behind the connecting door at three o'clock she'd been like a kettle that had been put on the hob to boil and then been forgotten: no longer steaming, but red-hot and molten.

He'd not been able to go five nights without a woman.

Because what else did a man do in the country until three in the morning?

"Shall I tell Symond that his lordship may visit you tonight?" Spragg asked as she set down the hairbrush, snapping her from her trance.

Phoebe's face heated—a common reaction that she *hated*—and she met her maid's eyes in the mirror.

"Not today," she said, the words abrupt and sharp. She turned away from the other woman's curious gaze. "Please look at my emerald habit—I believe there is a rip in the coat pocket and I should like to wear it tomorrow. I find the blue one a trifle cool for this climate." Not to mention the fact that Needham had purchased the garment for her. Indeed, he'd bought several gowns and even new riding boots—the nicest she'd ever seen. Phoebe had no intention of wearing any of them ever again.

As Phoebe descended the stairs to the second-floor landing, she saw two figures coming out of the bookroom.

One was Needham and the other was the new housemaid, Samantha or Sarah or something that began with an S.

Phoebe had immediately noticed the girl yesterday because she was an exceedingly beautiful young woman.

And now she was standing close—far too close—to Phoebe's husband.

The maid said something that made Paul chuckle, and he flicked a finger over her cheek in a way that was achingly familiar as he'd done it to Phoebe on more than one occasion.

She must have made a noise because the two of them turned in her direction.

"Ah, there you are, my dear," Needham said, greeting her as if she'd not just caught him caressing the cheek of a servant girl. "Off you go, Sabrina," he said dismissively.

Sabrina dropped a curtsy that was so low that she was practically kissing Needham's boots. "Thank you so much, my lord."

She sashayed—because that was the perfect word for her hip-swinging walk—toward Phoebe, her destination the servant stairwell which was at the other end of the corridor.

She barely inclined her head and murmured, "My lady," and then she did something odd: she laid a hand on her midriff, the gesture caressing, her fingers resting lightly on a distinct bulge.

Phoebe's eyes bounced up just in time to catch the girl's smug, catlike smile.

"Good morning, my dear," Needham said, striding toward Phoebe when she remained rooted to the spot. "I was hoping to have a word with you before I left for the day. Is now convenient, or are you heading to the breakfast room?"

"No, I ate in my room," she lied.

She doubted she could keep down any food at this point. She stalked toward the doorway, avoiding his gaze, her own eyes strangely hot and almost *itchy*.

Once inside the pleasant room he waited for her to sit before taking the chair behind his desk.

"I shan't beat about the bush," he said. "I understand Mrs. Temple paid a visit to you yesterday."

"I had that pleasure."

He looked amused by her sharp tone. "I'm sorry I was not here. I know she can be... trying and she is hardly the sort of woman you are accustomed to receiving calls from."

She cut him what she hoped was a scathing looking. "I daresay I had better become accustomed to entertaining women of her sort."

His eyebrows rose and he leaned closer, resting his elbows between the tidy stacks of paperwork that filled the entire top of his desk. "Please explain that comment."

"I should think it speaks for itself."

"I don't think so. I wouldn't like to misinterpret."

"She was your father's mistress and bore him a child, both of whom lived in this house with you and your mother. Did I misinterpret any of that?"

"No, that was most... succinct."

"How many more women of her ilk should I expect to call upon me? How many other siblings will I encounter? Perhaps I might send out invitations for tea and have done with introductions all at once?"

He chuckled. "No, that won't be necessary. Mrs. Temple was the only one of my father's mistresses who raised her son in this house."

"I can't help noticing how carefully you state that. Did other women raise his sons in other homes?"

"If they did so, you can rest assured that he would have taken care of his... indiscretions. But then my father's infidelities are not really the issue, are they?"

"Not entirely," she agreed. "As to your own indiscretions, how do you anticipate managing them?"

He opened his mouth, but Phoebe couldn't keep her's shut.

"Wait—no, that is not the right question," she said, her voice a bit louder than she would wish for.

"Then what is, pray?"

He was no longer smiling and any amusement that had been twinkling in his pale eyes had faded away. Indeed, they seemed even paler and more silver in the daylight that filtered through a nearby window. He looked even more inhuman, his craggy, harsh features fixed and inscrutable, like a stone carving.

You had best curb your temper, the voice of reason urged her.

Phoebe ignored it.

"It occurs to me now that I should have demanded to know—before I agreed to marry you—just how many mistresses and b-baseborn children you intended to install in my house."

Surely it was her imagination that the air had chilled?

"It was as well that you did not do so, Phoebe," he said in a velvety soft voice, his brogue more pronounced suddenly. "I don't respond well to threats or demands."

She leapt to her feet. "And *I* don't respond well to you filling *my* house with your women and their b—"

"Careful, now," he said, as quietly as a snake's hiss. He came around the desk, not stopping until they were almost touching.

He towered over her.

Phoebe glared up at him, refusing to move back.

His face was cold and hard.

Fear made her limbs feel leaden but sped her pulse. Not fear that he would strike her or physically hurt her, that was not his way with women, she knew that instinctively.

What terrified her was how tenuous her hold on this man was. A man who held her future, her happiness, her very existence in the palm of his hand. A large, powerful hand that could easily crush her.

While he would not strike her, what else might he do to a wife who was willful, rude, and disobedient?

He did not love her, she knew that.

All she had was his regard, and that, once lost, would be impossible to regain.

But it wasn't only fear which froze her spiteful tongue. She was disgusted with herself for what she'd almost said. It was not the children of men like her husband who deserved scorn and she'd been unjust to even *think* the word bastard.

"I apologize for what I was about to say," she forced the words out not for him, but for her own dignity and peace of mind. "Thank you for stopping me."

She'd rarely seen genuine surprise on her husband's face, but she saw it then.

"What?" she demanded. "You think I like turning into a virago who vents her rage on innocent children? It is you and your behavior I deplore, my lord, not people like poor Lucy."

"Deplore all you like, my lady, but you would be best served never again to mention my daughter's name in anger."

Phoebe forced her mouth to stay shut.

"Now, was there anything else you wished to say?"

"No."

He nodded.

Phoebe turned on her heel, but his voice stopped her before she reached the door.

"Have your courses finished?"

A wave of heat swamped her at his indelicate question. Especially after the argument they'd just had. What a callous oaf. How *dare* he!

Phoebe became angrier the more she thought about his question.

Anger for him *and* herself, as well as self-loathing for the way her sex clenched and her thighs tightened at the thought of him returning to her bed.

Right behind that infuriating lust was rage at her body for betraying her.

And it was her rage that had, once again, lured her into opening her mouth and demonstrating ill breeding.

She refused to turn around. "Yes," she said through gritted teeth, her voice pulsing with anger and loathing. "You may rest assured that I am once again available to be bred like the bloodstock I am, my lord."

When a low chuckle came from right behind her she jumped. *How* did he move so silently!

Her scalp tingled as he leaned close enough that she felt the heat of this next words. "Then I will come to you tonight."

Phoebe reached for the door handle, desperate to get away from him before she did something rash—like throw herself into his arms.

His hand landed on top of hers and kept her from turning the handle. "It would please me to see you wear one of the nightgowns I chose for you. I especially want to see you in the black one."

Her stomach fluttered at his provocative words and it was all she could do to retort, "Is that a command, my lord."

"If it needs to be."

"It will be as you say, my lord."

He hesitated a long moment before opening the door for her.

Phoebe waited only until the door closed behind her and then she ran, her eyes blurring with angry tears she could no longer hold in check.

She hated him! Never in her life had she hated a man so much!

Thankfully she saw nobody on her frantic flight to her room, where she found Spragg closely examining the green habit for a non-existent tear.

"Leave me," she ordered.

The startled woman scurried from the room and Phoebe locked the door and flung herself onto her bed like a child of ten instead a woman of almost twenty-one.

She squeezed her eyes shut, but the tears still came, her emotions so raw and confused she didn't know whether to laugh hysterically or sob.

Thankfully she did neither.

Instead, she wept quietly into a pillow, fiercely refusing to allow anyone to hear her

Phoebe had been the one to make a bargain with this—this *hellbeast* and now she would have to pay the piper and take him into her bed and her body.

You can lie to yourself all you want, but the fact is that you are aroused and wet from only ten minutes in a room with him, the voice in her head mocked.

Indeed, just thinking the words was enough to make her sex clench, which in turn sent ripples of pleasure out to the rest of her body.

Phoebe *hated* that the sly voice in her mind spoke the truth. And knowing that he was coming to her tonight would make the hours in between drag.

She ground her teeth and pressed the pillow harder over her mouth and nose. Was it possible to smother oneself?

Phoebe sighed and flung away the pillow, glancing at the clock.

And then sighed again. She would be receiving callers today and she knew, thanks to a subtle warning from Mrs. Hodge, that the neighborhood luminaries were all atwitter to meet her.

Indeed, Needham had told her there was to be a supper at the end of the week.

She snorted when she recalled the brief conversation. He'd been so concerned that she would be overwhelmed to host a dinner party that it had been amusing.

"I managed my family's house for years," she reminded him. "Organizing a dinner that doesn't rely on stretching one small joint of meat to feed eight people will be a pleasure by contrast."

And of course, it was only northern provincial merchants they would be entertaining.

"There is also the fact they are eager to be pleased, for many it will be the first meal they've shared with a genuine peeress," Needham had pointed out, reading her thoughts with unnerving accuracy.

She'd opened her mouth to say… something, but his next words had stopped her.

"Don't take offense, my dear. I was only teasing you."

Phoebe realized she was smiling at the memory. It *had* been nothing but a little gentle ribbing. At the time it had cheered her that maybe they were moving beyond their initial awkwardness and bridging the gap between their disparate backgrounds.

And now *this*.

But what did you really see?

She frowned at the thought.

I saw my husband flirting with a beautiful servant girl. A pregnant servant.

No, what you saw was her flirting with him.

She chewed her lip, replaying the brief encounter.

Very well, she finally admitted. *But then why did he not deny my accusation?*

How do you respond to accusations? Especially unjust ones?

Phoebe cringed away from that question, her mind returning to that afternoon when her husband had encountered her with Dixon. She had been angry and had behaved afterward by flirting even more with Dixon, which had *not* been a way to ease Needham's concerns.

As Phoebe played back the course of their conversation from earlier, she was forced to admit that he had never said the maid's child was his. Nor had he said anything about other mistresses.

You immediately went on the attack.

That was true; she'd been so desperate to hurt him as badly as she hurt that she had simply launched an offensive.

Needham had reacted in a way she was beginning to see was standard for him whenever she insulted him: he became cold and unresponsive.

Phoebe cringed when she recalled her behavior when he'd asked if he might come to her tonight.

She'd been shrewish and accusatory—as if he'd used her as nothing but a broodmare when she had enjoyed those nights with him every bit as much as he had, if not more.

"Uuuhhhgg!" she groaned, thrashing her head from side to side.

And then there was the issue of the nightgown.

How could Phoebe explain her complex reaction to the delicate, erotic garments when she barely understood it herself?

She was Phoebe, the sturdy, squat, practical Bellamy sister. The gowns he'd chosen were sensual works of art meant for beautiful, willowy women, not ones like her.

And yet he had commissioned the gowns for *her*, so he really did wish to see her in them. Wouldn't he be offended to have his gifts so churlishly refused and rejected? Wouldn't she feel the same if he acted that way?

Phoebe massaged her temples while she tried to work through what had just happened downstairs.

Both of them were quick to anger and take offence and often spoke with the intent to wound—because *they* felt wounded.

Phoebe sighed. One of them would need to take the higher ground.

It was unjust that it would likely be her role, as the wife, to be peacemaker, but such was the reality of married life.

She would wear the nightgown tonight. And she would pretend as if this morning's hostilities had never happened. And then she would see if that worked.

Because she had to try something new. These arguments led only to more unhappiness.

Feeling a bit calmer at having made a decision, she glanced at the clock on the bedside table; she had only an hour to make herself decent for callers. No doubt her hair, which poor Spragg had just dressed a short time ago, would be a rat's nest thanks to her thrashing on the bed.

Phoebe pushed the thought of the new maid—and Lila Nott—from her mind and prepared to face the curious neighbors.

But first, she needed to ring for Spragg and apologize for behaving so rudely.

It would be good practice for tonight.

Chapter Twenty-Two

The day had started out wretched and miserable and hadn't stopped yet. Paul had spent the entire ride from Hill House to his newest blast furnace—which he hoped to have up and running by the end of the day—castigating himself for his idiotic behavior with Phoebe.

If he'd not been such a stubborn, proud, prickly arse, he could have dissipated the argument with a few assurances.

But she'd come at him with all her cannons blazing and his reaction had been kneejerk.

He was ashamed of himself. He'd behaved like an ignorant brute.

He knew how Sabrina must have looked, batting her lashes up at him, *my lording* him in that sinful bedroom voice of hers.

Thank God Phoebe hadn't seen the girl ten minutes earlier when she'd dropped to her knees and covered his hand with grateful kisses.

She was a trouble-causing minx and Paul had needed to speak sharply to her, demanding that she quit trying to manipulate him with her body.

Sabrina had been sulky and mulish after that and it had taken Paul far too much time and effort to gain the truth from her.

He'd almost wept with relief when she'd admitted that Gideon wasn't the father of her unborn child.

Unfortunately, the truth had been almost as bad: the father was one of the bloody Nott brothers. Not either of the unmarried ones, but the one who already had a wife and *nine* bloody children.

Of course, nobody could know that, so Paul would have to find some young man willing to marry Sabrina and be a father to another man's child.

Paul had been frazzled by the time he'd chivvied Sabrina out the door, only to find Phoebe seething in the hall.

After he'd cocked up that, there'd been a nasty surprise waiting for him at the new blast furnace.

"What happened?" he'd demanded of Gerry Thompkins when he'd arrived to find the blast furnace not merrily puffing away but cold and dead.

Gerry's green-gray complexion told him the answer before the man spoke: somebody had damaged the furnace.

While it had been an annoyance and expense to repair the beehive ovens, the blast furnace was a significant setback.

Paul had spent the rest of the afternoon arranging to have yet more men brought in to guard the furnace, which would cause tempers to rise even among men who *weren't* engaged in the mischief because the miners were insular and despised outsiders. Especially ones who were armed with truncheons.

After Paul had taken care of that problem, he'd ridden out to the Nott property to confront the brothers, only to find the place empty.

Next, he'd gone to Robert Nott's hovel, where he'd found only Nott's unhappy wife and her filthy, shoeless brood.

"Don't know," had been her sullen answer to where the men had gone and when they'd return.

So, that had been that.

And now, with scarcely two hours before he needed to be home for dinner—which he could *not* miss again after this morning's skirmish with Phoebe—he was going to face what was certainly the most unpleasant part of his day: his brother.

It had been three years since Paul had last seen Gideon, not since he'd given him the property in Cumberland, telling him that would be the very last time.

You owe me this, Paul!" Those had been Gideon's last words to him before Paul had capitulated and signed over the large tract of coal-rich land.

Just as he'd financed a pottery in Manchester, funded a canal scheme in Birmingham, and provided money for a half dozen other ventures before that. Each and every one of them had been failures, some of them spectacularly so—like the cloth mill that had suspiciously burned to the ground.

According to the men he'd spoken to since arriving in Middleton, Gideon had re-surfaced almost a month ago—which coincided with the recent spate of vandalism—and was now living off his mother.

The door to Suki Temple's imposing new mansion opened before Paul even reached it and Poundstone, her butler, greeted him with genuine warmth in his eyes.

"It is a pleasure to see you again, my lord."

"Thank you, Poundstone. I hope Mrs. Temple has time to receive me—despite the odd hour."

"Madam has gone to visit her sister in Wolverhampton, my lord."

Paul almost laughed—not in amusement, however. Suki loved her boy, but she'd known there would be fireworks when Paul discovered that Gideon had returned to a place he'd been forbidden to visit.

"Where is my brother?" he asked the butler, handing over his hat and gloves.

"In the library, my lord."

"I know the way," he said shortly when the elderly butler began to escort him.

Indeed, he *should* know his way as he'd been the one who'd paid for the construction of the house. The structure was a monument to excess, as was everything in it—from the garish *objets d'art* cluttering up every flat surface to the truly horrific carpet beneath his feet.

Paul entered the library without knocking.

"Hello, brother," Gideon said when Paul hesitated in the doorway, squinting to make out the other man.

"Why are you sitting in darkness?" Paul demanded, striding to the fireplace where he could just make out a gaudy brass bowl full of spills.

"An active imagination requires no excess illumination." Gideon chuckled at his own wit as Paul lighted a small brace of candles.

Paul scowled when he could see his brother better. "Now that I see you, I understand your desire for darkness. When is the last time you shaved or bathed?"

Gideon grinned, unoffended by Paul's observation. "You, however, are looking in the pink of health old man."

Even scruffy and dirty, Paul's slightly elder half-brother managed to look like an angel come to earth.

Paul's father—who'd been no fool, for all that he'd been infatuated with Suki Temple—had often jested that Gideon, who resembled an angel, was rotten to the core, while Paul, who was brutishly ugly and villainous looking was largely virtuous.

"I understand from Mam that you've come with your wife," Gideon said, holding his glass out to Paul. "I'll wait for my dinner invitation to meet her, shall I?"

Paul ignored Gideon's dig and refilled his empty glass without comment before pouring a whiskey for himself.

"You need to stop what you are doing," Paul said, sitting down across from his brother, who gave him a wide-eyed innocent look.

"You mean drinking Mam's fine spirits?" he teased.

Paul went on as if he hadn't spoken. "It will kill your mother to see you sent to prison or transported, Gideon."

Gideon slammed down his glass, spilling amber liquid all over the hideous gold-leafed sphinx end table. "And you would just *hate* that, wouldn't you?"

"I bear your mother no ill will."

That was true. Now.

But when Paul had been a child, he'd both feared and hated her.

It had taken years to forgive the ignorant harpy for terrorizing him. Not until Paul was an adult could he see her character clearly. She was a beautiful, jealous, thwarted woman and his father had put her into a position of power in his household, and over his legitimate son.

Jonathan Needham had been wise enough to know better, but he simply hadn't cared.

"That which don't kill you, will make you stronger," his father had said the one time Paul complained about Suki's rough treatment.

Paul supposed his father had been right, although Suki Temple had come damned close to killing him on more than one occasion.

As had her son.

Paul took a sip of his drink and looked at the drunk and broken creature across from him.

Thanks to his own machinations, Gideon now had very little to lose, which made him a very dangerous man in Paul's opinion.

"What will it take to stop you sowing discontent?" Paul finally asked, too weary to beat around the bush.

Gideon chuckled. "I'm enjoying myself too much. I find it refreshing that not everyone who lives on your bounty licks your boots like a dog." He smiled evilly. "It is good for you, I think, to realize you are only a man and not a god. You've been accustomed to buying everything you want for too long." He sneered. "And now you think to *buy* me?"

"It has always worked in the past," Paul reminded him dryly.

Gideon's eyes briefly widened in surprise, and then he laughed. "I suppose you are right."

Paul had to smile; his brother always had possessed the ability to laugh at himself.

But Paul had not come there to laugh.

"The Notts have become more and more reckless, Gideon. I am not going to wait until they kill somebody before I stop you."

"I'm offended that you think I am the one behind these recent acts of sabotage," Gideon said, smirking.

"We both know that you are far too lazy—and too wily—to wield the sledgehammer, yourself."

His brother cocked his head. "A compliment, from you? Are you trying to turn me up sweet, Paul?"

"The Notts are not stable," Paul continued. "You have chosen weapons which might very well malfunction and end up hurting people. You, included."

"And that would make you even sadder than hurting my mother, wouldn't it?"

Paul sighed and set down his glass, largely untouched. "I am tired of having this same conversation with you."

For all that Gideon looked as languid as a predator that had just feasted, he moved remarkably fast, his arm a blur as he flung his glass at the mirror over the mantle.

The explosion was ear splitting and Paul, who was five feet closer to the mirror, did not turn away fast enough to avoid a series of sharp pricks along the side of his neck, cheek, and temple.

Paul stood and carefully brushed the shards of glass from his hair and clothing.

"That is what I think of your *weariness*, Paul."

The library door flew open and poor Poundstone stared around with such a wild look that Paul knew the older man had feared one of them had killed the other.

That was still a possibility.

"Get out!" Gideon snarled.

"The mirror broke—it was an accident," Paul lied. "It can wait until I'm gone to clean up Poundstone," he assured the poor old man—who was obviously hesitant to leave them alone together.

The butler nodded and closed the door.

Gideon turned on him. "You have a great deal of nerve to order my mother's servants about as if they were your own, don't you?" He gave a bitter bark of laughter. "But then they are yours, aren't they? Everything is." He plucked at his none-too-clean shirtsleeve. "My clothing, the mirror that is all over that hideous rug," he paused. "Do you think I ruined that damned rug?" The question seemed genuine.

"We should be so fortunate," Paul said.

"She'd just buy another one—probably worse—even if I did." Gideon laughed and Paul joined him.

And for a heartbeat, it was like it had been all those years ago, before Suki had poisoned relations between them, and before their father had left not so much as a farthing to one son and all of it to the other, effectively murdering any chance that they could ever patch things up.

And before you stole even more from him, Paul's conscience reminded him. *All without Gideon knowing just how badly he'd been robbed.*

"How is Ellen?" Gideon asked, the question eerily close to what Paul had just been thinking.

"She is not well."

Anguish, intense but fleeting, flickered across his brother's face. Gideon glanced about him, looking for something—probably the glass he'd just hurled—and then sighed when he didn't find it.

"How long does she have?"

"The doctors say she will not last the year."

"Does she still love me best of the two of us?"

Paul had to laugh. "It isn't a subject that has come up of late, but I'm guessing the answer is still the same."

Gideon snorted, his expression sullen. "She loves me best but it is with you that she had a child. Oh, the irony."

Paul did not comment on that. Instead, he looked at the full-length portrait of Gideon on the opposite wall. The artist had managed to capture both sides of Gideon's character, depicting both the angel and the demonic imp, lightness and darkness, good and bad—bad, not evil. He didn't believe that Gideon was truly evil, just deeply, deeply troubled.

"I want to go to America."

Paul turned from the painting back to his brother.

"I am told there is enough room that a man can live without falling within another man's shadow," Gideon said.

Paul felt genuine fear for the first time in ages.

It wasn't Gideon's departure that he feared, but his own hope that he might finally be free of the other man.

He glanced down at his clenched fingers and forced them to relax, praying that Gideon had not seen the hope in his gaze and guessed what it meant.

When he looked up again his mask was firmly in place. "Do you have anything in mind?"

Gideon's hyacinth blue eyes sparkled with sudden excitement. "I spoke to a man—an ex-soldier—who fought there. He said there is free land for the taking. He said it is near impossible *not* to become wealthy."

Paul sincerely doubted it was that simple but held his peace and waited.

His patience bore fruit quicker than he'd hoped.

"I want a fair slice, Paul."

Paul looked into his brother's eyes.

"I know what you are thinking," Gideon said, when Paul didn't immediately answer.

Paul laughed. "I doubt you'd guess the whole of it." At least he hoped not. The truth was that he'd pay a great deal to put an ocean between himself and his brother.

"So, then what *are* you thinking?"

"How much do you have in mind?" Paul asked.

Gideon named a figure that made him smile.

"That might be a fair share now that I've been in charge a decade, Gideon, but do keep in mind that our father did not have even half the holdings I now possess."

"Fine. I'll take a quarter, then."

It was still a great deal too much and they both knew it. Jonathan Needham—desperate for ennoblement—had gifted the most lucrative of his patents to the Crown some years before he'd died.

While it was true that he'd left Paul a very wealthy man, it was also true that Paul's empire was far vaster, and much more diversified, than his father's had ever been.

Paul's wealth was not in a bank vault but sunk into more than a dozen ventures.

He would need to sell more than a few holdings to get the money, but it would be well worth it.

But only with certain guarantees.

"I have several requirements," he said.

"Of course."

Judging Gideon's gleeful expression, he already believed that he'd won.

Not that it mattered. Gideon's removal to America would be a bargain at twice the price.

"You will get *nothing* until this sabotage stops."

That wiped the smirk from his face. "But—"

"I don't care."

"You don't even know what I was going to say!" Gideon protested.

"It doesn't matter—I still don't care. I want a year without any destruction before I transfer the entire amount."

"A *year*! But how will I survive an entire year?"

"I shall give you a sufficient amount to live on. And you needn't stay here—in fact, once you've convinced your compatriots that it is unwise to continue, you will take yourself off to Bristol and hop on the next ship bound for America."

"A year," Gideon muttered again.

"That is the first condition. The second is that you do not return to England for seven years. Anything of value will take at least that long to establish. You will sign a statement to that effect."

Gideon waved a dismissive hand. "I hadn't planned to ever come back. Is that all? Or is there more?"

"That is all."

"Well, I have a condition of my own. I want to see Ellen before I leave."

"No."

"What do you mean *no*?"

"I mean *no*. You go within one hundred miles of Ellen and I will go to the magistrate and lay an information on you myself."

An ugly, hate-filled look took over Gideon's handsome features. "You really are an inhuman monster. She doesn't *love* you, Paul. She never did. The only reason she's with you is because of your money."

Paul shook his head in wonder. "You really are self-deluding, aren't you? You *know* why she is with me. She never would have come to me in the first place if you'd not laid hands on her, Gideon."

Gideon winced. "You will never stop throwing that in my face, will you?"

"You are correct, I won't. Not as long as you pretend the past never happened."

Gideon shoved a hand into his greasy gold curls. "You don't understand. I couldn't help it. It wasn't as if I *meant* to do it. It was a mistake—an accident, I didn't—"

"Having too many pints is a mistake. Tripping and breaking your mother's favorite shepherdess figurine is an accident, Gideon. Beating a woman so badly you break her arm, fracture her skull, and cause her to miscarry your own child is unforgiveable brutality."

Gideon's face crumpled like a sheet of parchment. "I regret it more than anything else in my life! Why won't either of you forgive me?" He covered his face with his hands just as a sob tore out of him.

Paul stood. "You are drunk and maudlin, Gideon, and it turns my stomach." He strode to the servant cord and pulled on it. "Sober yourself and go talk to the Notts *tonight*. Do not wait until tomorrow. I don't want another day like today, where I am dealing with wreckage and trying to find work for people thanks to your idiocy. Are we agreed?"

Gideon nodded, his eyes red-rimmed and puffy.

The door to the library opened and Poundstone looked in. "You rang, my lord?"

"Bring lots of tea and food for my brother."

"Of course, my lord."

The door shut behind him and Paul took out his billfold, removed all his money, and tossed it onto the desk. "That is all I have on my person. Tomorrow, if you've done as you promised, I will give you more."

Gideon sniffed and nodded. He hesitated and then added, "I really do appreciate what you are doing, Paul."

"And I really hope you find what you are seeking in America, Gideon."

"I'd—I'd like to meet your wife before I leave, Paul."

"I think that would be a bad idea."

Gideon grinned, looking more like his old self. "Worried she'll fall in love and run off with me to America."

Paul snorted. "Tonight, Gideon. I want you to put an end to this tonight."

"I'll see to it. You can trust me."

Paul would believe that when it happened and not a minute before.

***

"That is a very pretty gown on you, my lady."

Phoebe wrenched her eyes off the peas she'd divided into three separate units—or perhaps they were battalions or maybe brigades, she could never keep the various military designations clear in her mind—and looked up at her husband.

"I'm sorry?" she said.

"I said that shade of pink suits you."

"Thank you, my lord."

He ate a mouthful of peas rather than forcing them to do military maneuvers.

Once he'd swallowed and taken a sip of wine he said, "I saw the cards on the table in the foyer. You must have had a busy afternoon?"

"Yes, quite busy."

A busy, dull afternoon that had been entirely forgettable. Were morning calls always so insipid? It seemed unlikely that this group of ladies should be any worse than any other. Phoebe had been ready to fall asleep by the time she'd exchanged the same pleasantries with the tenth woman.

"Are you not hungry this evening? Or is the food not to your liking?" Needham asked, making her aware that yet again she was staring at her plate.

"No, the food is delicious." She cast a glance at the footman behind her husband's chair; it would *not* do for Cook to hear that the mistress did not care for her food. "I daresay it is because of all the tea and cakes I had this afternoon."

Needham chuckled, but Phoebe had not been speaking in jest. The afternoon had been interminable and she'd been positively awash in tea by the end of it.

"And how was your day, my lord?"

His eyebrows rose, as if the question surprised him. Did she really never ask about his day?

"Busy." He gestured for the servants to remove their plates. "Too full for dessert?" he asked.

Tonight's dessert was floating islands, her favorite. "I think I might have room."

He looked amused and nodded at the footmen, who left to fetch the desserts.

"Busy with what, my lord?" Phoebe asked after the silence began to stretch. "Your day," she clarified when he looked confused.

"Just business matters."

The door opened and two servants entered and set a floating island before each of them.

Needham smiled. "Thank you. You may leave us."

"I feel like you are avoiding answering me, my lord," Phoebe said when the door closed behind the servants.

"Not at all. I just don't think you'll find it of much interest."

"Why don't you let me be the judge of what interests me?"

He flashed her one of his rare smiles. "Very well. I had some breakage at my new blast furnace. That brought the work to a halt until it can be repaired."

Phoebe savored a bite of sweet, creamy custard, considered another spoonful, but decided against it.

When she looked up, she found her husband watching her with the oddest expression.

"What is it?" she asked. "Do I have something on my face?" she daubed at her mouth with the damask napkin.

"No. It is nothing."

"So was the breakage the result of carelessness on the part of a worker?" she asked.

A scowl flickered across his face. "No."

Her eyebrows rose. "You mean it was deliberate?"

"Yes."

"Is this like those workers who broke weaving looms?"

"No, this was not like the Luddites. It was not disgruntled workers seeking better condition or pay or reacting from fear of losing their livelihood. This was a malicious act of vandalism that was personal."

"Aimed at *you*?"

"Yes."

"So you apprehended the person who did it?"

"Not yet, but I hope to do so."

Phoebe took up her spoon and enjoyed another bite.

If it were up to her, she would have floating islands every night. Of course, she would soon be twenty stone because she was positively greedy for it.

It was a struggle to set her spoon down between each bite, but she mastered herself.

Once again, she found her husband watching her.

"You are looking at me very oddly," she accused.

"I'm just enjoying watching you savor your dessert."

She gave a small, mortified laugh. "My mother always scolded me for too obviously *savoring* my food."

Except the countess had been far crueler. "You are fat, Phoebe," she had said on more than one occasion. "You are the sort of woman who should never eat dessert."

Needham frowned. "What is wrong with enjoying one's food?"

The last thing she wanted to do was confess that her mother called her fat.

So she said, "There is nothing wrong with enjoying it. But showing one's enjoyment is—" Phoebe bit her lip, suddenly not wanting to say the word.

"Vulgar?" he suggested with a faint quirk to his lips.

"I was trying to think of another word—given our recent history with *that* one."

His smile broadened. "How about crass? Crude? Indecorous? Rude? Plebeian?"

Phoebe laughed. "I am impressed. Hmm," she tapped her lower lip with her spoon. "I think you missed ill-bred."

He grinned. "Unseemly."

Phoebe almost choked on her second-to-last mouthful of dessert. "Boorish."

"Brash."

"Unrefined."

She wracked her brain. "Oh, no! I can't think of another but I know there must be more."

"Improper, indecent, unbecoming."

"You are so good at it!"

"It?"

"Yes, we played a similar game at home—but in reverse, where somebody thinks of a word and the rest try to guess it. You have an impressive lexicon."

He looked thoughtful and then said, "Gauche."

Phoebe dissolved into laughter at that point, amazed and pleased when her husband joined her.

***

Paul felt lighter *after* dinner than before it.

That wasn't because he hadn't eaten enough to feed a horse. Rather, it was because Phoebe hadn't been furious or cold, as he'd dreaded. True, she had been a bit distant, at first, but they'd ended the meal by laughing together.

Indeed, it was one of the best evenings he could recall. And it wasn't close to over yet.

Paul skimmed the razor down the side of his nose and examined the results in the mirror before setting down the blade.

He then took the steaming hot cloth his valet held out for him. "That will be all for the night," he said, reveling in the delicious heat.

"Very good, my lord." Symond gave a last, yearning look at Paul's shaving kit but left without another word.

He knew the man would have liked to shave and dress him, but Paul drew the line at such coddling. He shaved himself and kept his own kit in order, his razor sharp and keen. He also tied his own neckcloths and fastened his own coats.

After checking his face and neck for cuts—there were none—he snuffed the candles and opened the door to his wife's room.

And then stopped, his jaw sagging open like the end-gate on a farm wagon.

It was his wife, but not his wife. At least not like he'd ever seen her before.

She was wearing the silk net gown as he'd requested—or, he admitted, boorishly commanded—and it exceeded his fantasies, which themselves had been... excessive.

Her face darkened and she began to sit up and cross her arms. "You are making me feel—"

"No, don't move," he ordered, his voice already thick with desire. "As you were," he added when she hesitated.

She gave him a mulish look but obeyed.

"Thank you," he said, slowly approaching her, enjoying the view every step of the way. He stopped and expelled the breath he'd been holding.

"You are feminine perfection, Phoebe."

If he thought she'd been red before, he was mistaken. He swore he could see her rosy flush spreading even beneath the silk netting of the gown.

He could certainly see her erect nipples, which were pressed against the nearly transparent fabric in a way that made his mouth water so copiously he had to swallow repeatedly.

She had draped herself on the chaise longue, giving him a view of the entire front of her body.

The neckline was cut so low it skimmed her nipples and the sheer fabric cast interesting shadows over her voluptuous curves, making the dark V between her thighs even darker.

She looked more naked than naked.

She shifted and squirmed, embarrassed by his lustful gazing.

Although that made him throb even harder, he knew better than to push her too much. So he held out a hand and she took it with amusing alacrity.

When she was standing, he was, once again, reminded of how small she was, the top of her head not even reaching his shoulders. Indeed, her mouth was the height of his nipples.

That was a thought that made his already erect cock leak like a spigot.

He set his hands on her waist. "Look at me, Phoebe."

The look she gave him from beneath her lowered lashes was shy and yet there was a hint of daring.

"I have never seen anything more beautiful in my life than you on that chaise longue."

The effect of his words was electric, her full lips parted in wonder and her large hazel eyes softened. Quite suddenly he understood that she would not have heard those words before—not in a family in which she was always considered the plain sister.

He cupped her flowerlike face in one hand, his palm dwarfing her. "I adore your body," he murmured in a low voice. "You are perfect."

He claimed her mouth, then, thrilled when she not only pressed against him, but wound her arms around his neck and returned his kisses in a way that was still adorably innocent.

Paul allowed his hands to roam while they reacquainted themselves with each other's bodies.

Those nights without her had been barren. For once, he'd not just wanted *any* woman. Only Phoebe.

Although Paul had never given the matter much thought, he knew he would never treat his wife the way his father had treated Paul's mother. But until that moment, he'd not realized just how little he wanted any other woman.

Paul lifted her easily and carried her to the bed, their mouths still joined. Only when he'd set her on the mattress did he pull away.

"You mentioned your love of games," he said, stroking her sweetly rounded jaw with the backs of his fingers.

She blinked, her eyes dark with lust. "Er, yes. We have always played games as a family."

"I have an idea for one."

"You wish to go to the study and play one *now?*"

Paul grinned at the disbelief and frustration in her voice; his little sensualist wanted her pleasure and she wanted it *now.*

"No. This is a game we would play here—in your bed, without any clothing."

She caught her plush lower lip with her teeth, her glance darting around the room as she considered his proposition.

He waited patiently; he would not force her to do anything she didn't wish to do.

After a long moment, she turned to him and said, "How does one play this game?"

***

Needham's beautiful eyes shone with humor and something else. Could it be affection?

Phoebe's heart—already pounding—sped at the thought.

"It is a simple game," he said. "You touch me on my body where you'd like to be touched on yours."

It took Phoebe a moment to untangle that sentence.

When she did, she gulped. "That—that is all there is to the game?"

He nodded.

"But…"

"But?"

"How does one win?"

His pupils, already large, swelled even more. "This game will have two winners, I think."

Her cheeks heated so quickly she felt dizzy. "Oh."

"Would you like me to go first?"

She nodded, not trusting herself to speak, afraid she might squeak or cough or otherwise embarrass herself.

"I will undress you." His gaze dropped to her chest, which was rising and falling far too quickly. "Although it is a pity to take this off," he muttered, more to himself.

Phoebe had felt positively wicked when she'd seen herself in this gown. She'd had Spragg dress her in her regular nightgown and then waited until the maid left to quickly change into this one.

She had almost changed back when she'd seen her reflection in the mirror.

How could clothing be more naked than bare skin?

But it was.

It was still the same old Phoebe—short and plain and with too-large of a bottom and thighs—but she'd somehow looked… *potent*. Yes, that had been the word for it.

She'd not believed she could feel more naked, but when he raised the gauzy gown over her head and tossed it aside, she knew she'd been wrong.

His lips parted and a low humming noise rumbled in his chest as he looked at her bare body.

That was when it struck her that it was *Phoebe* who was causing her husband to flush and breathe harder.

Exultation surged through her like sweet, slow-moving honey at the realization.

She was the one making this man—who always appeared so untouchable—shake and sweat and gaze with hunger. Yes, that was the expression—she recognized it because she felt the very same thing: hunger. For him.

A rare moment of indecision flickered across his face, as if he couldn't decide what to do—where to touch her—first.

It was such an intoxicating feeling that she closed her eyes and savored it, amazed that a mere feeling could be more delicious than her favorite dessert.

His touch, when it came, was warm and gentle, his huge palm closing around her right breast.

She shivered and opened her eyes to find him looking at her, his expression similar to the one he'd worn at dinner.

"You make me so hard, Phoebe."

Her lips parted in shock and his gaze—suddenly black—dropped to her mouth.

"It was sweet torment to watch you eat your dessert."

"It w-was?"

He nodded slowly, his hand gently caressing her breast, which was growing heavier, her nipple already so hard that it hurt when his thumb grazed it.

"When you licked a bit of custard from your lower lip, I feared I might spend in my pantaloons."

Phoebe gasped. "Needham!"

He shook his head, his fingers tightening on her nipple. "Paul. Say it."

"Paul!" she gasped again, but this time in pleasure rather than shock, astounded by how good it felt to be *pinched* in such a sensitive place.

"Good girl," he praised, soothing her aching nipple with a caress. "Lie back for me now."

She moved to obey, but then recalled something as she looked up him. "Wait. Isn't it my turn?"

His eyes widened and then he chuckled. "You are correct. I was trying to cheat."

Phoebe's gaze lowered to his body. As usual, he wore no nightshirt, only his gray silk banyan.

At first, it had shocked her that he slept without a nightshirt, now she was thrilled to know only his robe stood between them.

"I am to undress you?" she asked, darting a quick look at him.

He nodded.

Phoebe swallowed and then reached for his sash. Her hand was almost touching the silk when she allowed her gaze to drop. His membrum virile was jutting, somehow looking even bigger enshrouded by the heavy silk.

She had seen him many times already, so she should have expected what greeted her when she opened his robe.

But it robbed her of breath the way it had the very first time.

Perhaps even more now, because she knew that it *would* fit and that he would bring her sublime pleasure with something that looked so blunt and terrifying.

Emboldened by that thought, Phoebe tugged his robe down and he bent his knees so she could shove it off his shoulders.

Then he stood before her, naked and magnificent.

What was it that she was supposed to do?

She chewed her lip, darting a quick look at his face. "I don't remember—"

His lips were curved in that slight smile she found so… arousing. "You touch me where I touched you."

Oh. That was so simple—how could she have forgotten. But then her mind wasn't precisely operating normally.

Neither was her hand when she reached for his right nipple, which was tiny and erect, just as hers were. Her fingers shook badly and he took her hand and held it in his.

"Phoebe?"

She made herself look up again.

"Is this frightening you?"

"No—it's just, well, I don't know what I am doing. I'm afraid I'll do it wrong."

"There is no way to do this wrong, sweetheart."

Sweetheart.

Had any word ever sounded so... well, *sweet* to her? If so, she couldn't recall it.

"This is just a way to discover each other's bodies," Paul went on. "We don't have to play. We can get beneath the blankets, snuff the candles, and—"

"No. I want to play. And I want the candles."

She could see her words pleased him.

Well, they were true. She was intensely curious about his body, but usually too shy to do anything about it. Tonight he'd given her *carte blanche*, in a manner of speaking.

He released her hand and she set her fingers on the muscular bulge that was his breast.

He hissed in a breath and pressed against her fingers, just as Phoebe had.

His skin was so hot and silky soft, while the muscles underneath were rock hard.

When she cut a glance at his face, she was stunned to see his stern, thin lips were suddenly slack with pleasure and... anticipation.

She swallowed again and turned back to her task, trying to recall what he had done to her.

Her nipple. He'd first stroked it—she grazed the tiny little nub with her thumb and his body jerked, a growl rumbling deep in his chest.

He laid his hand over hers. "More."

Phoebe was entranced by his slitted gaze and flaring nostrils. She could actually *feel* his desire, which roared like an inferno.

When she pinched his tiny, pebbled nipple, he groaned and dropped his hand to his thick shaft.

Phoebe's lips parted when she saw the tiny slit was already leaking. Why did such a crude thing excite her?

He squeezed himself hard enough to make the thick ropes on his forearms bulge beneath the skin, forcing out yet more pearly liquid.

She swallowed the moisture that flooded her mouth.

Phoebe decided to take his reaction as a sign that he liked what she'd done.

He lifted his eyelids. "My turn."

"No," she argued. "You got to go first. Now *I* get to go, and then you." In a burst of daring, she pinched his nipple *hard*.

He gasped, the muscles in his chest and abdomen flexing in a way that was positively *entrancing*.

She bit her lip to keep from laughing. How could such a tiny thing affect him so?

"You vixen." His heated gaze burned into her. "Very well, take your *next* turn or you earn a forfeit."

"You didn't mention that rule," she argued.

"Phoebe."

"I'm thinking—just thirty seconds," she begged, her gaze flickering over her. Where did she want him to touch her?

You know where.

She squeezed her eyes shut. Could she be so bold?

"Ten seconds, Phoebe."

She opened her eyes and looked at *it.*

"Seven, six, five, four—bloody hell!" he shouted when she reached out and grabbed *it.*

Chapter Twenty-Three

I'm sorry!" Phoebe squeaked. "Was that too hard?"

She began to withdraw her hand and Paul quickly closed his own hand around hers.

"No. It was perfect." Paul tightened his fist and then slid their joined hands slowly down.

Her wide-eyed gaze was fastened to his crown as he stroked back up, until only the slit peeked from his foreskin. On the next downward stroke, he thrust his hips at the same time, making himself look huge as he shamelessly preened for her.

"It's so soft," she marveled.

He stopped. "Soft?"

"Yes, the skin."

"Oh." Paul resumed their stroking.

"This was supposed to be my turn," she reminded him, but she sounded amused rather than put out.

Paul forced himself to release her hand. "You are right." He rested his hands on his hips and watched her with interest.

She chortled and resumed stroking, her grip deliciously tight. "I'll wager you don't say that often."

"And I'll *wager* you learned to say *wager* from your brother."

"You would lose, my lord," she said, her eyes on what her hand was doing. "It was our old stablemaster who started almost every sentence with *I'll wager*." Her brow furrowed. "Am I doing this too hard?" She cut him a quick look.

"Harder."

Her small hand tightened and Paul moaned. "Yes, just like that, Phoebe."

For a moment, all that was heard in the room was the raspy sound of breathing and the wet sounds of friction as she worked him dangerously close to his climax.

"My turn," he said abruptly, removing her hand and then lifting her beneath her arms and moving her higher up on the bed before climbing up after her.

"Wait! I wasn't finished."

"I almost was," he muttered.

She laughed, clearly taking his meaning.

Paul pushed her legs apart and parted her petals with trembling, eager fingers. "My God I've missed you." He slid his thumb through her slick, swollen folds, circling her little nub, which was already engorged and thrusting from beneath its protective hood.

"I think you're—oh!" she gasped as he slid his middle finger into her, his thumb still caressing.

It took only a few deep thrusts before she quivered and cried out, the already swollen walls of her cunt clamping around him as she surrendered to her climax.

The game rather lost its structure after that.

***

Somewhere at the back of her mind Phoebe knew her husband was cheating again. But this time she let him.

His mouth was so soft and hot, his lips firm and his wicked tongue teasing at the entrance to her body. Because she was a wanton, depraved harlot, Phoebe spread wider for him and canted her hips, desperate to feel his tongue inside her.

"Please," she whispered.

Without hesitation, he thrust into her, and Phoebe whimpered, the mere thought of what he was doing almost as erotic as the hot, wet stroking itself.

Once again, he drove her mercilessly toward bliss, pushing her over the edge into ecstasy.

"You cheated again," she said, when she finally came back to herself, smiling woozily up at him.

He smirked as he rose up above her. "And now I'm going to cheat again."

Her inner muscles clenched hard at the sight of his red, swollen lips, which were slick with her juices, and they both groaned at the exquisite sensation.

But when Phoebe tried to do it again, she couldn't seem to find those same muscles.

"You will learn how to control them," he said.

"How did you know what I was thinking?"

"I just know." He positioned himself at her entrance and then impaled her, burying himself to his root.

Phoebe moaned and arched up to meet him.

"You have no idea how good you feel, Phoebe."

Oh, she had some idea.

"Six days without you—without being inside your body—was a torment."

She swallowed at his raw words, forcing herself to meet his gaze.

"I missed you, Phoebe. *You*," he added, punctuating his words with a sharp pump of his hips.

She whimpered and caught her lip, her body rising to meet his.

"Good girl," he praised, his face hard and stern. "Grab your legs behind your knees and lift them as high as you can," he ordered in a breathless voice. He nodded when she hesitated. "It will bring you even more pleasure."

Phoebe complied, feeling naughty when she realized that pulling on her knees opened her wider.

He glanced down between their bodies.

What must she look like?

"You look so beautiful taking me," he said, as if she'd spoken aloud. He shifted slightly and rolled his hips in such a way that he touched her even more deeply.

Phoebe squirmed at the ache such deep penetration created, each thrust echoing through her body.

"So good," he murmured, his hips pumping harder, his pelvis brushing against that wonderful button of flesh with each thrust. His eyes were glazed as his hips hammered into her, his thrusts becoming more savage and uncontrolled.

Phoebe wanted to watch him because she never got to see him come apart, but, yet again, he drove her over the edge of pleasure first.

"Can't wait any longer," he gritted out, pounding into her with several hard, driving thrusts and then hilting himself and flooding her with warmth.

Phoebe could actually feel his shaft thicken with each spasm and she gloried in their connection. Although their joining was so raw—almost primitive—it still felt like something more than just physical pleasure.

He shivered, groaned and then lowered his body over hers.

Phoebe didn't hesitate to close her arms around him, even though she'd never embraced him before.

Something had changed between them tonight and Paul had mirrored her thoughts when he'd admitted the days apart had been torment. Phoebe had missed not just his body and his presence in her bed, but *him*.

Already she was attached enough that it would be painful if he stopped coming to her at night.

And if she were foolish enough to allow her burgeoning infatuation to turn into something more—like love—then it would be agonizing when he tired of her and went back to his mistresses.

"Mmmm." He rolled onto his side and pulled her into his arms, shifting until they were both slotted together like two spoons. "S'good?" he mumbled.

"It's good," she whispered back.

It was better than good; it was delicious and wonderful. Phoebe had never felt so… cherished.

She squeezed her eyes shut, caught on the horns of a dilemma: how could she continue to have him in her bed and *not* fall in love with him.

What if she already had?

Chapter Twenty-Four

Phoebe nibbled her toast and studied Paul from beneath lowered lashes as he flicked through the third newspaper he'd brought to her room.

He'd woken her at dawn and taken her on her side, lying behind her. She adored the slow sensuality and how she'd drifted in and out of sleep, sliding back into her dreams after she'd climaxed.

The next time she woke up he was dressed in his riding leathers, the faint smell of horse telling her he'd already been out.

She glanced at the clock and goggled: it was almost eleven.

"Look who is finally awake," he teased, looking up from the paper as he closed it.

Phoebe glanced around for her robe—or any clothing.

Paul shook his head. "I want you to have your breakfast in bed this morning." He pulled the bell and then brought her the black silk dressing gown that had come with the nightgown.

Her face scalded when he held out the robe for her to slip into.

She hesitated and he smiled at her, clearly unwilling to look away.

Phoebe fumbled out of the bed, trying to hide as much of herself as possible, even though it was the bright light of day.

He wrapped the luxurious garment around her and then encircled her with his arms, pulling her back against his fully dressed and hard—yes, even *that* part—body.

"You feel so good," he murmured, nuzzling her neck and covering the sensitive skin with hot kisses and then cupping her breasts, squeezing and plucking at her nipples until they were tight and tingling, just like her sex.

Phoebe allowed her head to fall back against his chest as she luxuriated in his sensual fondling, forgetting all about modesty or daylight or anything but his expert touch.

"I wish I didn't have to leave you," he said, the words hot on her scalp, his fingers teasing and pinching and tormenting her nipples until she *ached* for him to fill her.

A frustrated whimper slipped out of her before she could catch it.

He chuckled and ground the hard ridge of his arousal against her lower back. "Poor darling." He slid a hand between the flaps of her dressing gown and stroked her swollen sex as if it were perfectly natural to do such a shocking thing. "Wet and hot and needy," he murmured, gently pinching the source of her pleasure with one hand while penetrating her with a finger from his other hand.

He pumped her slowly and the wet sounds of her own arousal causing her face to burn.

"I wonder," he mused, pushing another blunt finger up alongside the first and thrusting harder and deeper. "Can you come for me before the servant arrives with your breakfast, Phoebe?"

Phoebe squeaked and bolted forward a step at the horrifying thought of being caught in such a position. She pulled her robe closed and spun around.

He grinned and then put the two fingers that had just been inside of *her* into his mouth.

"Mmm." He sucked them clean, as if he were eating the most delicious thing he'd ever tasted.

Phoebe gasped and stared, her head buzzing with shock and arousal.

He smirked. "Get back into bed," he ordered, turning her as if she were a doll and then swatting her behind.

She yelped and clambered up the bed steps onto the high mattress. Before she could scold him, the door opened and she had to hurry to cover herself.

"Set it on the table here, Sabrina," he directed. "And then you may leave. I will be her ladyship's servant this morning." This last part he said while grinning at Phoebe.

She wanted to strangle him and knew her face would be flaming.

Sabrina gave him a sour look when he didn't spare a glance for her.

"That will be all," he said abruptly when she lingered.

She flounced—yes, that was the proper word—from the room, but Paul didn't seem to notice, his interest taken up by the contents of the tray.

"Coffee or tea?" he asked. "I've seen you drink both at breakfast."

She was charmed that he'd noticed. "Coffee this morning, please."

"And very light with two sugars?"

Her lips parted.

"I don't know why you are so surprised. Do you think me an unobservant man?"

Phoebe smiled her thanks when he brought her cup and saucer to her. She took a sip and sighed. "Perfect. As to your question, *no* I don't think you unobservant, at all. In fact, I think you are always watchful."

Where Phoebe was concerned, at least.

"I'm observant, too," she said. "You drink your coffee *and* your tea black. Although you have a weakness for macaroons, cream cakes, plum tarts, and butter biscuits."

He laughed—a genuine laugh rather than a brief chuckle—and she realized how rarely he did so. And how attractive it made him look.

She shook herself. If she wasn't careful, she'd be fawning over him just as badly as Sabrina.

"Are you not working today?" He'd worked every day they'd been there—even Sunday, albeit only at his desk.

"I must go out for a short while to check on something. But hopefully I will return in time to take you for a picnic lunch, or a picnic tea, rather, as I expect I shan't be back until three-ish. How does that sound?"

"It sounds delightful."

"Sorry, I suppose I should have asked if you had plans first."

Phoebe raised her eyebrows. "Two apologies in twenty-four hours!"

"You shouldn't become accustomed to it," he teased, tossing aside the paper that still sat on his lap.

"Do you read so many different papers *every* day?"

He sat back and sipped his coffee. "Yes, I like to get them from all over the country. Although the *London Times* purports to report stories from all over the nation, I find they do a less than impressive job of it."

"What sorts of stories are you looking for?"

"It is difficult to describe, but I know it when I see it. That is how I found my most recent venture—which is a partnership in two new warehouses in Liverpool. I discovered the opportunity when I read an obituary. The gentleman who'd died had been in the process of constructing the warehouses. It seemed logical that his partner would need a replacement." He smiled faintly. "Ghoulish, perhaps, but effective."

"Warehouses for what?" she asked, nibbling a corner of toast.

"For whatever people need to store. Ships come in and need a place to store cargo. Or merchants need somewhere to keep their goods while they await shipping." He shrugged. "Any number of things."

"Is there anything you don't do?" she asked, only half teasing.

He smiled and set down his cup and saucer. "If I don't tear myself away there is at least one thing I won't be doing—which is getting back in time to take you on a picnic." He leaned close enough to kiss her and then take her chin when she would have looked away, startled yet pleased by the gesture of affection.

His pale eyes bored into hers. "You gave me a great deal of pleasure last night, Phoebe. Normally when I come to Hill House I work late into the evening and only dine with other men of business. I am always eager to leave. Thanks to you, I find it hard to tear myself away." He kissed her again, this time on the lips, lingeringly. "Thank you," he said when he finally pulled away, leaving her breathless.

She was still reeling when the door shut behind him.

He was always a tender, thoughtful lover, but never had he been so affectionate when they weren't in bed.

His behavior this morning felt like something completely different. Could it be that he was coming to care for her?

Her mind raced in about ten different directions at that startling possibility.

The next time Phoebe took a sip of coffee it had gone cold. She glanced at the clock.

No wonder! She'd been staring at nothing and re-living last night for almost twenty-five minutes. She sighed. It was probably time to ring for—

"*Everyone says you're lying, Breena.*"

The voice was so loud that Phoebe jolted and looked around. For a moment, she was at a loss, but then recalled the servant corridor that contained a linen room and broom closet was just on the other side of her dressing room. There was a transom window between the two rooms, which Mrs. Hodge said had been installed to keep air circulating and fight damp.

"*I'm not!*" a familiar voice retorted.

"*Shh, keep your voice down. The mistress will hear you.*"

"I don't care if she does. His lordship won't let her punish me or—"

There was the sound of clanking and Phoebe missed the rest of what was said.

Normally Spragg shut the window when she woke Phoebe in the morning, but this morning Paul obviously hadn't done so.

Phoebe pushed back the covers and slid off the bed, not bothering to put on her slippers as she strode toward the dressing room.

Just as she reached for the chain to pull the window shut, she heard Sabrina say: "It is *too* his lordship's!"

"Then why are you still cleaning chamber pots? Why aren't you like Dotty Nolan who has her own cottage and even a maid of all work to do for her and the babe? Or like old Suki Temple who lives like a queen?"

"Paul wants to keep me close at hand—for when *her ladyship* bores him."

The other woman gasped at the same time Phoebe did.

"If Mrs. Hodge or Norris hear you talking like that you'll be out on your tail, Breena."

"No I won't, because *he* won't let anyone dismiss me. He needs me too much to let that happen. You've heard the stories about him—they're true." She gave an earthy chuckle. "He's like a beast who can't get enough."

The other servant gave a scoffing laugh, but her words, when they came, bore more than a tinge of respect, "You had better mind your step even so. It won't matter if you're his favorite if you cause mischief between him and her ladyship."

"Oh, *her*." Sabrina laughed, and Phoebe heard the sound of a door opening.

The next words were fainter. "Once he's put a bun in *that* oven, he won't have to go to her again until the next time. He's already told me he'll leave her down south—where her sort belongs and"—the door shut with a loud *click* cutting off whatever else she'd been about to say.

Phoebe realized her hands were still on the chain and dropped them. Her heart was pounding so hard she felt faint. She barely made it to the basin before emptying her stomach, which continued heaving even after there was nothing to bring up.

She staggered to the nearest chair and slumped into it, shaking her head in disbelief. Suki Temple had spoken the truth; like father like son.

Phoebe sat staring at nothing for almost half an hour before fury rose up in her—so thick it almost choked her.

She got to her feet and charged into her dressing room where she yanked down the smaller of the two portmanteaux, almost braining herself with it in the process. Once she'd fumbled it open, she began throwing clothing into it, willy-nilly, filling it so full she had to sit on it to buckle the straps.

She did the same with the second, until there wasn't a stich of clothing remaining in the dressing room.

Which is when she recalled that she was only wearing a dressing gown.

Infuriated beyond reason, she yanked open the bigger trunk and threw everything onto the floor until she found what she wanted—one of her older morning gowns, a dress she could put on without a maid's assistance.

Once she'd shoved herself into that, savaging a few buttons in the process, she rammed her feet into her ankle boots, forgetting all about stockings because they were at the bottom of the other trunk, and then went to the dressing table and ruthlessly brushed her hair, until tears streamed down her cheeks.

She dropped the brush on the table and stared at her reflection in shock.

What was she going to do? Why was she packing? Where would she go? She was his *wife*. His possession. If he wanted to, he could have her locked up in the cellar and beat her daily and nobody would make so much as a peep.

He wouldn't do that.

You don't know what he'd do if you displease him.

What am I supposed to do? Tolerate his mistress under my nose? Watch as she raises his child in my house?

Perhaps you'll be fortunate and—

Her head jerked toward the window when something struck it.

Phoebe frowned and stared stupidly, jolting when a second pebble *pinged* against the glass so hard that she was surprised it didn't break.

It was the window that looked out over the back garden.

Outside, near the hedge, was the red-haired woman from a few days before, Lily—no, Lila Nott—and she was waving.

Stupidly, Phoebe pointed to her chest and the woman gave an exaggerated nod and used both hands to make a *come here* gesture. She wasn't carrying her child today.

Paul's child.

Her gestures became more and more frantic and she kept looking around, as if she were afraid of being caught.

Phoebe stared for a moment longer and then snorted. Why not go talk to her? She had at least one mistress inside the house and another back at Wych House; what did one more matter?

She made a *stay and wait* gesture and then quickly plaited her hair before tucking it beneath a bonnet. She rooted around in the trunk until she found her old cloak, the one she always wore when she went walking.

Less than five minutes later—after dodging two footmen and a parlor maid—Phoebe squeezed through the hedges.

Lila hovered on the other side. "Finally!" she hissed, grabbing Phoebe's arm and pulling.

"Wait! I'm not going with you. I just came to see what you wanted."

"I wanted you to come with me."

Phoebe dug in her heels. "No! I'm not—"

"It's my baby! They're going to take him away."

"Who is?"

"My brothers sold him 'cause of who his da is."

"They *sold* him? But—that's not legal. They can't just—"

"Help me! You're his lordship's wife. They'll listen to you. I came looking for Needham, but the servants drove me away."

"He's not at home. But let me go and—"

The woman was weeping openly now. Up close, Phoebe could see she was younger than she'd thought—perhaps even younger than the maid, Sabrina.

It sickened her to think of Paul using these powerless girls as if they were his own personal brothel.

"Please!" she wailed. "We've not got much time. If you'll tell them to stop, then we can get his lordship and magistrate after. But I need you *now*!" She grabbed Phoebe's arm and this time she didn't fight her.

"How far are we going?" Phoebe demanded as the other woman pulled her into a near run.

"By the road it's three miles but—"

"Three miles! I can't run three miles. Slow down!"

"It's shorter through the waste."

Phoebe didn't like the sound of that.

"What sort of waste?"

"Just old bell pits, slag heaps, and few collapsed adits, but nothing to worry about."

Since Phoebe had no idea what any of those things were, she was hardly convinced. But at least the woman had stopped sobbing.

"Tell me about these people who've come for your baby."

"It's a banker's wife—she can't have a baby of her own and so her husband paid for mine." Lila pulled on her arm. "Please," she begged. "Just run, if we're too late, he'll be gone and I'll never find him."

Phoebe jerked her arm away. "Let go of me and I'll move faster."

The woman hesitated and then took off at a half run-half walk.

Phoebe stared after her for a moment, torn.

What else do you have to do today?

She scowled at the thought.

But it was true.

She had good boots on and her gown wasn't binding and she'd run with Doddy plenty of times, so…

Lila stopped and turned. "Please!" she shouted.

Phoebe took a deep breath and ran as fast as she was able.

Chapter Twenty-Five

Paul threw his gloves into his hat and handed both to Andrew.

"Where is your mistress?" he asked.

"I've not seen her ladyship this afternoon." He paused and then added, "Miss Spragg said she's not rung for her yet."

Perhaps she was still lounging in bed?

Paul grinned to himself at the thought and took the stairs two at a time, imagining her sleepy and warm and willing.

His cock, which had been painfully tumescent on the ride home in anticipation of this afternoon's picnic—where he planned to fully debauch his wife under the open sky—hardened the rest of the way.

He opened the door quietly, so he wouldn't startle her if she was still sleeping.

Paul gawked at the scene that met his eyes; it looked like a whirlwind had struck the room.

The bed was empty and heaps of tangled clothing were strewn out the dressing room door and across the floor.

There was a basin sitting in the middle of the floor and when he approached it, he saw it contained a good deal of vomit.

"Phoebe!" he shouted, suddenly frightened.

He strode through the chambers, flinging open doors and calling her name.

The carnage was the worst in the dressing room, where two portmanteaux were in the middle of the room, both open with their contents flung about.

His wife was nowhere to be seen.

Paul pulled the servant cord, yanking it hard enough to burn the palm of his hand.

He strode through the rooms again while he waited, as if he might have missed a full-grown woman.

"My lady?" the abigail's voice came from the bedchamber.

"She's not here," Paul yelled as he stalked toward the cringing woman. "Where is she? Have you seen her?" he barked.

"Not this morning, my lord—not since you told me to let her sleep. I kept waiting for her to—"

Paul pushed past her and went into the dressing room again. He threw the remaining garments out, onto the floor.

Once the trunk was empty, he looked up to find her watching him as if he were a lunatic. "How many habits does she possess?"

"Er, you mean how many are here?"

"Christ, woman! I'm hardly going to care about the ones that are elsewhere!"

"I'm sorry sir. Er, two, my lord. Just two." Her teeth were chattering and she backed away.

"Check the pile out there," he ordered, going through his own pile again.

The maid's voice came a few seconds later. "They're both here."

So, she hadn't gone riding, then.

Paul strode out of the room and encountered Mrs. Hodge and Norris, who'd no doubt been drawn by his bellowing.

"What is it, my lord?"

"Assemble the indoor servants immediately and find out who last saw my wife. I'm going to the stables myself."

Five minutes later Paul had questioned every stable worker and gardener and nobody had seen Phoebe that day. The hack she preferred hadn't been ridden.

"How the *hell* is it possible for a woman to simply disappear?" he raged at the men, all of whom looked back at him with wide, worried eyes.

"My lord!"

Paul turned at the sound of Norris's voice to find his normally expressionless butler dragging Sabrina toward him, his face grim as he glared down at the squirming maid. "I think we might know *why* she left, my lord. Although not how."

"What have you done?" Paul thundered at the girl, who quailed, her normally willful smirk nowhere in sight.

"I didn't know! I didn't mean it! Please, my lord—it wasn't—"

He grabbed her by the shoulders and leaned down until their eyes were on the same level. He didn't shout, he didn't shake her—which he was mad to do—he didn't even squeeze her.

He held her gently but firmly and said, in a calm, level voice. "What. Have. You. Done?"

***

"Stop!" Phoebe gasped. "I can't go any farther."

She bent over at the waist, her lungs heaving, and fought down the urge to throw up for the second time that day.

"We're almost there. It's just around those overgrown briars." Lila's hand landed on her arm. "Please, we're almost there."

Phoebe stumbled after her.

"I should tidy myself," she mumbled. "Nobody will take me seriously looking like this."

"We can go into the barn first before going into the house."

Phoebe didn't like the sound of that, but she didn't like the idea of facing a banker and his henchmen looking like a demented woman, either.

The barn looked more like a shack, the second story of the structure listing dangerously to one side.

Phoebe hesitated. "Er."

"Come on," Lila flung open the door and yanked her inside.

Phoebe couldn't see a thing going from the bright light into the dimness. The smell of old straw and sheep was almost overwhelming. Lots of sheep.

Phoebe turned around, but the door slammed shut, cutting off the light. "What are you—"

"I've got her!"

She jumped at the sound of Lila's voice, which was loud and *right* behind her.

"Took you long enough," a male voice snarled before two men stepped out of the gloom and into the faint light that was cast by a lantern on a hook.

Phoebe wasn't entirely surprised to see it was two of the three men she'd seen that first day—both gingers like their sister, but neither handsome. Or perhaps that was only the twisted snarls on their faces.

"Will you let Mr. Gideon go like you promised now that I've brought her?" Lila asked in a wheedling voice.

One of the men's hands flashed like a blur, his open palm connecting with his sister's face hard enough to knock her to the ground.

"Good God!" Phoebe shouted, dropping to her haunches to help the woman.

But before she could reach her, strong hands closed around her arms and yanked her to her feet.

"You don't worry about that slut—you worry about yourself," he snarled before turning to the man who was standing gawking. "You go fetch Robert. *Now!*"

Lila pushed to her feet, blood oozing from her split lip. "Nate? Please, this won't—"

"You shut it!" Nate—the one holding Phoebe—ordered. "Make yourself of use and grab that lantern and come along." He yanked on Phoebe so hard she stumbled as he dragged her deeper into the rank, stale smelling building.

"Why are you doing this?" she asked. Cobwebs slithered across her cheeks and she flinched.

He pulled her again and this time it hurt so badly it felt like he'd yanked her arm from its socket.

Phoebe cried out. "Please! Stop, you're—"

Nate shook her so hard her teeth rattled. "Shut up! You give me any trouble and that slap Tom gave our sister will seem like a love tap. Get over here, Lila!"

The woman brought the light closer and Phoebe saw, with more than a little dismay, there was a rude door with a bar on it.

"Hold up the light," Nate ordered as he lifted the bar with one hand, holding the back of Phoebe's neck with the other.

There was the loud creak of a hinge, and then a new voice came from the darkness, "It's about bloody time! I'm parched and need some water."

"You shut yer gob," Nate said.

Lila raised the lantern, illuminating the voice's owner.

Phoebe caught her breath at the sight of the angel—crumpled and filthy, but still beautiful—huddled on the floor of the cupboard.

She barely had time to take in a pair of tilted hyacinth-blue eyes—familiar eyes she'd only ever seen in one other person—when Nate shoved her.

Phoebe tripped over her own feet and fell on top of the angel.

The door slammed behind her and the man beneath her thrashed and squirmed. "Ow! Get off me! Those are my jewels you've got your bootheel on. Bloody hell!" He shoved her roughly aside, knocking her into the wall.

Phoebe bit her lip to keep from whimpering as pain shot from her shoulder.

The bar fell into place with a dull *thunk* and another slap came from beyond the door, followed by Nate's voice, loud and vicious, "You get back into the house, slut. Go see to your precious bastard."

Lila said something, but the voices moved away from the door and dropped to a murmur.

"Well, I take it you're the new Lady Needham." The voice was not precisely uncultured, but neither was it polished, like Paul's.

"Who are you?" she asked, although she could guess.

"I'm your bastard brother-in-law, Gideon Temple."

She flinched at the ugly word, her mind spinning with the implications of what she'd seen a moment earlier: this man was, without a doubt, Lucy's father.

Another suspicion sprouted right behind that thought; it was tiny but growing rapidly.

"I don't suppose anyone knows you're here—my brother, for example?" Gideon asked, a sneer in his voice.

Phoebe squeezed her eyes shut, grateful for the dark.

She heard a dry, mirthless chuckle.

"Walked right into it just like a rabbit into a snare, eh?"

"I'm so pleased my predicament amuses you."

He whistled. "Don't *you* sound just like a lady."

"What a stupid comment. I *am* a lady, you buffoon."

He laughed and this time it was genuine. "Say that again."

"Say what?"

"Stupid—only say it the way you did: styouuupid."

Phoebe felt as if she were in a strange dream—a nightmare, in fact.

"Have you yelled for help or tried to escape or done anything of use?" she demanded frostily.

"The door is barred and we're in a cupboard in the middle of a sheep barn in the middle of nowhere." He hesitated and then added, "The last time I yelled Tom Nott opened the door and kicked me in the ribs for my pains. I doubt he'd be any gentler if you tried it."

Phoebe knew he wouldn't—she'd seen the way he'd struck his sister, the rage in his face. These men were so furious, they looked almost mad with it.

"So… you have no plan?" she asked. "You just intended to *sit* here?"

"My only plan is to do nothing to anger them and hope they decide to let me go now that they have you."

Phoebe gasped. "You are *despicable*."

"So I've been told. Often."

She seethed in silence, carefully rotating her shoulder. It hurt like the dickens, but at least she could move it.

Once her breathing settled, she appraised her situation.

As much as she loathed having to speak to him, Gideon Temple was all she had at the moment. "Those men are the ones damaging the, er, the facility, aren't they?"

"The very same."

"Did you catch them? Is that why they put you in here?"

He laughed. "Oh, you *are* an innocent darling, aren't you? Let's just say my plans went badly awry." He spoke the last few words in an accent she assumed was meant to be hers.

Phoebe ignored his mockery. "That woman—Lila—she is, er, you are—"

"Lovers is the word you're so clumsily searching for."

Naturally she blushed like a naïve ninny at the word.

"Yes, how very astute you are, my lady. However did you guess the fair Lila and I were making the two-backed beast, as the Bard would say?"

It took her a moment to puzzle out the meaning of his words.

Once again, she was grateful for the darkness. "It was not difficult to discern," she snapped. "She begged for them to release you—to trade you for me."

He grunted. "That was damned foolish of her."

"The child is yours." It wasn't a question.

He snorted. "You're a great deal wiser than the Nott lads are. They refused to believe their eyes, even though the little bastard is my spitting image."

Phoebe thought about Lucy, and now this child. How many others had Paul been blamed for? And why did he claim them?

"And you just allowed everyone to believe that—"

"That dear old Paul is the father?" he supplied. "Oh yes! And I daresay you believed it, too, didn't you?"

Phoebe swallowed her shame and said, "There is a girl who has recently come to the Hall—Sabrina something—she is pregnant. Is she—"

"Lord! Don't tell me Paul hired the little slut!"

"I don't care for that word," she retorted coolly.

"That's a shame, darling, because it fits too well not to use on little Sabrina Whitten. I wasn't the first and I doubt I'll be the last."

"She can't be more than sixteen!"

"If that," he agreed.

"You are a vile, odious swine."

"I daresay you're right about that," he agreed cheerfully. "But you're dead wrong if you think she didn't beg for it. I brushed her off the first few times she offered herself up to me, but her sort come into heat early. Have you ever seen the way a bitch behaves around a pack of male dogs, my lady?"

"I don't wish to hear this—you are—"

"She'll squat for any and all of them, but she especially wants the dominant dog to take her. I daresay that's what happened with Sabrina; she went after Paul, first, but he is far too virtuous to get up to any rantum-scantum in his own back yard, so she had to settle for second best." He chuckled, the sound bitter. "Why, I've seen a greedy bitch take it from as many as five male dogs, one after another. *That* is Sabrina Whitten."

Phoebe knew she should cover her ears, but she was too transfixed.

"I threw her out of my bed when I was finished with her, hoping she wouldn't get any ideas. But the little minx was naked between the sheets the very next night." He snorted. "I could see where *that* was leading. So I had to drop a hint in dear Suki's ear." He laughed. "My mother is a right match for young Sabrina since the two are cut from the same cloth. Suki would never have hired the girl if she'd known I was coming for a visit and she was glad for a reason to send her packing."

"You impregnated this girl and then had your *mother* sack her?"

"That's exactly what I did. Why? Did you think I should get down on bended knee and offer my heart to the little tart?" He scoffed. "I wouldn't even if I could. I may be a maid's bastard, but I've still got a little pride."

Phoebe didn't doubt that; the repugnant man was positively stuffed with all the deadly sins.

"I don't understand—why does Paul allow it?"

"And here I was starting to think you were a clever girl"

Before Phoebe could think of something equally rude to say, he gave another of his unpleasant laughs and said, "Paul allows it because he knows that it is better for a woman to have the wealthy lord's bastard than the feckless, impoverished half-brother's."

"And you chose not to disabuse people and own up to your responsibilities."

"And cheat Paul of playing the gracious lord? God no!"

Phoebe needed a moment to leash her disgust before asking, "How many are there?"

"Oh, there are quite a few."

"You are *proud* of yourself for what you're doing—victimizing these poor girls as well as your own brother."

"Don't pity Paul, he could deny his paternity, but he chooses not to. That's because accepting blame and playing the great, moral lord, feeds both his guilt and martyrdom."

Phoebe stopped asking questions about the matter before she kicked him. Instead, she said, "Why do the Nott brothers want *me*?"

"Because they want to hurt Paul."

It was her turn to laugh. "They've been dreadfully misinformed if they believe hurting me will do much more than inconvenience your brother."

"That's not what I hear," he said in an infuriating sing-song voice.

Phoebe didn't want to give in to his baiting, but it was impossible not to ask, "What have you heard?"

"That my cold-hearted beast of a brother has finally been hit by cupid's arrow."

"Which one?"

There was a pause and then, "Which one what?"

"Cupid had two arrows in mythology. One filled the recipient's heart with love and one rendered the heart devoid of love."

"Is that so?"

"If you are going to spout mythology perhaps you might have a better grounding in it." She hesitated, and then couldn't stop herself from adding, "You unlettered dolt."

He laughed so hard that she thought he might choke on it. Which would only serve him right.

When he could finally speak again, he said, "I can see why my brother is finally in love; he has met his perfect match: a woman who is bossier and more irritating than he is."

Her heart fluttered at his words—not about being bossy and irritating—but about Paul being in love.

"How do you even know this? You've not seen us together."

"No, but the servants have and they talk. And what they say is that the mighty has been brought low by a homely little dab of a woman."

Phoebe clenched her jaws.

"Oh," he added after a significant pause, "that was rude of me, wasn't it? Well, what can you expect from an unlettered dolt?"

Phoebe supposed she'd earned that one.

"Are these men thinking to ransom us?" she asked.

He laughed and this time it was grim. "Nothing so direct or simple. They hate my brother with a passion. I would say their hatred of him is what keeps them going."

"They hate him for what they think he did to their sister?"

"God, no! Lila's fall from grace is just an excuse. They hate him because their feckless father drank and gambled away their land—rich with coal—and Paul stepped in and saved them by assuming the old man's debt. Without Paul, the Notts would be homeless."

"You're saying they hate him because he saved them from being dispossessed? That makes no sense."

"Has nobody ever saved you?"

"Yes, as a matter of fact—your brother."

"And how did it feel to know your future was dependent on his good will."

Phoebe opened her mouth to retort she was grateful, but then stopped.

She *had* been angry at him at first. But that had been because she was being forced to marry a man who kept his mistress under the same roof as his wife. Hadn't it?

You thought him a vulgar cit from that day on the road. You hoped even then—*weeks before you met him*—*that he'd not lease Wych House.*

You hated the fact that a merchant was the only one who could save your family.

Gideon snorted. "I can tell by your silence that you take my meaning. And you are a genteel woman who was raised to accept such assistance. For poor, hard-working men like the Notts, it robbed them of their most prized possession: their pride."

Phoebe was the last person to scoff at pride, which was surely the worst of the seven deadly sins, at least for the bearer.

"So then… what? Are they going to use us as bait to lure him here?"

"They might do that," he said agreeably, as if they were discussing the Notts taking them all out for an ice at Gunters.

"Unfortunately," he went on, his voice taking on an edge of fear, "I believe they have a surprisingly diabolical and clever plan."

"How do you know what plans they have?"

"Because I might have been the one to give them the idea."

"What idea?"

"To make both of us disappear. Forever."

Phoebe frowned, confused. "But how would that bring them any money? And why would you have put that idea into their minds?"

"Oh, my idea didn't involve our dying—it just involved removing you from my brother's possession for a while. Making him believe that you had run away with me."

Phoebe gasped. "Why would he believe such a ridiculous thing?"

"Because it happened once before, when his wicked stepbrother ran off with his betrothed right before their wedding."

"Good God," she whispered. "You did that to him? To your own brother?"

"Not once, but twice. Not the running away part, but I did *take* away both women he was betrothed to. Although the first one was such a calf-love that my father would never have permitted Paul—his heir and the jewel in his crown—to marry a mere village maiden. So perhaps I actually did my brother a favor with poor Christine." He sounded proud and vindictive rather than remorseful.

Phoebe had no words.

"Except this time, it would be different," he went on, relentless. "This time the happy couple wouldn't be running toward the Scottish border. Instead, their bodies would be moldering in one of the hundreds of abandoned adits that litter the area and Paul would *never* see them again."

His words echoed in the silence for several moments before she could scrape together the will to ask, "Why would they want to do such a thing?"

"Because they could then sit back and watch as my brother suffered and grew more and more miserable and bitter.

"It wasn't pleasant for him the two times before, but this time it would be so much worse since the woman in question was also the love of his life." He laughed, the sound filling the cupboard. "It is the perfect revenge, my dear. Absolutely perfect."

Chapter Twenty-Six

She's not anywhere on the road within ten miles. She didn't go into town and rent a gig or hack from the inn. Nobody has admitted to giving her a ride anywhere or to seeing her."

The Runner stopped speaking, his gaze anxious. "She just seems to have disappeared."

Paul scowled at Humboldt. "People don't just—"

The door to the library opened and Norris hovered in the opening. "I beg your pardon for interrupting, but Mr. Poundstone is here, my lord. I think you will want to hear what he has to say." He gestured the butler into the room.

"What is it?' Paul demanded.

"Mr. Gideon didn't come home last night, my lord."

"So? I can't imagine that is too unusual."

"No, my lord, that isn't," he admitted, but then hesitated.

"Speak freely."

"His traveling valise and curricle are gone, sir, but his favorite hack—Dash—is still here."

"What is so unusual about that?"

"He always has Dash sent along after him, sir. He is exceedingly fond of that animal. His groom said Mr. Gideon would never leave him behind."

"When is the last time the groom spoke with Gideon?"

"Almost two weeks, my lord. Mr. Gideon had given him a holiday." He cleared his throat and then added, "Mr. Gideon has not been able to pay him for some time, my lord. Grayson said he would have stayed with Mr. Gideon without pay, but he sent him home."

Paul considered that information for a moment.

This morning was the first time in weeks there'd been no new acts of sabotage anywhere. Paul had assumed that his brother had, somehow, stopped the Nott brothers.

Except for Gideon's horse, the information all seemed to point to Gideon holding up his end of the bargain and then toddling off to Bristol.

"Did he leave a message for his mother?" he asked.

"Not that I found, sir."

That would be like Gideon, too. Thoughtless to the end.

Paul turned to Humboldt. "I want you to go to Bristol and see if he purchased passage on any of the ships bound for America."

Poundstone gasped. "Should I tell Mrs. Temple that is where he has gone?"

"That was his plan," Paul admitted. "But I'm not sure that is what happened."

His brother might have left without his horse, but only if he'd sold it, not just left it behind. Gideon was skint, so he'd have sold everything he possessed before leaving the country.

Paul looked up and found Norris, Mrs. Hodge, and Poundstone all giving him the same look, and he knew what they were thinking.

All three had known him all his life. They'd been around for both the lesser debacle with Christine as well as the widely known disaster with Ellen. All three believed that Gideon had met Phoebe and charmed her the same way he'd charmed his two fiancés.

But Paul knew enough about his wife to say, with confidence, that Gideon was the last sort of man she'd find attractive—he was far too much like Sebastian Lowery—and he would wager his fortune on that.

Besides, last night had been… different between them, a turning point of sorts. She'd taken the initiative in bed more than once, welcoming him into her body with eagerness and open arms.

Phoebe wasn't a liar, nor was she adept at concealing her feelings; she wore her emotions on her face, for Paul to see.

If she'd been planning on running away with Gideon today, she never would have laid a finger on Paul last night.

His brother was still in the area, and so was Phoebe.

Gideon had needed to have one critical conversation before he left.

That was exactly where Paul would start: with the Notts.

***

"I'll wager that Paul never told you about the two women he was betrothed to marry, did he?'

Phoebe jolted at the sound of Gideon's voice and then gasped when she jarred her shoulder. He'd subsided into blessed silence after blurting out his horrifying prediction and his part in contriving it. She had hoped he was finished talking and she could die without having to listen to any more from him.

Apparently, that was not to be.

The room was stuffy, smelly, cramped, her shoulder screamed, and she was going to die alongside the most loathsome man she had ever met.

At least she could refuse to engage in any conversation with him.

"I suppose it is almost twenty years, now" he went on, evidently needing nothing from Phoebe to continue. "During the Christmas break—when Paul was down from Harrow."

Phoebe wanted to plug her ears rather than listen to this man talk about her husband, but she couldn't make herself do it.

"Little Christine Fowler was the butcher's daughter." Gideon gave one of his loathsome chuckles. "She was a right comely piece and virtuous, to boot. Paul took one look at her and fell head over heels. Of course, he treated her like a vestal virgin, not so much as touching the hem of her gown. He told our father he was going to marry her when he was old enough. If you'd have known our Da, you'd know how humorous he found that. *She's the sort you keep on the side, Son—not the sort you marry,* he said. Paul was furious."

He paused, and Phoebe had to bite her lip not to ask what happened next.

"By the next Christmas, when Paul was still as staunch as ever, my father began to get nervous. When Paul went back to school Da offered to buy me a curricle and pair if I could put an end to it."

"Good God! What do you mean?"

He laughed. "I knew you were listening."

Phoebe didn't care about his mocking. "What did you do?"

"What do you think I did? I showed little Christine a bit of charm, gave her a promise or two, and she lifted her skirts just like any back alley trull."

"You... *pig.*"

"Aye, it does make me look bad. But my father never would have allowed his heir to marry a village lass, so I decided—and still contend—that I did my brother a favor."

If Phoebe could have seen him, she would have slapped him.

"So, the second time. Well, that was a bit more... difficult. After that business with Christine Paul didn't come home again for years, not until he finished Cambridge."

"He went to university?" she blurted without thinking.

Gideon laughed. "Ah, that is priceless."

"What is?"

"You're another one of those, are you?"

"Another one of *whom?*"

"Those people who underestimate Paul because he's a great hulking ugly beast of a man who—"

"He is my husband," Phoebe snapped. "I would thank you not to insult him."

"He is my brother and I'll say whatever I damn well choose about him," Gideon shot back. "Although it is adorable that you leap to his defense."

Anger and guilt swirled inside her. Anger because she was forced to sit and listen to his cruelty and guilt because he was only saying what she had, herself, said and thought on more than one occasion. It shamed her that she'd ever been so shallow. And she hated to have anything in common with this despicable man.

"I grant you that he has grown into his features now," Gideon went on, his tone musing. "But Lord! He was an ugly sod when he was fifteen, towering and all gangly knees and elbows. And that *nose* of his looked positively obscene on his narrow face."

Phoebe didn't know when she'd started to see Paul's nose as regal and distinctive, but she couldn't understand how she'd ever thought it ugly.

"I still recall that summer—forgive me while I digress a moment, my lady," he explained. "To the summer before Paul met Christine, when he was still amusing to knock about with. Women, young and old, were lining up for me when I was fifteen," he boasted. "Poor Paul, on the other hand, was not so fortunate. It was almost his sixteenth birthday and he still hadn't shed his tiresome virginity. He was so hideous and awkward that not even our obliging kitchen maid, Cora—a girl who'd spread her legs for more men than a jockey does for horses—would consent to give him a jump."

Phoebe gasped at his crudity, but he went on as if he'd not heard her.

"I decided that I'd have to take a hand in things and dragged him to a place in Leeds to get the deed done. Even then the whore wanted double—not because he was ugly, mind, but because he was so prodigiously... endowed." He laughed. "The old doxy claimed she'd not be able to work the rest of the night after taking him. But then I suppose the matter of Paul's endowments is old news to you, isn't it?"

Phoebe was surprised her face didn't glow in the darkness.

"I'm sorry," he said, his voice dripping with insincerity. "But it occurs to me that perhaps this story isn't the sort a gentleman should tell a gently bred young woman."

"You needn't apologize. I'm not laboring under the misapprehension that you are a gentleman."

He snorted. "Ah, touché my dear sister."

"I suppose that imposing on kitchen maids and servant girls somehow makes you admirable."

"Imposing? I think not."

"Oh, they gave themselves to you willingly? I believe that is a story many masters tell themselves to excuse their behavior."

He chuckled. "Well, let me put it this way, my lady, in the pantheon of the gods I'm Apollo and Paul would be Vulcan. Or perhaps Hephaestus."

"They are the same thing—one is Roman and the other is Greek," she retorted. "*Do* leave off boasting about your skill with servants and mangling mythology."

He chuckled. "I'll move on to, shall I?" He continued without waiting for a response. "Paul came back from Cambridge where he managed to finish whatever it was he did with honors and—"

"Didn't you go to school?"

"Now who is getting distracted?"

"I only ask because you sound positively green with envy at his lordship's academic achievements."

"Oh, do I?"

For the first time since she'd been thrown into the darkened hole, he sounded angry.

Phoebe suddenly wished she'd kept her mouth shut. She had no way to stop him—nothing to defend herself with—if he became violent.

"For your information," he continued, raising his voice. "I never went away to a fancy school."

Phoebe pushed her back against the cupboard wall, as if she could somehow get away from him that way. Her shoulder ached and something dug into her scalp, so she pushed her fingers into her hair, most of which had fallen down when Tom had yanked her hat off and jerked her around—and encountered something sharp: a hatpin.

Phoebe plucked it from her hair and held it like a dagger. A very small, slim dagger.

Still, it was better than nothing. If Gideon laid a hand on her, she would take action.

"Don't you want to know *why* one son would go to Harrow while the other would go to the village school?" he asked a few minutes later, his voice so silky and dangerous she realized he'd become angrier, rather than calmer.

"Only if you wish to tell me."

He was suddenly close enough that she could feel the hot breath on her face. "Because I'm a *bastard*, that is why. "

Phoebe flinched away and bit back a sob when her shoulder twisted.

"That is how it was in Jonathan Needham's household," he went on. "My mother warmed his bed at night and scrubbed his house during the day. At least until his wife died, then she no longer had to work. At least during the day."

Phoebe closed her eyes, not wanting to even imagine such an existence.

"Once my mother took charge of poor old Paul, he had a rather hard time of it."

"Wh-what do you mean?"

"I mean Suki was a woman bent on retribution. She couldn't vent her anger on my father, so she punished Paul."

"Do you mean *physically*?" she asked, nauseated by the thought of beating a child.

"Physically, emotionally, mentally—if there was a way to punish, then Suki found it."

"Why didn't your father stop her?"

He laughed bitterly. "Oh, you clearly know nothing about our father. He cared about two things: money and status, in that order. What went on in the house was a woman's business. Besides, he believed that hardship built character and success. So, I suppose Paul owes my mother a debt of gratitude because he was black and blue by the time he escaped the house and went to school."

Phoebe closed her eyes, but the tears fell anyhow. It was all so dreadful. Her parents were remote and selfish, but neither of them had ever touched their children in anger.

"After what happened to Christine, I didn't see my brother for years. But I won't sully your delicate ears with any more of that."

Phoebe ignored the dig. She didn't want to anger him again. Also, she wanted to know about her husband. And listening to his stories had the added benefit of keeping her mind off whatever was happening with the Nott brothers. She refused to believe Gideon's grim prediction. Being murdered in a sheep barn in Yorkshire was simply too gothic and far-fetched.

At least she hoped it was.

"But back to the point of this story, which was Paul's betrothal. He came back from university covered in glory. Our father was a very sick man by then, but he clung to life because his precious son was betrothed to the diamond of the Leeds social scene, who was the daughter of an impoverished baron.

"What mattered to my father—with his shiny new title which clanked when he moved—was respectability and acceptance. And with his son marrying a blue blood—no matter how poor—he would finally gain *entrée* to those circles that had kept him out, even after the king himself, in a temporary moment of lucidity, conferred the viscountcy on him."

Gideon sighed. "Papa lived long enough to see them betrothed but died before they could marry. His final request was that the marriage not be put off. Paul was not to wear mourning. He was to marry and begin the process of getting heirs before my father's coffin—which was made of cast iron, you know—was lowered into the ground."

"Cast iron?" she asked.

"Oh, yes. He was John "Iron Mad" Needham all the way to the end. To make a long story short, Paul never obeyed our father's last wish because I swooped in and bore his bride-to-be off to the Scottish border." He laughed long and hard.

"You are despicable."

"Yes, shocking, aren't I? But will you forgive me when I tell you that our union was one of profound love. Indeed, Ellen took one look at me was lost." Phoebe felt him shift in the darkness, and then he asked, "Has Paul ever spoken about her?"

Phoebe's mind raced: if he was asking that, then he didn't know about Paul housing his wife and mistress in the same house. The last thing she wanted to do was expose her shame to this man.

"He mentioned the name once."

"I should warn you that he has her tucked away somewhere—although he won't tell me where. But you needn't worry that she's a contestant for his affections; Ellen is too ill to be his mistress. At least according to both Paul and Ellen's few letters."

Phoebe struggled to put the pieces together, but none of it made sense. Ellen was his *wife*? If he was still married to her, then Lucy was legitimate—no matter who her actual father was. And why did—

Loud, angry voices approached the door, along with the sound of a woman weeping.

"Can you hear what they are saying?" Phoebe hissed.

Before Gideon could answer the door shook and the voices outside grew louder.

Phoebe clenched her hand and then winced; she had forgotten all about the hairpin and had given herself a nasty jab in the palm.

Words like *whore* and *liar* were shouted beyond the door.

Phoebe clutched her feeble weapon, concealing it carefully in her fist just before the door swung open and three figures towered above them. The light was behind them, so their faces were not visible.

"Get up! Both of you."

Phoebe recognized the voice as belonging to Tom. She tried to stand, but her legs had fallen asleep.

"He said *get up!*" Nate, the other brother, shouted and then grabbed her injured arm and yanked her to her feet.

She yelped, the edges of her vision darkening with pain.

"She's gone into a swoon, you fool. Catch her!"

Brutal arms closed around her and Phoebe's face was pressed hard against homespun that smelled of old sweat.

"You get back, Temple!" Tom shouted. "Stay away from him, Lila." He gave a gasp of disbelief. "Good God, Lila! What do you have in your hand? Is that a *knife*?"

"Stop, Tom. I won't let you hurt him—"

The rest of what Lila said was cut off by the deafening cracking of timber.

Phoebe's captor's arms tightened around her and dragged her back a step, until he bumped into the wall.

"You there!" a familiar, beloved voice called out, although Phoebe couldn't see her husband. "Put Lady Needham down right *now*—gently," Paul ordered.

"Go to the devil!" Nate shouted, squeezing Phoebe so tight she couldn't even draw a breath to scream.

"Get away from that door or I'll smash the lamp and set the entire place alight!" Tom shouted.

Fire!

The word was like a vicious slap, snapping her from her pain-induced fugue state. If she didn't get away *now*, she would burn to death.

Without a second thought, Phoebe raised her good arm and brought the hatpin down as hard as she could.

Nate screamed when the long pin sank into his thigh. He shoved her away and Phoebe was momentarily free before her shoulder slammed against something hard and unforgiving.

White spangles exploded behind her eyelids and she sank to her knees.

All around her there was screaming and shouting. And then a blinding flash and the thick, acrid smell of smoke.

"Paul!" she called out, but her voice was barely a wheeze.

She pushed to her feet and took a stumbling step when something hard struck her in the head.

This time when she fell, darkness claimed her.

Chapter Twenty-Seven

I t was the sound of somebody moaning that woke Phoebe.

"Darling?" a low voice murmured as a large, warm hand closed over hers.

She forced her eyes open and groaned, which is when she realized that earlier groan had been hers, as well.

"Do you want some water?" Paul asked.

She nodded and then winced.

"Can you hold the glass? Or do you need me to—"

"I can—" she choked and coughed.

"Shh, don't try to speak just yet. The doctor said you inhaled quite a bit of smoke and you throat is probably raw. Drink."

She tried to raise her hand only to discover it was immobilized at her side.

"You'll have to use the other arm. The doctor said something in your shoulder has been strained, but there is no breakage. He predicted it would be tender for a while."

Tender. Yes, that was an understatement.

Phoebe let Paul hold the glass and greedily gulped the water.

By the time she'd had as much as she could hold, her eyes had adjusted to the gloom.

"What—" She swallowed. "What happened?" she asked in a raspy voice that sounded nothing like her.

He frowned down at her, clearly unhappy that she was talking.

"I'm fine—not so sore, just... scratchy."

"Tea?"

She nodded and he stood and strode to the door, murmuring something to whoever was waiting outside.

"Do you want to sit up?" he asked when he returned.

"Yes, please."

"Let me help you." He slid an arm around her and held her against him as he tucked several pillows behind her.

"Good?" he asked after lowering her.

She nodded and then wrinkled her nose. "Smoke."

"That's probably your hair. Mrs. Hodge wanted to wash it but the doctor told her you needed rest more than clean hair. She had to satisfy herself with washing the soot from your face and combing your hair."

Phoebe wanted to weep with gratitude for the woman's thoughtfulness. Even so, she was sure she looked a fright.

"Can I have a bath now?"

"The doctor will be here in a few hours and we'll ask if you can exert yourself enough for a bath."

"I can't tell what time it is."

"It is seven," he said.

"How long did I sleep?"

"Almost twelve hours."

She hesitated a moment and then made herself ask, "Your brother?"

A nerve in Paul's firm jaw twitched. "One of the Notts struck him hard on the back of the head. He was badly burned by the time I managed to get him out and he never regained consciousness."

"I'm sorry, Paul." Phoebe *was* sorry, for Paul's sake, even though Gideon had been a vicious lout. But she could see from his taut expression and tightness around his eyes that he'd cared for him.

Paul gave an abrupt nod, his features as stone-like and harsh as ever. He was not a man who found it easy to show emotion. And no wonder given the household he'd grown up in.

"Nate and Tom Nott never came out of the fire," he said.

Phoebe thought that was just as well for them. The men wouldn't have had much of a life after what they'd done.

"And Lila?"

"She has a badly burned arm, no hair on one side of her head, and she inhaled a great deal more smoke than you did, but Doctor Nicholson says she will be fine."

The door opened and Mrs. Hodge brought in the tea tray. "Oh, thank goodness you are awake," she said as Paul stood and took the heavy tray from her.

Phoebe made a subtle, desperate, gesture toward her face when Paul wasn't looking.

The older woman nodded and turned to Paul. "The magistrate has been asking for you, my lord. There are several questions that only you will have the answers for. I will see to Lady Needham."

Paul hesitated, glanced at Phoebe, and then nodded. "No letting her up and about," he ordered.

"Of course not."

"And do not let her tire herself."

"No, my lord."

Once the door closed behind him, the housekeeper gave Phoebe a surprisingly impish smile. "He hasn't left your side since the doctor went home."

Phoebe's face heated at that information and she didn't know what to say.

Mrs. Hodge went about preparing her tea.

When the older woman handed her a cup, Phoebe gestured to the tray. "There is a second cup. Won't you join me? Please," she added when she hesitated.

Mrs. Hodge nodded, sat, and poured herself a cup of black tea.

"I behaved rather foolishly yesterday," Phoebe said, not sure how to start what was going to be an awkward conversation.

"Oh, I think you probably had excellent reasons. Sabrina Whitten explained what she'd said—she knew you were in your bedchamber." Mrs. Hodge's face pinkened.

"The whole household knew. His lordship had scolded everyone to be quiet, that you were resting."

"She said all that on purpose?" Phoebe asked.

"She has always been a mischief maker. I wanted to strangle Mr. Norris when he asked the master to hire her. You see her father, Dick Whitten, grew up on the estate and was a good friend with his lordship when they were lads. Dick is ill and dying and—well, Master Paul wished to ease his concerns by giving Sabrina employment. She had already tried her tricks over at Mrs. Temple's and been sent off for her efforts."

"But—" Phoebe bit her lip. It didn't seem right to tell anyone what Gideon had confessed to her now that the man was dead. That was a decision best left for Paul.

Mrs. Hodge nodded, even though Phoebe hadn't spoken. "Sabrina confessed it all, my lady, how she went there to trick Mr. Gideon, but he turned her game back on her." Her lips twisted into a scowl. "Those are two peas in a pod, although I shouldn't speak ill of the dead."

"Gideon admitted the child was his."

Mrs. Hodge snorted. "Well, it *wasn't.*"

"What?"

"Yes, the master got the truth out of her. It is Robert Nott's child." She pursed her lips and shook her head. "And him with a wife and nine other mouths to feed."

"He wasn't one of the men who died in the fire?" Phoebe asked, horrified to think of a widow with nine children.

"No, he's the only good one"—she barked a laugh. "That is stretching it as he was breaking things like his brothers, but he came running over here last night—just as Master Paul was heading out to question Tom and Nate. After Robert explained what his brothers were planning his lordship knew to bring all those Runners with him. If Robert hadn't come it is doubtful that you would have made it out alive."

"In helping me he killed his own brothers," Phoebe couldn't help pointing out.

"No, that was their own foolish doing. They could have come out of the building, but they chose to burn for their sins. They were rubbish!" she said, suddenly vicious. "Breaking machinery and putting men out of work who are just trying to feed their families, and all for foolish, stupid pride. Everyone will be better off without them, especially that poor, silly Lila. Now *that* baby is Master Gideon's. It's clear to anyone with eyes in their head. But people can disbelieve their eyes when they've a wish to."

Phoebe thought about Lucy. She'd never even noticed the utter lack of any resemblance to Paul, but then why would she have suspected he would lie? Why *had* he lied?

Mrs. Hodge laid a hand over hers. "I saw how your pretty face was pinched and worried these past few days and I wanted to speak but I didn't feel it was my place to say anything."

"You needn't apologize. Instead of assuming, I should have spoken to my husband."

Mrs. Hodge chortled. "Or he might have come down from the rafters and explained the truth to his wife."

Phoebe smiled wryly. "I'll admit I wish he had done so."

"He's one who'll cut his nose off to spite his face. So busy showing he doesn't care about what anyone thinks that he pushes people toward the worst conclusions."

"So then, er—"

Mrs. Hodge smiled kindly. "The master has no children off his own people, my lady. 'Tis not his way. He likes to come the villain, but he is the protector, that one. Even when they were boys, he'd take Master Gideon's punishment for him."

"But... *why?*"

"Guilt, pure and simple."

"His brother said that, too—but what does he have to be guilty for?"

"Because everything—down to the last penny—went to him."

"That's hardly his fault!"

"No, you're right. But people don't always make sense, do they?" She inhaled deeply and pushed out a gusty sigh. "This house was a poisonous place. The old lord cared only for himself. He was one who should never have had children. Master Paul's mother might have made things better if she'd lived—she had a strong will— but Suki Temple was Sabrina Whitten all over again, selfish and spiteful and scheming."

"Yes, that is what Gideon said."

"I went to the old master more than once—risking sacking—and pointed out what she was doing to poor Master Paul. But he would only laugh and say it would make the boy tougher."

Mrs. Hodge turned her cup around and around in her saucer, her eyes vague as she looked into the past.

"It was better when Master Paul went away and didn't come back—better for him. But things grew worse here. Suki became more and more bitter as she realized Lord Needham would never give Gideon his name or treat him the same as he did Master Paul. She was a foolish woman and should have realized how things were years before when Lord Needham kept Gideon home while sending Master Paul to that fancy school. It about broke that poor boy's heart and it showed Gideon, even then, that he would always be his father's dirty secret."

Phoebe marveled at people's capacity for cruelty to their own children. To favor one child so much above the other was heartless.

At least her own parents had ignored them all equally, perhaps giving a bit more attention to their heir. But they had never purposely set their own children at loggerheads.

"Thanks to growing up with Lord Needham and Suki Temple, Master Paul learned how to hide his true feelings—even from himself. But make no mistake, my lady: he cares deeply for you. I've known him since the cradle and I've never seen it before. Master Paul is in love for the first time in his life."

Phoebe was torn between joy and disbelief.

"Ah, I can see it in your eyes—you don't believe me."

"His brother said this was not the first time he was to marry."

To her surprise, Mrs. Hodge laughed.

"Oh, dear me—he is still boasting about that, is he?"

"But he said his brother was in love with two other women."

She gave an unladylike snort. "It was nothing but calf love with Christine Fowler. As to Ellen Kettering? Master Paul was dazzled by her the same as every other man, young and old. She was a beautiful, dainty little thing, and sweet and mild tempered, as well.

"Master Paul was determined to obey his father, who is the one who wanted the marriage. But love? No." She leaned forward, as if to impart a secret. "I'll tell you what he felt when Gideon and Ellen ran off together: relieved."

"Surely not!"

Mrs. Hodge nodded. "Yes, he was relieved, but then guilty for feeling it. He saw it as a betrayal of a deathbed promise to his father." She scowled. "One of many the old lord was unscrupulous enough to demand from his son. The other being to take care of his brother and Suki Temple. What a burden he laid on Master Paul's shoulders! No," she said, sitting back in her chair and smiling smugly to herself. "He'd lay down his life for you—and he almost did, last night." Mrs. Hodge shook her head when Phoebe opened her mouth to ask what she meant. "No, no, I'll not tell you how he ran into that burning barn and almost died in the process. He'd be angry at me for doing so. You just take my word for it, my lady, Master Paul is in love for the first time in his life."

If that was true, then what in the *world* was her husband doing claiming Ellen Kettering as his lover and Lucy as his child?

Chapter Twenty-Eight

Five mornings later Phoebe was forced to send Spragg to speak to her husband's valet for a *second* time, as Paul appeared to believe she was so delicate and wounded and traumatized that he should not even come to her bed.

This time, Phoebe made the message mortifyingly direct: Lady Needham requested Lord Needham's presence in her bedchamber at eleven o'clock that night.

Her face heated just thinking about it, but really, what else could she do to convince the man that she was *fine*?

Besides, she had many, many things she wanted to ask him, the sorts of things that were best asked under cover of darkness after they'd both lowered their normal defenses.

Although Spragg had relayed Paul's assent to Phoebe's request, her husband had remained maddeningly aloof through dinner and in the library afterward, working his way through documents and ignoring her.

It was now two minutes until eleven o'clock and Phoebe was contemplating storming through their connecting door and confronting the frustrating man when he came through that very same door.

As usual, he did not bother knocking.

Phoebe decided that was a battle she would never win. Besides, she no longer really cared that he appeared to consider her chambers *his* chambers.

"Am I interrupting?" he asked as she hastily pretended to sand a letter that she'd only written five words of.

"No, I am just finished writing to my sister Hyacinth." She hesitated and added, "Neither Hy nor Selina answered my last letter and Aurelia said she hasn't heard from them either."

He leaned against the wall beside her writing desk and crossed his arms over his powerful chest, the action pulling his robe lapels wide and exposing acres of hard male flesh.

"Are you concerned that something has happened to them?" he asked.

"No—I can't imagine something bad would have happened and nobody told either of us."

"We can stop in London on the journey home to Wych House."

"Oh. Are we leaving soon?"

"As soon as you feel well enough to travel." He hesitated and then added with a faint, wildly sensual smile. "We shall see how you do after some exertion this evening"

Phoebe laid her palms on her flaming cheeks. "You do that on purpose, don't you?"

"I do," he said. He suddenly laughed. "I'll also admit that I find it amusing that you've decided to employ our body servants to exchange intimate messages."

Phoebe huffed. "It is what my mother told me is proper."

"Why am I not surprised by that? From now on, my dear, I'd prefer if we simply related such details or requests directly to each other."

"If that is your wish, my lord."

His smile grew a tiny bit broader. "It is my wish, my lady." His silver gaze dropped to the dressing gown she wore—one of the others he'd selected for her, a pale seafoam green with a nightgown even more scandalously transparent than the black one had been.

"Stand up," he said in his typically authoritarian fashion. "I want to see you—all of you."

Phoebe marveled at the sheer, unadulterated arrogance of the man; he spoke as if his wishes should be treated as *law*.

When she opened her mouth to argue, he stepped toward her and took her hand, lifting her to her feet. Once she was standing, he kissed her palm, a simple gesture that somehow managed to make her knees turn to water.

"Yes, my lord. Of course, my lord," she said, her tone mocking but also breathless.

Rather than look annoyed, he looked pleased. "That is better."

She snorted, although it was more of a gasp as he continued to lay soft kisses up to her wrist, which he then gently sucked.

"You are a throwback to feudal times," she said in a voice already thickening with lust.

He smiled and kept kissing.

"That was not meant as a compliment," she told him.

He took one of her fingers into his mouth.

Phoebe hissed in a breath.

His thin lips curled into a wicked smile as he sucked and tongued her finger, the sensation of soft, wet heat exquisite.

She would never have guessed fingers were so sensitive.

He released her with a soft, crude *pop* and then reached for the sash of her dressing gown.

"I wish to see you now. If I recall correctly, this gown has an interesting pattern that is perfectly placed to show—"

"Yes—yes," she said hastily cut in, before her head became any hotter. "It is openwork lace."

He smirked, clearly proud of shocking her into blithering idiocy. "Arms down, my love," he murmured when Phoebe tried to cross her arms.

Her body tightened—*all* of the interesting parts—at the *my love*.

She swallowed and obeyed and he opened the dressing gown and then slid it from her shoulders.

When he remained silent, she forced her eyes to look up and up; his expression was worth the kink she was likely to develop in her neck.

His eyes moved with glacial slowness over her, lingering on her breasts and sex.

His jaws flexed and he inhaled until his chest looked like it might explode. Finally, he heaved a sigh of deep masculine satisfaction before meeting her eyes.

"You are exquisite."

Phoebe floundered before she could manage to retort, "And you look so proud that you might have tatted the lace yourself. " She had wanted to come across as wry and sophisticated but had ended up sounding breathless.

Predictably, he threw back his head and laughed.

***

Paul watched his wife as he dropped his robe, hungry for her reaction.

It never failed to amaze and please him that she liked to look at his big brutish body. But the swelling of her pupils and deep pink flush that spread over the pale skin of her chest did not lie.

Once he was naked, he took her hand. "Come, up on the bed."

She scowled at him in the way he adored but climbed the two steps that led to the high mattress.

Her scowling stopped when Paul raised the hem of her nightgown—he'd left it on tonight—spread her thighs wide, and then lowered his mouth over her.

Lord but he had missed her the past five days!

And it had pleased him that *she* had been the one to come to Paul.

He smiled against her hot swollen sex, lazily tonguing her bud in a way that was too light and teasing to be entirely satisfying.

She squirmed and muttered something beneath her breath as she lifted her hips higher.

Paul grinned and tormented her a bit longer, not relenting until she grabbed his hair and snarled his name.

And then he made her shatter not once, but twice before he finally released her, moving up to her nipples, which were pebbled and charmingly thrusting through the small holes in her gown.

Paul had already discovered that she had the most sensitive breasts and nipples he'd ever encountered. It didn't take much suckling and pinching and nibbling to send her toward yet another orgasm.

His own body was shaking with need by the time she floated back down to earth.

God, but she looked lovely with her legs splayed and nightgown hiked up to just beneath her breasts.

He gave her sex a light swat that made her startle. "Up on your hands and knees, Phoebe."

She scowled adorably as she brought her knees together.

Before she could turn over, however, he stopped her. "Unless—wait, does your shoulder."

"No, I don't hurt. Really," she assured him, and then rolled her shoulder to prove it.

Paul studied her face for any sign of pain. When he saw none, he said, "Raise your arms, I'm going to take this off."

Once she was naked and on all fours, he positioned her so that they were both facing the large mirror that hung—not coincidentally—at a very convenient angle on the adjacent wall.

It took Phoebe a moment to notice their reflection. "Oh!"

Paul pulled her bottom up higher, still needing to spread his own knees a great deal to bring their bodies to a matching height.

Once he had her the way he wanted her, he reached between her thighs and pushed two fingers into her tight heat, watching her expression like the greedy, debauched swine that he was.

Because only a swine would use his gently born wife like a harlot, mounting her in beast fashion.

But Paul didn't care—he could admit it—he'd been fantasizing about taking her in this position since before their marriage. Imagining how her lush bottom would look offered up to him, full and spread, and the way her plump tits would jiggle and bounce as he fucked her.

Paul found the slightly rough spot inside her and stroked until she was grunting and riding his hand, begging for more. Their eyes locked in the mirror as she sped toward yet another orgasm.

"You look so beautiful, Phoebe."

She whimpered and arched her body at his words, thrusting her bottom up at him in a submissive yet demanding way that went straight to his aching balls.

"Shoulders down, eyes on me," he growled as she struggled to keep her glazed eyes open.

She obeyed without hesitation, her eyes never leaving his.

"Good girl." He withdrew his fingers, licking them clean while she watched, red-faced and rapt.

"Are you ready for me?" Paul murmured, positioning himself at her opening.

When she nodded, he entered her in one long, hard thrust.

Phoebe moaned, her tight sheath clenching around him and her eyelids fluttering shut as he buried himself to the hilt.

"My God you feel delicious," he rasped as he pulled her back against his pelvis, keeping her full and stretched as she squirmed to accommodate him.

"Eyes open," he ordered, his voice strained from holding back his orgasm for the last forty minutes.

Her lids raised slowly and Paul began to pump.

Because of the position, he was careful to work her slowly and shallowly at first. Even so, she still whimpered softly after his first few thrusts, her body struggling to adjust.

It didn't take long before her eyes began to glaze over and she forgot to be self-conscious or embarrassed, instead pushing back at him, using her body to beg for more.

Paul gave in to his need, sliding in deeper and harder with each stroke, until she was taking every inch, grunting and bucking and surrendering to her animal side.

"That's right," he praised, staring at her wild, lust-filled eyes as he reached between them and stroked the place where they were joined, caressing her unspeakably soft flesh as he slid in and out of her body.

God! How he wished he could see her wrapped around him.

But feeling her tighten around him as she began to orgasm was even better.

"Yes," he urged. "Come for me, Phoebe."

Her face contorted into an expression that was somewhere between pleasure and pain and she cried out, her sheath contracting hard enough to hurt.

Paul relinquished control and let go, flooding her with hot spend.

It was the most intense orgasm he could recall and seemed to last forever, spasm after spasm wracking his body, until he was wrung out, exhausted, and limp.

Once the last wave of pleasure had washed through him, Paul lowered them both to their sides, his arms naturally sliding around her body.

But when he closed his eyes, sleep did not come.

Paul sighed. He owed her some answers.

***

Phoebe could feel the change in Paul's big body. One minute he'd been as warm and loose as she felt, the next, he went as rigid as a board.

And then he rolled onto his back, taking his lovely weight and heat with him.

Phoebe opened her eyes and turned her head to find him looking at her.

"I need to tell you something."

It was the first time she'd ever heard any doubt in his voice.

"Lucy is not your daughter," she said.

His eyes widened and Phoebe couldn't help laughing. "I thought *I* was the naïve one," she said when he looked startled by her response. "She looks like the very image of your brother, Paul, how could I not make the connection?"

He grimaced. "Is the resemblance really that pronounced?"

"Yes."

He sighed. "Ellen had suggested we keep her away from Middleton for that very reason," he admitted. "I suppose I am willfully blind since I wanted her to be mine. To me, she has always been herself and not an image of her father."

"Why did you lie?"

"To hide her from Gideon—her own father." He raised a hand and squeezed the bridge of his nose between two fingers, turning to face the canopy overhead.

Phoebe propped her head in her hand. "Your brother told me about Christine and Ellen."

"Did he gloat about how she loved him—Ellen, not Christine?" he clarified.

"Yes."

"It was true. The moment Ellen saw Gideon, she lost her heart to him."

"Did you love them?" she asked when he went silent.

He hesitated a moment before saying, "I think I loved Christine—not that I ever really knew her—but it is so long ago I honestly cannot remember clearly. I recall my hatred for Gideon far better than my love for her. I feel like that must say something about the strength of my feelings."

Phoebe wasn't so sure about that, but she kept that thought to herself.

"As for Ellen? No, I never loved her."

"*What?* Then why did you—" Phoebe sputtered, unable to find the words to express what she was thinking. "I don't understand," she finally said.

"Don't you see? Not loving her made everything worse."

"No, I don't see at all! How did you come to that conclusion?"

"I never wanted to marry her—I didn't love her and only agreed to please my father. I was disgusted by my own weakness and *grateful* when Gideon ran off with Ellen." He clenched his jaws. "I knew *exactly* what he was and I let him take her."

"What do you mean?"

"Gideon was like a pendulum that went from sunshine to darkness. When the sun was shining, nobody was more charming. But nobody knew what would set him swinging into the other direction. And then he became vicious and cruel, determined to smash and ruin everything. It was as if two men shared his body."

"Are you saying he was mad?"

"Not all the time—but... yes, a sort of madness overtook him. Sometimes not for months and months—once, when we were younger, almost a year. But then he slashed my father's favorite painting—something expensive and rare that he loved to distraction. My father was enraged and he took a crop to Gideon. He wanted an apology, but Gideon—when he was in that frame of mind—only laughed and goaded him. Father beat him bloody, until Norris and Mrs. Temple managed to pull him off."

Paul turned to her after a moment, his brow deeply furrowed. "We lived in a state of constant tension, just waiting for the next episode. My father sent me to Harrow soon afterward, mainly to get me away from him. It took my father years and years to accept that Gideon was dangerous. He had planned to send Gideon to school, as well; not Harrow, but somewhere that would accept a boy with his background. But after the incident with the painting, he feared turning Gideon loose on the world. Naturally that only made matters worse."

Paul grimaced. "Coming home during school breaks was... nightmarish. Gideon hated me and his mother just encouraged his bad behavior, in addition to contributing some of her own. Father insisted I learn to manage them. *With great wealth and power comes great responsibility, Paul. You will be head of this family when I am gone.*"

Paul rolled his head from side to side and snorted. "I can't tell you how often I had to hear that, or some variation, from my dear father.

"All the while Suki believed I was scheming to do her son out of his inheritance. She was... well, she was a mother protecting her cub. I know that now, but it was unbearable. And so I stayed away for years, not returning until after I finished at—" He broke off and then cut her a swift look.

"Cambridge?" she asked, cocking one eyebrow. "Yes, Gideon told me that, too. And then crowed when he realized I didn't already know. Why didn't you tell me you'd been at university—and took honors—Paul?"

"Do the men of your father's class make that announcement to each other?" The look he gave her was so cold she shivered.

Even a week ago Phoebe would have been offended and hurt by such a look. Now Phoebe knew that expression only meant that he was protecting his tender underbelly from snobs like Phoebe.

"I am sorry, Paul," she said softly.

He gave a dismissive snort and Phoebe could see it would be better to drop the subject. "Finish your story," she said.

"I came home to see my father, who was very ill, and then I capitulated to his pressure to marry. I knew Ellen feared me and found me repulsive—although she'd been too kind to show it—so I insisted on a long betrothal. It was my hope she could be convinced to break the engagement after my father died. Ellen did not want me, and no matter how beautiful she was, I did not want to marry a woman who loathed me." He gave her a wry smile. "And yet I did, anyhow, didn't I?"

Shame rose up in her at his words. "Please don't—"

"Shh." He caressed her cheek. "I'm sorry. I should let it go. But you've probably discovered that your husband is a thin-skinned man who bears a grudge. But that was the last time I shall allude to what happened before we married. I give you my word."

She nodded.

Tell him how you feel about him now! Tell him how drastically your feelings have changed. Tell him!

But Phoebe couldn't make herself say it. What if Mrs. Hodge was wrong about how Paul felt about her? After all, *she* had never seen Paul look at her with love.

And so Phoebe bit her lip and waited for the rest of his story.

"Ellen and Gideon hadn't been married long when she became pregnant. Gideon was delighted—almost alarmingly so—and he came to me and demanded we bury our differences. He also demanded money to support his wife and child." Paul paused, his expression unusually pensive. "She lost the child several months later, after falling down some stairs."

Phoebe gasped. "How dreadful!"

He nodded but didn't look at her.

"I didn't believe Gideon so I went to see Ellen. She insisted it had been an accident. They'd been arguing and she turned and ran and slipped. Gideon was furious when he learned I'd gone behind his back and the two of them disappeared the very next day.

"Ellen came to me six months later. She had a black eye, a broken arm, and she was pregnant."

Paul turned to her. "She still loved him—she does even now—but she knew it was either her child or her husband, because Gideon would never share her. Ellen chose her child."

Phoebe set a hand on his shoulder and he took it and kissed the tips of her fingers, his gaze distant as he pondered his next words.

"So we decided to say that she had lost the child—it was the only way to keep Lucy safe. Gideon refused to give her a divorce—even as recently as a year ago he'd denied her request. Because he had always believed that I was in love with Ellen it was easy enough to convince him that she had come to me and to become my mistress.

"Gideon was too proud to beg her to come back, of course, but if he'd have learned about Lucy, he would have taken her away to make Ellen go back to him and the law would have allowed it. Even though I only wanted to keep them both safe, it made me sick with guilt to keep Gideon's child from him. It's difficult to explain,

Phoebe, but I still loved my brother—even after everything he'd done. That doesn't mean I condoned his behavior, but I couldn't stop loving him. Even though I lied to him until the end."

"Don't second guess what you did, Paul. It was a child's life at stake. *Lucy's* life."

He nodded. "I know. And Ellen—bless her—remained staunch even though I know she still loves him." He took Phoebe's hand and pressed it against his cheek. "I wrote to Ellen and told her what happened. I'd rather have told her in person but I know Suki will have written, too. She will delight in blaming Ellen for Gideon's downfall."

"Do you want to leave sooner to go back to Wych House? You could leave me to follow if you want to ride Coal—it would be faster."

He lowered her hand, kissing it before releasing it. "No. I don't wish to leave before Gideon's funeral. Nor do I wish to leave you alone on the road."

"Hardly alone—with six outriders!"

"I'm not leaving without you," he said firmly.

"I am glad." Phoebe took a deep breath and then reached for his hand. She lifted it to her mouth and kissed his palm the way he'd done to her.

He looked startled.

"I don't want to be without you, Paul."

He turned on his side slowly, his lips parted, fingers tightening almost painfully hard on her hand. The hesitant wonder in his eyes was all the courage she needed.

"I love you, Paul."

Years later she would still recall the first time she saw the expression—the one she came to know as his *loving* face—blossom on his harsh features.

She took his face in both hands and kissed him the way he'd kissed her so often—soundly and thoroughly.

When she pulled away, he looked dazed.

"I love you," she repeated.

A delightful flush spread across his cheeks and—although he did not say the words back to her—he demonstrated, in his own way, that he loved her just as deeply.

Chapter Twenty-Nine

Paul was finishing up the last meeting he'd have with his Hill House bailiff, a phlegmatic man named John Johnson, when the door to his study banged open and his wife stormed into the room.

"How could you!" she demanded, waving a crumpled piece of parchment in the air. "You—you vile, odious, lying, sneaking—"

Johnson couldn't stand up fast enough and tripped over his own feet in the process. "I'll be on my way then, my lord."

"That is probably best," Paul said wryly.

Johnson moved with incredible speed for a man in the middle of his eighth decade.

Once the door shut quietly behind him, Paul's wife wadded up the letter in her hands and threw it at him.

Her aim was true and it struck him dead between the eyes.

Fortunately, it was only paper.

"Won't you have a sea—"

"No!" she stamped her foot. "No, I won't sit and you can't *make* me!"

"Perhaps you might tell me—"

"Read my mother's letter!"

Paul bent to pick it off the floor.

Before he could open it, the bailiff's notebook—which Johnson had left on the table beside his chair in his haste to leave—came flying at his head.

Paul easily ducked the projectile and strode toward his wife.

"Don't you touch me!"

"I think it might be best. At least until you calm—"

She reached for a marble paperweight.

"No," he said firmly, seizing both her wrists and holding them in a gentle, but unbreakable grasp before asking, "What is wrong, Phoebe?"

"You contemptible, sly, sneaking—"

"Detestable, despicable, deplorable,

"Reprehensible—"

"Unspeakable, revolting, heinous, contemptible—"

"I already said contemptible."

Paul cocked his head. "No, I don't think you did."

"I *did*."

"No, I don't think that's right, darling."

"*Don't* call me darling ever again."

"But you arc my darling."

Her nostrils flared, making her resemble a miniature bull that was preparing to charge.

"How could you?" she demanded.

"I didn't recall you'd already said *contemptible* or I never would have—"

"Not that you—you *swine*! How could you plot and plan to steal Wych House from Doddy?"

Paul grimaced. "Ah, yes. That."

All the color that had rushed to her face fled so suddenly she looked faint. "You admit it?"

"Yes, I did plot and plan to buy Wych House and help your father break entail in the process."

She gave a choked sob that tore at his heart.

When she yanked her arms away Paul slid his hands around her waist and held her lightly while she punched and kicked him, not bothering to defend himself and earning a bloody lip, ringing ear, and tear-inducing punch to the nose in the process.

"Let me go!" she cried, and then collapsed on his chest.

He held her while she wept.

"Listen to me," he said, quietly.

"I don't want—"

"Hush. What did your mother say?" he asked sternly.

She made a gulping sound. "Some dunning agents came and showed that Father had used something—paperwork or a contract or—*I don't know* what—but she learned about some loathsome thing called common recovery."

"Yes, that is the term. And I directed my solicitors to halt all work on the matter the day after we were married."

Her body stilled, but she didn't look up.

Paul sighed and held her at arm's length before lifting her tearstained, puffy face.

"Don't," she muttered and tried to pull away.

"No, look at me while I say this."

She glared up at him, her lashes spiky with tears.

"I saw the error of my ways almost as soon as we were betrothed, Phoebe. I only waited until after our marriage to stop the process because I thought your father might forbid the wedding. I'm sorry I ever contemplated the action to begin with, but to tell you the truth, your father was dead set on doing the deal with me or somebody else. At least now that I know about his plans, I can make sure he doesn't succeed."

She had stopped squirming so he risked releasing her to wipe the tears from her cheeks and then hand her his handkerchief.

She snatched it from him. "That was very underhanded."

"Yes, I know," he agreed meekly.

"I hope you've not done it to anyone else."

"No, I haven't, and I shan't in the future."

She frowned at him. "You are not just condescending to me?"

"No. Never."

"Don't lie. You find my ignorance of business matters convenient."

"Perhaps I do on occasion."

She gave a watery, disbelieving snort and then sagged against him, laying her head against his chest. "I was so... disappointed when I read her letter," she finally said. "I thought I could trust you—and that you cared for me."

"No."

Her head whipped up, her eyes wide and shocked. "You—you *don't* care for me?"

Paul smiled down at her. "No. I don't just care for you. I love you, Phoebe."

Her jaw dropped.

Paul smiled smugly, pleased with the effect of his declaration. He would have to use it sparingly in the future. But not *too* sparingly.

"You do?" she asked, her voice adorably squeaky.

"Yes."

"Since when?"

"I think for a while, although I was not familiar enough with the emotion to recognize it." He kissed her softly. "But I was fairly sure it was what I was feeling the other day when you told me your own feelings."

She colored prettily and he knew she was recalling the *very* erotic evening in question. "When you didn't say anything, I thought perhaps—"

"That I was a coward?"

She gurgled. "No, not that. Just... cautious."

"No, cowardly is the correct word." He kissed her again and took her hand. "Come and look at something." He led her to the desk and unlocked the drawer where he kept papers of importance. Not too far down the stack was a letter from his solicitor.

He handed it to her.

"What is this?"

"Read it." He smirked. "Or would you prefer I ball it up and hurl it at your forehead."

"I'm sorry about that," she muttered, unfolding the letter.

A few short seconds later her head whipped up. "You *bought* Queen's Bower! But why?"

"I thought it might be the only way to keep your father from losing it and leaving your mother and sisters and Doddy homeless. Keep reading, darling."

After a moment her head whipped up again, "They are living there without having to pay rent and *you*—not my father—are paying for all the roof repairs?"

"Yes, and any other repairs that might need to be done in the future."

She smiled mistily up at him. "Oh, Paul."

"Please don't cry again."

She shook her head.

"If you are compelled to think me heroic," he said, "which I can see from your expression you are, I want you to recall my more, er, odious, domineering., dictatorial—"

"Bossy."

He nodded. "Bossy, feudal, and so forth, characteristics."

"Oh, I'm sure you'll remind me of them soon enough. But right now, just let me appreciate this rare, gallant, sterling—"

"Yes, yes, yes," he said dismissively, his face heating in a most mortifying way. "Now, up on the desk," he ordered. "Quick," he barked, when she gazed up at him, slack-jawed.

"But—it is the daytime."

"Indeed, and it is ticking away as you disobey your lord and master."

"Oh! Right away, my lord."

"Good girl. Now up." He took her by the waist and lifted.

"But there are papers and I am sitting on—oh! My lord, that is most naughty. And it tickles—not there, lower—yes, almost—"

"For a feudal conquest you certainly dictate your terms, don't you?" he asked, nuzzling behind her ear.

"Mmm," she hummed, and then slipped her hands down to his breeches and did some conquering of her own.

Epilogue

Wych House
A short time later

Y ou've been frowning at that letter for ten minutes," Paul said, glancing up over his reading spectacles.

He'd taken to wearing them more often, now. An impulse which had occurred, not coincidentally, after Phoebe had won a wager and then demanded, as her spoils, that he make love to her wearing nothing but his glasses.

"It is the oddest letter from my sister Hyacinth," she finally admitted.

"Oh? What has she to say?"

"Well, that's the thing—there is nothing." She held up a sheet of writing paper only a quarter full. "I cannot believe she would abuse my uncle's frank so grossly by sending a letter that is scarcely worth writing. And she answers none of the questions I asked in *my* letter. Nor does she mention our visit to my aunt and uncle's house while she and Selina were at that country house party. Do you imagine my aunt forgot to tell her that we visited."

"Well, she did seem rather, er, scatterbrained, but you left a letter," he reminded her.

Phoebe shook her head. "It is the oddest thing. I feel as if she isn't getting *any* of my letters."

"Perhaps London has distracted her. Perhaps they are both having such a jolly time they don't have time to write."

"I *might* believe that of Selina, but Hy had never gets excited or carried away. At least not about balls or parties or fancy dresses."

"Do you wish to pay another visit?" he asked.

"I can't. Not now that Doddy is coming to stay. He will only be here a month before going off to wretched Eton." She chewed her lip. "Are you sure we did the right thing by bringing him back from his crammer early?"

Paul chuckled. "Judging by his last letter, I think we did the *only* thing."

"Yes, I fear so—he was quite bitter about having to study all summer. In any event, I want to spend as much time with him as I can before he goes to school. I wish he *weren't* going, Paul."

"It will be good for him."

"Will it?"

"Yes. And remember that we shall have him on the holidays," Paul pointed out.

That was true, since Phoebe's father showed no sign of leaving his lodgings in London any time soon, and her mother was just as entrenched in Bath, where Paul had leased a house for her, complete with servants and a handsome allowance.

"Trust me, it is worth every farthing to keep her there," Paul had said when Phoebe had protested the expense.

Phoebe didn't mind her parents' absence so much, but she missed her sisters and brother dreadfully. Suddenly her family was so scattered!

"I wish Katie had agreed to come home. I cannot believe she prefers a trip with Aunt Agatha to staying here at Wych House."

"She just wants to stretch her wing, darling. She is seventeen and a trip to the Continent is an adventure for a girl who has never been anywhere."

Phoebe knew he was right. But it was disturbing how spread out they all were. Aurelia wrote regularly, but her letters were so... distant and guarded it was difficult to know what was happening with her. And she'd refused Phoebe's offer to come live with them.

"I am content here, Phoebe. I find the work stimulating and the environment... interesting."

Whatever that meant. How could a draughty castle in rural Scotland be... interesting?

As for Hy and Selina? Well, who knew what was happening with them?

A shriek shattered the quiet morning and a loud crash of glass followed it.

They looked at each other and both said, "Silas."

"I *told* you he would be a problem," Phoebe said mildly

A smile pulled at Paul's lips. "Well, he's turned out to be quite a mood-lifter for Ellen, so I can't really be that angry."

It turned out that Ellen Kettering, as frail and dainty as she looked, was delighted by the little rodent.

On Phoebe's daily visits to Ellen's chambers—which she'd begun making as soon as they'd returned from Yorkshire—Phoebe more often than not found the squirrel reclining alongside Ellen.

"It's not fair!" Lucy had complained. "Mama is fattening him horribly. Just what will Doddy say when he finally sees him? Not only that, but Silas likes Mama better than me!"

"I think he might like her better than Doddy," Phoebe had shot back.

The two of them had shared a snicker at that thought.

As for Lucy, she had settled into the house and neighborhood so quickly and easily it was as if she had always lived there. Phoebe had been relieved to learn their neighbors had decided to treat Lucy as if she were truly a daughter of the house, no doubt afraid to anger Paul if they did otherwise.

Paul and Ellen had decided it would hurt Lucy more to learn the truth at this point—that Lucy wasn't Paul's daughter, nor was she illegitimate—than it would help her.

"Paul can tell her one day—when she is grown," Ellen had said. "I've written some letters about Gideon so that Lucy might know the best about her father when the time comes."

Now that Phoebe knew Ellen wasn't in love with Paul and had never been his mistress, she quite liked spending time with her and the two of them were becoming close.

Not only did she enjoy her company, but she found it amusing to scandalize the neighborhood with the unconventional friendship.

Ellen had stunned Phoebe by confessing that she'd been relieved by Gideon's death. "He was a lost soul—wandering from place to place, but never happy. Even when we were together, he was looking to the horizon. I regret that he is gone, but he would have ruined Lucy's life if he'd known about her and he was a terrible weight on Paul."

Phoebe had silently agreed.

She had been amazed by how much of her husband's dour, stern disposition had been due to his worries about Gideon.

He was so much happier now and his love for Lucy was a joy to behold.

"I'm sorry I was so suspicious of you when you visited me that day," Ellen had confessed to Phoebe a few days earlier. "I felt torn between guilt and shame for what you must think of me and fear that—"

"Fear that I wouldn't allow Paul to care for Lucy when you were gone," Phoebe had cut in quietly.

"Yes. And I must admit that knowing that is not true has made me far easier. Which, I believe, has made me stronger."

But she was still failing rapidly.

Phoebe privately prayed that Ellen at least made it until after Christmas—which was Lucy's birthday.

But she knew that whenever the other woman died, Lucy would be positively devastated.

"She will grieve," Ellen said. "But at least now she will have you to help her through it, as well as Paul, Doddy, and of course Silas," Ellen had said when Phoebe had voiced her worries about Lucy.

Phoebe knew the other woman was right; there was no way to protect anyone against death. They best they could do was love Lucy, who was very easy to love.

Another crash came from the corridor, pulling Phoebe from her grim musing.

The door flung open and Davis, white lipped and vibrating with anger, stood on the threshold.

"What is all that racket out there, Davis?" Paul demanded, cutting Phoebe a quick wink.

Oh, how he loved to rattle his proper butler.

"That... *creature* is loose in the dining room and is savaging the fifteenth century epergne from the fourth earl's sojourn to India," Davis said tightly.

"Oh, no. Not the epergne," Paul said, a look of unholy glee in his eyes as he prepared to tease the poor servant, who believed—like so many—that an inability to trace one's lineage back to the Conqueror meant a lack of intelligence. "Er, what is that, exactly, Davis? A fruit of some sort?"

Phoebe choked back a laugh and got to her feet. "I will be there in a moment, Davis."

The butler cut Paul a frosty look and shut the door soundlessly.

"You are a beast to taunt him," Phoebe chided as she strode past him. Or at least she attempted to stride past.

But Paul caught her hand and then pulled her into his lap. "Yes, but I am *your* beast, darling" he murmured, claiming her with the sort of deep, languid kiss that she would never grow tired of.

"You are my beast, Paul—all mine," Phoebe murmured against his lips when he came up for air. "And I am grateful for that fact each and every day, my love."

And then Phoebe commenced to show him some of that gratitude, ignoring the sound of breaking glass and shouting, and kissing him properly—or improperly, rather—even though it was broad daylight.

Dear Reader:

I hope you enjoyed Phoebe's story and enjoyed (briefly) meeting her siblings.

I had so much fun writing this book and imagining ways for each of the Bellamy offspring to try and save their family's future. As you all know, there were few respectable options for a woman back in the Regency Era. Basically, she could marry well if she wanted to pull herself out of poverty. Anything else—working, for example—would mean losing her position in the *ton* hierarchy.

Some books are easier to write than others, and I found this one a joy to put down on paper. Phoebe and Paul were both so clear in my mind's eye that I often felt like an observer of their relationship, rather than an instigator.

I absolutely love a romance with opposites, although in this case, Phoebe and Paul proved more than a little alike in personality—both were headstrong, opiniated, and determined to have their way—even though their backgrounds were very different.

I also adore "age-gap" romances and older heroes as there is a sixteen-year difference between myself and my husband.

I *very loosely* based Paul and his father on John "Iron-Mad" Wilkinson, who did indeed marry two wealthy women and conduct an affair with a housemaid, upon whom he fathered his only children when he was in his seventies.

As usual, I spent way too many hours burrowing down rabbit holes. My husband was a geologist for his entire career, so he was overjoyed to assist me with all the mining details.

For the purpose of the story, I simplified coal mining in the Nineteenth Century—so you may thank me for that now;>)

It was really tough to decide which sister's story should come next, but Hy just caught my attention first.

As usual, if you read my book and enjoyed it—hell, even if you hated it—I'd love it if you gave me a review.

Have a great year and stay safe!

Minerva

P.S. I've got a treat for you if you keep reading—an exclusive look at the next book in the series, *HYACINTH…*

Chapter 1

London

Even with a half-naked woman on his lap Sylvester Derrick, eighth Duke of Chatham, was bored.

But that wasn't unusual—neither the boredom nor the half-naked woman.

No, what was unusual was that Sylvester hadn't simply gotten up and left hours ago—when he'd first begun to *get* bored. He blamed his inertia on the weather rather than laziness, but he knew that was a lie. While it was true it was wretched outside, it was truer that his arse had been in this chair so damned long the two seemed to have become fused.

He shifted the girl's plump bottom from one leg to the other and she made a soft grunting sound, like a sleeper disturbed, her arm tightening around his shoulder.

"I'll stick," Sylvester muttered over her shoulder when the dealer gave him a questioning look.

The young buck next to Sylvester took a hit on a four showing and received a ten. The boy stared at the two cards and savagely chewed his lip before—amazingly—asking for another card. It was a knave, which meant twenty-four showing.

Sylvester snorted.

The idiot gave a gurgle of surprise and dropped his head into his hands. "Bloody hell!"

"No hysterics," Fowler, who sat on the boy's other side, growled. The cantankerous merchant shook his leonine head at the dealer, "I'll stick."

The version of *vingt-et-un* at Number Nine Leeland Street—known more commonly, but less flatteringly, as the *Pigeon Hole*—was different than most versions played in other London hells, not that every hell didn't have its own variations on the popular game.

This version was played with two decks, the dealer was allowed to double, the second card was dealt face-up, and—most interestingly—the dealer was required to take a card on anything less than fifteen. Sylvester found the variant more entertaining than any other he'd played and, therefore, compelling enough to come to such a godforsaken part of the city.

The dealer flipped his card, revealing a queen to go with his four, and then dealt himself another: a second queen hit the table.

"Bloody hell!" the young fool beside Sylvester groaned again, louder this time. "I could have won if—"

"Shut it or leave," Fowler snapped, scraping his winnings across the green baize with a scowl.

The younger man shoved back from the table and lurched unsteadily to his feet, glaring down at the gargantuan merchant. "I'll—I'll—"

"You'll go eat some supper," Sylvester advised the boy before Fowler did something everyone would regret.

The younger man turned and blinked blearily down at him, his gaze flickering to the right side of Sylvester's face. He grimaced and then coughed. "Ah, yes. Supper."

He staggered away and Fowler chuckled.

"It must be bloody nice to be a *dooook* and scare little boys away with a glance," Fowler taunted. "We poor commoners usually have to give them a boot in the arse to be rid of them."

Sylvester smiled, even though he knew it was not a pretty sight. He liked the other man a great deal, as harsh and uncivil as Fowler was. Not only was he clever and amusing, but he elevated plain speaking to an artform.

The whore who was sitting on his lap, Delia he thought her name was, shifted restlessly, her hand going to Sylvester's face. The unscarred side.

She stroked him and whispered into his neck, her bottom rubbing suggestively over his groin. "What about you, Your Grace? Have you worked up an appetite? Are you... hungry."

Sylvester knew that Delia wasn't talking about the surprisingly excellent supper the Pigeon Hole provided its victims.

But her carnal words did nothing to stir him, so he ignored her offer.

The deal passed to the lugubrious Lord Framling, a man who'd been losing as steadily as Sylvester and his friend Angus Fowler had been winning. Sylvester had at least two thousand in his pile and Fowler even more.

"You going to supper or staying?" Fowler asked, as they waited for fresh packs of cards—which was Framling's prerogative.

Sylvester opened his mouth to say *neither* when the door to the card room swung open and a newcomer hovered in the doorway.

"Ah, fresh meat." Fowler paused in the process of stuffing some of the bills on the table into his pocket to scrutinize the young man. He snorted disparagingly. "Although he doesn't look like he'll have much to contribute to my purse."

Sylvester had to agree. The newcomer was a stripling who couldn't have been more than eighteen. He was a spindly lad, his well-made clothing hanging on his thin frame and thick, over-large spectacles perched on a long, boney nose that looked out of place above a full but tight-lipped mouth.

As he came closer, Sylvester readjusted his estimate—the boy looked closer to fifteen than eighteen. He was nothing but sharp angles and fine-boned fragility.

Surely he was too young to be out and about by himself at such an advanced hour in such a dangerous part of London?

"Here then," Fowler said, eyeing the boy with a look harsh enough to strip the bark off a tree. "I think you took the wrong door, lad. The nursery's one door down."

The others chuckled and even Sylvester smiled.

The boy's freckled skin—pale and not yet sprouting hair—mottled an ugly red. He took off his hat, exposing hair that was the shocking orange-red of an actual orange, and dropped his skinny carcass into the chair where the last youngster had been sitting. He placed his hand on the table and when it came away, there was a tightly rolled wad of bills in its place.

Fowler chuckled. "I guess that shuts me up."

Sylvester studied the boy's flushed profile. Strawberry blonde eyelashes grew thick and without any curve from lids that rode heavy over pale green eyes. His fine hair was overlong and brushing his collar. Even a heavy dollop of pomade could not stop the frizzy curls, except around the boy's temples, where the hair had been brutally scraped back to expose fair skin with blue veins pulsing beneath.

He turned toward Sylvester, obviously aware of his scrutiny. Not by a blink or even a change in breathing did he show any surprise at Sylvester's hideously scarred face. That, alone, was unusual in Sylvester's experience. In fact, it might be unique. Even Fowler, as rough and tough as he was, had gawked at the scar the first time they'd met. But the boy just fixed him with a pale, fishy stare.

Well.

But then his eyes drifted to Delia and his flush—which had just started to recede—rose up with a vengeance, flooding his narrow face. The boy swallowed so hard it looked painful.

Sylvester chuckled at his obvious discomfort and gave the girl on his lap a nudge. "Up you get, darling." She was putting his leg to sleep and wasting her time on him; it was better for both of them—not to mention the nervous boy—if she found a lap that paid better.

Delia unfolded herself from Sylvester's lap with the languid stretch of a cat, making sure to thrust her substantial breasts up against him in the process. He pressed some money into her hand and her sleepy eyes widened at the amount.

"Coo, much obliged, Your Grace." She licked her full, rouged lips. "Are you sure you don't—"

"Not tonight," Sylvester said, his gaze still on the boy's wide-eyed stare—which had become even wider when Delia had turned the full extent of her charms in his direction. Really, the lad was looking at the woman as if he'd never seen one before.

A waiter came to deliver fresh packs of cards and take orders for drinks.

"Brandy," the boy said in the warbly uneven tone of a young male in the process of becoming a man.

Sylvester nodded at the waiter to indicate he would have the same.

Framling gave the waiter card money, split open two fresh packs, and commenced to shuffle.

Outside the wind blew hard enough to rattle the shutters on the building.

***

Hyacinth Louisa Bellamy, the second oldest daughter of the Earl of Addiscombe, carefully turned up the corner of the face-down card: an ace.

She flipped it over and pushed more money toward the dealer. "Split and double down."

Hy ignored the low murmuring that came from the other players. She couldn't blame their irritation; she had enjoyed an unusual number of splits this evening.

The dealer dealt her two cards: a nine and an eight.

"You lucky little bastard," the big gruff player—a Scotsman called Fowler—grumbled as he stayed with his hand, a five showing.

This was a better group of card players than Hy usually encountered, but then again this wasn't a group of grooms, postilions, and footmen in a stable; this was one of the highest dollar hells in London. Complete with prostitutes.

The dealer flipped his cards to grumbles all around the table: seventeen. His hand beat all but Hy's and the scarred man next to her.

Hy glanced at her winnings, several towers of neatly stacked coins and a small collection of bills. She'd increased her stake money by three hundred and twenty pounds. It was the most profitable evening of cards she'd ever had. She could have earned a lot more if she'd wagered more aggressively, but her naturally cautious nature was difficult to suppress.

Besides, this was only her fifth night out and she had plenty of time to accumulate the funds she needed without becoming reckless.

Hy would have liked to continue playing, but it was late and she had to be careful about returning home.

"I'm out," she said.

She took the small leather purse her younger brother had given her and began to put away her winnings.

"Leavin' already?" Fowler growled, leaning back, one huge arm slung over his chair, his dark green eyes as hard as agates. He was a ginger, too, although nowhere near as red as Hy.

Nobody was as redheaded as Hy.

Hy nodded at the man and then remembered what her sister Selina was always telling her: "You've got to *speak* to people, Hy. Even if it's only to say *hello* and *goodbye*."

"Yes." That answer seemed far too bald so she added, "Thank you, sir, it was most enjoyable."

Hy stood and tucked the purse inside her coat, the fat roll of money making a bulge over her left breast. She stopped her body from dropping a curtsy at the last minute, turning the action into a rather awkward bow.

Fowler laughed. "D'ja hear that Chatham? The lad has *enjoyed* takin' our money."

The Duke of Chatham looked up at her, his light brown eyes glinting with humor. The wound in his cheek—an odd, circular scar—pulled the right corner of his mouth up, exposing his canine tooth and the ones on either side of it, giving him a perpetual sneer.

The longer he looked at her, the more Hy relaxed: he did not recognize her.

Hy should have been ecstatic about that, but she couldn't help feeling a bit insulted: this was at least the fifth time they'd been introduced—or *re*-introduced, rather—this Season.

Of course the other four times Hy had been wearing a dress.

Besides, why *should* he recognize her? Hy was... well, *Hy* and the duke was one of the *ton's* preeminent connoisseurs of women, and a matrimonial catch who'd been pursued by some of the most marriage-mad mamas in the *ton*.

And those were only the proper rumors she'd heard about him.

The *im*proper rumors—those she'd overheard in the various hells she'd visited—described Chatham as a libertine with sexual appetites of Roman proportions.

Hy had heard enough women complain about his mutilated face—even while they were setting their caps at him—to know it was his wealth and title that attracted all the interest.

Personally, Hy didn't think his scar was horrifying—unless you thought about how badly it must have hurt when it happened; *that* was horrifying.

She thought it gave him an air of danger and improved an otherwise average face. But then she was odd that way, liking ugly or damaged things. She was hardly a diamond of the first water, herself, so it didn't seem fair to expect perfection and beauty from others.

"What's your name?" The duke's soft voice, unlike Fowler's, was of Hy's own class.

Hy and Selina had already discussed this eventuality—although she'd never imagined she'd have to put her lies to the test with the Duke of Chatham, of all people.

They had decided that a name as close to her own was the wisest choice. "Hiram Bellamy, Your Grace." She cleared the froggy sound from her throat and added. "But I answer to Hy."

The duke's shrewd gaze made Hy's skin prickle beneath the men's clothing she wore.

"Any relation to the Earl of Addiscombe?"

Again, Hy had anticipated this question. "None that I know of, sir."

Fowler laughed. "He sure doesn't play like Addiscombe!"

The men at the table, all except the duke, laughed with him.

The duke's speculative gaze made Hy feel more than a little uneasy. But it seemed she was worrying for nothing because, after a long moment, he smiled faintly and said, "No, he most certainly does not."

Hy experienced a pang at hearing her father's skills—or lack of them—spoken of so derisively. However, she wasn't surprised. The earl was a dreadful card player, no matter how much he loved gambling. Or perhaps *because* he loved it so much.

The duke kept her fixed with his piercing stare, so Hy held his gaze, unwilling to back down. After all, it wasn't too often that she had an excuse to openly gawk at such a man.

The Duke of Chatham was that rare beast: a wealthy, bachelor duke of marriageable age—not that he appeared to be looking for a wife, much to the chagrin of her Aunt Fitzroy and every other matrimonial minded mama in England.

In addition to being a well-known libertine with voracious appetites—which would explain the prostitute he'd had balanced on his lap—he was also accounted to be top of the trees when it came to hunting, shooting, fencing, and was a pugilist of some renown—a Corinthian, in other words.

Hy wasn't certain what, exactly, a Corinthian was—although her brother Doddy was wild to belong to the group. She could only assume a Corinthian was the embodiment of masculine ideals.

Strangely, the duke did not *look* like a debauched pugilistic rake. Well, other than the prostitute he'd had on his lap. He was only slightly above average height and of normal build, although his shoulders and chest appeared well-developed.

The unscarred side of his face was neither handsome nor ugly. He looked, with the exception of the scar, shockingly normal.

Especially when compared to his friend Baron Fowler.

As if reading her mind, Fowler gave one of his noisy, good-natured guffaws. "There, see what you've done, Chatham? Cut off the boy's garrulous flow."

Again, the others laughed, all except the duke. "Do you play here often, Bellamy?" he asked.

Did twice count as often? Hy shrugged.

"You must join us again sometime and give poor Mr. Fowler an opportunity to win back some of his money." When the duke smiled the undamaged side of his mouth pulled up higher, exposing a second pointy canine. "If you do come back, you will need to arrive earlier—we begin our play at eleven o'clock. I know it is an unfashionable hour, but we are elderly and must start our entertainments early in the evening."

Fowler laughed.

Hy exhaled the breath she'd been holding. "Thank you, Your Grace, I shall bear that in mind. You honor me with your invitation."

Which I shan't be accepting any time soon.

Hy had been lucky to escape recognition once, she might not be so lucky again. "I bid you goodnight." She turned away, forcing herself to move slowly, rather than run from the room—and the duke's disconcerting stare.

***

Sylvester watched the boy leave, his gait the awkward, self-conscious walk of a very young man who was newly on the town.

"Quite the cool-headed little bastard, wasn't he?" Fowler asked, holding up two fingers for the hovering waiter.

"Too cool-headed for you," Sylvester said, his gaze flickering to his friend's much diminished pile of money.

Fowler thought that was hilarious. "Aye, but I think I wasn't the only one taken in."

Fowler was right, the stripling had worked the table more skillfully than men who'd been playing for thirty years. While Sylvester had no way to prove it, he knew the boy was aware at all times of what had been played and what remained in the deck—an impressive skill when a person was counting into not one, but two packs of cards.

Not only that, but he'd employed a strategy that was logical, consistent, and unemotional. It had been a pleasure to watch him play even though Sylvester had lost money to him.

To be honest, it had been a while since Sylvester had enjoyed much pleasure at the card tables—or anywhere else—which must have been why he'd issued the unusual invitation to the lad.

"An odd humor to invite him back here to play, wasn't it?" Fowler asked, as if reading his mind.

"I enjoyed watching him take your money."

Fowler gave Sylvester's diminished pile a pointed look. "Aye, I know what you mean."

Sylvester smiled and gathered up his winnings.

"What? You leavin'?"

"I have an early appointment tomorrow."

Fowler looked at his watch. "It's already half past two o'clock in the bloody morning. You might as well stay awake and go to your meeting from here."

Sylvester stood. "Do you want a ride?"

Fowler scowled. "I'm staying."

"As you wish." Sylvester headed for the door.

"Don't forget that I'll be wantin' you to go with me to Tat's to look at that pair of chestnuts," Fowler called out behind him.

Sylvester didn't bother answering; Fowler would show up at his house and drag him off whether he agreed to go or not.

His carriage was ready and waiting for him when he stepped out into the horizontal wind and rain. He'd told John Coachman to be ready at two-thirty and the man knew Sylvester valued both his servants and cattle too much to keep them standing in the cold and rain.

A burly footman opened the carriage door and Sylvester leapt into the plush interior, which was warm thanks to a cast-iron brazier set in a special slot in the floor. Sylvester put his booted feet on the brass lid of the warmer and relaxed against the soft leather seat, his mind sorting through the evening.

The Pigeon Hole offered interesting games and some of the highest stakes in London, but it was in a part of town Sylvester wouldn't want to ride through without armed men.

Fowler had convinced him to go the dangerous gambling hell because of the play, but normally Sylvester would not have bothered.

Still, there was not much he could seem to be bothered to do these days. Even bedding his mistress seemed like a chore—which is why he'd not paid a visit to her in over two weeks. He was disgusted by his moodiness, but no longer surprised by it. His father—as Sylvester knew all too well—had suffered from a similar melancholic disposition. Unlike his father, however, Sylvester did not have the luxury of eating a bullet. At least not until he produced an heir.

Sylvester's lips twisted at the overly dramatic and self-pitying thought.

Poor, hideous, rich you, his inner critic mocked, coming out from wherever it lurked; never far away.

Sylvester yawned, wincing as he stretched out his sore body. He'd gone to Jackson's for the fifth day straight. It was excessive behavior and he'd known as much even without looking at the famous pugilist's frown. Not that *The Gentleman* would dare to say anything other than, "Welcome, Your Grace" to him.

He massaged his shoulder and smiled; one of the few benefits of being a duke—never having to argue with anyone.

Except with your own mother, his mental companion whispered gleefully.

Yes, except her, Sylvester conceded.

A grown man afraid of his mother!

Sylvester refused to be drawn into another tedious mental argument with his own conscience.

Instead, he rested his head back against the soft leather and thought back to tonight, and the odd young man at the gaming hell.

I hope you enjoyed your peek at HYACINTH! Look for it in February 2023!

Who are Minerva Spencer & S.M. LaViolette?

Minerva is S.M.'s pen name (that's short for Shantal Marie) S.M. has been a criminal prosecutor, college history teacher, B&B operator, dock worker, ice cream manufacturer, reader for the blind, motel maid, and bounty hunter. Okay, so the part about being a bounty hunter is a lie. S.M. does, however, know how to hypnotize a Dungeness crab, sew her own Regency Era clothing, knit a frog hat, juggle, rebuild a 1959 American Rambler, and gain control of Asia (and hold on to it) in the game of RISK.

Read more about S.M. at: www.MinervaSpencer.com

Follow 'us' on Bookbub:
Minerva's BookBub
S.M.'s Bookbub

On Goodreads

Minerva's OUTCASTS SERIES

DANGEROUS
BARBAROUS
SCANDALOUS

THE REBELS OF THE *TON:*

NOTORIOUS
OUTRAGEOUS
INFAMOUS

THE SEDUCERS:

MELISSA AND THE VICAR
JOSS AND THE COUNTESS
HUGO AND THE MAIDEN

VICTORIAN DECADENCE: (HISTORICAL EROTIC ROMANCE—SUPER STEAMY!)

HIS HARLOT
HIS VALET
HIS COUNTESS
HER BEAST
THEIR MASTER

THE ACADEMY OF LOVE:

Made in the USA
Monee, IL
29 September 2023

43675286R00152